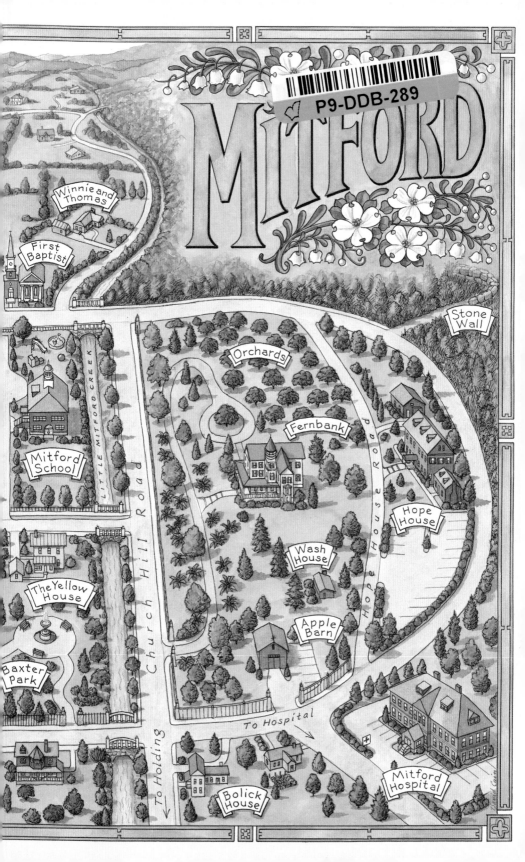

To Be
Where
You Are

FATHER TIM'S COLLECTED QUOTES

Patches of Godlight:
Father Tim's Favorite Quotes

A Continual Feast:
Words of Comfort and Celebration, Collected by Father Tim

CHILDREN'S BOOKS BY JAN KARON

Jeremy:
The Tale of an Honest Bunny

Miss Fannie's Hat

The Trellis and the Seed:
A Book of Encouragement for All Ages

G. P. PUTNAM'S SONS

New York

To Be
Where
You Are

JAN KARON

PUTNAM

G. P. PUTNAM'S SONS
Publishers Since 1838
An imprint of Penguin Random House LLC
375 Hudson Street
New York, New York 10014

"When They Sleep" by Rolf Jacobsen, translation by Robert Hedin, from
The Roads Have Come to an End Now: Selected and Last Poems of Rolf Jacobsen
(Copper Canyon Press, 2001). Translation reprinted by permission of Robert Hedin.

Library of Congress Cataloging-in-Publication Data

Names: Karon, Jan.
Title: To be where you are / Jan Karon.
Description: New York: G. P. Putnam's Sons, [2017] | Series: A Mitford novel; 14
Identifiers: LCCN 2017026335 (print) | LCCN 2017030276 (ebook) |
ISBN 9780399183751 (ePub) | ISBN 9780399183737 (hardcover)
Subjects: LCSH: Kavanagh, Timothy (Fictitious character)—Fiction. | Mitford
(N.C. : Imaginary place)—Fiction. | Episcopalians—Fiction. |
Clergy—Fiction. | Marriage—Fiction. | Weddings—Fiction. | Domestic
fiction. | BISAC: FICTION / Family Life. | FICTION / Christian / General. |
FICTION / Contemporary Women. | GSAFD: Christian fiction.
Classification: LCC PS3561.A678 (ebook) | LCC PS3561.A678 T63 2017 (print) |
DDC 813/.54—dc23
LC record available at https://lccn.loc.gov/2017026335

Printed in the United States of America
1   3   5   7   9   10   8   6   4   2

Book design by Gretchen Achilles

For my mother
1921–2016

To Be
Where
You Are

1

I t was the first day of October, and all things considered, Mitford was pretty quiet.

Around the tenth of the month is when it would hit the fan. The chlorophylls of summer foliage would have degraded into non-fluorescent chlorophyll catabolites, and hidden pigments would explode in a pyrotechnic extravagance of scarlet, gold, vermilion, and out-loud yellow.

While the display would be rampant throughout the Blue Ridge Mountains, Mitford was proud to offer its very own autumn expo:

A brace of mature *Acer rubrum*, which paraded from Town Hall to First Baptist. Such annual spectacle would not be missed by tourists in the thousands, steaming up the mountain with the ubiquitous cell phone and occasional Nikon.

There was, however, a caveat. There were now two gaps in the parade of maples. One where lightning had struck in 2005 and the other where trunk rot had finally dealt its fatal blow.

The Council had ordered the stump ground and the vacant sites disguised with mulch. Mitford had not enjoyed a furor in quite a while and somehow, collectively, had decided the time had come.

A party of locals demanded that the maples be replaced, full-size, which would cost the town a bundle. Others campaigned to replant with beds of pansies, historically known as the town flower. A group calling themselves the Vocal Locals objected to pine bark mulch as too acidic for the soil and pressed for cocoa bean hulls, which others rejected outright as 'too foreign.'

Esther Cunningham's copy of the weekly *Muse* hit the porch at seven-thirty sharp; she read the feature on the trees while cranked back in her recliner.

She hadn't served as Mitford's mayor, albeit former, for nothing. She knew about such things. People were right about th' pine bark—get it offa there and go with th' pansies. How often did they get a blank spot to drop in a couple flats of pansies? As for replacement, no. Nobody in their right mind would go for the cost of spading in mature trees, and young stock would look ridiculous among their elders.

After sixteen nose-to-the-grindstone years, she'd been retired for how long? Too long! She had sworn never to run for office again, but didn't people change their minds all the time and so what if she was gaining on ninety?

Take th' woman in England who was a hundred and still tendin' bar—pullin' pints, she called it, three days a week. And that hundred-year-old gal writin' for a newspaper, askin' people, Got any news?

And how about th' mayor who was still mayorin' at a hundred an' two, bless 'er heart? Just lately, she dropped dead comin' out of a council meeting, which was no surprise. How many of those monkey shows had she, Esther Cunningham, barely escaped with her life?

She located the remote in the pocket of the recliner, cranked upright, and reached for her iPad.

Havin' an iPad had opened a whole new world. Her daughters could no longer accuse her of bein' Stone Age; she knew what was goin' on out there with people livin' longer.

. . .

At seven thirty-five, Father Tim Kavanagh dropped a frozen banana, half a package of frozen acai berries, and a handful of frozen mangoes and peaches into a blender. The mélange was followed by a container of Greek yogurt, a spoonful of tahini, and a long pour of almond milk.

He hit the Blend button while firmly holding down the lid. Completely new to the smoothie regimen, he was alarmed by the possibility of the lid flying off and splattering stuff all over the kitchen. But the blender wouldn't blend. It sounded like an eighteen-wheeler spinning tires on a sheet of ice.

He hit Off and reviewed the options.

Puree, Whip, Mix, Stir, Grind, Frappé.

Grind did not work. Same with the other options.

Okay, so some of the contents were frozen like a rock; maybe they had to partially thaw. When the nurse gave him the recipe after his physical, she didn't say the ingredients had to be thawed. He did not have time to wait for something to thaw. He hit Blend again. A sound like tires screaming on a NASCAR track.

This would be his first morning without caffeine. Whether he could live up to the caffeine-free regimen recommended by Dr. Wilson, he couldn't say. He was totally hooked on coffee and had been for decades. Cut him some slack, for Pete's sake. Let him cling to this harmless vice.

He removed the lid and looked in. Maybe if he stuck a knife down in there and broke up the frozen chunks . . .

So, okay, you cannot put in big chunks, they have to be broken up first, because that worked pretty well and now the blender was sort of blending. This smoothie business was no walk in the park. He'd had trouble opening the package of frozen acai berries and resorted to sawing through the wrapper with a bread knife. Acai berries, whey, tahini—such exotic items were not available at the Local; he'd been forced to drive to the neighboring Wesley, a college town in which such products thrived.

He emptied the contents of the blender into a large glass for himself and one for Cynthia, who would be coming downstairs any minute, and since Puny was taking a few weeks off, he was careful to do a cleanup.

He carried the glasses to the study, glancing beyond what they called their 'picture window' to a view of their own *Acer rubrum*. The crimson was as yet a mere blush, and there were the blue mountains beyond, illumined by the blast of pure, clean light that happens when the earth does its autumnal tilt.

He put the glasses on the table, sat on the sofa. To be honest, he wasn't completely excited about today's agenda.

They would be lugging the contents of Cynthia's workroom up the hall to the dining room, now vacant of the pool table, which had recently moved to Meadowgate Farm, hallelujah.

He visualized the countless tubes of paint and brushes, boxes of colored pencils and pens, and the tons of finished art that had happily leaned against a wall for a decade or two, plus the contents of a massive wooden file cabinet wherein resided the complete history of her life as a writer/illustrator of children's books. Then there was all the stuff pushpinned to the wall that had served as images of encouragement: faded prints of Matisse paintings, her grandfather on a pony at the age of nine, newspaper and trade journal accounts of her many awards and recognitions, innumerable photos of white cats in various poses . . .

Lug, haul, schlep, tote—that was the way of marriage. As a bachelor, he had never moved anything. Every item in the rectory had been deeply, and for his money happily, rooted in place.

He checked his watch.

They would have to be dressed and out of here at twelve-fifteen for Esther Cunningham's birthday luncheon at the club, and after the big bash, come home and have at it again. But he wouldn't grumble. The new workspace would be reviving for his wife, who had for years hunkered down in quarters the size of a shoebox.

He looked across the room where Truman slept in a wingback chair, undisturbed by dreams of preying hawks or the one-upmanship of barn cats. A cat as white as chalk, except for a black ear, was a red flag to rural predators, including fox and bear. Clearly Truman had considered the odds and made a decision to leave Meadowgate Farm. He was discovered yesterday on the backseat of Cynthia's new Mini Cooper. When she arrived home and opened the car door to take out a sack of squash from the farm garden, Truman had jumped down and dived for their kitchen door. Home free!

And here was his wife, a vision in sweats and fuzzy slippers.

'This is the day the Lord has made!' she said.

He lifted his glass. 'Let us rejoice and be glad in it!'

She thumped onto the sofa, took her glass from the table. Smelled the contents.

'What is this?'

'It's a smoothie, the first of ten commandments from Wilson. It contains calcium to help restore bones.' *Osteo* was the dark word the nurse had used. *That's where this is headed if you don't shape up, Father.*

Cynthia took a sip and looked at him, wordless.

'I think I forgot the whey,' he said.

'*Whey?*'

'The recipe calls for whey, but I forgot. Here's lookin' at you, kid.' He drank half the stuff, just to show that he could.

She tried again. 'There's a blob of something in here.'

'I think there's supposed to be a blob or two.'

'But a smoothie is supposed to be smooth.'

'Blobs are good for you.' It was his final argument.

She took another sip, tentative. 'I can't do this. I'll settle for the bones of Elijah, dry as they may be. But thank you, sweetheart.'

'We also have to start walking, Kav'na. Every day. A hundred and fifty minutes a week, total. Should be easy. Oh, and do weight-bearing exercises.'

'Is this your medical protocol or my medical protocol?'

'Mine, really, but your bone density test is due next week and you'll need the same treatment, trust me. It's an old-age thing.'

She gave him a look. 'I can't believe you're caving to the notion of old age.'

'Not caving, just being realistic.'

'Realistically, I must begin painting today. The Children's Hospital auction . . .'

'Realistically, the auction is nearly six months away. April!'

'Six months will be gone in a blink. Irene and I are committing to fifteen new paintings each. The work sold so well last time, we want to be even better this year. It isn't easy to be better each year.'

'Tell me about it.'

So she would be absent from this galaxy until the last brush was cleaned and put away. For years he'd been jealous of her creative passions, but in recent years had learned to support and encourage her—a strategy which, ironically, returned her to him in surprising ways.

He heard the *Muse* truck slow down, then roar away.

'The *Muse*!' he cried. 'Drink up, girl, we have work to do!'

He went to the door and brought the newspaper in; he would just take a minute to check LOL, aka the laugh of the week.

He didn't have to look far.

'Mitford School Students,' declared the front-page headline, 'Make Delicious Snacks.'

Mitford's police captain shocked herself by running a red light— indeed, the only traffic light in town.

She was mortified. She looked both ways on Lilac Road, ahead on Main, and into the rearview mirror. Had anyone witnessed this? All clear, thank the Lord. That was unusual for a weekday morning, but in a town like Mitford, even the bushes had eyes. She was born with a lead foot, and she'd been hauling to make it to the station for a special meeting of the day shift.

She wheeled into the parking lot as the church bells at Lord's Chapel began their eight o'clock chime. *Bong . . . bong . . .*

She was an honest woman; should she write herself a citation? Adele Hogan, MPD police captain, grandmother, churchgoer, wife of local newspaper editor . . .

She was struck then by something like an aftershock. She realized she hadn't just run the light, she had been speeding. Her heart was kicking like a horse at the stall door. She got out of the patrol car and adjusted her holster with the new .40-caliber Sig Sauer. She hadn't been doing more than five or six miles per hour—okay, ten—over the limit, but still . . .

Two offenses. If her mama knew this, she would roll over in her grave. A citation would send her to court where they would march her fool self off to driving school. Her face burned. If she did not opt for driving school, she would have to pay court costs and a fine. Five hundred bucks. If she opted for school, the DA could probably be moved to reduce the charges for a first offender, but there would still be points on her driver's license, an increase in her insurance premiums, and nobody in town, much less the MPD, would let her forget it.

As if that wasn't punishment enough, the whole miserable incident would land on the station log, engraved in stone, which is when it would go from bad to worse.

Everybody knew Vanita Bentley checked the log five days a week, prowling for any scrap she could splash across the front page of the *Mitford Muse*, owned by the husband of the MPD police captain.

Her husband would sell his grandma for a good story. But even if it didn't circulate in the newspaper, it would definitely circulate by *word of mouth*. Roughly twenty minutes is what it took for news to spread through Mitford like a brush fire.

As she opened the station door, her heart was doing a number under the badge she had worn for six years plus change.

Why was she making herself miserable? Nobody had witnessed it. What was the big deal? Maybe it was her new blood pressure med.

She breathed in.

So, okay. No citation.

Really, all she needed was a reminder. Something she could keep in her sock drawer where J.C. would never lay eyes on it, but she would see it every morning.

She breathed out.

Yes. Good. She would write herself a warning.

Coot Hendrick was feeling entirely cured. Upper respiratory some-thin' or other—he could not recall exactly what had made him so sick. All he knew was, he had never smoked, so his conscience was clear. He stood at the big window in his upstairs apartment over Happy End-ings bookstore and worked out his list for the day.

He would finally be able to do everything that needed doin': Vacuum the store, wash the front windows, haul off the recycling, dust the books, an' whatever else Miz Murphy and Sister Louise wanted him to do, or even Grace, who sometimes asked him to catch her a frog or a housefly or a turtle so she could draw it.

Get stamps, he needed to get stamps for their mail-order business. An' put his bedclothes in th' washer in the basement. It would be nice to have clean bedclothes to look forward to when he finished his book tonight, and Lord knows, he hated to finish it. He'd got so used to that book, it was like he was livin' in a whole other place.

He remembered there was a piece of Miz Bolick's Orange Marmalade Cake still in the freezer. He would set that out to thaw and eat it tonight after he finished his book. He got a shiver of joy rememberin' how that cake looked settin' on his little table and how it was just for him, to help him get well. Miz Bolick had brought it up to the store and said to Miz Murphy, 'This is for Coot, who is one of Mitford's town fixtures.' It was a solemn honor to be called a town fixture.

He was turning away from the window when he saw the patrol car run the red light. He wondered if *police* had some kind of special permission to run a red light if nobody was comin' from a side street, which nobody was.

G race Murphy was writing a book.
It was a teachers' workday at Mitford School, and she had come really early to Happy Endings with her mom, who was unpacking a huge box with Aunt Louise and getting ready for the O for October sale. Usually she helped her mom, but her mom had said go write your book and we will call you if we need you. So she was lying on the new rug in the poetry section with her book bag and her notebook and pencils and writing at the top of page 4.

>The news today is not good said Samantha. Yesterday the news was good but today it is not very good.
>Is it sad news said Mrs. Ogleby?
>Not exactly said Samantha.

Her bifocals slipped down her nose; she pushed them back.

>Because I will go inside and close the shudders if it is sad said Mrs. Ogleby.

She wasn't using lined paper because that was for really young children, and she was six, almost seven.

Being six was neat. When you are five, you go to kindergarten and help the teacher with the children. But when you are six, you get to start first grade and dress yourself every morning and meet your friends at the corner and walk to school together.

Six was different from five in a lots of ways. When you are five, you like bugs, but when you are six, you do not like bugs because of the things they can do, like get in your hair and sometimes up your nose.

When you are five, you ride a bike with sixteen-inch wheels, but when you are six you get twenty-inch wheels because she was tall like her dad. She had wanted an even bigger bike, but the man said it was dangerous to have a bike too big for the kid and it was not safe to buy a bike for a kid to grow into. So that is why she had twenty-inch wheels, which were just right for now. Plus at five she had played with dolls, and now at six almost seven, she wanted to write books like in her mother's bookstore.

A million books were in their store and she had read a lots of them, at least fifty or two hundred, including *Charlotte's Web*, *The Secret Garden*, and *The Boxcar Children*. Her new teacher said Grace you're reading ahead of yourself! But she didn't know how anybody could read ahead of themselves or behind of themselves. She had just finished reading *Louisa: The Life of Louisa May Alcott*, and that is why she was writing a book of her own. Not on her iPad like at school, but with a pencil like Louisa. She was up to four pages in cursive, which her mother had taught her how to do when she was five.

Her book was about a girl who lived in a tiny town where only her family had TV and so she learned the news from her TV and went around in the town and told the news to people. She went out in rain and even snow and her puppy Morris went with her. As the writer of the book, she was mostly doing what her mom said to do, which is write about what you know, which was living in a tiny town even though other people had TV in Mitford.

She did not have a plan for how the book would end. She only knew it would not be sad and nothing bad would happen to the puppy. Her dad, who was chaplain at Hope House, said she could have a puppy soon. Luke and Lizzie were his Jack Russell therapy dogs and they were getting old, they had gray muzzles. They worked with him at Hope House and let the old people pet them, which made the old people truly happy. When she got her puppy, she would take it up to Hope House and everybody could pet it all they wanted to.

She would really like to have a brother and two sisters. Or she would take a sister and two brothers, either way, but her mother could not have a baby anymore and so a puppy would have to do. She was glad she had been born before the time her mother could not have a baby anymore.

Though the Local didn't open until eight, Avis Packard answered the store phone at seven-thirty and took an order for two roasters, a pound of thick-cut bacon, a dozen free-range eggs, two pounds of red potatoes, and two bottles of Prosecco, to be picked up at eleven o'clock.

Any business that rolled in before eight, he considered gravy. He wondered who was coming to see Miz McGraw, as she could not possibly eat two roasting hens by herself, much less a pound of bacon, and for sure, the Prosecco was a tip-off. This was an order that had 'company' written all over it. He liked knowing what his customers were up to, but would certainly not ask for details, no way, he didn't meddle in other people's business—what they shopped for usually told him all he needed to know.

So maybe it was Miz McGraw's twin sister, a Hollywood actress whose name he could not remember because he preferred old Westerns.

Pondering how he would answer the phone today, he stepped out to the sidewalk, lit an unfiltered Camel, and enjoyed a lengthy spasm of the familiar hacking cough.

At six-thirty this morning, he had taken delivery of fourteen pounds of livermush and twice as much sausage from his supplier in the Valley. Sausage was a sure seller. So in today's phone-answering blurb, he would promote livermush instead of hypin' the sausage, which would fly out anyway.

He inhaled deeply. Coughed. Recited aloud.

'Fall into the Local and get your first taste of Valley-made livermush.'

No. He needed to emphasize the first word, which was seasonal, and go more upbeat and cheerful on the word *livermush*. People who moved to Mitford from away, especially Yankees, didn't have a clue about livermush. *Liver* and *mush* were two words that scared people to death if they weren't from these parts.

He took another drag off the Camel and blew a smoke ring and re-cited today's phone greeting once more.

'*Fall* into the Local and get your first taste of Valley-made *livermush!*'

Right on.

'Slice it *thin* an' fry it *crispy!* Avis Packard here, how can I help you?'

It was a mouthful, but with the cost of newspaper advertising, a man had to do what he had to do.

As for knowing what he'd say to the big convention of the Home-town Grocers Association in November, he'd be et for a tater. They had called an' invited him to make a twenty-minute speech, and the very notion rattled him so bad he said yes without thinkin'. He knew exactly what they wanted to hear—it was how the little guy could make a de-cent livin' in a world of Harris Teeters, Food Lions, and Piggly Wigglys. In twenty minutes! As if he knew!

He regretted that he was not prone to pray.

A cross the street at Sweet Stuff Bakery, Winnie Ivey Kendall propped open the front door with a brick from the long-ago Sun-day school construction at Lord's Chapel. As the sun shone in, the aro-mas rolled out. Cinnamon. Oatmeal. Chocolate chip. Yeast rolls. Fig bars, still sleepy in their sugar-dusted wraps.

She shivered a little in the cool mountain air and drew in a lungful with something like joy. Summer had given them a black bottom line, followed by a sigh of relief when the tourists went home, and any day now, there'd be the big wave of leaf peepers to tide business over till the Thanksgiving surge.

Some would come up ahead of the color—she liked the first little ripple—and spread out around town like kids in a wonderland. They would want everything in the Sweet Stuff case; she could see their faces now. It was the same faces every year, though most of the time totally different people—she guessed it was the light in their eyes that was the

TO BE WHERE YOU ARE

same as they looked at the donuts or the cream horns, or the big slices of Orange Marmalade Cake, which this year would go for two-seventy-five a slice. The price was up twenty-five cents from last year, a huge hike that she and Thomas had talked about and also prayed about, and agreed it was the only possible way to make a profit on the OMC, which was complicated, time-consuming, and about as fun to bake as havin' a root canal.

She could not cut corners on the OMC or 'go commercial' in any way, as she had a typewritten agreement with Esther Bolick, who created the famous confection. She had promised to stay true to the original recipe and methods of preparation, and give Esther ten percent of all profits, and that had been faithfully done.

Over the years, Esther had eyed Sweet Stuff like a hawk, looking for the slightest variation or discrepancy, but not once had Esther enjoyed any *real* reason to complain of compromise. Though the agreement was not strictly legal, she, Winnie Ivey Kendall, would stick to it no matter what.

On the west side of the town monument, Lew Boyd pumped twenty bucks' worth of regular into a 1982 Ford F-150 half totaled by rust. This piece of junk would not live to burn a half tank. Three gallons. Four. Five. He yawned; his mind went into dream mode. It was time for him and Earlene to go ahead and retire. Buy a camper. Head out west like Esther and Ray Cunningham used to do. Pull off the road by a little stream, haul in a trout, cook it over an open fire. Yessir. That was th' ticket.

Fall was here, he could see it in the way the light glimmered and changed in the beat of a mortal breath. He shut off the hose. He'd spent forty years pumping gas for people going somewhere. It was his turn.

He went inside, whistling as he ran the credit card.

See the USA in your Chevrolet . . .

. . .

Esther Bolick hung her dress on the hook behind the closet door—it was polyester that looked for the world like silk crepe—and selected her shoes.

Red. She hoped red shoes were not too loud for a lunch at the country club with Esther Cunningham, who was turning eighty-nine today. How Esther Cunningham had made it to eighty-nine was a miracle. Stents. Strokes. Arthritis. Bladder infections. Biopsies. Boils. Osteo. Ingrown toenails. She was a regular Job whose medical quandaries had half killed her husband and all of her daughters, but nothing slowed Esther down. Oh, no, Esther Cunningham had a whole *tribe* of people to lean on, boss around, and generally wear to a total nub.

She would never tell her age, but she, Esther Bolick, had been spared to live to eighty-seven last March. And what was she spared for? That was the question. Sometimes she even asked out loud, 'Lord, why did you put me here, anyway?' Would the Lord put somebody on earth just to bake cakes?

How many OMCs she had baked in this lifetime she did not know. Maybe six hundred, maybe two thousand, or maybe as many as the stars in the Milky Way, which Gene said were three hundred billion.

She tried hard to get her breath. It seemed stuck somewhere in her chest.

She would keep going till the cows came home, but right now she was just bushed, hung out to dry. She sat on the side of the bed and looked at her ankles, which were as big as lampposts. Swollen ankles, Dr. Wilson said, came from too much sitting. Swollen ankles, somebody said at the Woolen Shop, came from too much walking. She couldn't recall if she had been walking or sitting. What had she been doing, anyway? Her mind was a furball.

She couldn't just step into those pumps, she would have to lean down and stuff her feet in with a shoehorn. She hated leaning down—it cut off her breath and made her head swim. Maybe she should wear the little black low-heels she could slip into while holding on to the doorknob of the closet. But no. Anybody could wear low-heeled black shoes, which, if the eye trailed down that far, disappointed the onlooker. Red shoes gave people a lift. Maybe that's why she was spared—to give people a lift once in a while.

If it wasn't Esther Cunningham, she wouldn't go. She didn't know who else was coming, but for sure it would be the Roman legions. The Cunningham daughters, who rigged this celebration, were known to invite half the county to everything from baby showers to Tupperware parties, but right there was a reason to stay home, as in a huge crowd she would not get her proper recognition. No, she would be introduced to out-of-town cousins as 'th' lady who used to bake the famous OMC.' Used to bake? Hadn't she baked an OMC just a week or two ago and trundled it up to Coot Hendrick, who was livin' in the bookstore attic? Because he was sick as a cat and had a fever and in his delirium, according to Hope Murphy, had *cried out* for an OMC? Cried out!

Used to bake? She could hardly bear to live another minute on a planet full of people who gloried in willful ignorance.

So yes, she would definitely wear the red pumps. They picked up the red in the dress she bought two years after Gene passed. If he could see her in that dress—she could just hear him—'You look eighteen years old, dollface. I'm comin' over there an' give you some sugar.'

Who was pickin' her up, anyway? Was it Dora? Dora had borrowed her good fall hat, which she just remembered she wanted to wear. She did not like to borrow or be borrowed from. Or maybe she, Esther, was doin' the drivin' today. Seems like she had given up drivin' a while back.

She leaned down . . .

'Déjà vu all over again,' he said, recalling the armoire they once lugged to their bedroom.

The Yogi Berra line usually got a laugh, but his wife was in no laughing mood. For a woman who loved surprises and welcomed change, she

was morose as all get-out in abandoning her work habits of seventeen
years, give or take.

Since somewhere around nine o'clock, he'd endured the nagging
headache of caffeine deprivation. A curse, and for what? As for the workroom transfer, he'd rather unplug a drain or give a talk to the Rotary.

They had 'done' her enormous file cabinet—emptied all drawers,
moved the cabinet, sat on the floor and exclaimed over forgotten contents of the files, put the stuff back in the drawers—and were currently
wrangling her worktable before going upstairs to dress for the birthday
bash.

The worktable was an artist's contraption with a sloped drawing
board. It had looked to him oddly lightweight all those years, tucked
into the little room where she had illustrated and written so many books
for delighted children. Now it weighed like raw ore.

Midway to the dining room, the thing threw a leg that crashed to
the hall floor. Truman bolted for cover.

'Rats!' she said. 'I forgot to tell you about that leg.'

Married all these years and he'd never known about the bad leg on
his wife's worktable? He could have propped it up with a matchbook,
taken a screwdriver to the nut, something.

'We can't just stand here, Kav'na. Keep moving.' His headache was in
the process of rolling over to pounding.

'There goes the phone,' she said. Her husband enjoyed answering the
phone. It could be a former parishioner in trouble, someone passing
through town and needing a handout, or maybe a birth or a bride-to-be—
the possibilities for a priest, albeit retired, were virtually endless.

He set down his end of the table and made a dash for the kitchen
phone. Though working long hours as a new vet at Meadowgate, his son,
Dooley, was trying to help him buy a vehicle; he had been vehicle-less
since Lace and Dooley's wedding in June. 'It could be Dooley!' he cried,
which caused a blinding sear of pain over his right eye.

'Or Jack Tyler!' she said, brightening.

It was Dora Pugh.

'I'm glad you're home, Father, I ran by Esther's a little early to take back th' hat I borrowed in case she wanted to wear it for th' party today, you know th' one . . . '

'Ahhh,' he said. Dora Pugh sounded mildly hysterical, quite unlike herself. 'Is this Dora?'

'Of course it's me, who d'you think it is? I couldn't get her to th' door, so I ran in and looked around an' hollered an' there she was. In her bedroom!'

'Aha.' Explosives gouged a crevasse in his brain.

'*Dead*, Father! As a doornail! *Esther.*'

Good Lord! His thoughts went instantly to Ray Cunningham, who had aged considerably in taking care of Esther in her manifold ailments. He was a prince of a guy, he would be desolate . . .

'Is Ray there?'

'Ray who?'

'Ray! Her husband!'

'Oh, good grief, you think I mean Esther Cunnin'ham? Law, no, she was up to see Doc Wilson th' other day, he said she'd live to be a hundred! No, bless 'er heart, it's Esther *Bolick*. I don't know why people in th' same town have to have th' same name, have you ever wondered about that? It's confusin' . . . '

'Slow down, Dora. Where are you?'

'In her livin' room. I'm not afraid to be in th' house with dead people.'

He could hear Dora's teeth chattering.

'Hold on!' he said. 'I'll be right there.'

'She's on th' floor, half dressed, I covered her up with a blanket out of respect. I called th' funeral home, they're on their way, an' I thought I should let you know 'cause she always said she wanted you to conduct her funeral.'

That wouldn't do. Father Brad was her priest, but . . . he had to get over there . . . the prayer of commendation . . .

He heard a kind of moan followed by a dull thud and the phone crashing onto what sounded like bare floor.

'Dora! Are you all right?'

Silence. 'Dora!'

'Come with me!' he shouted to his wife, aka his deacon of many years.

'The table,' she said, holding fast to the one-legged side.

He took it from her and laid the thing on the floor. 'Dora Bolick has passed.'

'Dora *Bolick*?'

'Dora *Pugh*! No, *Esther* Bolick!' So much for the caffeine-deprived wits of the retired priest.

2

A t Meadowgate Farm, the Queen Anne's lace and bush honey-suckle of summer had given way to the ironweed and witch hazel of autumn. Gone were the lashing thunderstorms of August and the sultry rains that besotted highland meadows in mid-September.

In the west pasture, six head of Red Angus cattle cropped knee-high grass mingled with clover and lespedeza. A muscular fifteen-hundred-pound bull named Choo-Choo didn't meander far from the heifers. Two of the five were scheduled to calve in March and three were due late April, a month-long gap conceded to be a welcome breather on a busy farm with a demanding vet practice.

At the Kavanagh Animal Wellness Clinic, the wall clock in Reception gave the glad news: high noon—or dinnertime, as the locals liked to say.

Dooley Kavanagh, DVM, had just completed the repair of an aural hematoma in the left ear of a bluetick coonhound. Chester was pretty much a regular at the clinic, having gotten at various times on the wrong side of a bull terrier, a lawn tractor, and a tangle of barbed wire.

He liked this hound, he had charisma. Hounds in general were great guys; he wouldn't mind adopting one, but hounds and heifers weren't always the best fit. Being fully ninety percent nose, the breed could hound a heifer till she gave him a jaw-breaking kick. The old farm dogs and Charley, their year-old female golden, were dogs enough for now.

He soaped his hands and washed up at the sink in the prep room. Through the open window, he heard their vintage tractor bushhogging the north strip. That would be Willie, who'd been Meadowgate's farm-hand for thirty-five years and lived in the little house out back. Tomorrow Willie and Harley would be mowing hay.

He was still in a daze, as if the life of landowner and vet was a dream. He and Lace had it all, but they'd invested nearly all to have this life. Things would be plenty tight for a year or two.

After college and vet school and the hard separations from Lace and the long process of acquiring Meadowgate from his mentor, Hal Owen, and jumping through hoops for the adoption agency . . . after all that, there was this: his wife of three and a half months, their four-year-old foster son, Jack Tyler, his new practice, a payroll, the cattle, their farmhouse, a hundred acres . . .

Unreal.

And the dream had taken shape right here. He had come out to Meadowgate nearly every summer since he was eleven years old. This is where he had read and reread everything James Herriot had written, and pored over old editions of *Beef Cattle Science*. It's where he'd watched the birthing of calves and lambs, colts and piglets, pups and kittens, and given a hand to Hal in more than one crisis.

He remembered the blood on his hands from the emergency delivery of a bull calf turned crossways in the birth canal. He was fourteen, and had helped a living being come into the world. He had considered the delivery a badge of honor, and actually hated to wash up afterward. It was, after all, the crown of the veterinary profession—this giving a hand to life, to breath. Hal had trusted him to do it—a little anxious, maybe, but counting on the kid to get the thing done.

Hal, who was pretty much a hero to him, was now retired from his full-time practice and working part-time at the Kavanagh clinic. The clinic had also been able to retain Blake Eddistoe, Hal's longtime vet tech, and their receptionist, Amanda, who was also totally competent at everything else.

It was a perfect setup. Even Joanna Rivers's vet practice a few miles north was a benefit. Joanna didn't have the mobility constraints or expenses of bricks and mortar; she had a truck and equipment and was good to go wherever needed. Most of Hal's former clients had turned their large farm animals over to Joanna, which took a potential strain off the Kavanagh clinic.

Still, a few of Hal's old clients continued to haul in the occasional donkey, goat, or llama. Just last week he'd gone out to a horse trailer in the driveway and treated a mule—a fungus infection requiring a thorough hoof swab and a shot. It was 'a drive-by shootin',' according to Harley Welch, who lived with them now in the farmhouse basement room with the canopy bed.

He heard the horn blowing as the farm truck wheeled into the drive—Harley at the wheel, Jack Tyler in the middle, and Charley on the passenger side in full head-out-the-window mode. He watched Jack Tyler jump from the cab and run this way.

Their little guy had been pale and uncertain when he arrived in June. Now he was brown as a horse chestnut and wired with a confidence that was amazing to see.

Charley exploded into the room and dashed up the hall to beg a treat from Amanda.

'Hey, Dad!'

And here was their brown-eyed kid, grabbing him around the legs.

'Hey, yourself, buddy. How was your trip to the co-op?'

'Charley ate their ol' cat's dinner an' pooped at th' front door where people step an' I had to stick my hand in a plastic bag an' pick it up an' flush it.'

'Life's little dramas.'

'Charley jumped up on everybody.'

'What did they say about that?'

'They didn't like it, so we put 'er back in th' truck.'

'What else?'

'Mr. Teague was there, he told me to shut up an' sit down.'

'Ah, Mr. Teague. A sad old fellow. Did you shut up?'

'Nope, but I sat down.'

'Hungry?'

'I'm about starvin'. I got a jawbreaker in my pocket, Jake give it to me.'

'Jake *gave* it to you, okay?' He and Lace were in the throes of grammar lessons, the alphabet, numbers . . .

Jack Tyler ran to the ruler on the wall. 'Hey, Dad, come see how high I am. Jake says I shot up a foot.'

He would take a full lunch hour today; he had bolted lunch for two weeks. They wanted time to talk with Jack Tyler, plant the seed—December was coming fast . . .

'Hey, Dad, come see if I growed any.'

'Grew any. We measured and weighed you yesterday. Forty-two inches. Forty-two pounds. That's it for now.'

He was stumped about what to do with Harold Odom's terrier, Hobie, checking in after lunch. They'd run the initial fecal test for Giardia and got a negative, but he wanted to do the ELISA. Hobie had been immunocompromised as a pup . . .

Harley came in with a 'parcel,' as he called it, and set it on the sink top.

'There's y'r bag balm. Our rope ain't comin' in till Saturday.'

'For my swing!' Jack Tyler jumped around in scuffed cowboy boots, flapping his arms.

'We gon' have you flyin'.' Harley grinned big; he was wearing his dentures today. 'You gon' be seein' th' other side of th' mountain from that swing.'

Their Harley—sixtysomething and a hundred and five pounds soaking wet—was family. Years ago, he had shielded Lace from her violent, no-good father, but that was only one reason they loved this guy. The downside was trying to teach Jack Tyler good grammar with Harley butchering the language.

'Any news at the co-op?'

'Jake says tell you y'r other vet's sellin' up an' goin' west.'

'Joanna Rivers?'

'Jake says 'er dad's in a bad way, she's leavin' soon as she can sell up.'

He was smacked by this. Not good. No.

'I'll be paintin' th' glider porch this afternoon,' said Harley, 'an' goin' in town this evenin'.'

Dooley grinned. Roughly twice a month, Harley trekked to Mitford to visit Miss Pringle, a French piano teacher who rented the rectory from his dad. Harley had subleased Miss Pringle's basement for several years, and how those two had made a connection beyond lessor and lessee . . . he didn't get it.

'I'm gon' cook a mess of collards f'r Miss Pringle,' said Harley.

'Give her our best. And be careful. Remember the curve.' His dad used to worry about the curve; now he worried about the curve.

'I'm half starvin',' said Jack Tyler.

'Okay, buddy. Climb up here and wash your hands.' He pulled the step stool from under the sink. 'We're going to talk about something exciting after lunch today.'

'Is it a bike?' Jack Tyler was buzzed about a bike. 'With sixteen-inch wheels?'

'Way better. Use soap. And wash some more, it's lunchtime.'

Joanna's news was cutting into his gut like a worm.

With Joanna out of the picture, clients would be needing the services of his clinic. Dangerous work, large animals. A kick in the head, a hoof to the jaw, a foot crushed beneath the iron shoe of a horse. Farmers were mostly vetting their cattle themselves these days, so the business was running more to the equine side.

He checked his watch, his text messages.

Lace. *Painted hr + half! Love u.* Carving out time for her art was hard.

The whole place was going at a gallop these days; thank God for Lil, who helped at the house twice a week.

His dad. *Esther Bolick passed this a.m. will do funeral Monday cant look at trucks til next week. Praying for you & love to all.*

When he was a kid, Miz Bolick helped him bake an Orange Marma-lade Cake, which won a big prize in a flour company contest. He re-membered the bedroom slippers she was wearing while they were baking the OMC in her kitchen. The slippers looked like pink rabbits, ears and all, with plastic eyes that clicked when she walked. She had sent them an OMC for their wedding present. She was cool; he had liked Miz Bolick.

Joanna Rivers. *Dad's melanoma going wild. Heading to Colorado as soon as I sell the practice. Any interest in expanding yrs? Best.*

Just what he needed—to buy another practice. No way. It was tough to sell a large-animal practice like Joanna's, even with the mobility of a truck with all supplies onboard.

He walked outside with Jack Tyler and drew in a lungful of the aro-mas coming from the house. Maybe their tomatoes with some spices, and somewhere deep in that smell, roast chicken.

He took the hand of his son, grateful, and they headed to the house like a couple of bulls responding to the rattle of a grain bucket.

H is wife was a dynamite beautiful woman, but even more beautiful when she'd been painting. Her art opened her up in a way he couldn't possibly understand.

'How's Chester?' she said.

He liked that his family cared about his patients. 'Great. He'll bunk with us tonight. How's it going over here?'

'Hoed weeds. Painted. Paid bills. Canned four quarts of tomato sauce; we're done with canning except for apples and pumpkins.'

She had a way of looking at him; he loved coming home for lunch.

'Grammar lesson this morning,' she said. 'Seems to be working, but you know he loves to say *ain't*. I told him he could say it once every day, but only once.'

'Very generous of you.'

'Okay, Doc, you two clean up,' said Lily.

'We're cleaned up, thanks.' He was looking for the roast chicken. 'So where's the chicken we smelled comin' over?'

'That's for supper,' said Lace. 'I've just been invited to Irene Mc-Graw's, Kim is here from L.A. And I have a list for the Local and a lot of errands and won't get home till five. So we made supper ahead.'

Kim. Irene McGraw's Academy Award nominee sister. Kim had bought several paintings from Lace. He looked at her, inquiring, but she didn't look back.

'I'm takin' my plate to th' porch,' said Lily. 'We'll not see many more days like this. Y'all set down an' eat before it gits cold.'

'Hey, Lil. Sandwiches, potato salad, iced tea? It's already cold.'

'You got fried bologna in that sandwich. Still hot.'

'I like th' same as my dad. Is mine bologna?'

'Is th' Pope Cath'lic?' said Lily.

Jack Tyler piled two volumes of *Beef Cattle Science* on the bench at the table and climbed up. He held hands with his mom and dad and his dad said a blessing and they all went *Amen!* together. Amen was the start of getting to eat and he was really hungry from going to the co-op for salt licks and laying mash.

'When're we goin' to talk about what's exciting?'

'After lunch,' said his mom.

Jack Tyler did the two-thumbs-up routine learned from Amanda. 'I have a great idea!'

'He's a man for the great idea,' said Dooley.

'You could say what's exciting now. An' I would eat every bite and not leave any.'

She gave him a look; he picked up his sandwich.

'You'll stay with Lily today when I run to town. Harley will be painting the glider porch and you can help, so put on your overalls, okay?'

'Okay,' said Jack Tyler. 'An' I'm savin' my ain't to say at supper.'

The new vet was hammering down on his baloney and cheese when his cell phone thrummed in his shirt pocket.

'We need you,' said Blake. Their tech didn't call him at home unless it was serious. 'Better get over here.'

He got over there.

W hen?' said Jack.

'After supper,' she said as she kissed him on the cheek.

She speed-dialed Dooley as she walked to the car.

'Water coming in on the floor everywhere but Reception,' he said. 'The plumber's on his way. Don't worry, go to town. There's nothing you can do.'

'Is there anything Hal . . . ?'

'Hal and Marge are away 'til Monday. I'll let you know."

Water coming in on the floor? Why? Surely . . .

She caught her breath. 'Love you.'

'Love you back.'

She would do what he said and not worry. That's also what God was constantly telling her. Take no thought for the morrow, fret not; be anxious for nothing. In hundreds of ways, God was telling her not to do what seemed like everybody's favorite thing to do.

She was tired, really tired. Up before six and nonstop every day. But she was young, Lily said, as if that meant she was immortal or something.

She turned right onto the state road and there was the deep green swale and then the Hershell place on the hill with its herd of little heifers who looked like toys, and the ragged ribbon of blue mountains beyond.

She loved driving through the countryside in her blue Volvo wagon. Though the wedding present from her mom and dad was seven years old, it drove—and looked—mostly brand-new. Sayonara to her old Beemer that had totally croaked and was parked on blocks under the barn shed. Maybe they could get a few hundred for parts if push came to shove.

All through college and the years after, she had saved every penny and stretched every dollar. She hoped push would not come to shove, or if it ever did, that it would wait a long time.

She hated leaving Dooley and Jack even for a town trip. Though she liked a break, she felt she was driving away from part of herself. Jack Tyler was truly part of her; she couldn't imagine loving him more if he'd been their biological son. She rarely thought now about the crushing diagnosis that meant she couldn't have children. The pain was the only real reminder, and the pills.

She glanced at the two dozen eggs in the basket on the passenger seat. She loved giving away eggs; people's eyes always, always lit up. Who in Mitford would like farm-fresh brown eggs today? It was a favorite guessing game. Maybe Esther Bolick, who had baked one of their two wedding cakes.

At Jake's place next to the co-op, she turned left onto Mitford Road, hit Play, and sang along with the first tune on her country classics CD.

'Try as I may, I could never explain
'What I hear when you don't say a thing . . . '

H e realized this would also be a blow to Hal and Marge. They would feel pretty miserable, maybe even guilty, all unnecessary.

He was watching the kitchen clock—ten after five—and filling a bucket at the sink when she opened the screen door.

She looked pale. Shocked, somehow. He had had his own shock this afternoon, but hadn't texted her with details.

'What is it?' he said.

'Where's Jack Tyler?'

'In the library watching a movie. He missed you. I gave him a snack. What is it?'

'We need to talk,' she said.

Hal had warned there could be problems down the road, and the more-than-reasonable sale terms of the entire Meadowgate property had always been forthright: *As Is*.

The inspector had given them his own warning about the pipes. 'It was replumbed twenty, maybe thirty years ago. So maybe three, four years to go, no way to say.' And now water everywhere but Reception, which was two steps above grade.

She set the grocery bag on the table, afraid to ask. Dooley didn't look like himself. 'What's going on at the clinic?'

'I'll give you a clue if you'll give me one.'

'Kim wants me to paint something for her.'

'Great.' Tap water pounding into the bucket. 'But that isn't what's bothering you.'

'She wants me to paint a mural. At her house. In L.A.'

He sat down hard on the bench, wondering if he'd heard right.

'For a lot of money.' She drew in her breath. 'Now you. I just . . . I can't . . . Let's do the clinic first.'

'We need some new plumbing. And a new wall. A weight-bearing wall. We'll have to jackhammer a section of the floor in the prep room so we can install new copper pipes.' The wall would require a construction crew, but one of the plumbing guys had construction experience and had given him a ballpark for the combined jobs. Ten big ones easy, more likely twelve.

He gave her the low figure of ten thousand. The heaviness in his chest was oppressive. 'Maybe more.' This whole scenario was beyond.

He got up and turned off the water and took the overflowing bucket out of the sink and let himself feel the heaviness on his chest.

'There are things in the car,' she said, barely audible.

'I'll help,' he said. 'I'll get Jack Tyler, he can help, too.' L.A.? A mural?

'We'll all help. Help is good.' He set the bucket back in the sink. 'Really good.' He was babbling.

The shop vacs were getting the water up. Willie was standing by and Harley offered to stick close, but they sent him on, with a bag of fresh mint for Helene Pringle's tea.

He and Lace visited the patients and distributed fresh water and Jack Tyler let Pete the bulldog into the run.

He went alone to check again on Chester, who was sitting up in his e-collar and looking perplexed.

They were getting dunked into the big stuff right out of the gate, he thought. It was a sheep dip.

She and Dooley didn't talk as they washed up the dishes.

She was glad they didn't have a dishwasher; a sink full of hot water and soap gave her time to think.

She wouldn't leave Dooley and Jack. Not ever. But she would allow herself the thrill of being asked to do the mural. Just to be asked! Her wedding present to Dooley—the painting of him driving the red truck with the dogs in the truck bed—was the largest work she had ever done; she had liked working big.

'Jack Tyler could come with me,' she said. It was a terrible idea, but she had to say it and mark it off the list.

'But he just got here. The little guy is still figuring out the place.'

Don't go, don't do this, he wanted to say. The disruption at the clinic would be huge. Alarming to their patients, not to mention staff and clients. Hammering, sawing, drilling, tearing up a floor, trucks in the driveway.

'My parents . . .' she said.

'We can't do that. We promised ourselves we wouldn't do that. Hoppy and Olivia have helped so much already.' He wasn't running to his parents, either. They had been more than generous. The whole parent scheme was out.

'And we did the right thing about Miss Sadie's money,' he said. 'I'm glad we can't get to it.'

What was left of his inheritance from Miss Sadie was untouchable. They had told the trust officer, Bartlett, 'Don't let us withdraw anything more for five years, no matter how hard we beg.' Bartlett was tough; it was done.

'If I do the mural, it would solve everything,' she said. She felt the enormous conflict of it, her breath short.

Was this the way he was going to handle life with the only woman he could ever love? My God. He hung the drying cloth on the rack. 'I'm sorry.'

'For what?'

'Sorry that work has pretty much taken me over, that I can't think of anything else. Sorry that I seemed to blow the mural commission in the weeds. This is huge. I'm so proud of you.' He put his arms around her, comforting her, comforting himself. 'I'll do better, I promise.'

She didn't want to cry, she was always bawling, but the relief of this moment was manna, and she let the tears flow.

'Do whatever you need to do,' he said. 'We'll make it happen.'

At eight o'clock, he went to the clinic, checked the floors, made a call to a contractor he'd gone to school with in Mitford, and walked home, scraping his brain for some overlooked solution. There would always be revenue coming from Choo-Choo's on-site services, but nothing close to what they needed now.

The plumbers' trucks were backing out of the drive. The meter had been running since two in the afternoon at sixty-five bucks per hour per man.

The mural job would solve everything, but . . .

He said what his dad said when he couldn't pray, when his thoughts were too jumbled, when he couldn't think straight. 'Jesus.'

A rock and a hard place, he thought. As a married couple, it was their first rock and a hard place.

S he raced up to Heaven, the attic studio where her head could be in the clouds. She wrote swiftly in her Dooley book; it had been weeks since she opened it.

THURS OCT 1~ *A calamity~ that is the perfect word. I can't write about it now as I want to write only positive things tonight.*
   Three things.
   Kim has offered me a commission to paint a mural! In her house in Malibu! Dooley says we can make it work but I don't know how. I don't want to leave D and Jack~ I don't. But it would completely solve the awful thing which I don't want to talk about right now. I am crazy happy to be asked but really sad to think of leaving. I can't imagine leaving them. This is so good, but so hard.
   Two! Dooley has not been late for anything in months. I am so grateful he is working to break this old habit. Trait? Can we break a trait? Can we inherit characteristics like being late? Or on my side crying without good reason? Did we have ancestors who went around being late and weeping?
   Last but so not least~ our Jack Tyler is the light of our lives~ of everybody's life. We would go through all the waiting and testing and paperwork a million times to have our wonderful son.
   Thank you God for so many dreams coming true. Thank you for everything. Even confusion and hard decisions.

W hen, when, when?' Jack Tyler opened his arms in supplication. 'When are we goin' to talk about somethin' *ex-cit-ing?*'
   Suddenly there was too much to talk about. But they had to start somewhere.

'How about now?' said Dooley. He and Lace were sitting on the old sofa in Jack Tyler's bedroom.

'Now is always a good time,' said Lace.

Jack Tyler climbed up between them, smelling of soap and clean pajamas. 'I didn't say my ain't at supper.'

'Good.'

He held up two fingers to his mom. 'I can say it this many times tomorrow, okay?'

'Okay.'

Dooley put his arm around Jack. 'Just before Christmas, you will be our son. Legally. We've talked about it a couple of times, remember? And we will be your mom and dad. Legally. But things will stay just like they are now.'

They looked at the boy who insisted on being called by both his first and last names. Jack Tyler had been a mouthful, but they had gotten used to it. They wanted to avoid saying Jack Kavanagh a hundred times a day; they had even knocked a syllable off Lily's name.

'Only one thing will change,' said Dooley. 'Your name will be Jack Kavanagh.'

Jack Tyler blinked. 'What will happen to my Tyler name?'

'You and your mom and I will all have the same last name. We'll all be a Kavanagh. Forever.'

'When he was your age,' said Lace, 'your dad had another last name. It was Barlowe. Like Uncle Kenny and Uncle Sammy.'

'But I gave it up,' said Dooley. 'Because Granpa Tim was good to me and wanted to be my new dad.'

'What happened to your old dad?'

'He was never around.'

'Like my old dad?'

'Yes.'

'I was adopted, too,' said Lace. 'I was Lace Turner. But when Granny O and Granpa Hoppy adopted me, I was proud to be given their name.'

'Why?'

'Because they loved me and took care of me.'

Jack Tyler looked at his dad. 'Will I get red hair like you if I'm Jack Kavanagh?'

Dooley laughed. It felt good to laugh. 'You get to keep your own hair. And if you'd like to keep your Tyler name, it could be another middle name. You would be Jack Brady Tyler Kavanagh.'

Jack Tyler looked at his mom. 'You would say Jack *Kavanagh* if you called me to come in the house?'

'If I called you to come in the house, I would say . . .' She put her hands on either side of her mouth and called. *'Ja-a-ck!* But if I baked a pie and you and Charley gobbled it all up when I wasn't looking . . .' She put her hands on her hips. 'I would say, Jack *Kavanagh!'*

Dooley laughed. 'See there, buddy, you an' Charley don't want to go gobblin' up her whole pie.'

'But if I kissed you and told you I love you,' said Lace, 'I would say . . .' She kissed his cheek and looked into his brown eyes. *'Jack.* Just Jack.'

Jack Tyler's eyes were big.

'When December eleventh comes,' she said, 'we'll sign papers that say Kavanagh is your new last name. Forever.' They said *forever* a lot in this house. So much in their boy's life had been maybe, maybe not, whatever, we'll see, who knows, who cares.

'We'll be a true family,' said Dooley.

'Ain't we a family now?'

Jack looked at them, surprised, then threw his head back and laughed big. He had used up his ain't but would get another one tomorrow. They all had a laugh.

'In our hearts,' said Lace, 'we're a family now. When we sign the papers, we'll be a family all the way. Legally. And the next day, everybody will come and celebrate your new name. Officially.'

Legally. All the way. Officially. She wanted better words; this was hard. 'You don't have to decide now. And whatever you decide will be good. We love you with all our hearts.'

'The big day will be here in ten weeks,' said his dad. 'Think about a present you'd like to have. Just one special thing. Maybe it's a bike, maybe something else. And if we all agree, you'll get it the day you become Jack Kavanagh.

'We'll have a party and there'll be music by Uncle Tommy and his band, and great food and maybe, just maybe, the cousins will come and we'll all dance again. Like at the wedding.'

'Man!' Jack Tyler spread all his fingers and knew that was how long it would be. A present, a party, maybe even the cousins. 'The cousins!' he said. And dancing! He liked to dance.

He jumped down from the sofa and bolted to the middle of the room. 'Look at me!' he said, and did his boogie dance that everybody laughed about at the wedding—wiggled his hips, flapped his arms. Charley barked.

He liked better than anything to make his mom and dad go laughing.

Dooley watched Lace watching Jack Tyler. If his wife was happy and his boy was happy, he was happy. End of discussion.

They were doing the tuck-in.

'Because I would be Jack Kavanagh, we would do everything like at th' wedding?'

'Pretty much,' said his dad. 'But without the tent.'

'Could we let Choo-Choo out of th' gate again?'

'No way,' said his dad. 'That was a one-off, trust me.'

'How about this?' said his mom. 'Starting tonight we'll call you Jack. Just Jack.' She watched his face. 'We'll practice for the big day!' They had said everything there was to say. 'Okay?'

He blinked again, solemn. Then nodded. 'Okay.'

His mom hugged him and maybe cried and his dad gave him a high five.

'Jack!' they all said together, loud as anything.

He felt a smile coming on his face. When he got up in the morning, he would look in the mirror to see if he was still himself, because it seemed like he kept changing into another boy.

He pushed open the screen door to the glider porch and the odor of new paint on the railings. He was twenty-six—gaining on twenty-seven, as Uncle Henry would say. But he felt old tonight. Beat. The plumbers had reminded him that toilets as well as sinks would be shut down for 'a good while.' He had thought the rigor of vet school was grown-up, but no—this was grown-up.

'Any sign of Harley?' he said.

'We're not his parents, you know.'

'What time is it?'

'Maybe nine-fifteen?'

'That's midnight by Mitford standards.'

He liked to know where everybody was; he was a worrywart.

He sat next to her in the glider and kicked off his tennis shoes. They had sat in this old glider during a lot of visits from school, but they'd never thrashed out anything with three zeros behind it.

He wanted her to know he was proud, but bottom line, he couldn't make it without her.

It occurred to him that the mural money was probably close to what the practice would net this year. On the other hand, it was no small matter that she was a super hand at the clinic. He could always call her to come help and she loved helping—she had a sixth sense with animals. But no matter what, the plumbing work had to start immediately. They could not run a hygienic operation, any operation, without water.

'Listen,' she said.

A heifer bawling in the west pasture, katydids in the grass. His heart rate slowed a little.

Don't go, he said without saying it.

'There's my savings,' she said.

'We said we wouldn't touch it, we would only add to it, it would be for his education. We made a promise.'

'It's just sitting there, not earning anything. We'd do better to bury it in a jar.'

She didn't want to give up her savings for plumbing. All the scrimping like crazy and cutting corners . . . In college, she could have bought clothes and shoes like other girls, she had loved shoes; she could have done things that a lot of other girls did, but she had worked hard to build the savings account.

She remembered her mom giving her three cotton sweaters; she had felt like royalty. She had never asked for anything, even when her mom wanted to be asked.

Just before the wedding, the most amazing thing—she sold five paintings to Kim Dorsay for more money than she could have imagined. She remembered the huge thrill of having a head start on Jack's future. She and Dooley had agreed that the money wouldn't be used for anything but college—no matter what.

That said, she would withdraw the money. But to do it for water pipes . . .

'Are you saying you don't want to go?'

'I'm saying I'm not going.'

He leaned back, closed his eyes, breathed out. They heard Harley's truck pull in and the sound of the basement door closing.

She didn't say that Kim would have flown her home on weekends— all the way across the country on Thursday night and back again on Sunday—or that the mural could possibly take up to three months. Kim wanted farm animals in a pasture, with clover, and mountains in the background, a whole farm scene. It would be done on a large loft wall, for her many grandnieces and -nephews. Kim had lived most of her life not knowing she had a twin sister, Irene, with all those lovely children and grandchildren. The children and grans lived in cities, one family as far away as Munich. They all loved meeting now at Aunt Kim's, and for reasons not explained, they were crazy about everything to do with farms.

Both Irene and Kim were true fans of her work, and had seen a photo of a painting she did of Choo-Choo and the girls. Lace Kavanagh was 'the very one' to paint the mural, said Kim. 'The only one!' said Irene, who hardly ever made extreme statements.

She would love to paint a mural, it would stretch her skills and teach her something important. But no.

For years she had been dry as stone and now, tears at the drop of a hat. Glad, sad, whatever, there they came. 'We'll use the savings.'

She leaned into the curve of his arm. A quarter moon gleaming out there in the grass with the katydids, the glider a cradle rocking. They held each other in what seemed a dream.

She had worked hard for that money, and he admired her for being smart enough to put it away. He would help replace whatever the plumbing tab would be. They would build Jack's future together this time.

'Hey,' he whispered.

She looked up at him. 'Hey, yourself.'

They went inside and closed the kitchen door and turned out the lights and went up the stairs.

He toweled off from the shower and came into their lamplit room. 'You asleep?' he said.

'Wide awake.'

The bed creaked as he got in. He appreciated that about a bed. It was kind of like hello, I'm your bed, great to see you again, how did it go today?

'You know what we forgot to do?' she said. 'We forgot to pray.'

Her hair smelled of cut orchard grass and Jack Tyler and apples.

He turned off the lamp and pulled the cover up and drew her close. 'How about now?' he said. Now was always a good time.

3

If he had a cigar, he would smoke it.

J. C. Hogan sat at his desk in the *Muse* office, in a busted swivel chair bought at a yard sale in 1997. He was wired from the effects of an idea that would be nearly impossible to pull off.

Esther Bolick's passing was good. It was, in fact, great. Carpe diem! This would be more than a front-page obit. It would be the first-ever special edition of the *Mitford Muse*, and well deserved by the deceased. Hadn't Esther carted that cake to every down-and-outer in a ten-mile radius, including old man Mueller, now gone to his rest? She had even carried one to the *Muse* when it celebrated its twentieth anniversary, he would not forget her for that.

He had always wanted to do a special edition, and here was the perfect opportunity. Rotten luck that the *Muse* hit the street today, as it had done every Thursday for thirty-some years. By the time next week's edition was out, Esther's demise would be old news, sayonara, life goes on. So he would have to put this baby to bed by two A.M. tomorrow morning, run it to Wesley before five, and roll the presses.

He checked his watch. Two-fifteen in the afternoon. The fact that he'd loaded his plate today at the Cunningham party was not helping; he'd like to crawl up on his desk and saw a little wood. But no—this train was moving.

He could see it. Single-fold, four-color process cover. Big headline, full-page story with major photo.

Two years ago, he paid his features writer, Vanita Bentley, to do obits on all the important people in Mitford, a labor that gouged a few bucks out of his pocket, thank you very much. Plus she had gone into the *Muse* files and pulled photos to accompany the obits.

They had Tim Kavanagh's obit, of course—when he kicked, that would be a big one, and a piece on his wife, who was a famous children's book author and illustrator, and Esther Cunningham, their former eight-term mayor, and Andrew Gregory, current mayor, plus Winnie Ivey of Sweet Stuff, MPD chief Joe Joe Guthrie, you name it.

So the obit deal was nailed, including one for J. C. Hogan, editor of the *Mitford Muse*, with a backstory on his youthful days as a paper boy plus a photo with his Schwinn. There was, of course, one for his wife, Adele Hogan, Mitford's first female police officer, now MPD captain, who, he liked to remind her, was too mean to die, just kidding. And yes, they definitely had an obit for Esther Bolick, including a shot with her famous cake, a three-layer number. All he had to add were the essentials—headline, circumstances of death, funeral home, viewing hours, the usual.

He would like to pop this landmark edition in the mail, but by the time it arrived in a PO box, the news would be cold. So he had to strike while the iron was hot and send out the two delivery trucks. Not to his entire demographic of three counties, no; he would limit distribution to Mitford environs, where the deceased was known. His chair creaked as he swiveled. The distribution cutback would mean giving a few discounts to advertisers, so a special edition would be costly in every way. He'd have to sell major ad space, pronto.

Okay! The inside spread would be all ads.

They could be tribute ads like *We love you, Esther, rest in peace*, set in a flowery script. He could sell that to the Woolen Shop in a heartbeat. Or *Condolences from your friends at Lew Boyd's Exxon, your friendly one-stop for gas, air, snacks, tobacco, hot sandwiches, you name it.* He would set that in Times Roman Bold, with a coupon for a free refill on wiper fluid. Esther had pumped her own gas at Lew Boyd's Exxon for decades; Lew would definitely spring for a piece of the action.

He wished he could sell the back cover as a full page. But none of the turkeys in this town would go for a full page, no way, not even at the ridiculously low rate of five hundred bucks. The full pages he had sold in this lifetime could be counted on one hand. His competition was not the *Wesley Highlander* or the *Charlotte Observer*, which Florida people mainly subscribed to, it was the old-fashioned, totally reliable WOM, word of mouth. Fancy Skinner, for one, couldn't care less about main-stream advertising. Now retired, she had built her business via the grape-vine just like her sister, Shirlene, who was making a killing off that tricked-up spray tan machine.

He would call Mayor Gregory's restaurant, Lucera, and speak with his Italian brother-in-law who was head chef. That crowd had big money, they just didn't talk about it. A back page would be a great investment for a restaurant with an Italian name nobody could pronounce.

If push came to shove, which it probably would, he'd have to wrangle eighth-pages for the back cover. Wanda's Feel Good Café—there was somebody else who ran a business on WOM. Wanda Basinger had run one ad and one only; she was a bloody tough nut to crack. He'd remind her that he'd personally seen Esther Bolick having lunch there at least twice. Come on, show some respect for the departed.

Village Shoes—he'd have to cut Abe a special deal, of course. Fifteen percent, given limited distribution, but not a penny more. Then there was the Local.

Avis Packard was no fan of advertising. His idea of a strategic cam-paign was to tape a sheet of butcher paper to the window and print

RED POTATOES $1.05 LB with a felt marker. But this was a special edition, for crap's sake, and Esther was a primary figure in this town. The merchants needed to come together on this once-in-a-lifetime opportunity.

He swiveled around to his console and riffled through the Rolodex, which hadn't been organized alphabetically since 1996. That was the year he hired and fired an assistant features writer for using the *s* word in an interview with a construction worker about limited job opportunities in the highlands. 'It was a quote,' said the idiot writer. 'I didn't say it, don't blame me.'

The Local was filed under *T* for The; the Woolen Shop under *L* for Lois, the manager. He located the Feel Good Café under *W* for Wanda. He was accustomed to pounding the pavement to sell ads, but this time it would be phone contact all the way.

He was feeling nauseated. The special edition had to hit the street tomorrow, period. What were the burial plans, who was the officiant—Father Brad, of course, as Esther was a member of the Frozen Chosen, though somebody at last week's prayer breakfast said Father Brad was in Colorado running the rapids, or was it a marathon? He would get the details from Father Tim, who always seemed to know everything even though he was out to pasture.

Unfortunately, he couldn't lean on Vanita Bentley, who was vacationing in Tennessee, during which time she would produce a lead story on Dollywood and the Great Smokies. He was planning to debut a travel section next month—'Meandering with the *Muse*'—though his wife thought it was a dumb idea, since people in Mitford never went anywhere.

He reminded her that since the Grill closed, Percy and Velma had been on not one but two cruises. Two! Never went anywhere? How about Esther and Ray Cunningham, who had traveled around the country in their RV and smoked a peace pipe with Indians? And Irene McGraw, who had been to Europe many times? She was a year-rounder now, sold off her fancy Florida mansion to live full-time in Mitford. So come on. Mitford was very much in the travel game.

Down the street, the Lord's Chapel bells chimed three o'clock. He didn't enjoy being reminded of the time right now.

He plucked further names from the Rolodex, remembering that the special edition and upcoming travel section would be his last hurrah. He was planning to retire January first, quit while he was ahead, though he hadn't said anything to anybody, not even Adele.

But bringing off these two ideas practically back-to-back had him pumped; it was like being in the newspaper business back in the day when editors drank a fifth of bourbon before lunch and wrote late into the night on a Smith Corona.

And how about the lead story for next week? Full coverage of Esther Cunningham's birthday celebration at the country club, which everybody and his brother attended, including the lieutenant governor with his girlfriend, who was of foreign extraction.

A special edition, a travel section, and next week's birthday-bash front page—all practically in one pop!

He lined up the Rolodex cards.

He couldn't believe that just a few days ago, he'd made a decision to throw in the towel.

Retirement?

For sissies.

He went to the coffee machine and brewed a little extra caffeine for the road ahead. As he set the mug on his desk, ha! There it was. The headline. It just popped out!

Using his forefingers, he typed it into his computer document.

Mitford . . . Says . . . Goodbye . . .

To . . . Beloved . . . Town . . . Monument.

He swiveled around in his chair, which pitched to the right, and put his feet up on the desk that some people unkindly referred to as the Dumpster and—first things first—speed-dialed Father Tim.

. . .

No, Father . . . at all, it's . . . absolutely . . . by me.'

Father Brad was breaking up. He was said by a Lord's Chapel parishioner to be 'out west in a canyon.'

'It's what by you?'

'Fine, just fine. Great! Esther . . . you to do it, the attorney . . . her last will and testament.'

'You're breaking up!' said Father Tim.

'I'll move to another rock.' Wind blowing, voices shouting, something roaring.

'What would the bishop think?' he yelled into the phone. Bishops didn't like a priest flapping about in the old parish like a maverick crow. Besides, the last time he'd been in the Lord's Chapel pulpit, he had bawled like an infant. Embarrassing.

'For one thing, there's no reason . . . bish . . . to know. Remember he offered you . . . interim . . . don't think you need . . . concerned . . . '

'You're sure, then, that I won't be interfering?'

'I . . . owe you . . . greatly. Thank . . .'

'Sure. Right. Okay. Are you having a good time, then? Out in the wild?'

'Wonderful. My girls . . . husbands . . . a blessing. Mary Ellen . . . Maybe . . . Mash-up . . . December. If you know . . . would be good fodder for . . . wake-up call. This time . . . young women.'

'I'll think about it!'

'Maybe you and Cynthia . . . join . . . ?'

'We'll pass on that, thanks!'

A strong blow buffeting Father Brad's laughter.

'Safe travels, my friend. See you back here in a week.'

'God . . . with you!'

'And also with you!'

Good heavens, he was practically hoarse from yelling across the better part of a continent.

He wondered what Father Brad had been saying about Mary Ellen, the lovely Boston widow he met at Dooley and Lace's wedding in June. He hated to lose that part of the conversation to the caprice of a canyon wind.

As for Father Brad's famous Snow Camp Mash-up for troubled teens, he had been there, done that, and upon arriving home, caked with mud, half starved and exhausted, completely agreed with his wife in what the raven had so judiciously quoted.

G race Murphy felt really guilty for doing it, but she could not help it. While her teacher was reading aloud to them from a storybook, she was writing her own story on a sheet of paper in her lap.

Her story just kept coming, she never knew when it would happen. 'It breaks out like a rash!' said her mom, who was happy she was writing a book, and her dad, too. But she wished it would not break out at school for two reasons. One, she loved school and loved to learn something new. And two, she could get caught by the teacher.

'Grace,' said the teacher. 'Are you listening?'

She looked up, speechless.

The thing she had dreaded was happening. She hadn't been listening, not at all. If she told a lie, she was pretty sure she would be forgiven, like at home when she did something bad. But she did not want to tell a lie. She wondered if everybody could hear her heart pounding.

She opened her mouth to speak, not exactly knowing what she would say, and burst into tears.

A t four-thirty on Thursday afternoon, an email with a subject line reading *E. Bolick FYI* chimed into the inboxes of eleven Mitford women. It was from the Lord's Chapel church office.

Esther Bolick's burial service would be held on Monday in the town cemetery (take left lane upon entering gates) at one o'clock, followed by a funeral service at two in the nave of Lord's Chapel and a reception in the parish hall; Father Timothy Kavanagh would officiate; no flowers; memorial gifts would go to Children's Hospital. It was noted that the viewing would be held Sunday evening at six P.M. at the Wesley Funeral Home.

All committee members were impressed by the speed with which this information had been gathered and circulated.

While there was some distinction in being the first to know particulars, there was also dismay. Their committee would of course be responsible for overseeing the reception—namely food, drink, tablecloths, setups, flowers, the works—all this on top of next Sunday's scramble to do a reception after the eleven o'clock for a fancy supply priest with a British accent. As Esther did not have family, bless her heart, there wasn't anybody in that line to help organize, fetch, and carry, which was a signal to advise their husbands, ASAP, that they had been volunteered for duty.

As for why their old priest, Father Tim, was officiating, they had no clue. All they knew was, their regular priest, Father Brad, was on vacation in Colorado, living off the land or some such.

By six-thirty in the evening, thirty-two emails, text messages, and phone calls had been exchanged among committee members.

How could they make this solemn event special? That was the question. Someone suggested they ask congregants to bake OMCs, strictly following Esther's famous recipe, and bring them to the reception.

'Brilliant!' one member wrote, and hit Reply All. It was estimated that ten two-layers at eighteen slices per cake would get the job done, with leftovers they could freeze for choir practice. They would supplement with mints and mixed nuts.

This plan would involve the parish in a wonderful and heartfelt way. And there was a fabulous bonus—it would just be coffee, tea, and cake and not the usual folderol with finger sandwiches and shrimp salad or, thank heaven, deviled eggs and fried chicken like the Baptists.

One or two wondered why they had ever volunteered for an Episcopal Church Women, aka ECW, subgroup, which Father Brad once suggested they call the Life and Death Committee. Father Brad thought the fact of death needed to be faced as a part of life. *Death* was not a bad word to be avoided, he said, it was a word to be embraced.

'Where is your priest from?' a new member had asked. 'Colorado,' was the answer. 'That explains it,' replied the person who was from Michigan. In Michigan, people were properly frightened to death of death and didn't fling the word around.

On Thursday evening, he received the first of many phone calls.

No, his wife would not be able to bake an OMC. But he would certainly bake a ham.

'That would be great,' said Lilah, the committee head, 'but we're only having cake.'

No ham at a *funeral*? What was wrong with people?

'I always bring a ham to funerals.' That should settle the matter.

But it didn't. His offer was declined.

'Would you bake an OMC instead?'

He had been very fond of Esther Bolick, but this was beyond the pale.

'That would be a terrifying experience,' he said. 'Sorry.'

'I'm not supposed to tell this, but we're going to showcase an OMC in the fellowship hall. On a pedestal! In a footed cake plate! With a dome!'

'Aha.'

'Compliments of Winnie Ivey!'

'Good job,' he said.

'Three-layer!' she said, a mite breathless.

He was switching off the lights, securing the flap of the cat door to prevent any misguided notion of egress, shutting down the PC . . .

>Fr Tim, I guess you heard about Esther Bolick. I never know if
people who are retired really know things anymore. Harold is still
in the throws of retirement—it is the good, the bad, and the ugly.
I hope you are not too out of touch with people as that can lead
to depression. Here come the Peppers any day now. Remember to
do your shopping ahead of the crowd!

>Yrs,

Emma Newland
Typing, organization, and general office work
Tuesdays only, 9–2

The Peppers? Who . . . ah, yes, another of his former church secretary's exquisite typos. The *Peepers!* As in *leaf.* She was right, of course,
the parking spots were already being snapped up; he'd better get over to
Avis ASAP.

FRIDAY, OCTOBER 2

Emma and Harold Newland had not expected the *Muse* truck to roar by
on a Friday morning. It was a total surprise when they heard something
hit the door, though it was a lighter-sounding thud than the Thursday
thud.

'Not much to it,' said Harold, handing the parcel over to his wife. He
was glad to be retired and not out there delivering mail and dodging
dogs and *Muse* trucks while the dew was still on. He climbed into his
recliner and cranked it back a notch and looked at the ceiling fan, which
needed a new motor.

She peeled off the wrapper and unrolled the contents. '*Goodbye to
th' Town Monument?*' she said in disbelief. 'Why would anybody want to
get rid of th' town monument?'

As this was a moot question, her husband did not reply.

She remembered the fool thing they'd done down in Holding—just picked up their monument and set it over in front of th' bank like so much leftover grits. 'Why?' she said, distraught.

'Beats me,' said Harold, who had never cared much for municipal behavior.

'Maybe they just want to root it out an' store it somewhere. But th' headline says *Goodbye*, so . . . Come here, Snickers, what's that in your mouth?'

Their aging spaniel ambled over and bared its teeth in a grin. 'Good grief! A carpet tack! Give it here, give it!' The carpet tack dinged into a saucer.

'This used to be a nice town,' she said. 'Nobody messed with you. But th' council's gone too far this time. Take down perfectly nice trees, throw a handful of mulch in th' hole, and now? Haul off th' monument!'

'Montana,' said Harold.

'What about Montana?'

'That might be the place to live. Good fishing, they say. Private. Wild horses an' such. They don't have town monuments out there. They don't even have towns, most likely.' He had been there once when he was in the army; he was proud to know about other parts of the world.

'Wait a minute,' she said, slipping the glasses down her nose. 'This is about *Esther Bolick*, who was a town monument, bless 'er heart. Oh, for Pete's sake. But what . . . what in th' *world*?'

Harold sat up and peered at his wife.

'Lord have mercy! Th' caption under this picture of Esther Cunningham says she's deceased!'

'But you were just at her birthday party.'

She grabbed the magnifying glass she kept on the table in the napkin holder. She could not make heads or tails of this mess, but maybe she was missing something. It was too early to call Lois Burton at the Woolen Shop, who'd know what was going on. But why bother Lois when she could get it from the horse's mouth? As soon as she finished her coffee, she would call up to Esther Cunningham's and see if she was dead.

S o, Lew,' said Abe Edelman, 'did you hear about burglars breaking into the Methodist church office?'

'I didn't hear that.'

'They got away with over two thousand bucks in pledges.'

He could tell Lew Boyd not only didn't get the joke, he was grumpy as all get-out.

'So,' said Abe. 'I was sorry to see Esther Cunningham passed. Glad she got to celebrate a big one yesterday.'

'Esther Cunningham did not pass,' said Lew, who was trying out a pair of work shoes. He had not had new work shoes since '09. 'It was Esther Bolick who passed.'

'But th' special edition . . . '

'Don't pay any attention to that rag,' said Lew. 'I got stuck for sixty-three bucks plus wiper fluid on that deal. J. C. Hogan owes money back to half this town if we can find 'im. My mechanic put air in his tires this mornin', says he was headed to Chimney Rock—hidin' out would be my guess.'

Lew stomped around, test-driving the shoes and grinding his teeth like the dentist told him not to do. He had run his last ad, done his last duty to the local community as an honest, God-fearing merchant trying to make a decent living.

Abe felt a grin coming on, but stopped it dead. Down the road, he'd get a free half page out of J.C. Meantime, he wouldn't mention that he'd invested only fifty-one dollars plus change.

D ora Pugh was able to park this morning in front of her hardware store, a treat she had enjoyed in October only four or five times in recent years. In a few days, she'd have to take a helicopter to work and parachute onto the roof, as tourists would be parked all over the place, occasionally in somebody's yard. And how could she complain, really? Bottom line, at the end of the day, wadn't it tourists who helped put bread on Mitford tables?

She picked up the newspaper in its plastic bag. She knew for certain the *Muse* had come yesterday, yet this was clearly something from them. She remembered having a call from J. C. Hogan which she had not returned because she was busy dumping fake autumn leaves in the left-hand display window and setting out the rakes and tarps with a red vintage lawn chair. Though tourists did not buy a lot of hardware, they liked her displays, had even stepped inside and told her so.

She switched on the coffee, which she needed after a day like yesterday—finding one of her best friends dead and all that ambulance and funeral home business and Father Tim praying and taking charge and then missing the party she had desperately wanted to attend but couldn't since her nerves were shot.

She settled onto her stool and removed the newspaper from its shuck.

There was a picture of Esther Cunningham, topped by a headline.

Goodbye to the town monument? They were getting rid of the *town monument?*

She'd heard a nasty rumor about planting pansies where something had to be removed. Unbelievable! You could not get any satisfaction whatsoever by drivin' around a bed of pansies.

She liked driving around the *monument*; she had driven around the monument since she was a child; that is what people used to do for a good time. You drove around once or twice, then out to the country for a little picnic on the side of the road. If it was Sunday, which it usually was, you would sit on that big rock by Hoover's store and eat fried chicken out of a shoebox, with potato salad and deviled eggs and a Dr Pepper. After that, her daddy would buy everybody an orange Popsicle from Mr. Hoover and they would drive back to town and circle the monument a couple of times and go home and play checkers. That had been wonderful! That had been *enough!*

Wait a minute.

Good Lord. Esther Cunningham had passed! This had nothing to do with her party. And right on the heels of poor Esther Bolick! There was their old mayor, with her hair in the Carol Burnett style she wore in the eighties. *Passed?* Of all things! How terrible. All those beautiful daughters to mourn their mother, and her poor husband, who was a saint, and twentysome, maybe thirty, grans . . .

That's the way it was with people. Fine one minute, dead as a doornail the next. Well, she would be missed. Yes she would, they both would. She had cried her eyes out last night about Esther Bolick, but didn't know if she could do the same for their old mayor.

But wait. Under the picture was this story about the OMC. And the names of people who'd been the happy recipients of Esther Bolick's famous cake.

Oh, no. Oh. Lord. Surely not.

They had got their Esthers mixed up.

Just like she'd always said, it was confusing for two important people in one little town to have the same name. And now the chickens had come home to roost.

E sther Cunningham took a forkful of the scrambled eggs she was allowed twice a week while Ray cleaned up the kitchen. He had brought in some kind of junk mail in a plastic bag, and put it on the table.

'The parkin' solution a few years back was a Band-Aid,' she said to Ray. 'After years of wranglin', what did th' council do? Raze a condemned buildin' and put down an asphalt slab for thirty-five cars. Thirty-five! We need space for seventy-five, minimum!'

She slid the plastic bag off whatever it was, maybe coupons.

What would she run on, anyway? The old slogan she was famous for had lost its zing. Mitford takes care of its own? No. Something new, fresh, exciting.

'You know what this town needs?' she said.

'What's that?' He sighed deeply and noticed the faucet needed a new strainer.

'Excitement!'

He did not respond.

'Do you agree?'

'It wouldn't hurt,' he said, though personally, he couldn't take any more excitement.

'But that's puttin' th' cart before the horse. Th' real question is, what would be my platform?'

Again, no answer. So it had come to this, she thought—hearing aids at four thousand a pop.

'Maybe a community center!' she shouted. 'Every town needs a community center!'

He would like to open the window over the sink and jump out, but since it was ground level, he would only sprain an ankle. 'Daddy,' one of his girls said, 'just close your ears and don't listen.'

'So, what do you think? Ray! Are you listenin'? How about a *community center*?'

On top of everything else, his wife was losing her hearing and about to bust his eardrums. 'The bookstore,' he hollered, 'is our community center!' Somebody promised he'd get a crown in heaven. That would be the least they could do.

'Lord *help!*'

He turned around and saw that she was white as a sheet.

'What is it, buttercup?'

'I'm dead!'

'Now, now,' he said.

She held up the special edition. 'Read this.'

• • •

Coot Hendrick had finished his morning chores at Happy Endings, and at ten o'clock the store was spanking clean and ready for business. After saying hey to Miz Murphy and Louise, he scooted next door to take his break on the bench at Village Shoes.

Yessir, this was the best seat in town. A nice cool mornin' with th' leaves about four to five days off from peakin' as far as he could tell. Some said a week or more, but if he was to bet on it, which he wouldn't, th' color would be a little early this year.

He zipped open the plastic bag of apple chunks, which he ate each morning, based on the notion that an apple a day keeps the doctor away. And there came th' MPD captain, Miz Hogan, lookin' none too pleased. Tight-lipped, you might say.

'Mornin', Coot,' she said.

He saluted. 'Mornin', Captain.'

She hesitated, sighed. He moved over on the bench.

'No, no,' she said, 'I can't sit.'

'While you're standin' here,' he said, 'I have a question if you don't mind.'

She gave him a blank look.

'Want a piece of apple?'

Another blank look. 'No, thanks.'

'Do *police* get to run red lights 'cause they're *police?*' He had been wondering this.

She sat down. 'Why do you ask?'

'Well, I seen somebody do it, I don't know who it was, an' I wondered if it's a regulation for *police* to do what we cain't do.'

'You say you don't know who it was?'

'No, ma'am, it was too far away to see.'

She got up as quick as she'd set down. 'Have a great day, Coot.'

'You, too,' he said. 'An' thank you.'

He realized she had not answered his question. Probably a lot on the mind of a *police* captain.

He and Cynthia hated this for Esther Bolick's sake.

How had things gone so completely haywire? At least the basic information about funeral and graveside services was just as he reported yesterday to J.C.

He punched in the numbers.

Three rings. Four rings. Five. And a recorded message:

'Thank you for calling the *Muse*. We print *good* news! Please call again and have a nice day.'

4

She opened the box, dug into the packing material, and removed three objects swaddled in Bubble Wrap.

She unwrapped the small.

Then the medium.

Then the large.

Three pink pigs with battery-operated coin counters.

She lined them up on the farm table.

All through college and Atlanta and the nonprofit, she had used a shoebox or a Mason jar. She had loved the fun of counting out pennies and nickels and dimes and quarters and rolling them up and taking them to the bank. But there was no time at Meadowgate to count pennies; they would have to count themselves.

She had read that people won't pick up a penny anymore, and not many will pick up a nickel. But the dime was a game-changer. Seventy percent of people would pick up a dime, and everybody would pick up a quarter.

She would still pick up a penny. So she would take the large. After all, she was out there buying things and paying cash when she could, and maybe she would be selling eggs, which was nearly always a cash transaction. She would keep her piggy bank in the kitchen on the windowsill.

The medium was for Dooley, who didn't often handle cash; his bank could go in their bedroom. And Jack's would be the small and sit on the windowsill next to hers.

She found batteries in the storeroom and searched the kitchen tool drawer for three pennies and a dime she put there last week.

Yes!

One by one, she slipped coins into the big pig.

01 . . . 02 . . . 03 . . . 13 . . .

She remembered some pocket change in a soap dish in the laundry room and ran to fetch it. A nickel and three dimes.

The coins chimed into the counter.

18 . . . 28 . . . 38 . . .

Forty-eight cents.

They were starting over.

And it would be good.

I t was her best friend's signature thing not to cry, not even when her husband left at Christmas four years ago and never came back, not even for his Armani suits.

But Beth was crying now, while talking on a cell phone in Central Park and walking fast.

'All I've done for four years is work. I haven't gone out with anybody in forever. Two years, to be exact!'

'Remember what Astrid said? Beth doesn't cry, she works at Goldman!'

'The truth is, I do cry. A lot. Mainly because I work at Goldman! But I almost never cried . . . in front of anybody except my mom and dad.'

'Thanks for crying in front of me.'

Beth had been her college roommate and her matron of honor. She had known in June that something was wrong, but Beth hadn't wanted to talk. 'What will you do?'

'It's the first time since high school that I haven't known what to do. All I know is, I resigned on Thursday and I'm clearing out my office on the fifteenth. If I thought I'd stay in investment banking, I'd have given six weeks' notice, but I'll never work in this business again. I'm no good at being lashed to the stake and the VPs playing with matches.'

'Why don't you come live with us for a while?' The thought startled her. 'Until you know?'

'I couldn't come down there and sponge off you like some poor relative. What would I do with my Yankee self?'

'We could cook dinner together. You could play with Jack and help with his lessons while I paint. Or you could help put the garden down for winter. And the eggs . . . we have so many eggs . . . we could sell them instead of giving them away. You're good at marketing!'

She was off and running, her head a teeming nest of to-dos. 'Best of all, you could be an aunt! We're seriously short of aunts for Jack. That would be enough right there, more than enough.

'And you could help with canning pumpkin if you come soon, I would teach you how . . . '

Beth gave her nose a hard blow. 'I never knew it was so much work to live in the country. Everything was completely beautiful and peaceful for the wedding.'

'It took seven people and eight weeks to make it beautiful and peaceful.'

'It would be great to be there. Heaven.' Beth was walking faster, breathing harder. 'Okay, but if I come, I promise not to overstay my welcome. I love Meadowgate and you and Dooley and Jack Tyler, and I have lots of money saved because I never had time to spend it. Which means I can pay rent!'

How would Dooley feel about this? She had jumped in so fast, without thinking. 'Would you come straight here?'

'My lease is up on the fifteenth. I'm sending things to storage in Boston and will stop over with Mom a few days. So if it works with you and Dooley, I could be at Meadowgate on the twentieth.'

But of course he would be glad to do it. He liked Beth, and after all, it was only temporary. 'This is so good! I'm so happy! You'll be the best country girl!' She'd almost forgotten what it was like to have a friend her age.

'How is Tommy? We texted a couple of times, but I was so overwhelmed with making this decision . . . '

'His grandmother died, he was very close to her. He's been really sad.'

'Oh.' Beth slowing down. 'I'm sorry.' Two dogs barking; a pause. 'Are you sure about this, Lace? I won't stay forever, just till I can think things through. And I promise to be useful.'

'I'll call you tonight.'

'I'll be in a meeting all afternoon, then I need to finish a proposal, then have dinner with clients from Dallas who don't know I'm leaving . . . '

'But this is Saturday.'

'That's what I mean!' said Beth.

Through the open windows of the clinic, he heard the backup singing of their vintage mowers.

He was addicted to the sounds of this place—the bawling of cattle, the barking of dogs, the bilingual stuff of mockingbirds, the occasional yowling of a mountain cougar—the whole symphony of living in the country.

Jack had come over to watch his dad work, lugging a bucket of water. These days, no trip to the clinic was allowed to be made empty-handed.

The hit of the morning had been the llama, with its seductive eyelashes and imposing physique. Jack had gone nuts over the big guy, and so had Charley. Hal's old client, a woman who lived pretty far up the cove, had delivered the llama, ready for shots, in an open trailer. She had tied ribbons and small bells in its impressive mane. 'I'm an old hippie,' she said, 'here to meet the new vet and get a break from cannin' apple butter.' She had come bearing two quarts of the same as a gift to the new doc.

Around eleven, Amanda rang his office. 'You have a visitor.'

'Who?'

'Come see,' she said.

His red-haired seventeen-year-old brother was grinning big. 'Hey,' said Pooh.

'Hey, yourself! What a surprise!'

Hugs, backslapping.

'You're my uncle Pooh!' said Jack.

'All th' way. How's our Jack Tyler?'

'You can call me just Jack now.'

'Okay. Just Jack.'

'No, I mean *plain* Jack.'

'Plain Jack. I like it.'

'No-o-o-o!' said Jack, laughing. 'Can you put up my swing?'

'That goes up later,' said Dooley.

'I'd like it up now, please, please.'

'We all want stuff up now. As soon as we can. You're tall as me, dude.'

'Six-two,' said Pooh.

The marvel of it, having this kid brother. He had been so busy since the wedding he hadn't thought much about family. 'Come on back. Perfect timing. What brings you to the sticks?'

'I'd like to run something by you, if that's okay.'

'Better than okay.'

'It's kind of . . . personal.'

'We'll go in my office. Jack, take Charley home and ask your mom to set another place at the table.'

'Thanks. I didn't come for that, but I'm starvin'.' Pooh looked around the prep room. 'What's goin' on?'

'Plumbing problems. We start tearing the place up on Monday.'

Pooh thought his big brother suddenly looked pretty serious. He guessed that whatever it was would cost money, but Dooley had money. Dooley had everything. He was rich from what Miz Baxter left him.

Ever since he was a kid, he thought his big brother could do anything, he was perfect. Dooley had been his hero when they were little, and he was still his hero. But there had been that flash of something in his expression just now and he thought that maybe, down deep, Dooley was like everybody else, even like Pooh Barlowe—Dooley had feelings, things didn't always go right, he wasn't perfect.

H e sat in the glider, looking up from the spreadsheet on his laptop. Pooh and Jack and Charley were fooling around in the yard.

'You're some little guy with that football,' said Pooh. 'How about a ride on my back before I bust out of here?'

'I'm not little!'

'Yeah, but we need somebody in th' family to be little, just for a while, okay? You'll be big way sooner than you think. Besides, big guys can't climb on my back and ride around, but little guys can.'

Pooh squatted; Jack climbed.

'Go fast!'

And off they galloped to look for Choo-Choo and the heifers.

U nbelievable.
      She had forgotten about Kim and Irene coming tomorrow afternoon to see the farm.

She literally ran to the freezer in the storage room.

Apple pie, blackberry pie, the inevitable banana bread, the hoarded piece of their wedding cake . . .

She grabbed the blackberry pie. She and Dooley and Jack had picked the berries in August. They had given a free ride to a bunch of chiggers just like when they were kids, and they all had berries with cream and sugar for supper. Jack had gotten wired from the sugar, they all did, and they danced on the porch to Dave Rawlings and wound up itching like crazy.

She would heat the pie and serve it with ice cream if they had any. They couldn't keep ice cream in the house, it was Dooley's favorite thing, but here was a pint of Ben & Jerry's vanilla behind a pork roast. Vanilla was Dooley's sworn favorite in the ice cream universe; he had inherited his vanilla addiction from Father Tim.

As for the house being ready for company. Dismal! The worst was the living room, which nobody ever lived in. The upholstered stuff needed slipcovers; it looked like a yard sale.

A dust rag, a carpet sweeper, and a handful of zinnias from the garden—she caught her breath. It was the best she could do for someone who had a fabulous house in Malibu and was nominated three times for an Academy Award.

She figured this wasn't the best time to talk about the phone call. Dooley had just built a fire and was sitting in Doc Owen's old chair in the kitchen with a vet magazine in his lap, probably hoping for rain. That would be another thing on his mind right now.

She used to just blurt stuff out any time, anywhere, which was not a good idea. Their counselor had taught them to pray before big talks, to be sensitive to timing.

She didn't want him to say yes just to please her. This had to please everybody. Beth was a hit with Jack; during the rehearsal and the wedding, she'd been a safe place for him to run during a strange, even scary time. And Harley and Willie were keen on Beth—among other things, she was lots of fun.

She was as collected as she was going to be, so she told him.

He was getting this wrinkle between his eyebrows. She didn't remember noticing it before.

'There's a lot going on,' he said.

'I know. But she'll be lots of help, and I think we can help her. It's just temporary.'

He really didn't want to share his wife right now. He was beat, she was stretched. Yes, they had a wonderful life; things could have been worse, a lot worse. How could he possibly complain? He couldn't. So he didn't.

He would lose a part of her, just as he had lost a part of her with Jack, but what he got back from that more than compensated, more than repaid. Her best friend was another thing. They would talk, they would laugh, he would be . . .

He stared into the fire.

She didn't ask for much. He didn't want to mess this up. He hated feeling jealous, didn't even like the word. Or maybe it was fear.

'She'll be useful to everyone,' said Lace. 'I promise.' She had told him about the rent money, but didn't want to mention it again. Money shouldn't be a deciding factor.

'Where would she bunk?' he said.

'I don't know yet. We could clean out the junk room upstairs.'

All his stuff from eight years of college. Data! Artifacts! Stuff he needed to go through. At a time when he really needed to let go, he was holding on. To Lace. To his stuff. Let go, let God. Come on, man.

'Okay,' he said. 'Sure, that would be great.'

She didn't hide her excitement. 'Is Tommy in town?'

'I think the band is on the road. But I don't know. Why?'

'I'd like to tell him Beth's coming.'

Her best friend, Beth, who sang with Tommy at the dance after the wedding . . . and Dooley's best friend, Tommy, who had driven Beth and her mother to the airport the next morning . . .

She moved to the chair and leaned down and put her arms around his neck. 'You know what?'

'What?'

'I'm goin' to hug you and kiss you till you holler for help.'

He cackled his Dooley laugh and pulled her into his lap. She was crazy about her husband.

. . .

S he and Beth were laughing like they laughed in school. Over every-thing and nothing. The whole idea of what they decided to call their 'merger' was so out of the blue. It was like the planet was spinning on a completely other axis.

'I meant to tell you before,' said Beth. 'Mom is on a rafting trip with Father Brad. With his two daughters and their families.'

'How amazing. And wonderful!'

'I loved my dad,' said Beth.

'I know. But it's been a long time for Father Brad and for your mom, too. Everything will be okay, I promise. Bring warm clothes. Lots of people say it will be a hard winter.'

'I'm totally prepared for winter. I grew up in Boston and I've lived in Manhattan since college. Winter can't scare me!'

T hey were making soup tonight from the last of the garden. Dooley was reading, Jack was zooming around on the kitchen floor with his cars and dump trucks.

'We can't put Beth in our junk room,' she said. 'It's piled with tons of old clothes and things from your apartments at school and my stuff from all over. And we can't give her my studio because I work in there.'

'Right . . .' He was focused on a Beef Cattle Science book. He kept a stack of magazines and textbooks close by at all times, and was a total student of surgery procedures on YouTube. He had just watched an agonizing procedure called enucleation, where the vet had to remove a dog's eyeball. Lace could help him at the clinic in a lot of ways, but never that way.

'Are you listening?' she said. 'I wish she could have Harley's room. With that great bathroom and big closet, it would be perfect. He's over at Willie's a lot and I don't think Willie would mind if . . .'

'I know what I want for the day I get official!' Jack sat up amid the fleet of vehicles. 'A really big dump truck.' He used his loud voice, spread his arms wide. 'This big!'

'Make a list, buddy,' said his dad.

'I mean, they enjoy each other's company,' she said, 'they're like brothers. And Harley hates Rebecca Jane's old canopy bed. It embarrasses him, even though nobody sees it.' She stirred the soup. 'I guess we could ask?'

Dooley glanced up. 'Don't look at me. You ask.'

'Why do I have to ask?'

'I can do a lot of things, but I can't do that,' he said. 'Willie has lived in that house for thirty-five years. It's his territory. And Harley is settled in downstairs. I can't do it.'

She saw that Dooley's leg was jiggling.

'Or it could be a yellow backpack like Granpa Tim's. Or a pony!' Jack zoomed a truck under the table. 'But mostly a bike with sixteen-inch wheels if it would be red. Or it could be blue.'

She walked over and took Dooley's hand. 'Come out to the porch with me.'

There was a great cooking smell wafting around that wasn't their own.

'Cornbread!' he said. Willie's house with the green shutters and screen porch—it was coming from there. 'And collard greens. Pretty nice setup.'

Now and again, Harley joined them for dinner at the farmhouse, but typically he and Willie cooked supper together across the yard. Willie's longtime specialty was cornbread—thin and crispy. Harley's skill set was more extensive and somewhat mixed: brownies, lasagna, various greens with ham hock, and more recently, banana pudding. Harley had seen a TV chef make banana pudding and had since turned out two or three, including one for Miss Pringle.

'Willie has that whole other bedroom,' she said. 'It's neat as a pin, like it's just waiting for someone to move in.'

He gave her a grin. It was the first she had seen in what seemed ages. 'You're right,' he said. 'It could work.'

'Or even a tractor,' said Jack, standing with Charley on the other side of the screen door. 'But one my size that me an' Charley could ride around on, or even a new jigsaw puzzle with a lots of pieces like forty.'

'Just tell them it's only temporary,' said Dooley. 'I'll give you cash money to ask.'

'How much?'

He dug into his jeans pocket and pulled out a five-dollar bill.

'No way,' she said.

He dug into his other pocket and examined the contents. He folded two one-dollar bills with the five. 'Seven bucks,' he said, grinning. 'And not a dime more.'

She put her hands behind her back. 'Done! But please give it to me in change.'

As for the roomful of junk, how did two so-called young people start out with so much baggage?

Hadn't she always heard stories about starting with nothing, like her dad when he was in medical school and married to Carol? They had lived on the third floor in one room with 'a hot plate, two chairs, and a Beach Boys poster,' as he loved to say.

Cleaning out the junk room for guests would be a pain. And what would they do with it all, anyway?

She paused on the stairs. Why hadn't she thought of this before? And at the same time, they could park the Beemer by the road with a FOR SALE sign. Awesome!

Jack was asleep, Dooley was finishing his deep-dish pizza for tomorrow, and she needed to put the leftover soup in the freezer.

Yes! she thought as she ran down the stairs. Piggy banks, rental income, eggs, Beemer sale, yard sale! Rebecca Jane Owen could help; there would be plenty of hands to make it happen.

Yes, yes, yes, yes, yes!

Everything was going to be all right.

He carried over two buckets of water, did last rounds, visited the patients.

A text from Joanna.

Planning what to sell and what to leave behind. Have dental equipment, IV pump, oximeter, etc, a few things u may be able to use, some free. Call Monday if interested.

It would be cool to jump in a truck with all you need already stowed and drive around these beautiful back roads. If he bought her practice, he could do it Monday through Wednesday, while Hal and Blake tended the clinic here, then do the Thursday/Friday swing back here. But both practices would suffer. That was inevitable. And he would be on call 24/7, just like Hal and Herriot had warned against. No time for Lace and Jack, and worst of all, he would be in debt, big-time.

So why was he wasting energy even thinking about it?

He would pray for her dad. That was the best he could do with Joanna Rivers's inconvenient news.

The grass was getting crispy in spots. Thank God for hay in the barn.

5

H e opened the side door and heard the wistful morning piano of
Miss Pringle.
Once in a blue moon, they got an October morning like
this. It was a day when he could almost smell the ocean, when a gull
might wing overhead. He wasn't the biggest fan of sand and sea, but occasionally some hungering gnawed at him for the visual feast of the
Atlantic plain and the knowledge, more like a secret revealed only to
Tim Kavanagh, that over there were Ireland and England and Scotland
and Italy and . . .

The chiming of the church bells. Eight A.M.

His insulin shot was done and he was writing a sermon in his robe
and pajamas.

Except for the headache, it felt good to be back to his old routine.
The only thing missing was Barnabas, who always had an ear for the
read-aloud excerpt or, now and then, the entire homily.

He left the door open and looked across to the sofa where Truman
was sleeping off a night out. Clearly, Truman had been nostalgic for the
wilds of Meadowgate Farm—the narrow misses by a renegade fox, the

aggression of male barn cats twice his size—for he had shot through the cat door at six A.M. with a torn ear and a gimp leg.

Wearing oven mitts against the resistance of an insulted cat, he had vetted the torn ear and bandaged it. About the leg, he wasn't so sure. He would call Dooley around nine and get a little free advice.

An email chimed into his desktop PC.

>Got to get out there and face the bloody music. Drop what you're doing buddyroe and help me out here. High noon. Feel Good.

Their local desperado had returned from his hideout.

H e slid into a chair at their usual table at Feel Good, where J.C. sat with his back to the door.

'Tell me who's comin' in,' said J.C. 'I've got to work up to showin' my face, I can't do this all at once.'

'Who is it you don't want to see?'

'Half th' town. But especially th' churchwomen who pitched in and took th' back page.'

'Which churchwomen? There are five churches in these immediate parts.'

'That ECW crowd. They could wrangle elephants with Genghis Khan.'

They gave their order to a college student from Wesley who would rather be hiking with his beagle. He drank half a glass of tap water and waited for the confession.

'Okay.' J.C. wiped his perspiring face with a paper napkin. 'By mistake I pulled Esther Cunningham's photo out of the file. So sue me! Is it my fault those women have th' same name? Come on, I was in a hurry, I had no help, I had to get th' blasted thing to bed. Look on the positive side—how many people could turn around a special edition, full color, in under sixteen hours, ads and all?

'I didn't sleep, man, I was cockeyed, give me a break. And think about it—it was a very flattering shot of the old mayor. With th' birth-day front page comin' next week, she gets her picture in the paper twice in a row! One with the lieutenant gov'nor! She loves that stuff.

'As for Esther Bolick, I hate that it wasn't her photo, she was a very nice woman. I'll run a correction next Thursday, and a photo with th' cake. But—and here's a mega plus—the obit was a masterpiece. Vanita at th' top of her game!'

J.C. maneuvered another napkin around the moonscape of his face. 'So I made a mistake. One little bitty mistake in thirty-five years! And what happens? I'm a leper in this town . . .'

'A group just walked in,' he said. 'One, two, three, four women. Part of the ECW committee for the Bolick reception.'

'Don't make eye contact,' said J.C., sliding down in his chair.

Wanda Basinger plowed through the lunch crowd in full cowgirl gear, her coffeepot a six-gun.

'How about you, Father?' She ignored the *Muse* editor.

'Not for me. I'm off coffee.'

'How long?'

'Two and a half days and counting.'

'You're gettin' more oxygen to your brain, your brain don't know what to do with it.'

'True. The headache from Gehenna.'

'Did you go cold turkey?'

'I did.'

'That's your problem. You don't cold-turkey a caffeine habit.'

'What do you do?'

'You come off easy. Use a blend of decaf with your regular joe and keep taperin' th' regular. Do that for a month and bingo. You're unhooked.'

There went the lightning flash over his left eye.

'Too late,' he said.

Wanda turned to J.C., gave him a look, eyed his coffee mug. 'You?'

'If you don't *mind*,' said the editor.

'So, Wanda, who is the woman who came in with friends a couple minutes ago?'

'Lilah somebody from up north. She's on th' committee to bury Miz Bolick an' tryin' to get a handle on th' way we do things down here.'

'That ought to keep her rollin' in the aisle,' said J.C.

Coffee poured, Wanda Basinger was on to greener pastures.

'Did you see that? If looks could kill, I'd be pushin' up daylilies . . . '

'Maybe you should think about doing what Ben Franklin said: *Never ruin an apology with an excuse.*'

'. . . which is the thanks I get for bein' a Feel Good regular.'

'Just tell people you're sorry. Be sincere. Keep it simple. It'll blow over.'

'Not to mention cuttin' her a deal on an eighth page and recommending her fries in an editorial last year.'

'You recommend fries in editorials?'

J.C. grunted. 'It keeps me offa politics.'

He recalled that last year J.C. said he would retire when pigs fly. Maybe pigs should hop to it.

D ooley had dispensed vet advice for Truman's paw and invited them to come out Sunday morning around ten-thirty.

He would celebrate Morning Prayer and Holy Communion, and Dooley would make his famous deep-dish pizza, which they would enjoy on the porch. Then home to Mitford to finish his sermon for Monday's funeral, after which he and Cynthia would be present at the Sunday-evening viewing.

He liked having a plan.

He thought it would be good to sing a hymn after Morning Prayer at Meadowgate. A cappella, of course. He noodled his noggin, as Uncle Billy used to say. Ha! Yes. Hymn 686. Three glorious verses! He would stash the hymnals in his yellow backpack, including a hymnal for Jack Tyler's very own.

He sang as he changed shoes for their walk.

'O to grace how great a debtor / Daily I'm constrained to be! / Let Thy goodness, like a fetter / Bind my wandering heart to Thee.'

His spirit lifted.

Twelve years out from a weekly pulpit, he was beginning to like retirement. He no longer needed the drama of full-time priesting, the mile-a-minute mishaps and consternations of the human horde. His end of the horde was all he could meaningfully hold up.

O kay,' he said, offering his arm. 'We're off.'

'Three walks per week divided into a hundred and fifty minutes. How much is that?'

Artists! They could never do arithmetic.

'Fifty minutes per walk. Piece of cake. You've been sitting at a drawing board for four decades, you can afford to sacrifice fifty minutes for your heart.'

'I have a good heart.'

'You do. Everybody knows that.' He patted his bulging jacket pocket. 'I've got our mesh bag, we should stop by the Local before the Peppers, um, the Peepers arrive.'

'How about what I'm wearing?'

'What do you mean?'

'What do people wear to walk for their health? Is this a power walk? Will these jeans work?'

They could stand here chatting all day. 'You look great, not to worry.' He reproffered the arm. 'Here we go.'

Up the sidewalk they trotted to the corner of Wisteria and Main, hooked a right, did a promenade past the Collar Button, Sweet Stuff, the glum office building, Village Shoes, and Happy Endings, then hooked a left on Lilac Road.

Left on Ivy Lane, left on Wisteria, stepping lively, and right into the alley behind Feel Good, where his wife slowed to a crawl. Looking at birds, coming to a complete standstill to view cloud formations . . .

'Cardio!' he said. 'They want *cardio!*'

Trooping past the unkempt rear garden of Edie Adams's old house and Mitford Blossoms's trash cans and the back lot of Melvin's Bike Repair, where Melvin was working on a ten-speed and tipped his cap to Cynthia.

He almost never got to parade his good-looking, much-younger wife through town; he was having a wonderful time.

'How's your heart?' he said.

'Beating,' she said, breathless.

'Great! Wonderful!'

Warmer this afternoon than expected. He had broken a sweat.

A lot of cars in the Lord's Chapel parking lot. Getting ready for the reception on Monday, of course, and setting up for tomorrow's service and the fancy supply guy from Morganton with his Cambridge lauds. In days of yore, yours truly would have been up to his elbows, if needed, in arranging altar flowers, sweeping the vestry . . .

'So,' he said, 'while we're here, let's run in and check things out.'

Her cheeks were flushed, her blue eyes bright, her hair in that sort of askew way he was crazy about.

'Five minutes,' he said.

There appeared to be a small meeting going on in the parish hall, so they stood in the doorway, respectful.

'When you die,' Lois Burton was informing Lilah, 'your body is usually hauled over to Wesley, where the funeral director if you see him on the street in off-hours is wearing a T-shirt. I just saw him rigged out in one that said *Make Cornbread, Not War.* Some people find this sort of behavior refreshing, but I find it tacky.'

'If your standards are higher,' said a committee member he didn't recognize, 'they ship you down to Holding. Holding has a funeral director in a suit and tie who even carries a handkerchief.'

'That,' said Lois, 'is where they should have sent Esther, bless her heart, she had high standards.'

'Ladies,' he said, 'I know we're interrupting. Forgive us, please.' He introduced his wife to those whom they hadn't previously known. Lois was a former parishioner, sprung from the Methodists some years ago.

'Have you heard the talk about a funeral home coming to Main Street?' said Lois.

They hadn't, actually.

'To th' bike repair. I don't think a funeral parlor would be good marketing for our picturesque village. People do not want that kind of place in their face. On a back street, maybe, but not on Main. Besides, what we really need in this town is a dry cleaner.'

'The Wesley funeral home called me this morning,' said Lilah. 'Wanting to know what she would be buried in.'

Lilah, he thought, appeared to be a caring and thoughtful woman.

'A dress, not a suit,' said Lois. 'Something floral. She liked mauve. Doris Pugh would know all that, she's at th' Hardware today, we could ask her.'

'That would be good,' he said.

His wife had claimed a chair and was fanning herself with a pew bulletin.

'What to do about her hair is the question,' said Lilah. 'She doesn't have family to think of these things. The funeral home is asking.'

'I don't know why they bothered to ask,' said Lois. 'In Wesley, they automatically do up your hair like the queen if you're over fifty-five. Even if you're a *day* over fifty-five, you get the part down the middle and a curl on either side. It's company policy.'

'That settles it,' said Cynthia. 'I'm being cremated.'

Up Main, passing Oxford Antiques and Dora Pugh's Hardware and the Irish Woolen Shop and the drugstore and the bank. Crossing Wisteria and whizzing past the Collar Button and Sweet Stuff and the glum offices and Village Shoes and hooking a right into Happy Endings and their O for October sale.

'Fifty minutes of shoe leather!' he said, tapping the face of his watch. 'On the dot! Plus we'll add a few bonus minutes to stop by Avis and cut through the alley to home. Today's route will be our plan.'

'Your plan.'

'Somebody has to have a plan,' he said.

C oot was vacuuming the floors at Happy Endings to the rhythm of something he memorized this morning.

He threw up his hand to th' preacher an' Miz Kavanagh without missing a beat.

'The corkboards are so full,' Hope said over the roar of the machine, 'we're writing quotes on the wall. You really started something, Father.'

Grace took his hand and Cynthia's. 'I'll show you mine,' she said.

They were led to the poetry section, where there was a great scribble on the wall. Dozens of scribbles.

'Here's mine,' said Grace. 'Under a quote by Dr. Seuss.'

He stooped and read her quote aloud. 'Next to Sarah and Leslie, a book is my best friend. Grace Elizabeth Murphy.'

'Well done!' said Cynthia. 'Succinct and charmingly stated.'

'Thank you,' said Grace. 'And that one is my favorite.'

It was a sketch of a dog quoting J. M. Barrie. *It is all very well to be able to write books, but can you wiggle your ears?*

'Okay, let me at it,' said Cynthia. 'Is there a special pen?'

'A Sharpie.' Graced handed it over.

'Either . . . write . . . something . . . worth . . . reading,' Cynthia quoted aloud as she inscribed the wall, 'or . . . do something . . . worth . . . writing. Ben . . . Franklin.'

'Amen!' he said. He had once tried writing a book of essays and scrapped the worthless project.

Grace looked at him through her bifocals. 'Now you.'

'I don't know if I can recall a good quote this very minute.'

'You can just think about it if you want to.'

'Give me a minute. Maybe I can come up with something.' He was a big quote collector, had two books full of the stuff. He scratched his head.

'Yes! Got it! Here's one.'

'Write big,' said Grace.

'A . . . classic . . . is . . . a . . . book . . . that . . . has . . . never . . . finished . . . saying . . . what . . . it . . . has . . . to . . . say. Italo Calvino.'

'I love that,' said his wife. 'Perfect.'

'That makes thirty-four quotes on the wall,' said Grace. 'I'm counting. When we run out of space that people can reach, Mom or Aunt Louise will get on a ladder and write the person's quote up there. Coot can't do it because he can't write as good as he can read.'

'Aha.'

'And customers can't go on the ladder. Do you know why?'

'I don't.'

'Because of insurance.'

'Good thinking,' he said. 'Now, moving along to business. What O titles are sailing out of here?'

'*Oliver Twist*,' said Grace.

'We have it.'

'*Our Town*!' said Grace. 'But I think that is a play.'

'We have that, too,' said Cynthia. 'So let's buy an O title for Coot. How about *Old Man and the Sea*?'

Grace nodded, approving. 'He's making a library and doesn't have it. I'm writing a book myself. I have four pages totally in cursive.'

'Wonderful!' said Cynthia. 'I'm always thrilled to have four pages.'

'I don't have a title yet. When I have a title, I think I should put my name on the front as big as the title. Because if I had not written the book, there would not be a title, and so these two things are equal.'

'Agreed. Absolutely.'

'Would you like to hear a joke?'

'Always.'

'How do chickens bake a cake?'

'How?'

'From scratch.'

Cynthia had a laugh.

'Aha,' he said. 'Very good.'

'You didn't laugh.'

'True,' he said. 'I forgot to laugh. But it's a good joke. Really.'

'I could tell you one more.'

'Tell away,' he said.

'Where do cows go on their first date?'

'I give up,' said Cynthia.

'The mooovies.'

They had an extra laugh on their way to the Local. Grace Murphy in her bifocals. Her curly hair. Her ardent solemnity. And to think the world might have lost this perfectly unique human being.

'A nerdy little kid,' he said with affection.

C oot Hendrick liked being what they called a town fixture.

His people had settled Mitford and he knew its early history as good as the back of his hand. He liked how his great-great-great-great-great-granddaddy had rode up th' mountain with his English wife settin' behind him on his horse. He had once known the name of the horse but forgot it, an' since his mama died, there was nobody to ask. Maybe it was Trigger, but he didn't think so.

He liked the way his place above th' bookstore creaked when th' wind was blowin'. It had scared him on his first night three winters back; it sounded like th' old buildin' had the shivers. He'd been tryin' to read *Where the Wild Things Are* to put his head to sleep. But he'd laid awake, froze as a Popsicle, hearin' sounds an' scared to breathe. Nossir, he would not read any more scary stories, there was enough of scary in this world.

Except for the whisper of tires on the nighttime street below, things up here was quiet as a settin' hen. He didn't have a TV; he'd set the bloomin' thing on th' street when he sold his mama's place. Besides, Doc Wilson said he was losin' his hearin'.

'Do you hunt?' asked the doc.

'Nossir,' he said. 'I don't kill nothin'.'

'Listen to loud music, play drums?'

'Nossir.'

'Then it's very likely genetic.'

'Very likely what?'

'Comes down your family line.'

'Say I'm gon' have a good time?'

He and Cynthia had made a darned good dinner, cooking and cleaning up as a team.

And now, what could be better than a handwritten honest-to-Pete letter in a hand-addressed envelope, with transit recompensed by an Elvis stamp?

He inserted a kitchen knife under the flap and sliced open the envelope and removed three crisp pages. A feast. He was happy.

Dear Brother,

Allow me to abide by an old rule for letter writing, which commands that I leave unmentioned what you already know and instead tell you something new.

I have found Eva's grave.

The joy of this discovery is beyond my powers of description.

For nearly forty years, I dared hope that by some miracle she may still be living, though every trace of her had vanished. Greater,

however, than my hope to find her alive was the unrelenting need to
find her at all.

To discover her grave has been to discover a somehow deeper
love. She is now in a mysterious sense more than alive, more than
real to me. You will understand how impossible it is to make such
feelings comprehensible to another.

Dunbar wrote in 'Love's Apotheosis':

> I care not what the circling years
> To me may do.
> If, but in spite of time and tears,
> You prove but true.

In the visit to her grave in Tuscaloosa, Alabama, I find that she
has somehow proved true.

I sat on a bench by her headstone and talked, spilling every grief
and happiness, then drove home to Holly Springs in a daze from
which I may never recover. Indeed, I find myself keen on clinging
to it! God has redeemed sorrow and given unbounded gladness
for loss.

I believe I have succeeded in telling you something completely
new! Further, the way in which I discovered her grave deserves a
letter all its own. I will write again in a few days as soon as we get
the garden cleaned out.

Tuscaloosa is but two hours and fifty-three minutes from
my door. In the months prior to spring, I shall spend the days
figuring which rose variety may work best at her grave site.
The churchyard is of fertile river-bottom soil with good drainage.
I hope you will give me your horticultural wisdom on suitable
varieties.

I also hope you notice that in this letter I haven't once
mentioned my health—now that is new indeed! I confess it is
extremely good.

You and Cynthia and Dooley and Lace and young Jack are ever in my prayers. Mama and Sister send love, as do I, your faithful brother in Christ,

Henry

P. S. Please write and tell me the many miracles on your end.

6

MEADOWGATE

SUNDAY, OCTOBER 4

The Feast Day of St. Francis of Assisi, the congregants kneeling on porch cushions by a wooden bench . . .

'The gifts of God for the people of God. Take them in remembrance that Christ died for you, and feed on him in your hearts by faith, with thanksgiving.'

He pressed the wafer into cupped palms. All those years of a parish family, and now this small, private family—his truest brethren, his cup overflowing.

'The Body of our Lord Jesus Christ keep you in everlasting life, Cynthia.'

'Amen.'

The wafer dissolving into the chamber of the heart.

' . . . in everlasting life, Lace.'

'Amen.'

' . . . in everlasting life, Dooley.'

'Amen.'

Joy upon joy.

The smallest palms lifted, baptized to receive. ' . . . in everlasting life, Jack.'

. . .

G ranpa Tim! My new pig bank. For keepin' money in.'
He dug deep—no change. Peeled off a five.

Jack shook his head. 'It only takes th' other money.'

'I'll give this to your mom. She'll get it changed into quarters for you. How's that?'

'How many quarters will it be?' Jack asked his mom.

'Um, let's see. In quarters . . .'

'Twenty,' said Dooley. 'Big money.'

'What can I buy when th' bank gets full?'

'Let's talk about that when it gets full,' said Dooley.

His mom smiled big. 'Or you can just take it to the bank and start filling up your pig all over again.'

Jack tugged at the sleeve of his granpa. 'Will you come swing with me?'

'I will!'

'You can push me an' I can push you. We can go to th' moon an' back.'

'Good plan,' he said.

'We need somebody to watch,' said Jack.

'That would be me,' said Granny C.

A fter lunch, he and Dooley walked together past the corncrib and chicken lot, through the barn shed where the Beemer sat on blocks, and down to the cattle gate.

'Great pizza, Doc.'

'Thanks.'

'You once said that music is in your head all the time. Still true? You sounded strong on 686.'

'There's a lot of other stuff in my head now. But yes, I miss singing.'

'We're looking for a soloist tomorrow. Esther liked 410, you used to sing it.'

Dooley laughed. 'No way.'

'I hope you'll sing again.'

'I don't know. That part of my life seems finished. I sing with the truck radio. That's a pretty cool way to do it, all that great backup. Sometimes Lace and I sing together in the truck.'

'Lace says she can't sing, but she sounded fine this morning.'

Dooley grinned. 'She's a fun singer. Sort of a female Bob Dylan, she says.' They stopped by the cattle gate and leaned on the fence, looking out to the tree line and the heifers.

'So, Dad. Some pretty profound news.'

'I'm a fan of profound news.'

Dooley grinned. 'Pooh wants to be a preacher.'

He was what the Brits call gobsmacked. 'Our Pooh?'

'Our Pooh. He doesn't know what denomination. He just knows he wants to go into the ministry, and wonders if you'd talk to him about it. I think he's had what you say is a call.'

He crossed himself, happy. So out of what Jefferson described as the sundered nest had come a vet, an engineer, a crack pool player, and now possibly a servant of God. An amazement, all of it.

'Then there's Jessie. She's in trouble, Dad. I don't know all the details, but pharmaceuticals are involved and it's not good. Pooh says she needs help, and Mom and Buck don't know what to do. Pooh says Mom won't call you because you've been the one who had to bail us all out.'

'You know who did the bailouts.' What timing. Father Brad and his famous mash-up for teen girls in a downward spiral—this year, snow camping, if they got any snow.

'Let's pray about it. You told me not long ago that it's hard to remember to pray. How's that going?'

'Spotty. I usually remember to thank him, but mostly I forget to ask.'

'Takes practice. A long obedience in the same direction, as Nietzsche said.'

They turned toward the house, walking along the fence line. Choo-Choo spotted them and came at a trot.

'That's a bull and a half.'

'He's th' man,' said Dooley. 'Beautiful coloration. Comes from a recessive red gene carried by the black breed. One in four calves—red. Since red to red breeds true, that's what we're lookin' for in th' spring.'

'How's it going at the clinic?'

'We've got a plumbing problem. Work starts tomorrow; things will be a mess for a few weeks. A prayer reminder for sure.'

'Can we help?'

'We've got it covered, thanks.'

We've got it covered. It felt good to say that, so he said it again. 'We've got it covered.'

'Well done.'

He liked hearing that, too.

H e and Jack had gone up to Lace's studio to move a chair down to the kitchen.

'Look, Dad!'

Jack was always buzzed about the height of the attic studio and the size of things below. 'There's Mom with th' ladies, they're talkin' to th' cows.'

Choo-Choo was in the chill pen, ready for a heifer coming their way this evening. He could have sold a couple of straws, but Fred Lewis was a farmer who liked getting it done old school. 'Nature's way,' said Fred, chewing a cud of tobacco. 'That's th' best way.'

Lace and Kim and Irene were walking toward the house, he could hear the faint murmur of their conversation through the open window, and his wife's laughter. There were no words for the love he felt for her, and for his son, a love so deep it was nearly painful.

When would he start believing all this was real? But if the current fiasco hadn't made their life real, what would?

S he ran into the kitchen. The room was instantly alive with her shining.

'I'm going to paint the mural! I'm going to paint the mural!'

She saw the look on his face.

'But right here at home! Up there! In Heaven!'

He couldn't take this in.

'The canvas comes eleven feet deep by as much width as we need, which is fourteen feet. We'll close up the window with plywood and install the canvas around the wall. It will stop just two inches to the left of the door. It will work, it will work!'

She was all eyes and laughter and long legs and hands clapping.

'Kim wants me to capture everything I can of everything they saw today. She loves Choo-Choo and the girls and the chickens and the barn with its smashed roof, even my old Beemer and Jack's swing. Everything. The mountains, the clouds, the beautiful clouds!'

She felt delirious, as she sometimes felt as a child when she was ill. 'We have to let it dry and roll it up and ship it to Kim by December twentieth; Irene and her family are going to Kim for Christmas.'

They high-fived; he took her in his arms and rocked her, stunned. There were no words in him. There were words, but they weren't coming out.

'Can I do it? Can I paint a huge mural?'

'You can do anything.'

'By December twentieth? How many weeks?'

'A little more than eleven weeks.'

She blinked. 'Jack's Name Day party on the twelfth. I just remembered.'

'We'll all pitch in. We can handle the party. Whatever it takes.'

She sat down at the kitchen table; breathless. There would be so many people in the house on Name Day weekend—Kenny and Julie and the kids, if they could come, which was doubtful, and Sammy, and Beth would probably still be here, she could help, and everybody from town, and the mural needing to be shipped by the twentieth. Her heart pounded.

'Tell me again.'

'What?'

'That I can do it.'

'You can do it. You can do anything. Whoa. Wait. We can do it, we can do anything.'

'Philippians 4:13,' she said. 'Can you believe this is happening?'

It was one more thing he couldn't believe. But he was happy for her, for the three of them, totally—he wanted to jump or shout or run or do something with all this, it was filling him up.

He pulled her to her feet and headed for the door. 'Let's go.'

'Go where? Where's Jack?'

'Napping with Charley in the library. Race you to the barn.'

S he was delivering sweet feed while Dooley and Jack rode the fence line.

'I'm doing the mural,' she said, holding a handful of grain across the hot wire. 'At home.' She was buzzing.

His eyes were the color of mahogany, his tongue sandpaper on her palm.

Five heifers lined up behind the big guy, waiting their turn. She dipped her hand again in the bucket, unable to say more.

H e looked up from a quick read of the article 'Grape and Raisin Toxicity in Dogs' and watched his son gunning cars around the kitchen floor.

It would be good if Jack had someone to play with. There were no kids his age in the immediate neighborhood, and school was a year out given his birth date. He needed to take Jack fishing. Yesterday had been a clinic and hay day; they needed a clinic and fishing day.

'Zoom, zoom!' said Jack. 'Look, Dad. It's a race.' Jack was putting his weight on a car in each hand and moving fast, following with his knees. A brother or sister would be great. But they didn't have the time it would take to pull off another adoption. Besides, Jack's adoption wasn't even official yet; they were fostering. His leg was jiggling. He needed to stop messing up his mind with the future and concentrate on what was at hand.

He got up and put on a jacket and stepped out to the yard. Cool. Nice. But parched. The crickets were louder in the thin October air.

The plumbers and construction crew would hit at seven-thirty in the morning. He rolled his shoulders and sniffed the air for what was predicted, and then heard the scream.

My God.

He'd seen plenty of blood, but this was Jack's blood.

The wheels of the cars had moved faster than Jack's knees could keep up and he'd gone down on his face. Charley was barking, Jack was screaming, sobbing, writhing in his arms.

'Need to check your nose,' he said. 'Hold still.'

'No! It hurts! No!'

'What happened?' Lace was breathless from racing downstairs.

He did a quick manipulation of the nose. Screaming.

'Not broken,' he said. 'He fell on his face playing with his cars. Need warm water and a cloth.' He held his son. 'It's okay, it's okay, it's okay.'

He suspected the sight of his own blood had frightened Jack as much as the incident itself. They cleaned him up on the sofa in the library; treated a cut on his forehead with iodine and a Band-Aid. 'Keep it moist for a couple of days,' he told Lace. 'He'll get some bruising and swelling around the nose, but he'll be fine.' Their boy would be growing up with two people who had never been consoled by their biological parents, had never heard the words *It's okay*. But he and Lace could do this; his heart was full of doing this.

Lace held Jack in her lap, rocked him in her arms.

'I hurt my face,' he sobbed.

'I know, I know. It will be better, I promise.' She kissed his forehead. 'I'm so sorry.'

'Skype th' grannies!' he wailed.

'We can't Skype the grannies. It's time for pajamas and prayers.'

'Skype th' grannies!'

'Why do you want to Skype the grannies?'

'To show them my face . . .' Sobbing. '. . . where I fell and hurt myself. They would want to see.'

'Tomorrow,' she said. She stood and picked him up and he laid his head on her shoulder, his arms tight around her neck. 'We'll show them tomorrow.'

'You promise?'

'I promise,' she said.

She would never leave Dooley and Jack; she could paint the mural. Everything was going to be all right, she thought as she left the room with Jack and Charley.

'I'll be right up,' he told her.

He took off his jacket, hung it on the coatrack.

'Man,' he said.

A little brother or sister; it was a tape playing in his head. Another adoption would take another two years, so there was an incentive to hurry even before they got in a groove with Jack. It was a total rock and a hard place.

The prognosis over a year ago was that Lace would never have children. Her father had kicked her twice in the abdomen. First time, she was seven years old. Second time, she was ten and the menstrual blood began. Thank God he had never laid eyes on the man; he would have ended up in prison instead of vet school. The hard blows had caused infections due to rupture in the abdominal cavity, a problem that was almost constantly painful and couldn't be detected by CAT scan or MRI imaging. Adhesive disease, they finally learned, though for years it had been treated as irritable bowel syndrome.

Bottom line, there was no way they could even think about another adoption. Not any time soon.

. . .

I t began around midnight.
    It would be a rain of long obedience in the same direction—
straight down. At two A.M., the temperature had dropped three degrees.
Tomorrow the high would be fifty-four, and soon, too soon for some,
temperatures would descend into the thirties, then the teens and
into the single digits. The time would come for snow on the roof, flame
on the hearth, smoke up the chimney.

    The rain fell steadily upon the big house and the small, the moss-
grown shingles of the corncrib, the corrugated tin of the barn. It fell
with a steady roar into the depths of the woods and thrashed the gray
waters of the pond. It sent rivulets into the bolt-hole of the groundhog,
the den of the fox, the burrow of the field hare.

    Across acres of alluvial fields once trafficked by glaciers, each drop
was a mallet pounding seed into its winter bed.

    Everywhere, everything . . . rain.

7

MITFORD

MONDAY, OCTOBER 5

F rom the get-go, the Local was a small-town grocery store ahead of its time.'

Avis Packard spoke to the mirror on the back of his bedroom door. He stood up straight in his sock feet and sucked in his gut, although, he was proud to say, he didn't have much to suck in. His Camel smoked in the ashtray by the bed. It was still dark out there and his sleep had been fitful.

He wadn't lookin' so good this morning. For all he knew, he hadn't been lookin' good for a long while, as he never examined hisself in a mirror.

He hiked up his britches, ran his fingers through his hair.

'Sourcing local has always been of utmost importance to me. Thirty-five years ago, I was on a mission to find the freshest, best-tasting food available for my customers. And I found it right in our own backyard. In a manner of speakin'.'

No need to describe his twelve-mile descent into the fertile valley below Mitford, on the switchback washboard road that had delivered him there without a tailpipe.

He smacked his head to wake up his brain. The whole business of makin' this speech had half ruined him at the store. He had stared at Father Tim a few days ago and could not remember th' man's name to save his life.

Father Tim looked worried. 'Avis?'

'Yo,' he said, dumb as a gourd.

'Are you in there, buddyroe?'

I need help, he wanted to say. But how would it look for a man to ask help for a speech about his own trade? Did Father Tim come to him for help on sermons? No. He would have to travel this road by hisself.

He wished he had somebody to turn to, but not a wife, no. He had never wanted a wife, that was as foreign an idea as walkin' on th' moon. He didn't understand a thing about women. Nothin'. One time he read what the teacher said on his report card. *Has difficulty with relationships.* Mostly nobody in his family paid attention to what th' teachers said.

A few years ago, people tried to fix him up with Shirlene Hatfield, who ran the spray-tan booth at A Cut Above. He'd only seen her on the street, but she scared him half to death in those funny clothes and he heard she wadn't too hot on gettin' fixed up with him either. He sent a six-pack of home-brewed ginger beer when she married Omer Cunningham.

Another thing. What if he passed out cold while givin' this talk and hit his head an' lapsed into a coma in a strange city? Just sayin'.

Travel was not his long suit, an' speakin' of—he had no idea what to wear for this shindig. Should it be a suit or jacket and tie? The people in today's small-grocery business were different, as he could plainly see in th' trade journals. Some had tattoos, one or two had piercings, and a good many had facial hair. They didn't look like moms and pops looked back in the day.

He opened the drawer of the bedside table and took out his comb and scraped it through his hair. This action occasioned a minor coughing fit, which he enjoyed. He turned his head to the left, to the right. He had not noticed before that his hair was longer on one side than the other; he could not see his right ear.

He ran a neat part along the center of his scalp, and combed his hair to either side. No.

Most of his farmers in the Valley worked town jobs in Morganton or Elizabethton, and had started out with a pig here and a few apple or nut trees there. But with the longtime ag training and instruction of yours truly, fourteen families now supplied the Local with Silver Queen corn, Big Boy tomatoes the size of dinner plates, Alberta peaches, wild persimmons, figs, walnuts, pecans, nine apple varieties, free-range chickens, grass-fed beef, and acorn-fed pork.

Boy howdy, they raised some awesome hogs in the Valley. If he was to take a couple of those big boys down to Charlotte and let 'em loose in the crowd, that'd be all the entertainment you'd want for an evenin'.

He trooped to the kitchen sink and ran water over his comb and took it back to the bedroom mirror and went at it again, this time with no part, just slicked straight back. He blinked and said a really bad word.

There was that sound again at the back door. Like somebody knockin' on th' screen. He went to the kitchen and turned on the yard light and opened the door and peered out. Must have been the wind, which was up pretty good since last night. One time he'd seen a wild boar in the yard, another time it was a black bear and her cub.

Ho! There was a little dog over in the bushes. It was pokin' its head out an' lookin' toward the house. Then it backed into the bushes and disappeared.

He switched off the light and went again to the mirror and grinned at hisself to see how that would go over with the audience. His teeth did not look like th' teeth on TV. TV teeth could blind a person, and no, he would not be settin' in a dentist chair to have his choppers bleached for five hundred bucks. People at th' convention would have to take him in the raw. What you see is what you get.

His life in the grocery business had been a good journey, even with that mighty battle he'd fought with Raleigh to sell homegrown Valley provender without callin' in troops and hound-dog regulators.

Th' Valley was like his baby, you might say, situated on a rich, dark, peaty soil you could eat with a spoon. He'd used all the farm trainin' he'd learned from his daddy, who'd been a county ag agent in Tennessee. His daddy had a green thumb like you wouldn't believe, and together they'd hauled home many an award from the county fair. Some of those awards were displayed right now over the fireplace he never used.

He checked the clock. Still dark. He had two pickup loads of apples comin' in at daylight—your Golden Delicious and your Red Delicious and your Rome Beauty and your Winesaps. It was pie time, cobbler time, juice and cider time; people were crazy about th' apples comin' in, hisself included, an' next would be th' pumpkins. What got him goin' was a truckload of fresh produce. Not women, not parties. He had never been to a party, much less thrown one; he'd been raised to work. Work, that was th' ticket.

He laid down the comb. He had just figured out what was naggin' him about this speech.

Since the Hometown Grocers Association was finally on the same farm-to-table page as the Local, what could he possibly have to tell these people?

He sighed and sat on the side of the bed and pulled on his shoes and tied the laces, and went to the coatrack and put on his green jacket and zipped it and saw that the wall calendar of food quotes was still turned to September.

In wine there is wisdom . . . in water there is bacteria.

—DAVID AUERBACH

He flipped up the page and stuck it on the nail and read the quote for October.

A party without cake is just a meeting.

—JULIA CHILD

I t was a perfect day for a wedding—*Happy is the bride the sun shines on*—or for that matter, a funeral. *No matter how rich you become or how powerful you are,* according to Michael Pritchard, *when you die, the size of your funeral will pretty much depend on the weather.*

Seventy degrees and not one cloud. The sky had been swept by an immense paintbrush loaded with Carolina blue.

Twenty-seven people gathered for the service at the rain-soaked graveside, then followed the Kavanaghs' car to Lord's Chapel.

Eleven ECW members, three husbands, and a bumper crop of lesser volunteers were standing by.

Lois Burton eyed the inventory, making sure nothing and nobody was missing.

Sugar bowls, creamers, forks, spoons, napkins, tea bags. Nine OMCs, counting the show cake on a Waterford plate with the glass dome, three pounds of salted nuts, three bags of party mints, two pale green brocade tablecloths, four candelabra with unintentionally mismatched candles, two massive flower arrangements donated by Mitford Blossoms, one hundred white dessert plates from China Hut and various Bane and Blessing sales, as many white cups and saucers of various pedigree, three industrial-strength coffeemakers: caff, decaf, and hot water for tea . . .

A volunteer husband, retired to his new handyman service, was missing.

'Where is Pete?' she asked Faye Dunlap.

'It was a last-minute call. He's helping set up umbrellas at Feel Good.'

Given the sober tenor of today's affair, she did not pursue this peculiar information.

• • •

E sther and Ray Cunningham arrived at one-thirty for the two o'clock
    service, seeking the more politically esteemed front-row seating.

She did not want to talk to people; she wanted to sit there and think
about her mortality. That's what a funeral was for.

She glanced through the Order of Service—Rite II; Esther was a big
fan of Rite II. For the first time in all the hullabaloo, she realized she
would miss Esther. Esther had been generous, upbeat, and opinionated,
and she liked those qualities in people.

Lois Burton popped down the aisle. 'I ran over to Shoe Barn this
mornin' for a pair of pumps an' was thinkin' of you. If you were still
mayorin', we might get those people to clean up th' trash in their parkin'
lot!' Though the old mayor was beyond her prime, Lois liked flattering
her just the same.

Esther gave her a look. 'Now that th' *Muse* has pronounced me dead,
I don't have to think about such as that.'

H e made the sign of the cross. 'In the name of the Father, and of the
    Son, and of the Holy Spirit. Amen.'

'*Amen.*'

'It's been estimated that everybody gets fifteen minutes of fame. Not
in Esther's case. Esther enjoyed forty years of well-deserved celebrity.

'In 1977, Esther's favorite aunt died. Aunt Margaret's last will and
testament gave Esther first choice of three items cherished by the deceased—a pair of diamond earrings in the shape of footballs—Aunt
Margaret was a Redskins fan—a 1970 Chevelle Super Sport with bucket
seats, or the recipe for her Orange Marmalade Cake.

'Esther said she struggled with this offer. She and Gene needed a car
and she had always wanted a pair of diamond earrings. However, she
admitted coveting since childhood the secret recipe her aunt had never
shared with a living soul.

'Esther claimed her inheritance and, in a manner of speaking, ran with it.

'For forty years, spirits were lifted when people saw Esther coming with her cake carrier. For forty years she demonstrated the gold standard for generosity. For forty years, she caused everyone who received her iconic cake to feel like a million bucks. After taxes.

'I'm not saying that Esther Bolick was entirely selfless or was doing it all for others. Esther also baked the OMC for Esther—for the mystery of it, she told me. She said that every one she baked had been individual, one of a kind, just like people. Further, she enjoyed creating something beautiful and rare. But let's not overlook the possibility of an even greater payoff: I think Esther did it for the joy of seeing our everyday faces light up.

'Proverbs 11:25 puts it plainly. *He that watereth shall be watered.* That simple. We got a blessing, Esther got a blessing. It was a win-win!

'All over town, people are telling their stories of Esther and the OMC. Coot Hendrick remembers the time his elderly mother was ill. It was Christmas and snowing out there on Route Four, and who showed up to deliver hope and good cheer? Esther and Gene Bolick, with chains on their tires and a two-layer OMC.

'There was the year Esther spearheaded the baking of fourteen OMCs, an endeavor that raised enough money at the Bane and Blessing to dig a well in South Africa. Fresh, clean water in a land gone dry. A lifesaver!

'Last June, Esther baked one of our son's two wedding cakes. There was nothing left of it but a few crumbs, which, loath to waste such treasure, I raked into a Ziploc bag and hid in my coat pocket.

'Indeed, the OMC has marked more life events for me and for Mitford than we can collectively recall. But there's one event I'll never forget. This dates back to B.C., Before Cynthia, when I opened my refrigerator to find what Esther had stashed by the milk jug. An entire OMC! For a bachelor! Although this diabetic priest knew better—yes, I did—I could not resist just one . . . small . . . slice.' Many of the congregants knew what was coming.

'I woke up from a hypoglycemic hyperosmolar nonketotic coma eight days later.'

Laughter.

'It was worth it!'

More laughter, followed by applause.

'We don't have to give the world the emotional spectrum of *King Lear* or the exalted praise of the *Messiah* or the figure of David released from marble. We don't have to do great things to make a difference. We can make a great difference by doing small things graciously. To that end, may we practice, as did Esther, this exhortation in Deuteronomy: *Let every man give—as he is able.* Esther gave as she was able. One cake at a time.

'Something occurred to me at the graveside. With Esther's OMC, you didn't just get cake. You got Esther. Esther delivered every cake personally. She couldn't wait to see our response to a labor of love that took four-plus hours to bring into the world.

'Indeed, creating an OMC requires a skill set of some magnitude.

'Baking the layers is easy enough. But then come the recipes for the syrup, the filling, and the frosting. As for the frosting—no yogurt, no way. OMC frosting is total heavy cream, full-bore sour cream, and high-octane sugar. And how you apply the frosting will tell the world all it needs to know of your patience and good humor. After decorating the top with orange slices, you may like to present the finished product on a paper doily. The doily, Esther told me, "adds to the cost—but is required for beauty."

'Our good Winnie Ivey has honored Esther by baking the OMC Bonanza, a spectacular three-layer which is on view today at the reception. She is honoring Esther further by donating ten percent of every sale of OMC, whole or in slices, to the Children's Hospital. Thank you, Winnie Ivey, you are a treasure.

'Immediately after the reception, the ECW will lead us up the hill—in cars, thankfully—to Hope House. There we'll do what Esther would have done—deliver Winnie's three-layer to our elders, personally.

'You're invited to join us in this loving tribute to Esther, and to experience with us the joy and exuberance of giving.'

He crossed himself, bowed his head.

'Lord, we thank you for Esther's life among us. It was beautiful and rare. Thank you for all those forty years of giving that modeled your son, Jesus Christ, who walks among us still, delivering—in person—the love, grace, mercy, and forgiveness we were created to receive and enjoy.

'Amen.'

And the people said, 'Amen!'

At one-thirty sharp, Avis Packard had left the store in the hands of Otis and Lisa James, his longtime help from the Valley.

Esther Bolick had not been one to do her grocery shopping in Wesley, like some people he knew. She'd been faithful to the Local, and the Local would be faithful to her.

He had walked home at a trot and changed into clothes laid out on his unmade bed. This would be a trial run.

At the reception, he got feedback.

'You're looking quite grand!' said Marjorie Douglas, who liked the fat cut off her rump roast, the skin removed from her chicken, and her bacon uncured.

Grand! So there you go, this was the outfit he'd be wearin' to th' Queen City. Jacket, dark britches, T-shirt sayin' *I'd Rather Be in Mitford*—which was true—an' lace-ups. He felt a good bit of weight roll off his chest and nodded his appreciation.

'How lovely to have cake!' she said. 'Don't you agree, Mr. Packard?'

'Yes, ma'am, I do. I truly do. A party without cake is just a meetin'.'

As clergy for nearly half a century, he was good at pegging people and he smelled a rat. The *Queen Mary*, aka Esther Cunningham, was headed his way in full sail.

'Lunch tomorrow at noon,' said Esther. 'We'd love to see you. I have somethin' to talk about that's highly confidential.'

'Ahh,' he said. He was a dash rattled by the rigors of the day and was unprepared for this. What was on his calendar? Where was his wife, he needed an excuse . . .

'It's been ages since you put your feet under our table, Father. Ray's makin' cornbread. Hot out of th' oven just for you.'

She eyed his hesitation.

'Fish or cut bait,' she said, tapping her foot.

Cornbread! His sworn favorite, but totally forbidden. Ray's recipe was secret, the best of the best. Cornbread!

F ollowing the reception, congregants passed through the lych-gates into the luminous October afternoon and the splendor of *Acer rubrum* come fully into its highest calling.

Inarguably, today was the peak—three days ahead of the predicted peak. The lavish, lovely, permeating rain had been the tipping point.

Selfies and group shots were made in the churchyard, beneath the branches of the spectacular October Glory. Several stood and watched as cars rolled out of the parking lot and joined the procession to Hope House. Others strolled up the street, where they were surprised to see tables and umbrellas set up outside Feel Good. All agreed that the umbrellas added a foreign touch, in a good way, to a mug of hot cider.

They couldn't yet force themselves to go home or back to work. The uplifting service for Esther, the sugar in the OMCs, the radiant afternoon—it was good to be alive.

In truth, the locals were happy to see the tourists, and the tourists were delighted to see the townspeople, whom they found to be generally sweet though somewhat peculiar.

Fall had officially arrived in Mitford.

TUESDAY, OCTOBER 6

On Tuesday, he woke with a good bit of self-recrimination. Lunch at the Cunninghams, not a good idea. As for cornbread—really not a good idea.

He consulted his wife. 'Go and be as the butterfly,' she said. 'Have only a very small piece.'

'Right. Absolutely. Of course.'

'But truly very small.' She gave him a look. 'And no butter.'

Without Cynthia, he would have been *morte* years ago.

A s I recently attended your birthday party, I know you're eighty-nine years old.'

He would be gentle, but she had asked for the truth. 'By the time the election comes around next November, you'll be ninety. It must be said, Esther—ninety is a somewhat advanced age to be mayorin'. Don't you think?'

'I most certainly do not think that, an' it burns me up that you do! I always gave you credit for havin' more sense than most people. Advanced in age? Look at yourself. Still meddlin' in people's business like you did before you went out to pasture.'

He hadn't meddled in anybody's business in months. Where did she get this information? 'While it's true that I'm long in the tooth, let it be said that my grandson and Puny's twins help keep me young.'

'Listen to me, Father. If we could depend on grandchildren to keep us young, I'd be thrown back to bein' a babe in arms. I have twenty-seven grans and great-grans and I don't need *them* to keep me young.'

Ray got up from the table and cleared the plates, declining help from their guest.

'One more thing,' said Esther, leaning in for what would likely be a reveal of the confidential matter. 'This is October.'

'It is that.'

'Th' perfect time to start plannin' for what I have in mind.'

There was Ray at the sink, grinning big, as if this was the most entertainment he'd had in years. Which, of course, it probably was.

'I want to make a little pre-campaign appearance,' she said, 'by ridin'
in th' Christmas parade.'

'Ah. Always a good thing.'

'But I've lost my clout.'

'That'll be the day. Clout is your middle name.'

'Is that too much to ask for a former mayor who gave all she had to
this town?'

'Not too much, no.'

'An' I want to ride with you.'

'I haven't been asked to ride in the Christmas parade.'

'Why not?'

'There's no reason for me to be in it. I'm still unclear why they asked
me to ride in the Independence Day parade a few years ago.'

'Because you're a majordomo. They gave you that award for bein' a
leading citizen. You have clout.'

'I do not have clout. Not one shred. Not anymore.'

'Don't make me call Andrew Gregory and beg him to let me ride in
that lineup of llamas an' kids on tricycles. They should be glad to get a
substantial participant. It's not like I'm askin' to be grand marshal. Let
that favor fall on other heads.'

'I believe it's Winnie this year.'

'Well deserved! She gives all those baked goods to th' poor. So you call
th' mayor for me. An' don't let him know I'm thinkin' of runnin' again.'

'For your info, it could be freezing that day, so there will be no kids
on tricycles. That's the Independence Day parade. Anyway, Andrew is a
good man, he'll do it. Just ask him.'

'Who kept th' big-box stores out of this town? Who steamrolled th'
council for th' Main Street Christmas lights that everybody loves? I
shouldn't have to ask. I want you to ask.'

He sat back in the chair. How had Ray survived?

'I'd like to ride in a Cadillac. Th' Cadillac is makin' a comeback, you know, it's not your father's car anymore.'

'That's Buick, I think. But there are no Cadillacs in Mitford, Esther. This is not a Cadillac town. It's more of a Chevy town, a Ford town. With a heavy dose of Asian influence and four-wheel drive.'

'Get me a Cadillac,' she said. 'Talk to th' dealership in Holding or Charlotte or wherever they are. Tell 'em who I am. They'll be flattered an' they'll come runnin'. A custom color would be nice. Lavender would be a showstopper, or an upbeat shade of pink. They'll do that if you tell 'em who I am.'

'Those are not campaign colors, Esther. Black is what you need for a political campaign.'

'There'd be no fun throwin' candy out of a black car.'

'Santa will be coming along at the rear, as you recall, throwing candy out of his own rig.' This was a root canal.

'Bah! What that turk flings to the huddled masses is pitiful! A handful! I throw candy in any parade, they expect candy from me.'

Then again, he may as well relax and enjoy it; the dessert course was still to come. He exhaled. 'Hardtop, I presume.'

'Of course, hardtop. Didn't you just tell me it would be freezin'?'

Ray set a bowl of fruit on the table, with a side of yogurt.

'Greek, Father. We hope you like it. An' th' fruit's all fresh. I even peeled th' grapes for you.'

He looked at Ray Cunningham, once the town's primo purveyor of baby back ribs and all things cholesterol. Ray was a little stooped now, and shriveled, like himself, but still smiling. Ray Cunningham was a sermon on two feet.

W hat the heck.

He knew the owner of the dealership, who was a parishioner of the Holding church he had frequently supplied. Thank heaven Jake

Tulley would decline such a ridiculous proposition and yours truly would be off the hook. Nossir, he would never have lunch with Esther Cunningham again. Not in this lifetime.

He rang the dealership.

Jake would be, in his own words, 'completely thrilled' to provide his wife's brand-new Cadillac CT6 with twin turbo engine, pedestrian collision mitigation, Bose sound system, five massage settings, heated seats—loaded. Sorry, no pink, this baby was a knock-out red. Red Passion, to be exact. 'Totally sexy!' said Jake.

'We wouldn't want to impose on your wife's . . .'

Not a problem! Jake would drive, and hoped they would allow his wife to ride with him. He and Tammy would look forward to it. Glad to do it! Thanks for asking!

I'm not doing it, Esther, and that's the end of it. You'll be riding in a great car, exactly what you wanted. Twin turbos, five massage settings, you name it, and that's the end of it. Done! I am not riding with you or anybody else in that blasted parade, so forget it.

Esther Cunningham looked shocked. So be it. And just in case she missed the point . . .

No! Absolutely not! A thousand times no!

'Wake up, honey.'

'What? What?'

'You're talking in your sleep,' said Cynthia.

WEDNESDAY, OCTOBER 7

He was up before six on Wednesday and called Father Brad, whom he knew to be an early riser. They would meet Friday at ten at the church office. Then he'd meet Pooh at eleven, in the nave. As for Jessie, he needed to talk first with Pauline, but didn't know how to go about it. He had adopted Dooley, found and mentored Sammy to the best of his ability, driven years ago to Lakeland to rescue Jessie. He had perhaps insinuated himself too deeply in that sundered family, it was an awkward situation.

But first things first.

He drove up to see Esther—to be done, once and for all, with the nuisance of the parade business. He'd contacted Ray, who was out doing errands, for clearance to drop by.

She was at the kitchen table in what she called her 'wrapper.'

'Have you seen what's goin' on at Feel Good?'

'What's going on?'

'Tables and umbrellas! On th' sidewalk! As if this is Paris, France, which it isn't. Think of th' paper napkins that'll be flyin' into th' gutter an' th' bird poop that comes from droppin' food all over . . . '

'We have the car you wanted.'

'What did I tell you, Father?'

'Totally available and very happily at your service. And, Esther, I will not be riding in the parade.'

She gave him a stricken look.

'Jake Tulley and his wife will be up front; you'll ride in back.'

'I'm not ridin' in th' backseat alone, I can tell you that. Who invited th' wife, anyway?'

'The fellow who's kind enough to provide the car you couldn't live without. Now listen to me, Esther. I have listened to you for a hundred years.' He leaned in. 'It's my turn.'

The wide eyes, the mottled face—her blood pressure going AWOL. If J. C. Hogan had to publish another special edition, this one citing Tim Kavanagh as perpetrator . . .

'I have a brilliant idea,' he said. 'Ride with your husband.'

'My *husband?* Ray?'

'The very one. The one, in fact, who has nursed you through every setback, entertained your every whim, put up with your monkey business, and generally earned *a crown in heaven.* The one who, even as we speak, is picking up your dry cleaning and bringing you a chocolate nut sundae from Wesley and driving home like a maniac before it melts. *That one. Yes.'*

There. He couldn't take it anymore.

'You know what I'd like to do?' she said.

'I can't imagine.'

'Croak right here and leave you to blame.'

'Exactly what I had in mind,' he said.

And then she laughed. Good heavens, he'd never seen anything like it. Over the decades, he'd pried a laugh or two out of her, but this was a gully washer.

T he kitchen counter was strewn with food items, and the blender was making its gnashing sounds.

His wife had a decidedly haggard look.

'I've been diagnosed with osteoporosis, just like you said.'

He gave her a kiss. 'I'm sorry. And?'

'Nurse Kennedy gave me this recipe to rebuild bone density.'

'Ha! The very recipe she gave me. We're in the same boat.'

'That's why growing old together is lovely. You have someone to complain to.' She patted his arm as if he were a house pet. 'I dragged out everything you put in the freezer, but all I get are these huge blobs. What vintage is your blender?'

When things worked, they were theirs; when they failed, they were his. 'I don't know. Maybe twentysomething?'

'That's the problem.'

'Okay, but remember that physical exercise is the true key to restoring bone loss. Put this stuff away and let's walk up the street, I have something to show you.'

'I'll take a rain check. I just bought art supplies in Wesley and the traffic was dreadful and I'd love a good sit.'

'Come, let's go. We'll drink this stuff later. Chop chop, Kav'na.'

She washed up, laughed, gave him a flash of her cornflower blue eyes. 'I love it when you're spontaneous.'

There was a virtual parade of tourists motoring along Main, with the occasional dog hanging out a window. Canada, Georgia, Texas, South Carolina, the welcome and inevitable Florida—a smorgasbord of license plates. Their spot beneath an umbrella at Feel Good was a hit with his wife.

'I've made a decision,' he said. 'I'm not going to buy a truck or any other vehicle unless you're tired of me using your car. I'll walk everywhere I can.'

'Not a problem, sweetheart, as long I retain first dibs on my car.'

'Absolutely.'

'You're back where you were years ago.'

'It's good to be back,' he said, proud once again of the notion to abandon wheels. 'Now. I've been thinking. I feel like planning something special for us. What is your heart's desire?'

'You keep asking my heart's desire and I keep telling you.'

'Ah, yes. The RV trip.'

He had avoided following through on this particular heart's desire by forgetting it each time it was mentioned. It was Cynthia who had the venturesome spirit. She could have settled the West while he contented himself with planting a lawn around their dogtrot cabin.

In truth, he was a somewhat trifling partner. He never took her to the movies in Wesley, much less to New York for the theater, though sometimes, of course, they drove on the parkway and stopped at an overlook.

And how long had it been since he sent flowers? A year? Two? And he was the man who, only minutes ago, she had called spontaneous? He could think of nothing he'd recently done for her, beyond bringing home fresh pasta from the Local, cooking it four minutes and grating Parmesan on top.

Life was short, his wife was youthful and good-looking—how could he afford to be boring? Her birthday trip to Ireland and the honeymoon trip to Maine were the extent to which he'd traveled with her in fifteen-plus years of making a life together. Holly Springs did not count as a holiday, for that was when his brother, Henry, was near death. She had come to Memphis and sat with him for days by Henry's bed; she had done everything and more to make things better by her living presence.

All she wanted, as she had repeatedly said, was to go on an RV trip, her husband at the wheel and she, the carefree passenger, wearing a ball cap and knitting. What a perfectly harmless and completely achievable ambition!

He looked at the woman seated across the table in the slanting October light. So beautiful, inside and out. George, Lord Lyttelton had said, *How much the wife is dearer than the bride.* His wife was a blessing, endlessly above all that he could ask or think.

'Let's do it,' he said. 'In the spring! After the auction!' They would drive into the sunset listening to audiobooks as she knitted away.

The church bells chimed the hour.

The deal was finally done.

He took her hand and kissed it.

But one question nagged.

How would he back it up, much less parallel-park the blasted thing?

I saw Father Tim and Cynthia sittin' under an umbrella at Feel Good,' said Lois Burton. She was fond of her view of Main Street and the surprises it rendered.

'He was kissin' her hand. I wouldn't have pegged him as a hand-kisser.'

'Awww,' said Nurse Green, who had stopped in at the Woolen Shop for a knit hat. She was loath to comment further, as she could not understand hand-kissing. Hands were where germs come from. As a nurse, she had to constantly wash up whether she needed to or not, it was regulation.

Sidewalk umbrellas were at the root of it. They called out a reckless streak in people.

H is mind was blank, his sleep hopeless.
   Avis stood at the screen door, looking over the backyard. Yellow leaves were falling from his neighbor's tree. They were coming down in a small wind that had kicked up before the local news. There'd be a big temperature drop tonight. He took his jacket off the hook and put it on and zipped it up.

The only way he could back out now was to die, which he'd be happy to do. Just not by his own hand, no way.

How could hometown indies possibly make it in a day of monster food stores? The big boys gave you an ATM, a gas station with car wash, kiddy slides, cooking demos, and fifty percent off everything. Plus the entire inventory was jumbo: Sixty-two buffalo wings per pack. Muffins the size of car tires. Toilet paper in rations bigger than his truck bed. Shampoo in gallon jugs.

He was resisting what had come to mind a few days ago—it seemed like foxhole religion.

He hiked up his britches and tried to get a deep breath.

But what did he have to lose in the privacy of his own home?

'God, if you're up there and you can hear me, all I'm askin' you for is what to say to these people. That's it. I'll give five percent to the Children's Hospital between now and th' trip to Charlotte. That's th' best I can do because of high overhead, an' thank you.'

He had a coughing fit and stepped out to the porch and turned his back to the wind and lit a Camel and there was the little dog, sticking its head out of the bushes.

He stood motionless for a minute and felt a strange warming in his chest.

'Hey.' He had no clue how to talk to a dog. He had never talked to dogs.

'What's goin' on?'

The dog looked at him.

Was its tail waggin'? People said that was a good sign. He couldn't see because th' tail was in the bushes. He remembered his mother and how she went and jumped off the bridge, just like that with no warnin' to anybody. It nearly killed him, though he tried not to let people know it, including hisself. She had always fed stray dogs, an idea his daddy did not go for.

'Do you want to . . . I don't know, come over for a bowl of soup or somethin'?' He wasn't doing test recipes these days. His cooking had fallen off th' cliff, he didn't have th' heart for it.

The dog crept out of the bushes and sat down.

'I don't know nothin' about dogs,' he said, apologetic. Like he knew zero about cars. A Plymouth or a Pontiac? A coonhound or a terrier?

Okay, the dog was waggin' its tail. He could tell because leaves thrashed around its haunches.

'Cream of mushroom, tomato bisque, chicken noodle,' he said. 'All canned, but say la vee.'

He took a long drag on his Camel. Blew out the smoke, coughed, spit. Somethin' in his chest. Maybe a sprained muscle from helping unload Mexican cantaloupes yesterday. Coughed again.

Leaves thrashing.

He went inside and fired up a gas burner and heated a can of chicken noodle and tested the temperature with his thumb—not too hot, not too cold, just right—and poured it into a bowl and stepped outside to set it by the bushes.

But the dog was gone.

He stood on the porch, the bowl cooling in his hands. He felt ashamed, somehow—ashamed that he'd been foolish about a dog.

Maybe he should just tip the bowl up and have the soup hisself.

But he set the bowl on the porch and stepped inside and stood away from the door so he couldn't be seen. He waited, holding his breath.

He was ready to quit when he heard it bound onto the porch and dig in.

Lap, lap, lap, lap, lap, lap, lap.

Then the dog was gone and the bowl was empty and everything was quiet except for the wind.

8

MEADOWGATE

THURSDAY, OCTOBER 8

THURS OCT 8~ *All furniture smushed to east side of studio~ mattress and springs upright against wall. Huge floor cloth arrived yesterday and already down.*

Canvas arriving tomorrow or Saturday~ Irene has worked with this art supplier for years and he's doing everything possible to make her happy.

Harley and Willie are great helpers. They cut a piece of plywood to fit inside the window frame and we'll stretch the canvas over the window and all the way to the door and staple it at the edges. Harley said he would be the boss of the job and Willie was totally relieved.

Harley and I will gesso the whole canvas. They're sending a tub of gesso and we'll use house painters' brushes or rollers~ they will send both in case we like one better. All we have to do is brush the gesso on the canvas like you would brush paint on a house and then let it dry and I will come back with a wash on top of the gesso.

Cynthia and I talked about whether to use burnt sienna or raw sienna for the wash. Raw seems earthier to me~ they are sending a gallon, and when that dries I will sketch in the images and it all begins!

H & W are making scaffolding out in the barn but the art sup-

plier says a ladder will work. I can work faster on scaffolding with all my stuff up there and not have to keep climbing up and down. We will install the canvas and they'll assemble the scaffolding in the studio.

The mountains and sky will require gobs of paint. Irene did the ordering but Kim is paying for all the supplies~ I am so excited and Dooley seems to be too~ I hope it helps take his mind off the clinic being a total wreck.

We have a litter of thrown-away kittens in a box by the kitchen stove and a sweet little pug named Teddy who's waiting to be adopted has a crate in our bedroom at night. And everybody is trooping over here to use the bathroom because I did not have the heart to let Amanda and Blake and Doc Owen use that awful outdoor toilet.

Jack and I sat on the floor in the kitchen and I drew images and he cut them out and we moved them around on a piece of cardboard 11 x 14"~ I think I finally know how to arrange everything in the mural. Mountains and clouds across the entire upper portion~ so many mountains it stops the heart, and all the shadows and nuance that mountains require. The elements: red truck the girls and Choo-Choo Truman though he doesn't live here anymore the farm dogs and Charley and the barn and the shed with the Beemer and Willie's house and the pond and the long stand of trees and the fence posts with their unseeable wires and the Hershell house way in the background and our old tractor and the corner of the clinic with the green sign.

Jack said Put in my swing! So we did~ which called for a tree. And put in a bike he said in case I get a bike and not a pony! So we will lean a bike against the railing of the glider porch. Put me in he said with my dump trucks! I said there are no people in this picture because the people looking at the mural will put themselves in. How will they do that he said and on and on and on!

A lot of elements in the mural will be placed differently than they are in reality~ like the pond which we can't really see from the house but we see in the painting. Kim says the point is to 'deliver the feeling and flow' of Meadowgate.

I think everything is now in my head in a more organized way and our parents are praying and Cynthia will do anything she can to help and Dooley and Willie and Harley and I'm on the prayer list in the pew bulletin at LC as 'Lace Kavanagh facing a welcome challenge.' And that is my team! Go, team!

This should get Jack through way more than a year of a good college. I'm excited but about to throw up too. Philippians 4:13.

P. S. Dooley picked flowers for me this morning~ a branch of witch hazel with its dancing yellow blooms and the last of the blue asters! The Latin for witch hazel is Hamamelis and means 'together.' xxxooo

P.P.S. I have $11.03 in my bank. When you start saving, all of a sudden change starts appearing out of nowhere~

The drilling, the jackhammering, the patients wailing in their crates—it was right up there with daily molar extractions.

And the mural. He was trying to get with the program. Because yes, it was a wonderful thing, but Lace's head was somewhere else, trying to whittle that huge project down to a size she could deal with. He wanted to help but felt helpless. The best he could do was check on the scaffolding project or take care of the supper dishes or pick up sandwiches from Jake's.

And now Homer was dead. How Homer had lasted beyond the wedding, he didn't know. Homer was valiant—that was the word. He had rarely seen such a noble, uncomplaining spirit as he saw in Lucy Bowman's pet pig. He had loved Homer, too, and complying with Lucy's wishes, he and Hal had done everything to keep him alive and make him comfortable, and that had likely been wrong. Old age, cancer, dental problems, vision and hearing loss—it was a blessing for Homer to be put down. But Homer had been Lace's favorite patient and he hadn't told her yet and he dreaded it because, by some quirk that was completely nuts, he felt guilty.

He was walking out to the barn to check on the scaffolding job, Jack running to catch up.

'Hey, Dad! I have a great idea!'

'It's not a good time for great ideas,' he snapped.

Jack stopped and burst into tears.

My God, what was happening? He walked back and stooped down to put his hands on Jack's shoulders. 'I'm sorry, buddy. Really sorry. It's always a good time for great ideas.'

Jack looked at him, blinking tears.

'What is your great idea? I want to know. Please.'

'I forgot.'

He picked him up. 'From now on, I want to hear all your ideas, okay? Please. Every one. Don't stop telling me your great ideas. Because they're important. Really important.'

Jack didn't know that dads could cry. He put his arms around his dad's neck and squeezed really hard.

He felt the softness of his boy's skin against his, the innocence and unguarded love.

'You'll run all your ideas by me, okay? And I'll be glad to hear them, okay?'

'Okay,' said Jack.

'Thanks, buddy. Thanks.'

He wiped Jack's tears with the heel of his hand, then wiped his own. Man. He needed that. 'Can you give me a smile?'

Jack's brown eyes and long lashes, then the smile for his dad. 'I remembered my great idea.'

'Tell me.'

'I want to be your name.'

'Jack Brady Tyler Kavanagh?'

'It's too many names. Just Jack Brady Kavanagh.'

'Are you sure? You can have it either way.'

'I don't even need Brady, what is Brady?'

'I confess I don't know, but it's a good name.'

Jack laid his head on his dad's shoulder. 'Just Jack Brady an' your name,' he said, glad to be in his dad's arms.

'Our name,' said Dooley.

'Our name,' said Jack.

I f he was goin' to move in with Willie awhile, he didn't want to be a burden. That sounded like his grandma. When the chicken platter was passed around, she took a chicken wing an' said, I don' want to be a burden. When she took the smallest piece of pie—when they was a piece of pie to take—she said, I don' want to be a burden.

Movin' in with Willie was Lace's idea and he agreed it was a good one. Nobody had time to clean out that bedroom upstairs, which was a mountain of pure junk; you could not repair or sometimes even recycle stuff that college students had anything to do with. The best solution was to open the window and shovel it down to a truck bed and take it to th' dump for a fifteen-dollar fee, which'd be money well spent.

On their afternoon break, he felt Willie out. 'What kind of breakfast does a man git at your place?' He said it in a jokin' manner, but he was serious.

'Any kind he wants,' said Willie.

Was Willie frownin' or what? He couldn't tell. He did not want to move in on a person that did not want to be moved in on. He and Willie had cooked many a meal together, but it was always supper and sometimes Willie let him fire up a pot of collards or bake brownies or whatnot. Mainly, he used his two-eye burner in his bedroom and a refrigerator that could hold one good-size bowl of banana puddin' and a six-pack of Cheerwine. The freezer could hold a pound of livermush, a pint of Ben & Jerry's, an' a Snickers bar, which was pretty much his housekeepin' provisions, total. Lace an' Dooley, they asked him up for supper pretty regular, but he didn't want to be a burden to young people.

'Just tell me what to do,' he said to Willie, 'an' Lord knows, I'll do it.' They had agreed to split th' food bill, but other matters had not been clear.

'Keep your bed made up,' said Willie, glad for the chance to talk about it. 'All white laundry together, all dark together. Laundry soap is four ninety-nine a clip, don't use more'n you need. Roll your socks up an' try to keep 'em separate from mine, don't you know. I'll wash, you dry like usual.'

'No problem,' he said. He was a clean-livin' man, he was regular military when it come to keepin' house, just ask Dooley or Miss Pringle how trim he'd kept his basement place in town. Of course Willie was plenty trim hisself; he Swiffered a mop around his kitchen floor every evenin'.

'An' no tobacco,' said Willie.

He didn't smoke, he didn't chew. Why was Willie tellin' him this?

'Just sayin',' said Willie. Willie leaned back in his chair and grinned. Then he chuckled and then he laughed. 'I'll be real glad for your company, Harl.'

Ol' Willie! What a joker! He could have hugged his neck but wouldn't want Willie thinkin' th' wrong thing.

H e came in for lunch and hung his jacket on the hook. 'The guys will be deer hunting for two days.'

'Deer hunting?' she said. There was the wrinkle, the little furrow in his brow . . .

'Bow hunters,' said Dooley. 'We've got a bunch of bow hunters workin' this job.' They were just getting started at the clinic and this would stall their work. Meantime, concrete jackhammered up, a hole in the floor, dirt piled on tarps in the X-ray room . . .

'What can you do?' she said.

He said all that he could reasonably say during deer season in western NC.

'Zero.'

. . .

H ave you seen the truck key?'
    'Don't you leave it in the truck?'
'I brought it in to change key rings.'
'When?'
'Last night.'
Dooley rummaging in the kitchen drawer, opening a cabinet door.
'You wouldn't have put it in there. Look in your jeans pocket in the
laundry. Lily does a big wash tomorrow. Where are you going?'
'Hey, thanks!' Blake, their vet tech, passed through the kitchen from
the hall, walking fast. 'Sorry.'
She felt sorry for them feeling sorry . . .
'I'm gon' love you an' leave you,' said Lily, flying in from the laundry
room with her handbag. 'I'm runnin' late to pick up Violet, we're cleanin'
th' mayor's house tonight, an' she's caterin' a party on Saturday—ten
dozen ham biscuits for starters, I'll bring you a couple. What can I git at
th' store on my way in tomorrow?'
'Umm,' she said. Her brain was mush. The acrylics and brushes and
all the supplies had just arrived by UPS; she was opening the boxes on
the kitchen table, and Jack was fidgety and the little pug they thought
was so sweet had just picked a raging fight with Bone Meal, their oldest
farm dog.
'Okay,' said Dooley. 'Gotta go.' He said something else but she didn't
hear.
'Love you,' she said.
'Love you back.'
'Corn,' she told Lily. 'Two cans of corn, no GMO. And a carton of
cashew milk and granola and blueberries.'
'Corn, cashew milk, granola, blueberries. Plus furniture polish, I've
got to do somethin' with your livin' room, it looks like it ought t' be
boarded up.'

'Polish can't fix the living room.'

'At least it'll look like somebody's been in there. If I could sew, I'd make slipcovers for th' whole mess.'

Maybe they would put it all in the yard sale. The old Beemer could be parked at the road, flanked by a couple of armchairs with their quaintly puzzled look . . .

'Where's Dad goin'?'

'I have no idea.'

'I could've gone with him.'

'You'll be helping me carry things up to Heaven.' Paint, big-time. Brushes, a lot of brushes. Two rollers. It was all real, starting now.

'I could feed th' kittens!'

'Not yet. I have to heat their milk.'

Two huge staple guns. Staples. 'And butter!' she called after Lily. 'Unsalted! And cocoa for hot chocolate!'

'I could give th' kittens their new names,' said Jack.

'You gave them new names yesterday.'

'I have a better idea.'

He went to the box and squatted beside it, pointing at each nearly hairless newborn. 'Moogie! Boogie! Frank! Bobo! An' you can be Pookie. Or you could be Boogie and th' one that was Whiskers can be Moogie.'

She heard Lily leave by the front door as Amanda came in the back.

'Sorry,' said Amanda. 'I just hate doin' this.'

Everybody hated trooping through their kitchen and down the hall to take care of business. But she hated it more. Her house was a zoo.

'Amen!' she said, closing Jack's long, rambling bedtime prayer.

'Amen,' he said, petulant. 'You say amen, too, Charley!' He shouted at Charley, who was sleeping on the foot of his bed. 'Say amen!'

Charley looked up, blinked.

'Don't speak like that,' she said. 'You're being rude and silly.'

'I want Charley to say amen.'

'You know very well that Charley can't say amen. I suggest you apologize for shouting at her.'

Jack was exhausted and she was frightened and angry. For a moment, she thought he would cry; she could see it coming. But he didn't.

A sigh of self-pity. 'I'm sorry, Charley.'

Charley jumped down and slunk into her crate.

'Charley is your best friend. She will protect you and love you always, no matter what. Never be hurtful to her.'

'Are you mad at me, Mom?'

'No.'

'Are you sad at me?'

'Absolutely not.'

Jack rubbed his eyes. 'When is Dad ever comin' home?'

'Soon.'

She hated lying to her son. But how could she say I have no idea when your dad's coming home—it's been hours, I'm frantic, I'm furious. Children did not need to bear the burden of grown-up craziness.

'Let's lie down now and tell your story.'

They read books together during the day, but he liked telling his own story at night. Now that he had learned it perfectly, they would begin reading to him at bedtime from the box of books her mom and Cynthia had sent: *The Berenstain Bears and the Spooky Old Tree* and *Mouse Soup* and *If You Give a Mouse a Cookie* and *The Velveteen Rabbit*. Even so, his own story was a liturgy that soothed when he was overstimulated and gave confidence when he was hurt or out of sorts. Maybe there would always be times when his own story, with its changes and evolutions, would be the best story.

'Let's look out the window at our stars, okay? Deep breath—in through the nose and out through the mouth, okay? Hold hands.'

Jack made all the breath gush out of his lungs and gulped air and fell back onto his pillow. 'Here we go!'

'This is Jack's story, the story of a forever family. Jack lives in . . . '

'A farmhouse!' he said. 'With green shutters. With my mom and dad!'
'Next door is . . . '

'Th' Kav'na Animal Wellness Clinic. Where Dad is the doctor for dogs an' cats an' sheep an' sometimes chickens an' even a goat an' th' big, big things with long eyelashes, which is llamas with two l's.'

'Jack loves his . . . '

' . . . big ol' slobbery dog named Charley!'

'Who loves him back and protects him. A lot of people work on the farm named . . . '

'Meadowgate.'

'And his home phone number is . . . '

'Two six six nine seven . . . I forgot.'

He repeated the two numbers she told him, then said it all over again. He did not like to forget the numbers or get them wrong.

'Besides us, the people at our farm are . . .' He liked to say this part in his loud voice. ' . . .Willie an' Harley an' Lily an' Uncle Doc Owen an' Amanda an' Blake!'

'Very good. Perfect. Every day, Jack does what?'

'Pulls Charley in th' wagon, goes with Dad to see th' heifers an' Choo-Choo, learns to talk better and not say ain't.' He shrugged. 'Hangs out with my mom and sometimes Amanda. Plays with my dump trucks an' stuff.'

'Jack has four grandparents and they all live in . . . '

'Mitford!' He held up four fingers and named each finger. 'Granpa Tim, Granny C, Granpa Hoppy, an' Granny O.

'An' my uncles are Uncle Pooh, Uncle Sammy, Uncle Kenny, Uncle Walter, an' Uncle Doc Owen, who is a fake uncle but I let him be real. Five uncles!'

'How many fingers?'

He held up five.

'Remember Uncle Henry in Mississippi.'

'An' Uncle Henry. Six uncles. An' my aunts are Aunt Jess an' Aunt Julie. Two is all.'

Just as she'd said, they were short on aunts.

'Jack's cousins are . . . '

'Etta an' Ethan! An' my fake cousin, Rebecca Jane.' He held up three fingers. 'Three cousins. I would like to have this many.' He held up ten fingers.

'Soon, Jack's last name will be . . . '

He yawned big and squeezed his eyes shut and spelled. 'K-a-v . . . n-a . . . h!'

She didn't tell him that he left out two letters tonight.

'When it's my name forever, I can have a pony or a bike.' He yawned again. 'Or maybe a Lego set with a barn and tractor or an iPad. Or maybe it could be a huge big dinosaur that you put together with help from your family like in th' catalog.' He couldn't keep his eyes open any longer. 'Or . . . it could be . . . a TV . . . in my room . . . '

The sweet opiate of his liturgy was working, and it was good.

She lay beside her son and listened to his breathing. So easy and natural, unlike hers which was shallow and uneven. Where was Dooley? Nobody knew. Why couldn't she reach him? Why wouldn't he answer his phone or text her back? Why hadn't she listened when he said where he was going? Or did he even say? He found his keys—that's all she knew.

She had called Blake, but he didn't pick up. Harley and Willie were at Jake's place, celebrating Harley's upcoming move-in, and didn't have cell phones. She had tried Jake's, but the line was constantly busy, as Jake liked to leave it off the hook and hang out with his customers. Amanda didn't know where Doc Owen was; there was a lot going on today, she said, and they hadn't communicated as they usually did.

Should she call the county police? Dooley was usually home at five-thirty unless he was needed at the clinic. She had texted Dooley at six-thirty, seven, and seven-fifteen, called him at seven-thirty and eight, and now it was eight-forty. His supper was in the toaster oven on warm, but it wouldn't be good now, he could want cereal.

Why would he do this? Being more than three hours late and not letting her know—it was the kind of thing that had broken them up twice; the second time had almost been the end. She had felt she would die from the pain they inflicted on each other. Out of hurt and anger and complete frustration, she had punched him, but she could never do that again, no matter what. A kick, a slap, a punch, a blow—all had been used by her biological father to terrify and intimidate her.

She would not imagine the worst. She refused. But the curve. If it was the curve, somebody would have come. She saw herself opening the front door and the county police standing there and the car in the yard with its flashing light . . .

No! Dooley was her heart, her soul, her blood. She prayed again.

Her head had been a fog bucket for days; all that was up there was the huge roll of blank canvas. Did he mention that Joanna Rivers had something for sale? Maybe he'd gone over to her place. Joanna was beautiful. And tall. Dooley liked tall girls. She had met her only once and wondered how she could make farm calls and wrangle big animals and still look stylish, even with mud on her boots.

But she would not go there. Going there was a guaranteed disaster.

Eight forty-five. Her heart was racing; she couldn't lie here and do nothing.

Teddy sat still while she snapped on the leash and took him downstairs and out to the yard. She kept her eyes on the dark road, looking fierce and resolute, as if that could produce headlights and the sound of his truck.

H e was crazy, but not too crazy to remember the curve up ahead and the fact that he was pushing eighty. Lace would kill him and he might as well help her do it and be out of his misery. God knows, he hadn't meant this to happen.

Joanna had been doing an intramammary infusion on a berserk first-calf Jersey that the farmer brought in on a rope. A rope! Was this the twenty-first century? Did the man not have a halter to walk his heifer a mile up the road to what he called 'th' vet woman'?

'This is Myrtle,' said the farmer, by way of introduction.

Any fool would have held on to the rope while the vet was down
there at his cow's teats with a needle. The heifer was in horrific pain;
he'd seen what mastitis could do. The moment the cannula was inserted
into the streak canal, Myrtle blew a fuse. Off she bolted, rodeo-ing past
the barn, cannula and plunger in the teat.

Whoever said cows can't run fast? And who would run after her? Not
Joanna, who had sprained her ankle yesterday on a horse farm, and not
the poor dope who stood there with his mouth open like the flap of a
county mail box.

No, the derp vet who had no vested interest in any of this—he would
run after the cow.

It was nearly dark and the pasture was a sludge bed. They'd kept
horses in here for years and the field was beaten to a pulp. Up ahead was
an open gate, and there went the cow sailing through the opening and
disappearing over the hill. He hammered the air with cussin' and threatening the beast with her life, the rope flying behind as she careened
down the slope toward a creek.

The marshy pasture bottom slowed him down, but on they went, the
cow walloping into the creek and churning upstream as if pursued by
demons. His left shoe made a bad connection with a slippery rock and
he sprawled into the water, hitting his hip hard on a stone, then scram-
bling to his feet and chasing her farther upstream, where he was able to
grab the rope and down he went again.

A dog barking. The cow stopped, suddenly timid. He hauled himself
up and felt for the teat and gave the cannula a quick jerk and out it came
and she bawled and reversed direction and splashed downstream at a
run. The heifer weighed 800 or 900 pounds; he clocked in at 154 soaking wet. Even with the rope, he could not bring her under control. He
was along for the ride and the fact that he hadn't broken every bone in
his body was a miracle.

Exhausted, they slogged up the hill and through the open gate to
the barn. My God, what a nightmare. He felt sorry for himself, and

even worse for her, for the serious pain she was in and the time they'd wasted.

'You're bleeding . . .' said Joanna. 'Let me . . . '

'This patient was here first,' he said, handing over the rope. 'I've got to get home.'

'I'll get you some dry shoes,' she said. 'Boots, I only have boots that would fit.'

No thanks. He was feeling around beneath his sopping jacket for his cell phone which he always carried in his shirt pocket, so he guessed it was in the truck and he was freezing his tail trying to collect the stuff he'd bought and Joanna was apologizing and the heifer's owner was holding the rope with his mouth still hanging open and then he was running to the truck in sodden gym shoes that weighed like concrete and feeling the wrench in his back.

As soon as he hit the highway he reached for his phone. He felt around in the console tray, but hello, it wasn't there. He felt around in the passenger seat. No.

So, okay, it was somewhere along the route of the blind chase led by Myrtle the Hellion. Maybe nestled between a couple of friendly boulders in the creek, iTunes leaking downstream.

And Lace with her eye on the clock, freaking out.

His phone had everything in it—it was his life, what could he say. All his contacts, notes, vet suppliers; Kenny's, Sammy's, Tommy's cells, he didn't memorize that stuff, it had been right there for years, one phone number after another, one school after another. And his notes, his lists, the works.

He'd never lost a phone in water, but if that's where it landed, it would be history. The phone store could maybe recover contacts and photos, he wasn't sure. If lost in the pasture, who had time to come back to Joanna's, a good hour-and-a-half round trip, and search for it?

He hadn't been this out of touch with Lace in a couple of years. The whole scenario was beyond. But here was the takeaway—he'd done what

had to be done; he was a vet, these things happen. Just not the phone
lying in the creek, please, God, engorging water. He did not have money
for a new phone.

He was driving like he stole this truck. If his dad knew his miles per
hour on a stretch famous for its sharp curves, he'd have a stroke. And if
there was a patrol car out here, as sometimes happened, he was dead
meat. But so what? He was dead meat either way.

T he hot shower on his beat-up bones; the sting of iodine, the smell
of bandages. The crazy little pug snoring in its crate.

He traced her chin with his finger, her skin light as air. 'So you never
want me out of your sight again?'

'Never. Not for a minute.'

'That's why I work next door,' he said.

9

I 'm keeping up with the laundry,' said Cynthia. 'And we've changed the bed twice and mopped the kitchen and vacuumed.'

'I'm keeping the garage swept out,' he said. 'And we organized the freezer and did some dusting.'

Puny had stopped by from a PTA meeting, and they were updating her on the condition of the household. They had fared well enough during her long-deserved housekeeping sabbatical, but there was another week to go before she came to work again. Being pretty much spoiled, they were flagging.

'I miss y'all,' said Puny.

'We miss you back!' he said, meaning it.

'Th' twins miss you, too. They want you to see th' chickens.'

'We'll see them on Sunday,' promised his wife.

Puny's two sets of twins, aka their unofficial grans, were doing a 4-H project he helped jump-start with the purchase of four Rhode Island Reds.

They steered her down the hall to Cynthia's old workroom, now the ironing room, where they had hung pictures of Sissy and Sassy and Tommy and Timmy. They had also installed a floor lamp, a philodendron, a rug, and a new ironing board topped by a pile of ironing. A big pile.

'Lord help!' Puny stood at the door, aghast. 'I never realized y'all had that many *clothes*.'

'It's just what happens when you wash something,' he said, apologetic.

'Do you like your new room?' said Cynthia.

'Oh, I *do*, I *truly* do. But th' *ironin*'!'

They had never seen Puny daunted by anything at all.

He drew his wife aside.

'She'll be fine. It's what vacations do to people.'

As a working priest, he'd taken exactly two real vacations in forty-some years. And when he returned to the church office after time off?

Whoa. A pile.

That had cured him, for decades, of vacations.

I t was their first hearth fire of the season, an event to be celebrated. But how?

Number one, by sipping an evening cup of hot cocoa, which would keep him awake until Advent. And two, by reading today's edition of the *Muse* to his wife who was a bona fide cheap date.

'*Musing on Main by Vanita Bentley*,' he read aloud. '*Will wonders never cease? That is the question being asked up and down Main Street these crisp October days.*'

He looked at his wife, who was already grinning; she loved this stuff. 'Have you been asking will wonders never cease?'

'Not even once,' she said.

'Nor have I. Let's see . . . *Wanda's Feel Good Café has installed umbrellas and tables on the sidewalk!!! When asked why now with cold weather approaching, she said, "I am rehearsing for SPRING!!!" Don't you love that???*

'*Speaking of, there's a prediction for a really hard winter. Dora Pugh at the Hardware has done up her left window with leaf rakes and her right window with snow shovels. BUMMER, Dora!!!*

'Just a friendly reminder. Today will probably be your LAST CHANCE to take pictures of the town hall maples at their BEST!!! This wonder will definitely cease, so GET OUT THERE!!!'

'We missed taking pictures this year,' he said. 'Maybe on our walk tomorrow.'

'Maybe I won't walk tomorrow. I'll paint.'

'Now, now, Kav'na, none of that. Painting does not increase the heart rate.'

'Not unless it's a very good painting. What is Mr. Hogan saying about his huge flub?'

'When it comes to apologies, he sides with Churchill, who said never complain and never explain. Below her front-page photo, very large and in color, he offers but two lines.' He squinted at the type size. 'He says he sincerely regrets the failure to run Esther Bolick's photo with her obituary, and calls her *a lovely and generous woman who will be missed by all.*'

Truman leaped into his lap, a feline behavior he had once disliked but now enjoyed. 'And . . . he's smoothing the feathers of our old mayor by giving thanks that she's still among us and looking—here's a word I've never known him to use—fabulous.'

'A silver tongue, that one!' She had taken up a book and was poring over it. 'Shall we move along to the classifieds where people are looking for mates? That's my favorite.'

'Patience, Kav'na. We're headed there.'

The fire crackled and spit. How many of humankind could make an evening's amusement from a cup of cocoa and a fifty-cent newspaper with no funnies?

He was only a page away from Vanita Bentley's weekly Helpful Hints and felt a dash of anticipation.

He had been embarrassed to offer her his hint. Being retired was one thing, but writing Helpful Hints was another. He confided that he had a great hint if she was interested.

'How exciting!' she said. 'I'll give you a credit.'

'Oh no, no, I don't need a credit.'

'Of course you do. Everybody needs a credit.'

'Here's the deal. If you use it, you must promise not to use my name. Okay?'

'Okay.'

He told her the hint.

'Great!' she said. 'How about the headline "Poaching a Successful Egg"?'

'No,' he said. 'Eggs are not by their nature successful or unsuccessful. How about "Poaching an Egg Successfully"?'

Ah, yes, and here it was. Vanita had pulled it off without a single typo. He would not mention his media exposure, albeit anonymous, to his wife.

He continued with Vanita's musings.

'Welcome to the tourists! We hope you will love our town. Here is the week's Lucky License Plate Bonanza—if you have a plate from Mississippi, drop by our town hall and get your free I'd Rather Be in Mitford T-shirt and maybe a coffee mug if there's one left from the Georgia license plate bonanza last week when we had three GA license plates in our picturesk town!!! Have fun and come back soon!!!*

And here was the announcement so many would be searching for. Long story short: New trees, no; mulch beds, no; pansies yes.

'Birthday coverage coming up!' he said. 'But you're not listening.'

'I'm multitasking. Listening to you and looking at this maddening knitting book.'

'Why are you looking at a knitting book?'

'I'm rehearsing for spring, sweetheart.'

'Whoa. J.C. got the name of the lieutenant governor's girlfriend wrong—I met the lieutenant governor on a previous visit; this is the name of his first wife. And girlfriend is spelled girlfiend. Oh, boy.'

'His goose is cooked in Raleigh,' she said.

'How about needlepoint?' His mother and Nanny Howard had done needlepoint. Piano bench seats, samplers, throw pillows.

'No needlepoint,' she said. 'I make pictures all day.'

'I always liked the pictures,' he said, wistful as any dowager. Nanny Howard's piano bench cover was of sheep in a glen. His mother's dining chair covers, roses in a Chinese vase.

'I've spent most of my life doing pictures. I'm looking for something useful, like an afghan. Or a *sock*.'

'Or maybe you don't need to be taxing your eyes with needlework. Look at the scenery while I drive. We'll play cow poker! We'll sing!'

'You know I can't sing.'

'Of course you can sing! Everybody can sing.'

Where would they park at night? In a church lot? RV parking could prove to be very interdenominational. How would they dispose of kitchen waste? Other? What if they ran out of gas? A monster vehicle would require more than a backup five-gallon can. Stranded on a road in the middle of nowhere, completely defenseless . . .

He turned to the classifieds.

Adele and J. C. Hogan were lying on their leather loveseat after an early supper, watching the local news. They half sat, toe to head, somewhat constrained by the limited space.

'My feet are cold,' she said.

'I'll get your socks.'

He slid off the leather, which was finally warmed by body heat, and headed toward their bedroom.

'No!' she said. 'Wait!'

He had never seen her leap off the sofa.

'What?'

'I'll get my socks,' she said, running ahead of him.

'One little thing I try to do for you who says I don't do much, and you want to jump up and get your socks?'

'I'm sorry,' she said, standing in front of the chest of drawers. 'Honey. Darlin'.'

'Honey darlin'?' J.C. was wearing sweat pants and a *I'd Rather Be in*

Mitford T-shirt. 'What's this honey darlin'?' He winked at the MPD captain. Maybe this was his big night.

'About you bein' sweet to want to get my socks.' She gave him a little shove. 'Now hurry back and turn on *Antiques Roadshow*.'

A vis carried home a chunk of grass-fed beef from the Local and set it on the kitchen counter. Maybe he'd fire up the grill tonight. Or maybe not.

He went to the bedroom and changed into his yard clothes. It would be pitch-dark in forty-five minutes.

He wasn't much on groomin' a lawn, but he had to do something fast or the town council would be over here with a warrant or whatever, as if this wadn't America.

'Are your blades sharp?' Omer Cunningham asked this morning. 'I can bring you a video.'

Don't bring me a video, he wanted to say. I will not look at a video of mower blades. So, okay, my blades chew th' grass—a mowed yard at my house looks trampled by cattle. But don't bring me a video.

He would make one last pass with rusted blades and next spring, hire th' job done. He would have hired out this evening's mow, but he needed the exercise, according to Omer. It was amazing what he could learn from his customers. They were up for managing his love life, ha-ha, his health, his finances, his marketing ploys, you name it, even his shoes. 'Clogs!' said Omer's wife, Shirlene. 'Good for posture and awesome for back support. You'll feel less tired from bein' on your feet all day, plus they promote circulation. I can send you a link.'

Don't send me a link, he thought. I do not need a link.

'I found a wonderful recipe for venison, really simple,' Adelaide Bush said today. 'I'll text you.'

He had literally felt his eyes glaze over.

He stepped out the back door and wrangled the mower off the porch and felt the squeezing around his heart, like his chest was stopped up with glue.

He coughed—what his daddy had called a rackin' cough—and couldn't seem to stop. He leaned on the handle of the mower and caught his breath. He was sweating. He'd gone to the doctor a year or two ago before the coughing set in, and tried to describe the same feelin' he just had in his chest. The doc wrote him a scrip for hypertension. He had taken the scrip home and put it in a drawer and never saw it again.

He looked up and ho! There was th' little dog.

Leaves thrashed.

'Well,' he said, hoarse as a frog. He stood for a long moment, stirred by something he couldn't name, and wiped his eyes on his jacket sleeve.

The little dog sat by the privet bush. The steak sat on the kitchen counter.

Timing, he thought, is everything. He didn't know much, but he knew that much.

Coot Hendrick enjoyed reading at night; he had a fine lamp in his upstairs apartment over th' bookstore and a pretty good wing chair from th' Bane an' Blessin' at Lord's Chapel. Since he sold his mama's place with all th' furnishings, Hope and Scott and Grace had made him a 'nest,' as they liked to say, where he was as warm as a mouse in a churn.

After he washed th' supper dishes, he'd finish readin' *Green Eggs and Ham*. Next he would read *How the Grinch Stole Christmas!*

How could anybody steal Christmas? It could not be done; it was a trick notion by th' writer to make you read th' book. Grace wanted to tell him th' story, but he didn't want to know. He wanted to be surprised on every page.

Fact is, he'd nearabout outgrown books with pictures and was now ready to read what they call chapter books. This would be a big jump, an' he would always thank Dr. Seuss for helpin' him learn to read an' for teachin' him it was okay to laugh out loud when you wanted to. Th' *Grinch* would be his last picture book.

After that, he aimed to tackle *Charlotte's Web*.

It will make you cry, said Grace. He did not mind cryin'. It was magic that a book could make a person laugh an' cry an' feel things they never felt before.

He'd come a long way from bein' a man with no job who couldn't read a lick—what they call il*lit*erate—to a workin'man with books to read anytime he got a notion. To top it off, he was even helpin' somebody write a book.

These days, he didn't want for nothin'—except gettin' to be Saint Nick again and stand in th' display window an' wave. He had done that a few years back and it was the best thing he ever done in his life. But Hope and Louise, they said they was too much goin' on for him to be Saint Nick again. The D for December sale, all th' gift-wrappin', bein' short-handed, plus runnin' th' mail-order business, which mushrooms at Christmas—they was just no way he could be Saint Nick again when they was so much for everybody to do.

E ight-thirty. Cynthia had gone upstairs for the nightly bath; he was switching off the lights. And there was Harley's truck backing out of Miss Pringle's driveway.

'Living proof,' he said to Truman, 'that wonders never cease.'

Their house phone, which seldom rang in the evening, was hammering away on his desk.

Caller ID: Connecticut. He didn't know a soul from Connecticut, but like the rest of the common horde, he couldn't resist a ringing phone.

'Good evening. Tim Kavanagh here.'

'Tim Kavanagh?' There was a pause of several beats. 'You aren't Jeffrey Simon, the journalist?'

'No, ma'am. Timothy Kavanagh, the Episcopal priest.'

'You're southern.'

'I am, yes.'

'Southerners say ma'am. We don't say that in Connecticut.'

'Is there something . . . ?'

'This is Brooke Logan in Stamford. You called me earlier, I believe. I thought it might be Mr. Simon . . . '

'No, I didn't call you. No.'

'I had a message from this phone number asking me to call.'

'I can promise it wasn't me.'

'I wrote the number down very carefully. I believe this is a North Carolina area code?'

'Yes; my wife and I are in the mountains. The Blue Ridge.'

'My grandmother was from Asheville; I went there as a child, on a train. There was a very long tunnel. I thought I'd gone blind.'

He laughed. 'A beautiful area. Our cathedral is in Asheville. So. Nice to have spoken with you, Ms. Logan . . .'

'Is anyone else there who may have called?'

'I'm afraid not. Only my wife and our cat, Truman, who isn't talkative.'

'I must have gotten a digit out of place.' Crisp. All business. 'Thank you, Father.' A dial tone.

He yawned, eyed the cat door, which was blocked this time by a wastebasket. 'Don't even think about it,' he said to Truman.

FRIDAY, OCTOBER 9

Christmas banners, Easter banners, all manner of banners adorned the walls of his old office, with poster-size photos of young families snowmobiling, hiking to mountaintops, and diving into various bodies of water.

He had to admit that Father Brad's smile was of the light-up-a-room variety. How many parishes could boast a good-looking priest—good-looking, it may be said, in a good way? Outdoorsman, gardenia enthusiast, ex-Marine, and all-around lover of life—he was the picture of health and enthusiasm, complete with a gardenia blossom on his desk.

'Kleim's Hardy!' said Father Brad. 'Blooms well into fall. Tolerates temperatures to zero.'

Father Brad poured himself a cup of fresh-brewed coffee and a cup of water for his guest. 'What do you hear from Talbot?'

'Volunteering at a soup kitchen in Toledo.'

While in Mitford, Henry Talbot had wrecked both his standing as a priest and his long-term marriage, then disappeared. On occasion, a postcard arrived in the Kavanagh mailbox. Postmarks from New Mexico to Ohio. Brief messages indicated he was pulling himself together. 'Peeling his onion,' Bishop Martin had said.

'Now here's a question for you. On the phone from Colorado, you mentioned Mary Ellen, but the wind carried away the context.'

Father Brad literally burst into laughter. 'You're worse than any woman, Father!'

'True! Ever hungry for context.'

'She was on the trip with us—my daughters, their husbands, my granddaughters. It was a wonderful time; she's a great sport. Had never rafted in white water, but was up for it and good job! Did I say she wrangles a mean breakfast skillet? On a burning log?'

'Terrific! Your daughters?'

'They were skeptical, didn't really want to include Mary Ellen. But all that has changed. Get this, Father. I prayed for someone like her, but never believed it could happen. We do that, don't we? Pray for something, but don't trust God for it.'

'Often guilty of the same offense,' he said, raising his hand. 'What's this about a skillet on a burning log?'

'It's called a Swedish fire torch. Split a big log in seven or eight pie shapes, leave about six inches of uncut wood at the base, dig a hole, stand the log in the hole. Pour oil or stuff paper around the pie shapes.

Throw in a match and there you go—a cooking fire that lasts several hours. Hope to introduce it this year at snow camp.'

'Snow camp is going forward?'

'There's one eternal problem with snow camping. We've got to have snow. And there's no way to know that yet. I find it exhilarating, but it can be pretty scary for the novice. It can make you search for something deeper in yourself. The year you joined us, it was mud camp.'

They had a laugh. He had definitely searched for something deeper . . .

When he signed on with Father Brad, there had been an inch of the predicted six on the ground, followed immediately by sheets of icy rain and not another flake. The campsite was a mud wallow.

They had taken refuge in a cabin built in 1914 by a moonshiner and converted into a way station for hikers. Historic! Sodden! Freezing! A misery of the first order!

So considering that they had no snow, could they please go home? No way. Father Brad had other ideas, and God had used the whole tribulation for good. Two of their party of five teenage boys, including Dooley's brother, Sammy, had turned their lives around.

'Dooley's sister, Jessie,' he said. 'What do you think?'

'I think she could sign on out of spite, to prove she's tough. But she may not be up to it physically. Overweight, a smoker, a problem with pharmaceuticals, barely managing to hang on at school. As you know, camp rules are no drugs, no tobacco, a note from the family doctor, cell phones checked at the church.'

'Who's going?'

'Mary Ellen was a Girl Scout leader and school counselor. She's very excited about this. Also, one of our youth group leaders.'

'Have you spoken with Pauline?'

'Pauline asked if I'd talk with Jessie. Jessie can be a pain to catch up with. I'll swing by her bus stop Monday morning, offer her a ride. If that doesn't work, we'll go to plan B.

'You know, by the way, that I'll carry my phone. There's the place on the ridge where you can get service. I'll give you a shout Saturday morning. You heard the news about Pooh?'

'Awesome, as they say. I'm meeting him in the nave at eleven.'

'He didn't want to talk with me, he wanted to talk with you. You raised Dooley, rescued Jessie, recovered Sammy, and Pauline says you hustled Pooh out of a desperate situation. You're the magic with the Barlowes.'

'Not with Jessie.'

'Nobody's magic with Jessie.' The Lord's Chapel priest looked uncharacteristically solemn. Then he smiled. 'Not yet, anyway.'

He believed in Father Brad, who conceded with Goethe that 'correction is good, but encouragement is better.' Bottom line, his friend was home from the canyons and in love, ready to pitch in for the youngest of the Barlowes.

He felt that his own smile may be lighting up at least a fraction of the room.

G od wants me to help people like my family. But I don't want to be a counselor. I want to be a preacher. Like you.'

'The right seminary gives you tools. The Holy Spirit gives you the user's manual. How the tools are used is different with everybody. A thousand priests, a thousand ministries. All glorifying one God.'

'I just want to help people.'

The seventeen-year-old sitting with him in the pew might have been a young Dooley or even a younger Sammy. Pooh was equipped with the long legs, red hair, and burning gaze typical of the Barlowes.

'This is wonderful. How did you come to know that's what you want?'

'God pulled on my heart.' Pooh's face colored.

'How did he do that?'

'I've been praying for a long time to be able to do something about

Sammy and Kenny and Jessie forgiving Mama. And for her to learn how to love them better.

'I finally realized there was nothing I could do. If it got done, it would have to be God.' Pooh cleared his throat, ran his fingers through his hair. This was hard. 'A few months ago, God said he . . . would walk with me through whatever it takes.' His heart pounded. 'I mean, he didn't speak out loud or anything.'

'I understand.'

October morning light illumined the stained windows of the nave— the infant in the manger, the boy in the temple, the man on the cross . . .

'I forgave Mama a long time ago. So it's been easier for me than for them. Probably my brothers and sister would like to forgive her, but they can't. And I don't know how to help people love each other.' Pooh looked away, then turned back to him with a level gaze. 'I think there are a lot of families like us.'

'There are. Yes.'

'Jessie is a freak. She does dope, hardly ever does her homework. I don't see how she can make it to graduation. And yet she's really smart. She hides how smart she is, like she's sayin' you can't know me, you can't touch me. She's at th' point of totally being kicked out of school. I feel like there's something I should do to help, but I don't know . . . '

Pooh leaned back, breathed out. 'I've been thinkin' maybe I should change my name.'

'I was reading just the other day about a Barlowe,' said Father Tim. 'Spencer is his name. A U.S. Air Force Pararescue officer. He received the Medal of Honor a while back. Not everybody gets one of those. Barlowe can be a good name.'

'I mean I should probably change Pooh to my real first name, Henry. I never heard of a preacher named Pooh.'

'A preacher named Pooh. Why not?' The idea brought a smile to his face. 'With an *h* or without? We've all been a little confused about that over the years.'

'With the *h*.'

'You'll get a few laughs, of course. But God can use your name to il-lustrate your humanity. I remember your nickname was inspired by a pool ball.'

'Mama brought it home; it was a seven ball and I thought it was the greatest thing in the world. I carried it around everywhere, called it a *pooh baw.*'

'Such a name will start conversations very handily. In fact . . .' He was intrigued by the thought. 'The name Pooh could be a great ice-breaker for the name of Jesus.'

Pooh's grin was big. He laughed. 'I've had to kick some butt over my name. Sorry I said that. Excuse me.'

'It's okay. Be yourself with me; say what you need to say. I won't be your judge, that's not my job. I'd like to be your helper.'

'I remember when you and Lace came and took me out of th' Creek—when Mama got burned. It was like being kidnapped; it was really excit-ing. I won't forget it.'

He wouldn't forget it, either. It had been a moonless night of barking dogs and a slippery bank and a chilling fear of what he and Lace were about to do.

'I know you and your parents attend services at Lord's Chapel. What denomination are you thinking about?'

'I don't know much about denominations. Really, I just want to learn to help people, and do it like you.'

'What am I doing that seems right to you?'

'You know how to . . .' Pooh hesitated, took a deep breath. ' . . . love people. I think that's what helps th' most.'

'Do you feel God's love, Pooh?'

'Yessir. I do.' Pooh wished his heart would quit beating so hard.

They were silent for a time. Father Tim watched the light come, then go. Amethyst, ruby, emerald; pools of color reflected on pews and floor. On the knee of his brown corduroys, a small lake of sapphire, cast from the Virgin's robe. It shimmered a moment. Disappeared.

'You must get an undergraduate degree, of course, then apply to grad-uate school. Eight years to get the job done.'

'I graduate from high school this year. Mom and Dad can't afford to send me to college, but I could work my way through. I've been working after school and in the summer and saving my money, and looking into scholarship programs with my school counselor. This is all new to me, so I don't know how to think about what to do.'

'Your grades?'

'Really, really good.'

Pooh's adoptive father, Buck Leeper, had often been out of work since the economic downturn, and Pauline's salary as dining room manager at Hope House would not fund higher education. College could be a rough go for Pooh.

But already he was thinking wrong thoughts. St. Luke had said, *What's impossible for men is possible with God.* That's the road he would travel with this.

'I'd like to do a kind of very unofficial discernment group. Four or five people. Just to ask questions, answer questions. Maybe help you hammer out your feelings and intentions.'

'Does that mean I'd be committed to the Episcopal Church?'

'No strings attached. Whatever path you choose, I feel it could be a positive early exercise.'

'Sounds scary,' said Pooh.

'It will be good; you'll find it helpful. Not to worry. Let me look into it and be in touch.'

'Is there anything I should be doing?'

'Praying. And reading God's word.'

'I'm doing that.'

'That's step one. As for step two, I have some fact-gathering to do.'

All things considered, the real step two was money.

He put his hand on Pooh's shoulder. 'Let me pray for you, son. And for your family. We'll all need to make this journey together.'

· · ·

The walk up the hill from Lord's Chapel to Hope House was not for the fainthearted. To think that until a couple of years ago, he'd run up! In any case, this should churn a little density into his bones.

'I been wonderin' when I gon' see yo' face.'

'I was here just a few days ago.' He stooped toward the recliner and gave Louella a kiss on the forehead. She had forgotten his visit when they processed up with the cake.

'You'd never guess who I was jus' now missin'.'

'Miss Sadie!'

'I miss Miss Sadie all th' time. Somebody else.'

'I give up.'

'Miss Rose! Gone how long?'

'Five years,' he said.

'She was what th' nurses call a hoot, bless 'er heart. Passed in her sleep. I'd like th' same, wouldn't you?'

'Either that or drop over in the garden by the rosebushes.'

She laughed her mezzo laugh, undiminished by ninety-plus years.

He sat next to her recliner on the low stool reserved for his visits. It was a seating arrangement guaranteed to make him feel ten years old.

'Every day, I miss th' one who raised me.'

'Helped raise you from an infant,' he said, fond of the old story.

'Bathed an' dressed me, pulled me aroun' in that little red wagon, cornrow'd my hair. You never *seen* th' like of ribbons she tied in my kinky hair.'

'I get a real sense of Miss Sadie when I come to see you. It's like getting Louella and Miss Sadie all rolled into one.'

'Rolled into a mighty stout one! They got me wearin' extra-large now.'

'And we thought that when we get old, we get shrunk.'

'Get drunk?'

'Shrunk!'

He liked laughing with Louella. Maybe the best way to honor the deceased was to laugh with the living.

V anita Bentley popped into the Local to shoot a picture of Chucky on his bed by the chewing tobacco display.

'I hope he doesn't take up the habit!' said Vanita, who expected Avis to laugh, but he didn't. 'What's he shakin' for? Is he cold?'

'He's not cold,' said Avis. He didn't know what made him shake, but his dog wadn't cold; he'd covered him up with a blanket last night and he kept shakin.' After a while, th' shakin' went away and he was fine.

'What's his name?'

He, Avis Packard, who knew zero about dogs, had named him Chucky. That was the name that just popped out from the get-go. It had sounded like baby talk, so he tried to think up other names. Bingo, Howdy, Bubba, Scooter. But when he said Chucky, the dog came over and licked his hand, so there you go.

He didn't have to answer her question because their police captain had arrived for her three o'clock sugar fix and Vanita Bentley went to snappin' what she called 'head shots and verticals.'

Adele Hogan popped the tab on her Coke can and eyed Avis's stray, who was trembling on the blanket. Probably kidney disease.

'Reckon you should put an ad in th' paper?' The captain hitched up her holster. 'Advertisin' a found dog?'

She and J.C. agreed a few weeks ago that Avis didn't seem fully with it these days. Haggard, thin as paper, work, work, work, a loner, nobody to go home to. And now a stray dog to feed, walk, whatever, plus carry to the vet. She was the first to admit she was nosy. She liked other people's business.

'He'll be right here in th' store in plain view every day.' He looked the captain in the eye. 'Which should be enough advertisin' for any-body.'

While it was out of the MPD's jurisdiction, she thought it worth mentioning. 'You probably know,' she said, 'that havin' a dog in a food store is a violation of federal and state food safety rules.'

He had a sick feelin' in his gut. Adele Hogan was a perfect example of why he had never wanted a wife.

'For th' police to get involved,' he said, 'a complaint would have to come from one of my customers. An' that's not goin' to happen because they're intelligent people.' He turned and walked up front. He'd like to knock that woman in the head, which was totally unlike him.

When he opened the mail yesterday, there was a letter from the Association. They were lookin' forward to what he had to say; did he have a title for his talk, which they could put in the program?

So there went another sleepless night, but it had nothin' to do with Chucky tremblin' at the foot of the bed.

He was relieved to see Father Tim and his wife comin' in with what looked like a list.

'Avis,' said Father Tim, 'before we get started, Cynthia and I need to tell you something.'

He couldn't handle any complaints or money-back guarantees today, he just couldn't.

'We really appreciate the Local and all you do for us. Like your pasta station on Wednesday, that's a winner. Who ever thought they'd find fresh pasta in Mitford?'

'A little triple-virgin olive oil,' said Avis, automatically reciting his pasta mantra, 'kosher salt, cracked pepper, lemon zest, grate a little Parmesan . . .'

'That's how we like it,' said Miz Kavanagh. 'And the way you design a meal for your customers—by putting the ingredients on display in one spot, with a recipe to take home. We just did your Tuesday-night meat-loaf.'

'Albeit on Wednesday!' said Father Tim. 'Very handy to have the onions and garlic and tomato sauce set out with the Worcestershire and bread crumbs. And there's the health benefit of your grass-fed ground beef, of course.'

'I admit we slip over to Wesley for a few items now and then,' said Miz Kavanagh. 'Everybody does, you know. But there's no place like the Local.'

'I'm just a little guy,' said Avis. 'I can't compete with th' honchos.'

'There was something else we wanted to say,' said Miz Kavanagh. 'Um, what was it?'

'Oh, yes!' said Father Tim. 'About your very small wine selection.'

Here it comes, he thought. 'I can't go up against th' chains with a hundred labels . . . '

'Right, and that's a good thing. Your wine selection is small and very thoughtfully curated. You keep it simple. We like that.'

'Ten red, ten white,' said Avis. 'Good values, all dependable.' He wanted to sit down, lie down, sleep . . .

Father Tim shook his hand. 'You bring a very personal touch to your business. It's a blessing.'

Miz Kavanagh was smiling. 'We've been wanting to say that.'

'Well, thank you,' said Avis, struggling to fight down a cough. 'I sure thank you.' He blushed, but asked anyway. 'Would you like to see my dog?'

Chucky stopped shaking as two people squatted by his bed.

'Good boy,' said Father Tim. He let the dog sniff the back of his hand, which conceivably smelled of Truman. The dog wagged its tail. 'Nice dog.'

'What kind, do you think?' said Avis.

'Definitely a good bit of terrier, with maybe a dose of spaniel. I'm not good at evaluating these things; we'll ask Dooley to stop by when he's in town.'

'I'd appreciate it. Much obliged.'

'How about if I look in your mouth, buddy? Any objection?' He pried open the jaws, gentle, peered in. 'Gums and teeth in fine shape.' He palpated the torso, a technique learned from Dooley. No lumps, yelps, or pained resistance. 'Around twenty to twenty-five pounds, I'd say. Muscular little guy.' A quiver ran through Chucky, but subsided. 'Looks like a fine dog. Congratulations.'

'How old do you think?' said Avis.

'Eighteen months, two years.'

'He shakes, don't you know. But not all th' time.'

'New people, new place. A little anxiety, I'd say.'

'He's not barked once.'

'I've seen that in a dog. Fearful, most likely. Time should take care of that, too.'

'He's very sweet!' said Cynthia. 'Beautiful coloration around the face and ears. Caramel, I'd call it. Where did you find him?'

'Pretty much what happened is, he found me.'

'I had a dog like that,' said Father Tim. 'You remember Barnabas.'

'Yessir, you wouldn't forget Barnabas.'

'What's his name?' said Miz Kavanagh.

Avis breathed out, felt the grin on his face. 'Chucky. Chucky's his name.'

He and Cynthia were on the sidewalk when he thought of something they neglected to mention.

He stuck his head in the door. 'Oh, and, Avis. Your home delivery. That's a marvel in this day and age. We don't use it often, but when we need it, it's champion. We don't know how you do it all.'

Honest to God, thought Avis, he didn't know either. As he sank onto the stool at the register, an odd notion entered his mind and rolled out into an actual idea.

It was crazy. Completely. And he probably wouldn't have the guts to go through with it. But if he did, and if it worked, he wondered it he'd still have to shell out five percent to charity.

Grace Murphy was learning that writing a book didn't just happen. It wasn't like it was left under your pillow by a fairy, already written. No. It was hard. You had to erase.

Beatrix Potter, who wrote *Jeremy Fisher* and *Peter Rabbit* and practically a hundred other books or maybe twenty, said she liked to have a hard word in each one. It would make children go ask their parents. So today she would pick a hard word out of the dictionary and use it. She was not afraid of hard words, because once you knew what they meant, they were easy. Ever since she was five, her mom would write down a hard word in cursive and tell her to look it up and make a sentence with it. Sometimes she gave her mom a hard word, but mostly she forgot to do this.

She took down the heavy dictionary. At school, she could look things up on the Internet, but at home, she used books to look things up.

It took a long time to find the right hard word, which ended up being in the R's.

The news today said Samantha is that very soon a lot of people will be coming to our tiny town and the not so good news is they will be ravenous! So I have a recipe for you in case you want to make something.

What people said Mrs. Ogleby? And why are they coming?

It is because the leafs are turning and looking at them turning makes people hungry.

What are they turning into?

Into mostly red and yellow said Samantha.

I will take your recipe said Mrs Ogleby. But I do not have a pen and paper to write it down.

I will tell you said Samantha. Get some bread and cut off the crust. Butter the bread then spred sugar over all the butter. Now spred cinnamone over all the sugar. Roll up the bread and cut it into a lots of little circles. Bake at 35o til you can smel the cinnamone cooking. They are called cinnamone stickies and you could get a dime apiece.

Oh said Mrs Ogleby that is a grate idea. I will make money to buy a cow which I have always wanted. Then we can all have ice cream!!!

Because she decided yesterday to illustrate her book, she stopped writing and drew a cow. She was disappointed that she could not make it look like a cow, so she erased it.

For the first time since retiring, he wasn't keen on the idea of another job. Which was fortunate, as job opportunities for old priests were virtually nil.

Indeed, he felt he had finally stumbled upon the elusive upside of retirement—known to many as home improvement.

Since the wedding in June, he had painted the interior of the hall closet, which had never been painted at all. He had lugged all the parkas and jackets and hats and gloves and boots to the living room and dumped them on the sofa, where nobody ever sat. Two coats of latex, brushed on. This closet would not see another paint job in his lifetime.

Then there was the garage floor, stained from years of leaking oil pans. Arizona red, according to the hardware guy, was the most popular color going for garage floors. Two gallons and a couple of new rollers. He had taken everything out of the garage and piled it in the driveway and scrubbed the floor with a wire brush and put in new shelves and organized and labeled everything that wasn't nailed down and recycled the rest.

While the stuff was sitting in the driveway, two cars stopped and people asked if there was a yard sale. 'Maybe later,' he said.

He had even restained the Adirondack lawn chairs, though they had never, not even once, been sat in. But just in case . . .

Life was full, life was good.

That said, he felt he was hanging around the house too much.

When Cynthia wasn't painting at Irene's place, she was working in her new home studio, aka former dining room cum billiard parlor. On such days, she was frequently up and down the hall, and so was he. In the odd moment, they bumped into each other in the kitchen, searching for a vagrant snack.

He found that he liked these accidental encounters. He liked it very much. When she wasn't in the house, he missed her. Nothing of abject longing, no, he just missed the sense of her in the rooms, the working of her blithe spirit. As for how she felt about the current arrangement, he had no clue.

They were sitting in the study, she with her knitting book and new yarn supplies and he with a library book on building a deck. They had a deck, but it was ancient and in the wrong place. A new deck would involve cutting a door next to the fireplace.

He had never cut a door in a wall and didn't know if he could. But why would he build a deck anyway? To be able, of course, to enjoy the spring and summer breezes and watch the maples turn color in the park. It would also add value to the house if they ever sold it. But why would they ever sell it? They could grow old and croak right here, completely skipping the retirement home.

'What are you thinking?' she said.

'Oh. This and that.'

'It's making your face pucker.'

'My face has been puckered for some years, in case you haven't noticed.'

'Seriously,' she said.

'Do you mind me being around the house quite so often?'

'Of course not! When Irene goes to Florida, I hope you won't mind *me* being around the house quite so often.'

He was silent for a moment. 'I have something to confess.'

She put her book down, ever eager for the provocative morsel.

Would he appear juvenile? Clinging? Even pathetic? Come now, this was his wife. If he couldn't confess to her, to whom might he confess?

'I like being around the house with you,' he said. 'I like to be where you are.'

'Timothy! Nobody ever said that to me.' She was beaming. 'How wonderful, sweetheart. Thank you.'

'You're welcome,' he said, relieved.

10

S he was walking single file with Dooley and Jack and the dogs, on the path to Marge and Hal's house.

In many of the books she read from the bookmobile—*Little House*, *Anne of Green Gables*, and later, the Jane Austen novels—people walked to visit neighbors. These fictional walks had been cinematic for her—lanes, paths, fences, cattle. Woodlands, orchards, birds' nests, meadows.

Worn in by the back-and-forth of Hal's trek to and from the clinic and of visits between their two houses, the path was their own pioneer mark on the land.

Rebecca Jane met them at the white oak.

'Did y'all hear about Danny Hershell gettin' out of home jail tomorrow?'

'What was he in for this time?' said Dooley.

'He made Mr. Teague's truck horn get stuck and nobody could make it stop till Dad went over and fixed it. It was blowin' half th' night and all morning.

'So his mom and dad gave him two weeks of time-out, which included his birthday. No devices, no TV, no radio! He learned to play th' mouth harp and went lookin' for Indian stuff with a metal detector. He found two arrowheads and sold 'em on eBay.'

'That would be Danny,' said Lace.

'I'm hungry,' said Jack.

'He gets out of bein' grounded tomorrow and I'm fixin' to play a totally big trick on him because I never got him back for stealin' th' rungs off my tree-house ladder. I'm goin' to get him back really, really good.'

'I'm starvin'.' said Jack.

'So what's your plan?' said Dooley.

'I can't tell. I'm just goin' to make up for all th' years I've done nothin' to him but be patient, kind, and long-sufferin'.'

'Man,' said Dooley. 'I can smell your mom's chicken pie all the way out here.'

They were crossing the footbridge to the house and its sweeping view of blue mountains.

Jack made a run for the back door. 'Race you, Dad!'

WEDNESDAY, OCTOBER 14

This was the easy part.

She and Harley were gessoing the canvas like a couple of buzzed house painters.

Stapled tight to the walls, the huge swath of linen commanded the room. Why bother to figure a more descriptive word for her journal when 'awesome' worked perfectly well? Dooley had seen it installed and was blown away. 'That,' he said, 'is a lot of real estate.'

The whisking sound of their rollers; back and forth, up and down. They had tried brushes, but rollers were faster. This was the final coat of gesso before the acrylic wash. The wash would dry quickly, then she could start sketching. She would sketch the mountains first. They would be her anchor, just as they'd always been in real life.

TO BE WHERE YOU ARE

Lily was already cooking and freezing for Beth's arrival next Tuesday, and gorgeous aromas were collecting up here. Skillet lasagna made with squash from their garden, a sauce of their sweet Sun Gold tomatoes for spaghetti with meatballs, and pumpkin pie.

Harley was quiet. She knew he had something on his mind—like maybe he wasn't keen on bunking with Willie?

'So how's the move coming?'

'I'm movin' over Saturday. Cleaned ever'thing out of th' dresser an' put it in a box. Cleaned up th' hot plate, defrosted th' freezer, wiped th' fan blades, an' I'll run th' vac th' mornin' I go over.'

'What do Lily and I need to do?' She would arrange asters and witch hazel in a Mason jar and put their best towels in the bathroom . . .

'You'uns don't need to step foot down there, I'll bring up th' bed-clothes an' put 'em in y'r laundry room. You'll want th' mattress cover, too.'

'Great! Perfect.'

'Warshed th' winders, took th' screen panel off th' door, put th' storm panel in. I'll clean th' toilet an' Swiffer y'r floors th' mornin' I go over.'

'You're the best, Harley.'

'It's trim,' he said.

He was definitely distracted; he had said all that like rote. Another long silence except for the whisking back and forth, up and down.

'Miss Pringle rented out her apartment,' he said.

'Good news! Who is it?'

'Professor from Wesley.'

'Tell me more.'

'Avis says white-headed, Yankee, romance languages, an' gluten-free.' When Avis explained th' meanin' of gluten-free, he couldn't believe th' answer. Bread made with garbanzo beans? That right there told 'im all he needed to know about Miss Pringle's renter.

'Any family?' she said.

'Just hisself.'

Up, down, back and forth. At this point, there was no such thing as a mistake, gesso was merely humble prep work.

Sometimes she was elated, sometimes nauseated with anxiety. This wasn't just any mural; it was for someone who believed in her beyond reason. That added an edge, for sure. She did not want to disappoint Kim Dorsay and she did not want to compromise the work because of a pressurized deadline. They had told her the parameters; she had signed off on all of it. Philippians 4:13, *I can do . . .*

'They say forty-two boxes of books come in a U-Haul.' A long pause. 'Educated. Her kind of people.'

She looked at the man who had saved her life on at least two occasions. The friend she would never forsake, as he had not forsaken her during those terrible years on the Creek.

As for his feelings for Helene Pringle, he'd never told her anything. But just now, the look on his face told her everything.

WEDNESDAY, OCTOBER 14

CROSSROADS CO-OP DANCE
FLATFOOT, SWING, ALL STYLES WELCOME
6:30 TO 9:00
MUSIC BY THE FAMOUS HAM BISCUITS
NO TOBACCO, NO ALCOHOL, NO CUSSING, NO KIDDING
TICKETS $6
KIDS UNDER 12 FREE
PROCEEDS OF TICKET SALES TO:
FARMVILLE ANIMAL SHELTER

He would have forgotten if he hadn't seen the sign just now at the co-op.

October 14. Do the math. He and Lace got married four months ago today. This was like—an anniversary.

TO BE WHERE YOU ARE

Jake ran a dual operation: a farm co-op that opened into an eating area with four tables and a booth. And while it was a stretch to call the adjoining room a café, it did have a grill, wrangled by Jake's girlfriend, Sugar, plus a coffeemaker, a drink box, and a seven-item menu that included pizza, grilled to order by the slice.

'Gon' be a mix tonight,' said Jake. 'Flatfoot, swing; I might call a dance if we get enough people to fool with it.'

'How'd you sign up the Biscuits? They're pretty famous these days.'

'Saw Tommy in town, told him what was goin' on. Said he'd send three of his band to help out th' shelter. Great guy.'

'The best.'

'Gon' do a special tonight. Grilled cheese, pickle, an' chips—in a basket.'

'You need to get some fries in here,' said Dooley.

'No fries. At Jake's, if you can't do it on th' grill, it don't get done.'

Y ou and Willie wear your dancing shoes,' said Lace.

'I don' have no dancin' shoes,' said Harley.

'The same shoes you wore to the wedding. Those are perfect for flat-dancing.'

He hauled the shoes out of the closet and hightailed it to Willie's with a can of polish and a rag.

They sat on the porch and did what had to be done.

'A man ought to have a day or two to get ready for a dance,' said Harley. 'This is a mighty quick turnaround.'

'I ain't never danced an' ain't goin' to,' said Willie. 'I'll set on th' sidelines with th' women.'

'Th' women will be dancin',' said Harley. 'Women like to flatfoot.'

'What kind of dance is flatfoot? I been flat-footed all my life.'

'I learned flatfoot when I was haulin' liquor back in th' day. Wadn't nothin' but a young'un, runnin' shine in a '34 Chevy Ute. Boy howdy, she'd go like a scalded dog.'

'What kind of dance is flatfoot?'

'With flatfoot, a man can dance by hisself or with somebody, either way. I mostly don't dance with nobody. Two left feet.'

'Fine,' said Willie. This was like wringin' blood from a turnip. 'But what kind of dance is it?'

Harley was in buffing mode. 'It helps to have taps on your shoes for flatdancin'. You got any taps around here?'

'Not a one.'

'So, flatfoot is pretty much . . . I can't explain what it is. Somebody said th' fiddle music goes in y'r ear down through y'r soul and comes out y'r feet. I'll be rusty as a nail, but I'll do y' a demo.'

Harley stood, cleared his throat, looked down. Work boots. Lug soles. Not good. 'Give me a little beat there,' he said to Willie.

'You're askin' th' wrong man for a beat.'

He thought Willie was mighty sour about goin', but prob'ly didn't want to stay home and miss anything, either.

Harley slapped his leg, laying down a rhythm. 'Okay, here we go, now. Look out!'

Harley did a few steps. Lug soles stickin' to th' floorboards; he could kill hisself dancin' in these shoes. Heel, toe, drag. Dadblame it. Not workin'.

'If this is what's goin' on at Jake's tonight,' said Willie, 'believe I'll stay home an' watch *Th' Voice*.'

Slap went th' screen door at th' farmhouse and Lily heading to her truck.

'Callin' it a day!' she hollered. 'See you Friday.'

'You comin' to th' dance?' said Willie.

'No way.'

'You might find you a man.'

'Not in that bunch of toothless wonders.'

'Leastways, you might git you some exercise,' said Harley.

'Like I need it after sawin' open nine pumpkins th' size of Volkswagens, scrapin' out two buckets of seeds, an' cannin' fourteen quarts.' Lily climbed in her truck and slammed the door. 'All I lack of bein' dead is th' news gettin' out!'

Willie and Harley looked at each other.

'Can't argue with that,' said Willie.

'When you gon' bake us a pie, Lil?'

'When pigs fly,' she hollered, gunning the engine.

Old Man Teague, first name Austin, was sitting inside the co-op door, his elderly redbone hound, Redeemer, asleep under his chair. Though ninety-one, Austin Teague might have been a hundred, easy. 'Wrinkles all over!' Jack once said.

'Evenin', Mr. Teague,' said Dooley.

Austin Teague gave the vet a curt nod.

'Evenin', Mr. Teague.' Jack hoped the old man would notice his new boots, but he didn't.

'I don't like 'im settin' at th' door,' Jake told Dooley. 'Bad marketing.'

The transformation of the Crossroads Co-op was a jaw-dropper.

Sacks of animal feed, bone meal, grass seed, and mulch were stacked against the walls, carts of blue jeans, overalls, and work shirts had been rolled into the stock room, and forty folding chairs faced a bare dance floor. Jake's girlfriend, Sugar, was wrangling the grill.

Over all, the familiar smell of hot dogs and fertilizer was made even more agreeable by the sound of Lonnie Grant tuning his banjo in the corner.

'It's a new day at th' Crossroads!' said Jake, who admitted he was nervous as a cat.

Grilled cheese and a pickle at th' co-op,' said Dooley. 'Is this life workin' for you?' He sat back in the chair and looked at her. 'Seriously.'

His wife could have gone places, lived in New York, had a whole other life. Sometimes he thought about these things.

'Are you really asking me this? Listen to me, Doc. This is all I could possibly ever want. Ever.'

He wiped Jack's mouth with a napkin. 'For richer, for poorer?'

'For better, for worse.'

'Just remember that worse is in there.'

'I'll take it,' she said.

Lonnie Grant was giving his mandolin a final tuning, Jesse O'Neill was strapping on his old Martin, and Buddy Ellison was at the bass, ready to ride.

'Find Harley and stick with him,' he told Jack. 'Mom and I will dance the first dance, then we'll all dance together, okay?'

'Okay!'

'You're th' man in your new boots.'

'Don't be shy,' Jake said to the crowd. 'This is th' first time we ever danced at th' co-op. It could be a monthly deal if you enjoy yourself. Let's have a hand for th' boys who volunteered to help us support th' shelter. Three of th' famous Ham Biscuits, folks! Fresh from their sold-out concert in Memphis, Tennessee!'

Cheers, stomps, whistles, applause.

'I don't know how to do this stuff,' said Dooley.

She laughed. 'You don't have to know—you can do anything to the Biscuits.'

He looked at his wife as they walked to the dance floor. Here was the girl whose hat he once stole and who'd laid him out for it, big-time. He took her hand, felt a grin going viral on his face.

'Happy anniversary!' he said as the music exploded into the room like a shot.

While Lace danced with Doc Owen, he sat with Jack and Lucy Bowman and stared, slack-jawed, at Old Man Teague burning up the floor. Taps on his shoes, the whole nine yards. Though his face remained a stone, Austin Teague was dancing solo and flatfootin' like crazy.

'I declare!' said Lucy. 'An' th' old coot gainin' on a hundred!'

The keys to the Teague smokehouse, tractor, truck, springhouse, front door, root cellar, hay barn, and storage shed hung on a chain from the old man's overalls pocket and jangled in time to the music. Though 'wrinkled all over,' Austin Teague was some kind of dance machine.

'I want to dance!' said Jack.

'Go,' said Dooley.

Jack grabbed his hand. 'But you come, too, Dad.'

'Go with your boy,' said Lucy. 'He'll be growed up an' gone 'fore you know it.'

'Only if you'll dance with us,' said Dooley.

'It's been a coon's age since I danced old-style.'

'Way too long. Here we go!'

The floor was churning. Rebecca Jane was showing off her skills from an Appalachian Studies class and hammering the floor, taps and all. Danny Hershell was dodging Old Man Teague and managing to flatfoot, though the soles of his tennis shoes were holding him back. Not liking to be held back, Danny whipped off his shoes, tied the strings together, hung the shoes around his neck, and danced in his bare feet.

'Do this!' Jack waved his arms.

He and Lucy waved their arms.

'Now do this,' said Jack, shaking all over.

They shook all over.

'Lookin' good there, Doc.' Jake hammered by with Sugar, who smelled of chili dogs and onions.

Judy the postmistress had dragged Harley onto the floor and was giving him a run, and there was Hal, bewildered but happy, dancing with Marge.

Joanna. He hadn't seen her come in. She was dancing with Mink and Honey Hershell and showing off her mountain roots. How easy she looked, as if no energy was required to be graceful on the dance floor or wrangle a breeched foal from a mare.

The Biscuits segued into a tune of their own and a local favorite, 'Do You Want Mustard on That?'

Cheers. Everybody dancing, taps talking.

The local vet decided that even though he didn't know what he was doing, he would give it all he had.

'What's that dance your husband's doin'?' said Linda Pritchard, who taught seventh grade in Mitford and commuted. 'Th' buck dance? Th' Virginia reel? What *is* that?'

'That's th' Dooley,' said Lace.

A t the band break, she thanked Joanna Rivers for her generosity to the clinic. 'More coming,' said Joanna. 'And thanks for praying for my dad.'

'Now let th' young'uns dance!' said Jake. 'All th' young'uns come up. Twelve and under, come on up. Parents can dance with th' little'uns if they want to.'

'Does that mean me, Mom?'

'It does.'

'You an' Dad will come with me, okay?'

Dooley took Lace's hand. Jack took her other hand.

It was good to be dancin' at the co-op. It was good to be happy.

P eople were talking and laughing in the parking lot; they had carried Jack out, sound asleep, and put him in the truck.

'Two minutes more,' said Dooley. 'Let's say good night to Lucy.'

They walked over to the old green Pontiac.

'Let me get that door for you, Lucy. I just remembered there's someone I'd like you to meet. Soon, I hope. He's dark, handsome, and amazingly intelligent.'

'Oh,' said Lucy, puzzled. 'Very nice. But why do you want me to meet him?'

'He's not picky about what he eats, either.'

'That's always a blessin',' said Lucy. 'I don't do much cookin' anymore. Nothin' to speak of, anyway . . .'

'That'll be just fine with him. And I must tell you that he likes to cuddle.'

She blushed. 'Oh, Dr. Dooley! Good gracious!'

'I know you have a small place, but he won't take up much room. His name is Teddy.'

'Teddy! Oh, my.' She sat down hard in the driver's seat, did a slow take, and looked up at him. 'Go on, now. You're teasin' me! I can see th' mischief in your eyes.'

Dooley laughed. 'I am teasin' you, Lucy, but there really is a Teddy.'

'Pay no attention to such talk,' said Lace. Her husband, the matchmaker! 'Teddy is an adorable *dog*. A little pug. We think you might love each other.'

'Which is what it's all about,' said Dooley, waxing philosophical. 'Whether man or beast.'

'A dog!' Lucy said with a kind of wonder. 'Which is a good thing in the end, as I have no space for a husband.'

THURSDAY, OCTOBER 15

She was sleeping 'the sleep of the dead,' as her mother once called it. She hadn't known she could be so exhausted. They'd come home from the dance and crashed into bed; the phone rang only minutes after they went to sleep. The Hershells' border collie, Chips, had been hit by a maniac pickup truck outside the co-op. Blood. A lot of blood. And Mink a basket case.

She and Dooley had done the pain meds and the sedation, and stopped the bleeding. Dooley would evaluate in the morning, with surgery following in the afternoon or Friday morning. The leg could not be saved—the arteries and veins that run inside the leg were severed, the limb dead. Dooley had her phone set to alarm at five A.M. so he could do a vitals check.

She felt something touch her shoulder and sat up, startled.

'What?'

Jack was sobbing. 'I'm havin' a 'mare!'

Her feet were on the floor. 'We mustn't wake Dad. I'll go lie down with you and you can tell me everything.' Charley was barking in Jack's room.

'I don't want to go to my room.'

'I'll stay with you till you go to sleep.'

She was hurrying him out the door and into the hall.

'I don't want to go back to sleep, ever . . . '

'Come, I'll pick you up.' He was heavy with sorrow and the business of life.

'. . . an' I don't want to go in my room again, ever. I want to be where you are.'

Charley barking.

'I'll carry you in your room so you can let Charley out. We have to let Charley out. I'm here, I'm right here.'

Charley was out of her crate like a shot and racing down the steps.

'We'll go to the kitchen now and you'll tell me everything, okay?'

'Okay.'

He had terrifying dreams too often. His granny locking him in the narrow toilet of her trailer. Hiding food and forcing a hungry little boy to search for it. Throwing away the baby from the pouch of his beloved plush kangaroo, now washed and put on hold in his closet. There were 'mares of his father, who he'd never seen, smashing into an oncoming train on a motorcycle that erupted in an inferno that 'boiled his brain.' His maternal grandmother and former ward had often told him this horrific story, sparing no detail.

'Some come out of crucifying experiences and actually blossom,' the social worker had said. 'Some don't do so well. Jack is doing well. Nearly all the kids have bad dreams. The remedy is love and time, time and love. Keep doing what you're doing.'

Three A.M. by the kitchen clock. She let Charley out and sat in the rocker with Jack in her arms.

'My ol' granny scratched my eyes out an' I couldn't find my eyes to put back in.'

'They're in now and always will be.' She kissed the lids of his eyes, tasting the salt.

'She said she was my real granny an' she would steal me back to live with her.'

He was crying again.

'No, no, no. You and Dad and I are family forever, you will always, always be with us. She is not your granny anymore. You have two wonderful grannies who love you dearly and forever.'

What to say? Where was a manual for this? She pulled up the tail of her sleep shirt and wiped his eyes and nose. 'You will always be with us and Charley and Choo-Choo . . . and the girls . . . and Harley . . . and Willie . . . always . . . forever . . . '

Rocking, rocking, his eyes closing, his head next to the gathered beating of her heart.

She recited fragments of a poem learned in school and written in her journal.

'All people are children when they sleep.
There's no war in them then . . .
They . . . open their hands halfway,
soldiers and statesmen, servants and masters. . . .
If only we could speak to one another then
when our hearts are half-open flowers
Words like golden bees
would drift in.'

Sleeping now, breathing his steady boy breath. 'Sweet dreams,' she whispered.

She rocked awhile, healing herself, too, then shifted his weight in her arms and stood and let Charley in, and they went upstairs.

She felt guilty when he had his 'mares, anguished that she couldn't love him enough to make the hurt go away.

F irst light. Moving fast, talking fast as they pulled on their clothes. Dooley was going over to check on Chips again and do payroll.

'He mentioned an iPad a couple of times yesterday,' said Dooley. 'No way am I into that.'

'I agree.'

'Why sit inside and play games on a device when you can play games on a hundred acres with your dog?' He put a foot on the windowsill and tied his shoelaces. 'When he gets into the world, there'll be devices enough.'

'Mitford School has computers in first grade now.' She ran her fingers through her long hair, gave it a twist, fastened it with a clip. 'I'll miss him so bad when he goes to kindergarten.'

'Next year,' said Dooley, disbelieving. It seemed Jack had just come to them, or that he'd been with them always, he couldn't say which.

More than anything, she wanted to homeschool Jack, but it was beyond her powers; she knew her limitations. She zipped her jeans, pulled on the shirt she wore yesterday. 'He really needs other . . .' She hesitated, searching for her tennis shoes.

Other children, he thought. Sometimes neither of them could say it. 'You're a blur,' he said. 'Slow down.'

'You're one to talk. Race you to the coffeepot.'

H e drank coffee while standing at the kitchen sink, looking out to a gray first light.

He needed to keep reminding himself that he had it all, everything.

Except X-ray equipment. Hal's old X-ray machine was shot. He hated sending clients over to Wesley for X-rays—it was a haul nobody needed and money he'd rather keep right here. Bottom line, he may as well forget it. There would be no money for new equipment until sometime late next year.

He reached to his shirt pocket. Gone. He kept forgetting.

Joanna had ridden her Gator over what she imagined his route had been. No phone. He had to get over there, but there hadn't been time. It was dark before he closed the clinic every day. The phone store said they could recover pretty much everything from the cloud, so maybe there was no reason to make the trek to Joanna's. Then again, maybe it wasn't in the creek. Maybe it was lying in the pasture with a dead battery, but still operational.

He had to do something, anything, and get it behind him.

The news of Joanna checking out to Colorado had gone viral; the clinic was getting calls. Hal had done inoculations at a horse farm yesterday, and a donkey, a couple of llamas, and a six-hundred-pound sow were scheduled for a farm call on Monday. A ballistic hog had once chased him up a tree; he didn't like to think about it.

Taking on large animals increased the incidence of emergencies. But the extra income would help pay pharmaceutical companies for drugs issued with a six-month grace period to his start-up practice. Last June, payback time seemed far away, but soon, in mid-December, he would owe serious bucks.

He filled two buckets at the kitchen tap, stuck a roll of paper towels under his arm, and headed to work. Twelve Flemish Giant show rabbits were due in today—a hundred and twenty pounds of pedigreed lapin. When he heard the symptoms, he guessed Pasteurella, but said nothing to the owner. If it was Pasteurella, they'd have to be quarantined in the crate room, and what would he do with the two patients recovering from surgery? Maybe the Persian in a crate in his office, the Havanese in the break room.

The plumbing job had advanced, but way slower than he expected.

Their need for water was constant. If they wanted it hot, as they often did, that meant heating it on the old apartment-size stove in the break room.

Without even trying, he could niggle around and find something to complain or worry about, like the searing pain in his left hip from the fall in the creek. And somehow Teddy had gotten out of his crate last night and ended up in their bed—the little guy was total Velcro, and his hip was worse this morning. He actually enjoyed a good whine now and then. But he had nothing to whine about, really.

This whole place was paid for—this beautiful farmland with the view of the mountains, now obscured by heavy ground fog, and their house and even his truck—all. Thanks to Miss Sadie.

It had been a while since he'd thought about Miss Sadie, and how he'd hauled her fireplace ashes out of that old barn of a place that he perceived to be a castle and scattered them around her lilacs. His job description included setting cook pots in the attic and the front hall if the weatherman called for rain. After the rain, he'd go up the hill and empty the pots in her fishpond.

He'd done jobs at Fernbank that he'd never heard of before, like polish silver doorknobs and beat rugs hanging on a clothesline and wash windows with newspaper and vinegar. Whatever he did, he tried to do his best.

Who would have thought that skinny little kid would be walking across rain-soaked grass this morning and unlocking the door of his own practice—all because of an old woman who, for no reason he would ever understand, believed in him.

They ran to the henhouse because running felt good.

She had asked Willie to let her collect the eggs for a few days; it would be a type of field trip with Jack. She didn't have time to collect eggs, but she needed to get the occasional breath of fresh air and Jack needed to burn energy.

'Where does eggs come out?'

'Where *do* eggs come out?'

'No!' he said. 'I don't want to talk perfect.' He was prickly this morning from lack of sleep.

She reached into the nest box without alarming the hen, and picked her up and showed Jack where eggs come out. This would launch the first semester of Meadowgate Ag 101. And right there—what timing!—was an egg half protruding from the oviduct.

Jack did a comic routine of staggering back with astonishment. 'Man!'

She thanked the hen for her nonchalance.

A touch of Indian summer today, following a quick, hard rain in the night. They walked toward the house with a full egg basket—fourteen of nature's most sublimely formed creations. Field trips, even mini, were good.

'Mom, look! Big clouds!'

Heaps, piles, banks of clouds.

'I see a pony!' he said.

She knelt beside him. 'Where?'

'Over yonder with th' long tail.'

'I see it! Yes!' And just above the pony, a gondola with its long-necked prow.

'We could lie down and look some more,' he said. Charley and Teddy came pounding toward them. 'Lie down, Charley, an' look at th' clouds. You too, Teddy, an' stop lickin' me.'

The cool October grass a cushion, the sky alive with cumulus. She was hungry to paint clouds. To float into their mystery, find them out. This moment in the grass would not be time wasted, it would be research for the mural. Didn't Constable study clouds for two entire summers? And look what happened! He became the best painter of clouds in the whole wide world.

She fought the temptation to close her eyes. She could sleep for a week. Two weeks . . .

'If clouds could talk, would they say they like my new boots?' He lifted his feet in the air.

'I think so. You outgrew the others zoom, zoom!'

'If clouds could talk, would they tell us about God?'

'They sort of do tell us about God, by helping make the rain that grows the grass.'

'Can they see us holdin' hands an' Charley's red collar?'

'In case they can see, we should wave. Here we are, clouds! It's us, Lace and Jack and Charley an' Teddy! Thanks for the neat mud puddle in our yard!'

He shouted at the top of his lungs. 'An' thanks for th' graaaaassss!

'Can clouds ever see inside of us?'

'Only God can see inside of us. He made us, so he knows exactly what's in there, and he checks it out all the time. He can look down inside me and see the big love I have for you. Big as the barn. Big as the sky.'

'Big as th' whole world?'

'Bigger!'

Kindergarten next year. She felt her heart hesitate, then beat again. She was missing him, missing him already.

A n Instagram collage from Beth.
      A selfie of Beth standing in her completely bare Manhattan apartment, a big window behind and a view of buildings. A shot of boxes and lamps and furniture in the back end of a moving van parked in an alley. A selfie of Beth with her beautiful mom, Mary Ellen, laughing on the terrace of a condo in Boston. How cool to think of Mary Ellen as Father Brad's girlfriend! A shot of Beth's new Kia Soul in front of the dealership, with Beth giving a thumbs-up from the driver's seat.

Getting there!

See you Tuesday, Choo-Choo!

Cant wait!

. . .

She was on the scaffolding again, working with Harley at the upper reaches of the canvas. If they kept their momentum, the wash would be finished on Monday and she could begin sketching.

'We're cookin', Harley.'

Harley nodded, doleful as anything.

She had never seen him so gloomy and pitiful, not even when she harassed him about misplacing his dentures. He was, she supposed, lovesick. She couldn't know that for sure, of course, because he never talked about his relationship with Miss Pringle. But she remembered her own lovesickness and how it really was a kind of queasy feeling. Didn't the poets go on about love and its awful effects even when it was wonderful?

'The rollers are easier,' she said. 'But not as much texture as we could get with a brush.' She hadn't wanted a completely smooth surface; she was painting life in the country, which had feeling and dimension. 'What do you think?'

'Whichever y' say.'

'Oh, for Pete's sake, Harley, what's the matter with you? I thought it was goin' to be fun workin' with you on this project, we haven't worked on a project together since the wedding. This mural will help send Jack to a good school, it is very important. So could you please just give me a break and *buck up*?' She was talking to him like she'd done when she was a kid, when she was teaching him math and American history and he was resisting but really eating it up and she was giving him A-pluses. 'You look like you've lost your best friend!'

Oops, shouldn't have said that.

Back and forth, up and down.

'I mean, have you *seen* this professor? Is he *handsome*? Some professors are, of course. But handsome would mean absolutely *nothing* to Miss Pringle, who is a woman of character and conscience. Besides, you're educated, too, Harley. For instance, you know all about the Lewis and Clark expedition. Do you remember who commissioned it?'

A heaving sigh. 'President Jefferson.'

'When did Lewis and Clark depart St. Louis?'

'Eighteen-oh-four. Spring of th' year. May.'

Glum was the word for Harley Welch.

'What did Mr. Jefferson send them out to do?'

'They was sent out to explore an' map th' territory. Mostly, they hoped to find a *di*rect waterway across th' country plus stake our claim before other nations got th' chance.'

'What else?'

'They was to study plants and animal life, as th' president favored plants an' animal life. Turned out they made a good many maps into the bargain.'

'How many?'

'Seem like it was a hundred an' forty-some.'

This was like old times. He'd had the benefit of nearly all her studies; it had been a regular two-for-one in the basement of the rectory when Father Tim and Cynthia still lived there.

'How do you spell Sacagawea?'

Oh, the sight of Harley spelling Sacagawea! One careful letter after another, as if engraving each in stone.

'Perfect! How many people do you think can spell Sacagawea?'

'I couldn't say.' He was grinning now. 'Nossir, I couldn't.'

And there was her old Harley again!

'Certainly not every professor, I can tell you that. Fancy education isn't everything. You don't need a doctorate to be an intelligent, sensitive, kind, and caring person which you truly, truly are, Harley. Forty boxes of books cannot equal that, I totally promise you.'

She dipped her roller. 'And I'd be willing to bet that he cannot, for the life of him, cook a pot of collards.'

The driveway was jammed with pickup trucks and the cars of clinic clients. She walked across the front yard from the mailbox, reading Julie's letter.

I was ten weeks when we came out for the wedding. We were so excited but—

How could we afford another baby? We couldn't, so we were embarrassed to tell anyone when we were there. Forgive us for keeping it a secret. It's time to tell the world and we are thrilled. Another thrill is that Kenny has been given a wonderful raise and a promotion! And we just learned we'll be transferred soon. A lot in one chunk. We have no idea where, but Oklahoma is a possibility. So much to be thankful for . . .

Dooley was washing up at the prep-room window when he saw her. She was standing in the yard holding a letter in one hand and their mail basket in the other. She appeared to be . . .

Something in his gut. He threw down the towel and went out to her. 'What?'

'Julie and Kenny are having another baby.'

She was fighting tears. 'I should be happy for her, I am happy for her.' He never knew what to say.

'Jack is enough,' she said. 'He's truly enough, he's so much more than enough.'

She drew away and gave him a smile. 'I just realized . . . Jack will have another cousin!'

'Three cousins! Okay!' He held up three fingers after the manner of his son, and they laughed. It really did seem okay.

Y ou won't believe this.'

He came in late from the clinic and stood at the kitchen sink looking . . . older, she thought.

'The entire toilet floor has to be replaced. A slow leak over a period of a few years. Two rotten floor joists, and we'll need a new flange once the subfloor is down.'

'How long? How much?'

'Two more weeks. Two more thousand. Maybe three.'

He turned and looked out the window above the sink.

She put her hand on his shoulder. 'We may as well get it behind us.'

'I'm the one who signed off on "as is."'

'You took me as is, I took you as is. It's not so bad.'

'Hal didn't know; there was no way he could know. The leak was under the floor, nobody could have seen it.'

'Man,' he said.

FRIDAY, OCTOBER 16

At seven A.M., she was at the ironing board they kept in their bedroom, wearing the ragged T-shirt that said *Love is an act of endless forgiveness.*

Chips's surgery was this morning; Mink and Honey Hershell would be there, both as shaken as if this were their child. Chips would be fine, of course, there were lots of happy three-legged dogs in the world.

She was ironing a shirt for Jack to wear to church.

'Date night,' he said. Her hair smelled of apples. 'I have a great idea.'

He put his arms around her waist, spooning his form to hers. 'Rebecca Jane can stay with Jack.'

'We just had a date night,' she said. 'The dance.'

'That was family night. This is our night. We'll ride around with the windows down. Sing along with the radio. Have a burger in Wesley.'

'All the way?' she said, smiling to herself.

'All the way. Definitely.'

He kissed the back of her neck; she maneuvered the iron around the collar of the shirt. 'Can we afford it?'

'I have a twenty I've been holding on to. An' keep your cotton-pickin' hands off it.'

A twenty! They were rich! She loved it when they laughed at the same time.

. . .

She was hand-washing her green date dress in the laundry sink by the open window and saw Jack. He was squatting in the driveway, playing with gravel—he loved gravel. Charley was sleeping on the warm stones.

'This is Granpa Tim . . .'

Jack moved a piece of crushed river rock to another spot. 'An' this is Granpa Hoppy. You can sit there for my Name Day. An' th' grannies can be here . . .'

He moved other pieces around, intent. 'This is Ethan an' this is Etta if they can come . . . No, this is Mom and this is Dad and here is me . . . and this is Charley . . .'

Telling his story. Coming into the fullness of his still-new life . . .

SATURDAY, OCTOBER 17

Chips was still sedated and sleeping in his cone collar, vitals good. After lunch and the all-hands-on kitten feed-up, they headed for the barn with Jack. The yard sale was on her mind and they were checking out the Beemer.

'Mice like car interiors,' said Dooley. 'Barn cats also have a way with parked vehicles.'

Dooley ducked his head under the hood, peered around.

She looked at the old Beemer, which she had driven for years. Even sitting under a bashed-in shed roof, it was beautiful, it had an attitude. She hated to sell it; it was part of her history. Maybe that's why there were so many junk cars parked in the weeds at people's houses.

'So what do you think? Two thousand? Twenty-five hundred?'

'You wish,' he said, kicking a tire.

On their way to the house, they stopped to admire the mud puddle where their tractor had trenched the grass.

'Me an' Charley want to jump in it!' said Jack.

'I don't know,' she said. 'It's pretty chilly now.'

'Not too chilly.' He looked up at her. Brown eyes pleading; that wonderful face. 'Please, please, please!'

'Give me your clothes,' she said, calm as anything.

Screaming, Jack splashed with Charley into the brown lake that had
popped up in the night. Teddy sat in the grass and barked.

'I'm pretty tired of bein' a grown-up,' said Dooley.

She loved seeing the frown line between his eyebrows sort of disappear.

'Did you know mud has healing properties?' he said.

'Mom, Dad! Look! I'm mud all over!'

Dooley was jiggling his leg. 'Opens up the pores. Antimicrobial.'

'Give me your clothes,' she said.

In a flash, he stripped out of his jacket and shirt and unlaced his
work boots and kicked them into the grass and peeled off his jeans and
socks and sprinted to the puddle and bombed in.

Charley barked; chickens squawked; Jack could not stop laughing.

She shot the garden hose on them afterward, which might be the
most fun she'd had in . . . ever.

SUNDAY, OCTOBER 18

It was a slow, cold October afternoon. As he walked across to check on
Chips, he smelled the woodsmoke from their kitchen chimney. Chips
would need one more night at the clinic; he would take him over to the
house for some family time.

He checked emails on Amanda's computer. A text from Joanna.

He bundled Chips up and took him home to the bed Lace had made
by the fire. He filled a water bowl and put a daub of peanut butter on his
finger, and squatted down with his patient.

'It's not looking good for Joanna to sell her practice,' he said. 'Her house goes on the market tomorrow. She decided to load what she can get in her truck and head out. She's offering me what she can't take. A Canon copier—ours is in midlife crisis. Some really great textbooks. Cautery supplies, a set of stocks—like new, she said, plus three hundred bucks' worth of radiograph equipment.'

'Can we afford all that?'

'Free, Lace. Free. *Gratis!* And we can really use it. Here's the deal. I'll leave at two on Tuesday—Blake can handle things, okay? It's the only day I can get over there. Plus I can drop Teddy off at Lucy's. I go right by her place.'

She watched his face. He was intense about giving her precise details.

'Lucy said if Teddy works out, she'll bake us a cherry pie. If it's a bust, no pie and we get Teddy back. I want it to work.' He gave his patient a scratch behind the ears.

Her husband loved cherry pie. Just now, when he laughed, there were crinkles around his eyes. Not many, and sort of new. But nice.

'I'll go to Joanna's, look for my phone, pick up the equipment, and be back for supper.'

'Beth gets here at five, remember.'

'Right. She'll want time to settle in; seems like a good day to get this done.'

'When would you be home?'

'A half hour to drop off Teddy. Forty-five minutes to Joanna's. Who knows how long to find the phone, if I can find it. Then a half hour or so to load up what Joanna's giving me, and home. Around six-thirty, maybe seven.'

'I'll send Joanna two quarts of pumpkin,' she said. 'She can surely find room to carry some pumpkin to Colorado.'

The wash coat for the mural was nearly done. She'd found a home for the kittens. They were getting free stuff for the clinic. And Beth was coming. *Yes!*

· · ·

I have a great idea!' Jack was out of breath from his dash up to Heaven with Charley and Teddy. 'I could go with Dad to take Teddy an' get things from th' other vet, okay?'

'What does Dad say?'

'He said ask Mom.' Brown eyes, long lashes, the hopeful face . . .

How can one's adopted child be so much like the adoptive parents? More than once, she had instinctively felt that Jack was them, they were Jack. His innocent trust, even after all he'd been through, and his honest, wide-open heart . . .

She wanted his heart to stay open, but of course, it could not. It would learn to close like a night flower at first light.

He was seldom away from her. Once, with the grannies in Mitford, he had begged to come home and she had driven in to get him and he'd not gone again. But it would be good for him to spend time with his dad and his dog. She had to start letting go even though she had just started holding on.

'Yes. All right.' She stooped and gave him a hug. 'But I'll miss you to pieces.'

'An' Charley can go, too?'

'That's a lot of passengers—two busy dogs and a boy.'

'Charley can ride in th' crew cab an' I can hold Teddy.'

'Ask Dad,' she said.

On his way downstairs, he thought that doing neat stuff took a lot of running back and forth.

11

He missed his morning coffee—the heft of a favored mug, the aroma of fresh-ground beans, the livelier conversation with his wife. Drinking water in the morning didn't get it.

He downed his glassful and eyed hers.

'Drink your water, Kav'na.'

She Who Was Already Dressed drank her water, gave him a look. 'I've tried to avoid the subject, since you dislike it.'

'What now?'

'You need a haircut.'

'I just had a haircut.'

'You had a haircut before Dooley's graduation. That was May, this is October.'

A sermon was brewing, and not from him.

'Hair is made up of protein, Timothy. It *grows*. Compare, if you will, the necessity of the regular haircut to the bed that must be made a thousand times over, the dishes that must be washed into eternity.'

Oh, boy. And where would he go to have the deed done with any semblance of skill? Considering the few hairs he had left, how much damage could anybody do?

"It's turning into curls at your neckline. Curls are darling, but these are way out of hand.'

'Curls are back,' he said.

'Back from where?'

'I saw it on the evening news.'

'All the evening news has to talk about in this broken world is curls coming back?'

'It was local news.'

Up and packing her painting gear, grabbing a bottle of water from the fridge . . .

'I could ride out to Meadowgate and ask Lily,' he said.

'Lily has been up to here with canning pumpkin and getting ready for Beth tomorrow and now I think she's working on a yard sale.'

His mother and Peggy had canned pumpkin. He didn't realize that people still canned pumpkin.

There was Shirlene, of course, who had taken over A Cut Above; she did what she called Mars/Venus cuts. Not a promising thought. Besides, she was still trying to sell him a go in her spray-tan machine. That would be a hassle.

'I think your Wesley barber is the one for the job. You can have the car tomorrow.' She gave him a peck on the cheek. 'Love you,' she said, collecting her car key.

'Love you back.'

'What are you doing today?'

'Umm. Lunch with the Turkey Club.'

'Great. The shower rod needs to be put back, the thingamajig fell off the wall. See you this afternoon, I'm painting with Irene.'

Always painting with Irene! Would it never end?

'The hospital auction will be here before you know it,' she said. 'And I forgot to tell you that Irene is going to Florida tomorrow and I'll be working at home.'

'Will I ever get to see what you've been painting?'

'Soon, sweetheart, soon.'

He followed her to the door. 'Are you happy with what you're doing?'

'Some days, yes. Some days, no.'

Right there was a profile of life in general.

He waved to his wife as she backed her Mini Cooper from the garage. He did not want to drive to Wesley tomorrow, and he especially did not want to drive to Wesley to get his hair cut. He did not enjoy the barber in Wesley, who was sour as a pickle.

He did what he usually did about seemingly insignificant matters: He prayed.

'G ranpa!' Tommy dumping his books in the chair at the side door.

'Hey, Granpa!' Timmy shrugging out of his backpack and hoodie.

'Our best chicken won a ribbon at school!' Sissy running in and giving forth a squeezing hug. 'We brought you an egg from her; her name is Loretta, remember?'

'I do.'

'It's in my coat pocket!'

And here was Sassy, wrinkling her nose and living up to her name. 'Granpa, your hair is all long and funny lookin'!'

Four faux grans who felt utterly real, all streaming into the kitchen at once. And Puny bringing up the rear and looking exactly like herself, freckles and all.

'Oh, hey, Father, 'scuse all this, I forgot it's a teachers' workday, it never entered my *mind* to check th' calendar this mornin'. They'll be good as *gold*, cross my heart an' hope to die. Sit down this minute, ever' one of you, an' start *readin'*.

'Have you had your breakfast, Father? Looks like there's your cereal bowl sittin' out. You should have more than cereal, it's good fiber but not nourishin', I can tell you that. How about we poach that egg for you? With a little whole wheat toast and sugar-free jam? Where's Miss Cynthy?'

'Off to paint. Missing all the fun.'

'Oh,' said Sissy, extending a hand dipped in yolk. 'Loretta's egg! It smushed in my coat pocket!'

'Yuck!' chimed a chorus of three twins.

'Go *wash*,' said Puny. 'An' do *not* use th' nice towels, those are for comp'ny. Here, use paper towels to dry your hands an' stick a wad in your pocket to absorb some of that mess. Then turn your pocket out an' I'll try to wash it.'

'Egg smusher, egg smusher!' cried Tommy.

Sissy burst into tears.

'Oh, for Pete's sake, Sissy! She'll listen to you, Father, please tell her not to cry.'

'Don't cry,' he said, dry as a crumb. Missing all the fun, that wife of his.

'And you, Tommy Guthrie—another word from you an' no more robot cars in this lifetime. Lord have mercy, let me git my head straight if I can. I've been gone so long I don't know where to *start*! Uh-oh, I see dust bunnies all around th' kitchen island.'

She swiped her hand over the top of the refrigerator. 'An' look at this. Nobody's dusted up there since . . . '

'Since the Boer War,' he said, unfazed by any reproof. 'Why don't I start by taking the troops to Sweet Stuff?'

'Yayyy!'

'Then for a good, long read at Happy Endings?'

Applause, backed by a whistle from Tommy.

'And last, to the Local to pick up a fryer to roast for supper, and say hello to Chucky, of course.'

'*Chucky-y-y!*' said Sassy, who was crazy about dogs, but had to be satisfied with chickens.

'Oh, *thank* you! Lord *bless* you!' said Puny. 'An' potato salad, would y'all like a nice bowl of potato salad to go with your roast chicken?'

'If there's time and potatoes, absolutely. And oh yes, the ironing. That would be a very good place to start.'

'Has th' ironin' basket toppled over yet from bein' stacked to th' *ceilin'*?'

'It's at the tipping point,' he said. 'At the tipping point.'

Things were back to normal in the Kavanagh household. Puny Guthrie's sabbatical was over, never to occur again if he could possibly help it.

A vis had walked home to get a bill he needed to pay. Maybe this was a good time to go through what he'd been thinkin' to do.

Chucky sat on the side of the bed next to Avis, who was speaking directly into the mirror on the door.

'I sure hate to ask you this . . . '

Not a good opener. Besides, he looked too worried when he said it. Best to look upbeat.

'I don't exactly know how to put it, but . . .'

He cleared his throat.

'This is the craziest thing I ever asked anybody to do . . .'

He stared at the doorknob for a minute, then went back to talking to the mirror.

'Just get to it, Avis. Don't beat around th' bush, okay? Here goes.' He hacked out a cough. 'I know it's a lot to ask, an' I know you're a busy man . . . '

No. He could not say what he had to say. He put his head in his hands.

Chucky looked at himself in the mirror. Tilted his head to the left, to the right, perked up his ears.

'Yo! Okay! Got it!

'A ham a month! We know how you like a good ham. Acorn-fed, fork-tender, sweet as sugar, low in sodium. Twelve Valley hams! Top of th' line! That'll get you through Easter, Thanksgivin', Christmas, birthdays, you name it. Here's th' deal . . .'

Wait a minute. A ham a month would kill both him an' his wife, so that was a bad idea. Pasta! All th' fresh-made, hand-cut pasta they could eat—for what? Two months? No, make it three!

But wait. Way too many carbs. On the other hand, wadn't it pasta that made Sophia Loren look so good? He still had her picture he'd saved off the front of a calendar.

'How about if we just wing it?' he said to Chucky. 'That's what we'll do. We won't try to figure out how to say it, we'll just cross our fingers an' go for it . . . '

He could hear it all th' way from Charlotte. Th' clock was tickin' at the Hometown Grocers Association.

H er mom and Aunt Louise were shelving books and she was sitting with Coot at the tiny table in the children's section. She loved teachers' workdays.

'Do you think Samantha should give out recipes or not?' said Grace. 'If not, I will have to erase a lot of the fourth page and come up with something new or maybe start over. I would hate to start over.'

'What's wrong with recipes?' said Coot.

'They are really hard to write and I only have two recipes that I know by heart. Plus they fill up a lot of room in a story.'

'People like to eat.' He held out his open bag of Cheetos, but she didn't take one.

'I could let the story do other things, but I can't think of any other things for it to do.' She had read an article in *Stone Soup*, written by someone eleven years old. 'Writer's Block: It Could Happen to You.'

'Maybe you're in too big of a hurry,' he said.

'I can't wait to finish and see it be a real book. I will draw the cover with a Sharpie.'

He thought twice before he said it. Shifted hisself on the little chair that was like sittin' on your fist an' leanin' back on your thumb. 'Maybe it needs more action.'

She did not like to hear this, but he pressed on.

'Dr. Seuss books is always full of action. Action was his big thing.'

'I am not an action person. Louisa May Alcott was not an action person except the fight scene but nobody got hurt.'

'Who is Louisa May what-you-said?'

'Somebody famous and dead.' She sighed. Why was she trying to figure this out when she had a pile of assigned reading? And a spelling test on Wednesday? Spelling was not exactly her forte, a word she just happened to know how to spell.

He felt a shiver that he recognized as an idea. He was respectful of an idea and whispered it. 'You could let th' cow git loose!'

She looked at him and blinked.

'You could let Morris th' pup chase th' cow into a fancy store if they have a fancy store in that tiny town.' He was excited and forgot to whisper. 'An' Miz Oglevy . . .'

'Ogleby,' she said.

'She could chase th' cow an' be afraid it would knock things over in th' store, but th' cow don't knock nothin' over, so guess who knocks things over?'

'Morris!' she said.

'Nossir! Not Morris.'

'Who, then?'

He thought her eyes looked big as walnuts behind her glasses.

'I ain't tellin'. You have to guess.'

Grace Murphy was a sober-minded young'un. He was happy to see her bust out in a big grin, all for his one little bitty idea.

Precisely like herding cats, he thought, as they poured into the sugared serenity of Sweet Stuff.

'I'll have, ummm, a napoleon!' said Sissy.

'Yum-o!' said Timmy.

'Yuck-o!' said Tommy.

'Napoleon was the leader of France,' said Sassy. 'But he didn't have anything to do with naming the napoleon with a lowercase n. It was an Italian dessert with a name that kind of sounded like Napoleon. I'll have, ummmm . . . '

'Cream horn for me!' said Timmy.

'Fig Newton for me!' said Tommy.

'Are you *crazy*?' chorused the girls. 'A *Fig Newton*?'

Everybody but Tommy was cracking up. This was the most hilarious moment of their lives now or in the foreseeable future.

'Get somethin' with *cream*!' said Sassy.

'Get somethin' with *chocolate*!' said Sissy.

'Shut up,' said Tommy. 'I'll get what I want.'

'Granpa,' said Sissy, 'he said shut up, he is not supposed to say shut up, especially as he is only seven.'

'I'll have a lemon square,' said Sassy, standing on tiptoe and pressing her nose to the bakery case.

'Ugh-o,' said Tommy. 'Sour ball.'

'Settle down!' he said in his pulpit voice. They turned and looked at him with something like wonder. 'And please demonstrate to me that you know how to say please and thank you to Mrs. Kendall.'

'Thank you, Miz Kendall!'

'Please, please!'

'Thank you and please!'

'Thank you very *much*, Miz Kendall!'

It was amazing what a good dose of pulpit voice could do.

'Granpa,' said Sassy, 'I want to eat my lemon square under the umbrella across the street.'

'We don't buy food from someone and enjoy it under the umbrella of someone else. We'll eat here, wash our hands, and move along to the bookstore.'

This decree, apparently, was the end of the world. Everybody was being raptured but Sassy Guthrie.

She pulled out a chair and *splat!* went the lemon square, upside down on the bakery floor.

Sassy burst into tears.

'Why all the crying today?' he asked, picking up the blasted thing with a napkin.

'I'll get that,' said Winnie, coming with a mop. 'We'll get you another. Not to cry, okay?'

'Thank you, Winnie, bless your heart. We're a handful.

'Now,' he said to those assembled, 'what's with the *crying?*'

'We don't cry,' said Timmy.

'Never,' said Tommy.

'Why not?' He broke his sugar-free donut in half. Coffee would be good, but c'est la vie.

'It's dumb to cry. Girls cry,' said Tommy.

'What do boys do?'

Timmy and Tommy looked at each other.

'We holler . . . an' stuff,' said Tommy, unsure of how to answer this.

'I cry,' he said.

'Granpa!' said Sissy.

'You *cry?*' said Sassy.

'I do.'

'What about?' said Timmy.

'Oh, the state of the world. The grace of God in my life. Miss Cynthy's oyster pie, when she makes it. Getting old. Feeling grateful. Crying is good.'

Timmy and Tommy looked at each other, rolled their eyes, shrugged.

And he had signed up for this!

At Happy Endings, his book-loving brood scattered to the four corners. Grace watched him climb onto the second rung of the step stool and inscribe the Thomas Mann quote he had discovered last night.

A writer is someone . . .

'You mustn't fall off the step stool,' she said, sober as a judge, 'or the insurance people will go insane.'

'I'm not going to fall off, I promise.'

'Hello, hello,' said their police captain. 'Anybody home?'

'Mama and Aunt Louise are in back. I can help you!' said Grace. 'Hey, Father.'

'Hey, yourself,' he said . . . *for whom writing is more difficult . . .* 'How's the police business?'

'Steady,' said Adele. She would not ask how's the retirement business; she knew he could be touchy about that.

'I need a cookbook,' said the captain.

'What kind?' said Grace.

'I don't know. Somethin' . . . how about somethin' spicy?'

Grace blinked behind her bifocals. 'Spicy.' She was in over her head. 'I'll go ask Mama.'

'What are you up to these days, Father?'

. . . than for other people. Thomas Mann.

'Nothing much. Just need to get a haircut.' That was all he had going in his life, getting a haircut. He stepped down from the stool and folded it and leaned it against the wall. He had been happy being up to something, if only a foot or two off the floor on the second rung.

'Where do you get it cut?'

'Ah,' he said, 'it's a long story.' He'd had haircuts by a fellow in a bait and tackle shop in Whitecap, by a former schoolteacher of a remote Episcopal mission school, by a woman wearing pink capris, by Harley Welch, Lily Flower, you name it.

'You name it,' he said.

She adjusted her holster belt. 'I cut J.C.'s hair.'

'Good, good,'

'Saves fifteen bucks,' she said. 'I'd be glad to give you a cleanup.'

'Oh, well . . . '

'Just need scissors and a little paper towel. Ten minutes.'

'How much?' It was common courtesy to ask, though of course it would be free and he wouldn't argue.

'Five bucks. Chocolate-covered popcorn for th' break room at MPD.'

'Done!' he said.

Aunt Louise delivered to the poetry section a pair of scissors, a roll of paper towels, a cookbook on North Carolina barbecue, and an entire volume on something called wasabi. She felt pleased to have collected everything the police captain could possibly want or need.

Grace stood by with a carpet sweeper as he popped onto a stool.

Adele draped him with paper towels, operated the scissors to see how they were working.

'Not rusty, I hope,' he said by way of conversation.

'You have a comb?'

He handed it over. 'Something spicy, huh?'

'Tryin' to perk up th' marital relations,' she said with a grim laugh. 'Okay, here we go.'

When he sat in any chair or on any stool for the purpose of being barbered, he immediately recited his wife's mantra:

'Get rid of the chrysanthemums on either side and leave it a little long in back.'

'How long is a little long?'

'Maybe a half inch? So it just misses the collar?'

'It's goin' to grow over your collar again in a heartbeat, you ought to let me cut it short.'

'No, no, really. Cynthia doesn't like me to look shorn.'

'Doesn't like you to look what?'

'Shorn. Like a sheep.'

He didn't know how to talk with somebody packing a Sig Sauer, standing so close he could hear her breathing. Was the trigger locked or did she leave it unlocked in case of emergency?

He felt what he believed to be her holster brush his right shoulder.

He made the sign of the cross in a way that could be interpreted as searching for his ballpoint pen or even scratching his nose.

The captain didn't know why she was so hardwired to stress over a little thing like runnin' a traffic light at ten miles over th' speed limit. Police were speeding 24/7, goin' to lunch, goin' home to watch football—siren, blue lights, pedal to the metal.

Maybe if she told somebody, it would help. Maybe the whole point was to confess, but since she was not Catholic she could not go into one of those little booth thingies and get it over with.

So right here was somebody ministerial, somebody who was not supposed to gab all over town what you told them. Grace had stepped away to find Margaret the cat, who had probably gone upstairs to sleep on Coot's bed, which was a no-no.

'I bet you hear a lot of stuff from people,' she said.

'I do.'

'I guess people bare their souls to you, right?'

'You could say that.' It had, however, been some time since anyone bared their soul to him.

Snip, snip. Stuff falling onto the paper towel and drifting to the floor.

As Adele opened her mouth to speak, Chief Guthrie's brood screeched into the poetry section. Sissy, Sassy, Timmy, and Tommy had each found a book and were ready to keep moving. But not before they thumped onto the floor and watched, wide-eyed, as their dad's police captain buzzed their adopted granpa.

A ll these years, people had called his franchise Lew Boyd's Exxon. Now it would be Jay Barringer's Exxon.

Lew had never really thought much about retirement since he was cured of his prostate cancer eight or so years ago. Then boom, before he could get the retirement notion completely fixed in his head again, up popped a buyer for his business, which he was sellin' *as is*.

He hadn't been much of a prayin' man since th' cancer. But while he hadn't necessarily talked to the Lord about this, he was sure thankin' him. Th' deal was, he would stay on for six months after th' closing in mid-November. That would get him and Earlene on th' road somewhere around th' middle of May, or June at the latest. He hoped he wouldn't miss th' bloomin' of his lilac bush over at th' air pump. Every May, that bush was a town fixture.

He wouldn't talk about the sale, because he didn't like to upset people. He would also be mum about what he'd call his 'spring vacation' with Earlene in a 'gently used' RV. Not likin' change, people would be ticked that he was sellin' up an' throwin' them under th' bus. They also wouldn't care to see him and Earlene ride off into the sunset for a bit of fun.

He'd never had a vacation unless you considered courtin' Earlene a vacation. He had run up to Tennessee every chance he got, usually on Saturday night after the station closed, and headed back Sunday evenin'. He was rode hard and put up wet courtin' that woman, but it was worth it.

There was a rumor that a funeral parlor was comin' to town. All they'd have to do if they'd bought his place was dig up the pumps— which was a very expensive undertaking, ha ha. But no, it had been Mr. Jay Barringer from Tennessee who jumped on th' deal of a lifetime.

People in this town didn't know Jay Barringer from Adam's house cat, and wouldn't get to, either. Mr. Jay Barringer would run his gas station from his gravel and cement monopoly across the state line. There would be no owner-hands-on, which was not a good idea, but who was Lew Boyd to say? His business was sold and hallelujah.

He checked his watch. Here in a minute, he'd run home and have a chili dog with Earlene and they'd go through th' RV catalog again, cover to cover. He was startin' to think new, not used.

See th' USA in your Chevrolet . . .

He whistled as he filled the tank of a vintage Suburban with slick tires and three coon dogs in th' hatch.

· · ·

Omer Cunningham noticed that some kind of ruckus was going on at the front of the store. He saw Otis move faster than usual to get up there.

He glanced out the window of the Local and there was a patrol car gliding up to the curb. Unlike regular vehicles, patrol cars seemed to glide. He took a pound package of livermush from the cold case and walked up front. Avis was talkin' to a ticked-off blond-headed woman with a dog leash in her hand.

'If you don't mind my askin', what's behind his right ear?' Avis asked the woman.

'I have no idea. What do you mean?'

'Like, if you scratch 'im behind his right ear—he likes that—what's behind 'is ear?'

Omer had scratched Chucky behind the ears and felt the mole that Dooley Kavanagh said was nothing to worry about.

'I don't scratch dogs behind their ears,' said the woman. 'And I don't have to prove anything to you. He's my dog, my brother gave him to me.'

MPD captain Adele Hogan, who had dropped in for her sugar fix, stepped closer. She got what was going on and was pretty sure Avis wouldn't ask the right questions—he was accustomed to pleasing people. The woman looked pretty tough and was way dressed up for this town.

'He didn't come with a collar,' said Adele, who found that standing with her hands on her hips was generally a good move. 'That could have helped prove who owns him.'

'He didn't come with a collar because he chewed himself out of it!' Chucky trembled, looked at Avis.

'Did you by any chance keep him tied up?' said Omer.

'Of course not! He lives in my house in the guest bathroom while I work.'

Sue Loudermilk was waiting to check out a bag of cat food. 'You work around here?'

'I work at the golf club in Wesley, eight to five. In accounting. You can call and ask—I am a very responsible and trustworthy person.'

'What's your name?' said Sue.

'My name has nothing to do with anything. Come here, Bouncer.'

Avis tried to swallow the knot in his throat. Chucky was looking to him for something he couldn't give or do. A terrible thing was happening and he could not open his mouth to speak, though all he wanted to say was Stop.

'Come, I said! And quit that shakin'!'

Chucky looked at Avis. They all looked at Avis.

'Be stubborn, then. I'm takin' you home.'

The woman slipped on a collar, attached the leash, and stared, furious, at the assembled group. 'Why I can't claim my own dog without the help of cops and a jury is beyond me.'

She pulled on the leash. Chucky sat. She yanked, headed for the door. 'Come, I said!'

Otis thought Avis looked like he might fall out. He moved toward him in case anything weird happened, but Avis turned away and was out the back door.

Coming in the front door as the woman stomped out was Father Tim with the police chief's kids.

'Chucky-y-y!' said Sassy, who stooped to pat his head.

The woman jerked the leash. 'This is not Chucky!' she shouted, pulling the dog behind her as she crossed the street.

'What's going on?' said Father Tim.

Omer set his livermush on the counter. 'Some dip-stick woman came in an' claimed Chucky. Said she saw his picture in th' *Muse*.

'Nine hours a clip in a bathroom?' Omer said to the assembled. 'Plus a dog can't chew himself out of his collar, right? Just sayin'.'

H e rarely went home during the day. If he did, he signed out with Otis and Lisa, but today he'd said nothing, just left.

He entered by the back door and sat down in a kitchen chair, trying to hold on to sections of himself that were flying apart. He was havin' trouble breathing. Heart racing. Light-headed. Hands trembling like an old man.

When he could stand again without his knees goin' to water, he went to his bedroom and took up the blanket at the foot of his bed and folded it and stood in the middle of the room wondering where to put it.

He walked back to the kitchen and placed it in a chair and stepped out to the porch, where he felt a strange and sudden confinement—the privet hedge surrounding the yard on three sides, the high fence of his neighbors, the sky sitting low and dark over the trees.

It was cold; he should go inside and put on a warmer jacket.

But he started walking.

Down the alley and across Wisteria and left onto Old Church Lane, where he stopped and had a prolonged coughing fit, and continued past the hospital and up by the stone wall, blind to the empty October sky.

He hadn't been along this route in years. Right in his own backyard, yet he might have landed on another planet. He slapped his shirt pocket—he'd forgotten his smokes—and kept walking. If he stopped— he was afraid to stop, he didn't know what might happen if he took a minute to look over the wall and into the Valley with the river like a ribbon laid out on the green.

Down Lilac past the maples, leaves crunching underfoot, and on past First Baptist and the town hall, where he hung a right. He hadn't walked this far at one time since coming to Mitford thirty-some years ago when his car broke down outside the town limit. He was a stranger to this neighborhood, the houses and lawns and trees and somebody's car backing out of a driveway, the radio blaring . . .

Chucky.

He was numb, as if from the cold, yet he'd broken a sweat. He stopped again to cough—a racking persecution that unlike the lesser coughs, he did not enjoy.

He had no idea where he was headed, he was on autopilot. But he was walking, okay? Which is what people had told him a hundred times he should be doing. Walk! Quit smoking! Walk! Get married! Walk! Wear clogs! Put some flesh on your bones, sharpen your mower blades, endless.

After the terrible thing happened with his mother when he was twelve, he had walked all night through his run-down mining town and around the fields and woods where he slept on a bed of pine needles. His daddy was on the way home from Montgomery, Alabama, and he'd been the only kin to see them fish her out of the river where she had jumped from the bridge. Hardly a splash, somebody said who saw her jump. A few ripples. And gone.

They had laid her out on the kitchen table with the little silver chain around her neck that he'd bought with two dollars earned at the feed store. The women had come and dressed her out for the coffin that three men and his daddy were building in the shed. He never sat at that table again.

He had not cried. He had never cried over the selfish thing she had done. She had come in and sat on the side of his bed the night before. He had waked up and there she was, like a ghost. She had taken ahold of his hand and said, I love you, boy. Please remember that. He had pulled his hand away as she'd never said such a thing before and it scared him. And she hadn't loved him at all, none, zero, else she wouldn't have done that to him as if he was nobody to her.

At Lew Boyd's Exxon, he slipped the key from the nail by the cash register and went around to the side of the building and unlocked the john door and sat on the lid of the toilet seat and put his head in his hands and felt it coming, coming like a train that he could not dodge, for he was tied to the tracks.

It was a kind of keening he heaved up, the howling of something wild and caged, and he couldn't stop it and it went on.

He was sliding off a high place into floodwaters and didn't know if he could sink that deep and come up alive.

. . .

H is haircut had been reviewed, Captain Hogan had received due
credit, and he was starving.

'Th' special today,' said Wanda, 'is tortellini primavera. Mr. Skinner?'

'Torta what?' said Mule.

'Come on,' said J.C. 'Get a grilled cheese, you like grilled cheese.'

'Fancy has me offa cheese. Too bindin'.'

J.C. mopped his face with a paper napkin. 'I don't know about you,
buddy. God knows, I don't know.'

'Mr. Hogan?'

'I'll have th' baked fish, coleslaw, cooked apples, an' th' banana
puddin'—but only if y'all remembered to put th' bananas in.'

The first zinger of the hour.

Wanda ignored this. Once, years ago, they had failed to put th' bananas in, and this goofball would never let her forget it. She pointed her
pencil at the cleric among them. 'Roast turkey with lettuce and tomato
on seven-grain with mustard an' hold th' mayo?'

'That's me,' he said. 'With iced tea, unsweetened.' Slipping in a little
caffeine . . .

He wouldn't mention the Chucky incident. The story would get
around soon enough. He felt for Avis; this was a tough one.

'How can you eat a turkey sandwich without mayo?' said Mule. 'I
don't get it. Why don't you have somethin' you'd actually like? Wait a
minute. What's this?' Mule pointed to an item on the menu.

'Biscotti,' said Wanda.

'What's a biscotti?'

'I'll bring you a sample.'

'Will I like it?'

'Probably not,' she said. 'It's a new item. And speakin' of new, startin'
next week, live music every Friday after eight o'clock. Tell your friends.
When it comes to advertisin' . . .' Wanda eyed the *Muse* editor. '. . . word
of mouth is th' way to go.'

Zinger number two.

J.C. raised an eyebrow. 'Umbrellas on the sidewalk. Biscotti. Live music. What next, Miz Basinger?'

'I'm an innovator, Mr. Hogan. How about you?'

J.C. gave her a dark look. 'I am a communicator.' This was code for saying he'd spread the word that he wasn't treated so good at Feel Good.

The cleric raised his hand, looking overly cheerful. 'This fall I cleaned out the garage and painted the hall closet. So I guess I'm a renovator.'

'Oh, boy,' said Mule. 'Let's see what I am. How about, let's see . . . '

'*Order*,' said J.C. '*Pick* somethin'. Anything.'

Mule looked dazed.

Wanda shoved the pencil behind her ear. 'You, Mr. Skinner, are a hesitator.'

He had checked with Father Brad. There would be five, including Pooh and himself, in the meeting on Thursday. If his similar experience of nearly sixty years ago in Holly Springs was any example, Pooh would be pretty stressed.

'Be yourself, son. Hang loose. And most especially, speak from the heart.'

A long exhale. 'Yessir.'

'Easier said than done—but don't worry. I'm available 24/7, and all your group will be praying for you.'

It took a moment, but Pooh managed a response. 'What . . . should I wear?'

'Wear what a preacher named Pooh would be comfortable in,' he said.

A small fire sparking on the hearth. An October wind licking their shutters on the Baxter Park side. And she liked his haircut.

What could be better?

He turned on the lamp by his chair and read aloud the letter he was happy to receive.

Dear Brother,

My nephew, Conrad, takes note of my pleasure in writing to you and in receiving your letters.

Why do you torment yourselves, he asks, with the time required to write so many words and wait so many days for your labor to strike its target? And then, he says, there's the persecution of waiting for a reply!

But that is the very reason for our delight, I say, as he sits nearby checking his text messages.

I promised to tell you how I found Eva's grave, a story that again proves how much stranger is truth than fiction.

I had gone up to Memphis to see my oncologist and stopped at a gas station south of town. (Perhaps you know that I'm still driving my old Buick!). I was running my credit card when I heard a lady on the other side of the pump, talking to an attendant.

My heart began to pound so alarmingly, it took my breath.

It was Eva's voice I was hearing from the lady at the pump. Everything about it—the tenor, the little uptick at the end of her sentences, the laughter. Eva!

I was in a state, brother, that cannot be described. I felt as if I'd had a blow to the knees, and sat down for a moment in my car.

She was pumping her own gas and her back was to me. I prayed and got out of the car and approached her.

Excuse me, I said. It was a whisper, really, and I realized I was 'trembling like a leaf,' as Mama says.

She turned and looked me straight in the eye and I found I could not speak! I was literally struck dumb. It was Eva—and yet it was not Eva.

She threw her head back and gave me a scrutinizing look.

Eva? I managed to say.

Eva passed in '79, she said. And then she smiled.

I tell you before God, Timothy, that it was Eva's bright and inquiring smile! And yet the eyes were different, and the way the face was modeled.

I'm Eva's sister, Lucille, she said. And who are you?

I'm the man who loved her beyond all reason, I said without thinking. What a ridiculous statement! I had humiliated myself with a bold and private truth.

She took my hand then, and there were tears in her eyes and she said, You must be Henry Winchester.

We stood there shaking hands like two politicians, albeit with true feeling. We couldn't seem to stop shaking hands in the most solemn and wordless manner. And finally I had to go for my handkerchief, at which point we both laughed for no reason at all. The amazement of it, brother!

I felt like someone had sloshed a tub of warm water over me, I was drowning in happiness.

I spent the night with an old friend and the next day drove northwest to Tuscaloosa, roughly four hours from Memphis.

Lucille told me how to find the house where she and her late husband lived when Eva came to them from Philadelphia. It was a humble place, now empty. I walked around it several times, though bullied by a neighbor's dog. I managed to find the spot where all those years ago, Eva had planted a little garden as her goodbye to this world. Lucille says the long months before her passing were very hard and that Eva spoke of me to the end.

After that, I went out to the little churchyard, a visit which I described in my previous letter.

Lucille lives in Memphis and teaches voice. I feel I have been reunited with a close family member and she feels the same. Her nine grandchildren are her mark of success, she says.

Lucille and I are exchanging letters and rose catalogs, eager to launch our beautification project during the first warm days of spring.

As for the home front, our vegetable garden is cleaned up and ready for the spade in March. I will have Conrad send you a photo of Mama with the gourd she grew this year. It is better than three feet in diameter! A covey of schoolchildren came out to see it.

With abiding love in Him Who loved us first, to you and Cynthia and the newlyweds and young Jack. Mama and Sister pray for you and the family faithfully as does

Your grateful brother,

Henry

B efore going up to bed, he checked his email.

>Dear Father,
>I have been waiting with baited breath to catch sight of you. Have not seen you in ages tho I hear you have lunch some days at Feel Good. Because Harold likes lunch at home since he retired, I have not had lunch out in two years!

>I have just read the most disturbing news. Did you know that depression and stress occur in wives whose husbands have retired? They call it RHS—retired husband syndrome! Retired husbands do not get out of the house enough. Are you aware of this? I hear you cleaned out your garage awhile back and were seen standing in the driveway, but that is NOT getting out of the house! Ha ha.

>It says that wives of retired husbands need an emotional playbook, but it did not explain what that is. Anyway, I hope you are not depressing poor Cynthia, who is such a bright, upbeat

person, and that you will GET OUT THERE as often as you can as
much for HER mental health as YOURS.

>Just a friendly reminder!

>Snickers sends love!

>Emma

He could count on more than death and taxes. He could count on
Emma Newland to meddle in his life for the rest of his days.

He was shutting down the computer when he noticed the message
blinker on their house phone.

But there was no message. It was merely the sound of . . . what?
Someone hanging up.

Caller ID, Connecticut.

12

S unrise.

'I can have th' bike with sixteen-inch wheels *or* I can have th' pony?' He was checking again. To make sure.

Jack had come down in his pajamas and joined them at the kitchen table.

'Yes. Only one present for your Name Day,' said Lace. 'One present that we all agree on.'

'You have a choice,' said Dooley. 'Choices can be hard sometimes, because your choice affects everything. A pony is a lot of responsibility. The stall has to be kept clean. He'll have to be fed and watered every day, and ridden regularly and given shots. Just so you know, a bike is easier.'

'An' I have to wear a helmet?'

'You do. House rule.'

'You'll also need to take care of a bike,' said Lace.

'You can't throw it down or beat it up. A bike is a big deal,' said Dooley. 'You need to keep it out of the weather; keep it clean, keep your tires inflated . . .'

He remembered his own first bike—it was red—and how diligently he'd cared for it. His dad had put it under the tree the first Christmas after he moved to the rectory; it had been everything he ever wanted. A bike was a life-changer.

Without telling his dad, he had wheeled out of Mitford and bombed down the mountain in frigid weather to find his mom. All those curves, all that traffic, all those miles, pre-helmet. And his dad going nuts with worry and the police investigating. But God had taken care of him.

Mostly what he remembered was the windburn. It was so bad that his face peeled for a week. He'd been completely, totally crazy, desperate to find his mother.

'It could be a bike,' said Jack, who looked worried about choices.

'Could be or will be?'

Jack pulled up his pajama top and covered his head. 'I'm hiding,' he said.

'Why are you hiding?'

'I'm prayin'.'

'Take your time,' said Dooley. He and Lace exchanged a look.

Jack pulled his pajama top down. 'A bike! With sixteen . . . '

'Got it. Red? Blue? Green?'

'Red!'

'Are you in?' Dooley asked Lace.

'I'm in.'

'Are you in, buddy?' Their boy was about to bust.

'I'm in! Are you in, Dad?'

'All th' way. But if you change your mind, there's still time.'

'I won't change my mind!'

'Sixteen-inch wheels,' said Dooley. 'Red. *Done!*'

High five.

Jack jumped off the bench and did his boogie dance.

But he hadn't found his mother. He went to the place she worked and the manager said his mama had a message for him if he came looking: Go back to the preacher.

The house trailer they'd rented, had barely been able to hang on to, was empty. He had pedaled down the dirt road and stood on a cement block and looked in the window. A squirrel ran across the kitchen floor.

He had five dollars and three Reese's Peanut Butter Cups. He bought a burger combo at Wendy's and put half the fries in a napkin in the pocket of his yellow windbreaker. Counting the time he slept in the woods and grunted his bike up half a mountain and hitched a ride in a truck with an old couple doing thirty miles an hour, it had taken a night and a day to get home to Mitford.

T he gessoing was finished.

Harley had been a big help; the rest was up to Lace Kavanagh.

She would let the canvas dry and begin the application of the wash. Harley could have helped with this, too, but she needed to be one-on-one now, with the great runway of her canvas. The wash would be the approach before the wheels touched down.

While Lily and Jack baked cookies, she put on her jacket and scarf and walked out to the October morning, awake to the chill air in her lungs, the ache in her roller arm.

Heavy dew this morning. Cirrus clouds creeping west to east. She leaned against a fence post.

'My dad is in Cameroon,' she said, 'near the Nigerian border. I worry a lot about his heart issues. Plus there are waves of suicide bombings and people burning villages and always the endless trauma surgeries. Malaria, too. There's always malaria.'

Her mom said they were to pray for the people her dad and his colleagues were treating, pray for his sound health and safekeeping, and trust God in everything. She knew such wisdom in her head, but complete trust was, as her mother said, 'yet to build a station in her heart and erect its flag of undisputed possession.'

There were things she couldn't say to Dooley right now. For example, she didn't bother him with the innumerable details of the mural because he had innumerable details of his own. Like twelve beautiful Flemish

Giant show rabbits that had tested positive for Pasteurella, a serious upper respiratory disease that can be passed to dogs and even children.

'The sketches on paper are clumsy,' she said. 'They look like a prep for a first mural. Which of course they are. Did you know that Adele, the famous singer, throws up before she goes onstage?

'Right now, the whole thing seems a joke, something I can't possibly bring off.' She shoved her cold hands into her jacket pockets. 'I want to give children an image they can walk into, a sense of place that will engage and expand their imaginations and be real to them.

'And I wanted to say that you'll be in it, okay? The girls will be in the midsection near the clump of cottonwoods. And you'll be in the lower right-hand corner in the foreground. Almost life-size—sort of the star, really.'

The whole time she talked, he had listened, doing what James Herriot described as 'that slow, lateral grinding that means contentment and health.'

On the other side of the fence, Choo-Choo was chewing his cud.

A nd we'll put the pond here.'

Jack shook his head. 'That's not where th' pond *is!*'

'It's not where the pond is in real life, but it's where the pond must be to fit in the picture.'

'Everything should go in th' right *place.*'

Whiny, tired; up too early this morning and too confined the last couple of days. Too much time with his antsy mom in an attic room smelling of paint.

She had eaten half a sandwich at two o'clock and continued with the roller. The wash was nearly finished; her right arm and hand were aching and stiff; she transferred the roller to her left hand.

'Go find Harley, please, and see what you can do to help.' Harley and Willie were picking up pecans today and working around the other nut trees.

'But I want to help *you*!' He gave her his best pleading look, palms upturned. 'When it's time, I could paint a cow or a chicken, I could *do* it.'

The fan whirred against the odor of acrylics. She looked out the open window to the oak hanging on to its leaves. Since the chill of morning, the air had turned soft and sweet. Jack needed to boil off energy. She needed to boil off anxiety. This project was swallowing her whole.

She stood away from the wall, feeling the pull of the deadline, the pull of her child, the pull of the clinic and its daily tribulations.

She hadn't run in months. She had run regularly in Atlanta and Chapel Hill, but only a few times on their hay road or around the pond where Harley always mowed a path for her. She was stiff, sore, cranky; she needed complete solitude to do this huge thing. No music, no interruptions, just the work. But that was not going to happen and she had to get used to it.

'Why don't we go for a really fast walk? Out by the pond and back again. Really, really fast. Would you like that?'

'Will I get my new boots dirty?'

She placed the lid on the paint can.

'New boots need to get dirty.'

W alking fast. Breathing deeper. Charley barking. Jack running. The sun warm on their backs.

And there was their old pond, temporarily populated by a couple of mallards passing through to warmer climes.

Two and a half years ago, she and Dooley had gone on a call for Hal—an injection of antibiotics for a pony—and there was Jack, two years old, squatting at the edge of a farm pond in nothing but a diaper. The weather had been cold, she was wearing her fleece jacket and running toward a child who was leaning dangerously forward, looking into the pond. Anything might have happened.

Charley dove into the water, startled mallards flew out, and there was Jack at the pond's edge.

'Don't!' she called, running to him. 'No!' she said, pulling him back. 'Never to the edge. Okay? Never.' Her heart pounding.

'Why?' he said.

'When you learn how to swim, then you may go to the edge. But only then. And only with Dad or me or Harley. Okay?' But wait, Harley couldn't swim. 'Just with Dad or me, okay?'

Insulted duck cries fading south . . .

'Okay,' he said, close to tears. His mom had scared him.

Tired. She realized suddenly how tired she was, how the loss of sleep had chipped away at her resources.

'Let's sit a minute.' They sat on a decaying log, mired in leaves. She could sleep for weeks, right here in the October sun beneath this gnarly oak.

And there came Charley bounding up and shaking pond water from her shaggy coat and delivering ardent kisses.

Jack covered his face. 'No, Charley, you stink!'

Just a moment to close her eyes . . .

Then Charley's screaming yelp and the snake winding itself out of the dry leaves and racing toward the pond.

Copperhead.

Stunned, she saw herself as if from above, picking up Jack and running.

'We've got to get her to Dad! Call Charley. Call Charley!'

'Come, Charley!' he screamed. 'Charley, come!'

The crazed, high-pitched yelping.

'Charley, come!'

Running hard, Jack clinging to her, and looking for holes that could catch her feet and send them sprawling.

'Run, Charley! Home, Charley!'

The snake was young. Some say the deadliest bite comes from the young . . .

Jack crying, Charley howling, their voices shredding the calm of the afternoon, her heartbeat hard against the weight of her son. It could have been Jack, it happened right where they were sitting, or it could have been her—the venom working so fast she couldn't have run for help. Hold yourself together, Lace, help us, God, thank you, God, Charley, Charley, run, Charley!

Run.

They couldn't go in by the crate room filled with contagious rabbits. They made it through the front door, her chest on fire. Charley sprawled at Amanda's feet, howling and desperate for air.

Amanda ran for Dooley and Blake who came with a gurney.

She followed the gurney. 'Take care of Jack,' she called to Amanda.

Two clients in Reception looked on with alarm.

Charley on the table, the frantic whistling of breath in and out of constricted lungs.

Dooley nodded to Blake. 'No antivenom.' His knees were shaky; not a good thing, but this was Charley.

What was likely the full load of the juvenile's venom had been injected into the left front leg by two rat-eating teeth, a forest of bacteria . . .

Pain meds. Then Blake setting up the IV and Dooley drawing blood to check clotting. The sixty seconds it took to test for clotting seemed to wind into eternity. She watched the hands on the wall clock. It was all passing in a blur. Clotting! Yes! Thank you, God. Charley whimpering, pawing air against the grinding pain.

'What do you think?' she asked Dooley.

'She'll need IV fluids for twenty-four hours, to flush out and dilute the venom. And a few shots of buprenorphine to manage the pain.'

Amanda at the door. 'How's her breathing? Jack needs a word.'

'Everything's going to be all right.' He didn't want to lie, but he didn't really know. The chances were good, but nothing was guaranteed.

'After the pain med,' he said to Blake, 'ampicillin every eight hours plus IV fluids, and more pain management through the night. What do you think?'

'Good,' said Blake. 'And we'll check the clotting again in twenty-four hours.'

His knees were fine now. They had a plan; he knew where this was going.

Dooley glanced at Lace and saw the whole scenario mirrored in her face. He needed to see her there, praying, backed into the corner as if for refuge. This had to work; this was Charley.

The IV pump he bought on eBay for $250—worth every dime. He needed all the help he could get.

Jack did not want to cry in front of people, but he couldn't stop. He crawled under Amanda's desk where he wouldn't be seen and tried to understand why part of him felt missing. While the people were talking to each other, Amanda crawled under the desk, too.

His dad was with Charley, right? And with his mom and Blake, and everything would be okay?

Everything would be okay, said Amanda, and she held him and made him blow his nose.

He took a deep breath and realized something new and amazing.

When he grew up, he would not be a dump truck driver. He would be a vet like his dad and save lives.

She can't sleep by *herself*,' said Jack. The usual big eyes; palms lifted in supplication. 'She will *need* me!'

'We're figuring it out,' said Dooley.

The rabbits would be released on Wednesday, after which everyone at the clinic would don masks and gloves and disinfect the crate room. In the meantime, a Persian was boarding in his office and the Havanese recovering from electrical burn was housed in the break room.

They had to make a spot for Charley, sleeping now in her cone collar. Taking her to the house wouldn't work. They needed the meds, the IV, the clinic amenities.

The plumbers still at it at four o'clock, the jackhammer decimating the toilet floor.

They would make camp in Surgery for the night—Charley in her crate. He and Jack would sleep where? They kept a folded cot behind the mech room door, but it wasn't built for two.

He went to the house and waded into the junk room off the upstairs hall. Piles like this were common in third-world countries without garbage disposal technology.

He wrangled the futon mattress down the stairs and through the kitchen and across the drive and into the clinic. He wouldn't ask Lace to join them; her sleep had been compromised for too many nights.

Jack hugged his mom's legs. 'Me an' Dad will miss you.'

'I don't think so.'

She smiled at him and reached into the big plastic bag she was carrying and took out a couple of blankets and three pillows.

TUESDAY, OCTOBER 20

Cool but sunny with rain coming in the evening, according to Willie's report.

She was on the kitchen porch, stacking logs in the carrier for tonight's fire, and feeling grateful. Beth was on her way from Baltimore, where she'd stopped overnight with a friend. Charley was sleeping in her cone collar, blood pressure good. And the sketch—wild, ragged, crude, spontaneous—was done. She was using the brush now, which felt familiar; she had sketched like the wind this morning, not stopping to correct or edit. The rough image would change as she progressed, but the components were loosely in place and it was working.

The mountains were purple today, the cows somewhere out of sight. Lily was in for a half day, there was Willie raking leaves in the backyard and Harley changing a tire on Dooley's truck and Jack playing in the gravel. A family; they had a family. Maybe not everybody's kind of family, but—

'Look, Mom!'

Two dirty palms upturned. A penny in one, a dime in the other.

'Where did you get it?'

'From th' driveway.'

'Terrific! Put it in your bank.'

'I could give you one for your bank. I would share.'

'Oh, thank you so much. Do I get to pick which one?'

'You can have th' penny.'

She took the penny, warm from the sun. 'I truly appreciate it.'

How earnest he was, and full of grace.

'I seen it in th' gravel an' I'm goin' back to look for more, okay?'

'Okay.'

'And I will prob'ly bring you another one, okay?'

'Okay! But you need to get your shampoo. You and Dad leave at two-thirty.'

'How much is two-thirty?'

'See the two? When the little hand gets to the two and the big hand gets right here to six, it will be time to go. Lily is ready to shampoo your hair and Harley will shine your boots if you'll bring them downstairs.'

'I want to shine my boots.'

'Will you rub them really hard with the rag, like Harley does?'

He nodded, eyes serious.

'I love you big,' she said.

'Love you bigger!' he shouted, and raced into the house.

She could hear him coming, her little steam engine pounding up to Heaven and counting at the top of his voice, 'Seventeen! Eighteen! Nineteen! *Twenty!*' and he was in the room and his forehead was sweaty and his eyes were big and her concentration was broken and she was glad.

'Mom!' Jack tugged at her shirttail. 'Come down, I have a great idea.'

'How exciting! But you can tell me out loud. There's nobody here but us.'

'Secrets have to be said in people's ears! It's a secret for Dad.'

She stooped to him, to the scent of his shampoo, and he cupped his hands and whispered the secret in his warm boy breath.

'Oh!' she said. 'How perfect!'

'But you can't tell anybody.'

'I won't, I promise.'

'People who tell secrets gets their toes cut off an' throwed in th' pond for th' big turtle to make *soup*!' He cackled with laughter. 'An' a huge tractor with a monkey on top jumps out of th' pond an' eats your brains out!'

'I will totally not tell anybody, okay?'

'Okay,' said Jack.

She laid her brush down. 'Now! I'm goin' to catch you and kiss you for scaring me!'

'No!' he said, racing from the room and down the hall.

'No, please!' he yelled. She was right behind him. 'You will kiss my skin off!'

She was laughing so hard. 'You better believe it!'

At two-thirty, Teddy was sitting by the kitchen door, eager to go on the ride he was promised. She would miss him.

'You and Dad will have fun.' She loved how he had polished his boots in such a solemn, grown-up way. 'Give Miss Lucy my love. Tell her we'll come visit.'

'Blake will watch Charley?'

'He will. And I will, too.'

'An' Uncle Doc will come and help watch?'

'He will.'

She didn't want them to go, not really.

'There's a food bowl for Teddy,' she said, handing Dooley a basket, 'and bottled water and snacks for the road and three quarts of pumpkin. It's ready for the pie shell. But remember to bring the basket back, okay?'

'Okay.' Dooley gave her a long look.

'Remember you have Teddy's kibbles in the truck.'

'Right,' he said, and kissed her. 'Love you deep.'

She walked to the driveway with them and waved as they backed out. There went her world—in a red truck. She watched them all the way to the road, where they headed north.

M eadowgate pecans on Beth's windowsill, in a bowl with a nutcracker and pick.

On the bedside table, a book they both loved in college: Knut Hamsun's *Growth of the Soil*, and its dense narrative of building a new life.

The bedspread turned down, pillows fluffed up, asters on the night table.

She ran upstairs and set Lily's pumpkin pie on a blue and white plate in the center of the kitchen table. Added three Mason jars of blue and white asters. Good, but needing a touch of red. A quart jar of their tomatoes. That worked, though maybe not the best thing with pie. All from their farm, that was the connection.

The loud knock at the front door. The farm dogs going nuts on the porch.

'Roses!' said the driver from Mitford Blossoms, looking personally responsible for such a windfall.

Coral, their petals tipped with yellow. 'They're gorgeous!'

'Runnin' late. Accident a few miles back. Tractor trailer.'

'The curve?' she said.

'You got it.'

She didn't see a card. From Beth?

In the kitchen she removed the quart of tomatoes, put the roses in their place—perfect—and looked again for a card.

Could they be from Dooley?

She remembered the intense, lingering look he gave her before they left. There was something different about that look. She didn't really understand its meaning; it seemed to come from a new place.

She laid a fire in the primitive style she learned long ago at Absalom Greer's summer camp for youth, then set out their best plates and glasses and flatware and two small red lanterns with candles. Jack loved these lanterns.

And there was Blake coming in the back door, on his way to the hall room. 'Sorry,' he said.

'It's okay. I may have to come over to your place sometime.'

A bit of a laugh.

'Will it never end?' she said of the plumbing job.

'Mid-November is the new end date.'

Always the meter running. 'How's Charley?'

'Vitals good. Awake and wanting out of there. I'll bring her over before I go home tonight.'

She checked her messages—Beth was a half hour away.

The sound of the flush in the hall room, and Blake walking fast through the kitchen.

At the door, he picked up a bucket of water to be carried over, required of any clinic staff using house facilities.

'Nice-lookin' table,' he said.

'Thanks.' She loved getting ready for her best friend and her husband and son.

Twenty-seven minutes past eight.

Rain pecking the kitchen window.

She had been looking at the wall clock every few minutes since his text.

Teddy looks like a home run. Loaded up & leaving Joanna 6:45. Home 7:45. Sorry. xo

Beth had arrived in her cappuccino-colored Kia, looking her pre–Wall Street girl self. All the dogs had greeted her car, sniffing every tire. Squeezing hugs, high five, the rain just beginning.

'Are you starved?'

Beth laughed. 'Seven hours on an order of fries and tenders. I only stopped once because I couldn't wait to get here!'

She and Beth had a history of standing by each other—through the hard times with Dooley, through Beth's loss of her dad and then Freddie walking out. With all their combined moving around since college—Beth to Boston, then New York, herself to Atlanta and Chapel Hill—they had remained close, like sisters, sometimes exchanging or lending clothes by mail or UPS, confiding the best and the worst of themselves.

They were devouring a plate of cheese and crackers.

'Honest, Lace, I think you're worrying too soon. And your supper smells so good I could weep.'

'It's sitting too long, but . . .' All she could think of was time. 'They're nearly an hour late.'

'They left at six forty-five. You said Joanna is about an hour away, that's seven forty-five and now it's eight-thirty. So that's really only forty-five minutes later than Dooley said. And with game traffic . . . '

'I'm so glad you're here,' she said. Maybe she should have gone with them to Joanna's; Beth could have let herself in and been perfectly at home. The rain was another reason this wasn't feeling good.

The text had come from RHH/llc, which she knew to be Rivers Herd Health. That meant Dooley had used Joanna's phone. Even if he'd found his, the charge would have been gone ages ago.

'The roses are beautiful. They even smell like roses. Who sent them?'

'No card. Maybe my mom, because she knew you were coming. I'm texting Joanna.'

Last time she'd been frantic about Dooley, but now it was Dooley and
Jack . . .

Hi, Joanna. Are Dooley and Jack still there? Thanks for everything. U
will be your dad's best meds.

'There's a good reason, I promise,' said Beth. 'They're okay, I just feel
it. Have you seen Tommy?'

'I think he's traveling with the band. I wanted to tell him you were
coming, but Dooley had his cell number in his phone, which he lost
chasing a cow.'

'I messed up by not texting him anymore. Things were so volatile
with me . . . '

'Do you care that you messed up?'

'I hate that I just sort of dropped him. Especially when he must have
been grieving his grandmother.'

'She pretty much raised him. He wrote a beautiful song about her.
Tommy said he loved singing with you at the wedding.'

'I've started singing again—around the apartment, in the car. It all
started at the wedding.'

Lace looked at the kitchen clock.

'You look tired, Lace Face. Your mural is amazing, I wish you could
know this. You've always struggled with knowing how good your work is,
but maybe that's okay. You've been working too hard, I can tell. But I'm
here now and I'll help. What's on for tomorrow?'

'I'm starting to paint clouds. Can you start being Jack's aunt?'

'I'd love that. What do aunts do?'

'Oh, I suppose they do what moms do, but with less worries! Work
with him on a secret project for his dad, read with him, help him learn
to count beyond twenty. He's a very quick learner. And I'll make
lunch.'

'Do you know what heaven this is for me? Thanks so much for letting me come. I'll do anything. Give me a broom! A shovel! A head rag!
Whatever you think.'

'I think we should eat.'

'Yes! Hooray! Let me help.'

Lace opened the warming door of the oven. 'Lil's famous lasagna! Bring the plates!'

M ost people were scared of the curve, he worried about deer. Frye Hickman hit a deer the other day—five thousand dollars' worth of damage to his new truck, a worse scenario for the deer.

No phone. He'd have to lay out four hundred bucks. He and Joanna and Jack and her farmhand had searched but it was no good—his phone was history.

They had pulled out of Joanna's at seven-fifteen—the farmhand had needed help with a trailer hitch, then the rain and the traffic from the game in Wesley held them up, so they were running late and he was making his wife crazy.

Dark on these country roads, but he liked that. He needed time alone with the light from the radio and the music to keep him company. Jack had worn himself out playing with a litter of collie pups, wolfed down a pimiento cheese sandwich, and was buckled into his booster seat, out cold.

He had loved the look on Lucy's face. 'I wouldn't think a dog could remind me of a pig, but that's exactly what Homer used to do.' After sniffing the territory, Teddy had leaped onto a low foolstool, curled up, and given them a satisfied look.

If he didn't get a cherry pie out of this deal, he'd be et for a tater.

Something moving at the side of the road. He threw his right arm across Jack as he braked. Not a deer. A man waving.

He rolled down his window, the rain spattered in.

'My wife's havin' a baby, I need a doctor! My cell phone don't have a charge. Can you call us a doctor?'

'I'm a doctor, but . . . '

'She's bleedin'. Please, God, can you help us? It's somethin' bad wrong, I can't move her like this.'

Jack stirred, opened his eyes.

'I'll look in,' he said. He wasn't the doctor for this job, but he couldn't leave the man standing in the road. He wheeled into the driveway, the man running alongside. A beat-up van. Stacks of firewood. Rabbit hutches. A light inside the house silhouetted three kids and a barking hound on the porch.

'It come on so quick, I couldn't git her out to th' van.'

Jack sleeping again. 'My boy's in here.'

'He'll be fine, he'll be safe. Hurry, for God's sake, she's in a terrible way.'

He heard screaming from the house, prayed for Jack to keep sleeping.

The children, roughly five years and up, were crying and clinging to each other. 'Is he gon' help Mama?'

'He's gon' help her. Go on, now, git in th' back an' don't come 'til I call you.

'She's thisaway,' said the man. 'We've birthed all our young'uns at home, ain't never had this happen.'

The smell of woodsmoke and fried ham . . .

'How long in labor?'

'Three hours. Water's broke.'

Walking fast down a dark hall, the air filled with a ragged, tearing scream, to the door of a room with the thick scent of blood and the woman lying uncovered, sweat pouring, the sheets beneath her a soaking red.

She turned her head and looked at him. 'Please.'

He was instantly pulled into her suffering; he felt faint as he walked to the foot of the bed.

Fully dilated, but the head hadn't crowned. If this was what Hoppy called abruptio or complete placenta previa, he, she, they were done for, he could not touch that. Could be the placenta was implanted in the uterus with an edge too close to the cervix. Could be anything. He had to get in there, locate the head.

Lube, he needed lube.

'I've got to go to the truck,' he said to the man. 'Hot water. Need to wash up.' He raced out, Jack sleeping. Lube, gloves, gloves, yes, and ran inside and took off his jacket and rolled up his sleeves.

Please, God, do not let me deliver a dead baby. Cover me here.

'Your wife's name?'

'Janette.' The man's voice was shaking.

In the bathroom, he lathered to his elbows with a sliver of soap, rinsed, dried, and went back to her.

She looked at him, wild with pain. He had nothing in the truck for this.

'Janette,' he said. 'It's going to be fine. Work with me.'

The smell enveloped him like a caul as he bent to her.

Gentle, very gentle, he instructed himself, feeling for the head. Right there! In place, but . . .

'Push, Janette. We need to get your baby out *now!*'

He was terrified. Yet in his terror, he felt a certain calm flowing in. Jesus, he thought.

'Help me,' she said.

He could stop somewhere,' she said to Beth, 'and use a phone. Two hours. And no message from Joanna.'

'I believe they're fine, Lacey. Somehow it's all going to be okay.'

'I'm calling the county police.' How many husbands out there were two hours late tonight? Surely hers was not the only one. But Jack—Jack was two hours late, also. If anything terrible had happened, she could not bear it. She could not.

Her mother had left her by looking the other way, her father left her by seeing his daughter as an object. Dooley's mother had left him, his father left him; somebody was always leaving, disappearing. Maybe two hours late wouldn't be a serious problem for other people, but . . .

She gave the dispatcher the model, the year, the color. Her name, his name, her cell number, whatever they asked for.

Her hand was shaking when she ended the call. She had just made her fears official.

H e checked the speedometer. He was flying,
      The whole thing had gone down in a blur.

He didn't know what the medical guys would call it. The word *abruption* came to mind. It had been dicey. But considering what it might have been . . .

In the end, mother and baby were fine.

Jack had been liberated from the truck by three curious kids. They had all shown up in the bedroom soon after Artie Johnson expertly scrubbed up his newborn daughter.

Jack had not been happy to come awake to three strangers staring in the truck window, and no dad. He wiped Jack's tears, picked him up. 'Look, buddy! A baby! Brand-new.'

The mother invited them to come and have a look. The young Johnsons were gathered close, exclaiming over the new arrival; the hound stood by, resting his muzzle on a pillow.

'He smells funny,' said Jack. 'Can he talk?'

'It's a girl,' said the mother. 'She cain't talk yet.'

'What's her name?'

'Angel.'

'Does she got wings?'

'They ain't growed in yet.'

'Where did she come from?'

'He don' know where Angel come from,' whispered the dark-haired boy.

'Your daddy made our little sister come out!' said the middle Johnson.

'She was stuck,' said the youngest.

'Gotta go,' said Dooley. He grabbed his jacket, shook Artie's hand.

'I thank you more'n I can say, Doctor. Sorry about your shirt. What do I owe you?'

'Nothing. Just the satisfaction of everything being all right. Maybe you should get them to the hospital in Mitford.'

'I'm fine,' said Janette. 'We're all right.'

'I think I should tell you, I'm a vet doc. Right up the road.' He was trembling. After tying off the cord with dental floss, his knees had gone weak and hadn't fully recovered.

'Well, I'll be,' said Artie. 'Did you hear that, Janette? A vet delivered our Angel. You done good, Doc, you done real good. Thank you. God bless you. I owe you for this. I'm beholden.'

'Artie,' said Janette, 'give th' doctor a quart of my pumpkin. It's ready to go in th' pie shell.'

Artie and the kids had waved from the porch.

'Bye, bye, Jack!'

'Bye, Dr. Dooley!'

'Thank you, Doc!'

'Y'all come again!'

The high beams picked out a long row of cedars in the rain.

Home in fifteen minutes. Lace would be a basket case. He checked the speedometer. Eighty.

'Your mom's not gon' believe this,' he said.

He glanced up.

In the rearview mirror, the flashing, freaking blue light.

While Beth was downstairs, she put on her jacket and walked out to the porch with her cell phone.

She was going to have to learn to trust God. Completely.

Something white in the gravel.

She dashed into the rain and picked up a small envelope, and re-turned to the porch.

She could not go on without trusting him completely. It was so hard, so impossible, this addiction to trusting yourself to do God's job. What could possibly have happened to Dooley and Jack? An absolute terror was upon her. Yet in all this, she was to trust God—and more than that, yes, truly more than that, she was to thank him.

Rain drumming on the roof.

She prayed the only words she was able to gather. 'Help,' she said. 'And thank you.'

She went inside and put a log on the fire, then took the wet envelope from her pocket.

In the light, she could see the logo. Mitford Blossoms.

She removed the card and peered at the blurred ink.

Welcome home.
Tommy

She went to the basement door and called down, using her old term of affection. 'Bethie! Something wonderful! Come quick!'

Willie didn't drive at night and she didn't trust Harley's truck for back roads. There was no one she could send out, and no word from the county. She should go looking, she knew the route he took to Joanna's . . .

She was torn in half; nothing in her life had been so unbearable as this unknowing.

'Lacey, come and sit down.'

As she sat in the rocker, she saw lights bounce into the backyard. They were coming fast up the driveway.

'They're home,' she whispered, and tried to rise from the chair, but she could not.

'See you in the morning!' Jubilant, Beth threw her a kiss and ran from the room.

And then the door flying open and energy pouring into what had felt all night like a void, and Dooley, with a long exhaustion in his voice, saying, 'You're not going to believe this.'

Jack running to her. 'Mom! You're not gon' believe this!'

And Charley barking and wagging her entire backside and racing around Jack in a circle of joy.

She looked up at Dooley and saw that something had been taken from him and something given back. On his shirt, blood . . .

'My God! What . . . ?'

'I'm sorry,' he said. The lines between his eyebrows, his hair damp with rain . . .

'Dad made a baby come out! It's a angel baby with its wings not growed in yet.'

Jack climbed into her lap. Unable to hold back the tears, she pulled him close and buried her face in his hair.

You're my baby,' she said as she slipped Jack's pajama top over his head.

He had eaten a bowl of cereal and she had taken him up to bed.

'I'm not a baby.' He blinked, tired and solemn.

'Just for tonight,' she said, 'Just for tonight, okay?'

He would do anything to make his mom go smiling. He thought about what she said, and nodded. 'Just *this* tonight, okay?'

'Okay!'

She kissed his head, his face, his neck, his belly—he shrieked. She kissed his hands, his nose, his knees—he whooped and hollered. Then his feet, his stubby toes . . .

'No, no, *no!*' he yelled, laughing. 'No more *kissin'!*'

Dooley had done an amazing thing. She would visit Janette one day and perhaps be allowed to hold Angel and inspect the tiny shoulders where wings would grow.

Four hundred for a phone. A hundred and fifty for the traffic court judge. Plus the million bucks he would pay, if he had it, for sitting by the fire with Charley, wolfing down a double helping of Lil's lasagna and hearing the laughter upstairs.

13

H e recognized the firm, rapid knock at the side door.
Helene Pringle handed him a newspaper from the town at
the foot of the mountain. 'The *Holding Times*, Father. I take it
because of the crossword. I thought you should see this.'

The paper was folded to reveal the obituaries; she pointed to a death
notice.

*Clyde Henry Barlowe, 57 years old, of 7216 Wild Cat Road, died
October 19.*

They looked at each other.

What should he do with this information? Dooley's biological father
was dead, survived by five children whom he had abandoned to tragedy
and turmoil.

Sammy may be the one most affected by this news. Clyde, known by
various authorities as Jaybird, had held on to Sammy into his sixteenth
year when Helene Pringle, of all people, stumbled upon a direct lead to
the boy's whereabouts. The damage done had been appalling, but not
irrevocable, no. As for Dooley, Dooley had washed his hands of his biological father years ago.

He made the sign of the cross. He would go to Pauline, who, he expected, would tell Pooh and Jessie, then he would drive out to Meadowgate and tell Dooley, who would spread the news to Sammy and Kenny. This seemed as fair as he knew how to make it.

F or years, Pauline had wept when she saw him.

'All you've done for her kids reminds her of what she couldn't do,' said her husband, Buck.

Needless to say, someone tearing up at the mere sight of him was a downer, but he had no power over it. Thankfully, the tears had ceased since Dooley's wedding, when Pauline gained courage to express her remorse to all five children. There had been no instant healing, no miracle, but something had shifted, if only a little.

He found her in the Hope House dining room, sitting at the table by the fountain, sorting meal tickets. She glanced up and smiled, glad to see him.

'You're looking beautiful,' he said, meaning it.

They talked for a time; he held her hands and prayed for her as he always did.

'Jessie,' she whispered.

Though conflicted about his so-called rescue of several of her children, she was asking for help with her daughter. He had gone to Lakeland to find Jessie when she was five years old, but that was the extent of his involvement in Jessie's life.

He had worked no magic with any of her children. Whatever had happened was by patience, interest, and certainly the grace of God. Jessie was out of control, and once again, Pauline was faced with her own seeming helplessness. She could not explain what she meant by uttering Jessie's name, but he knew.

'It's out of my hands, Pauline. Out of my hands. Let God have her, give her to him daily, hourly. I have no magic.'

He thought she might weep, but she did not. Believe in your capacity to love, he wanted to say. Don't give up. Believe. Trust. Oh, he could say any number of things because it was easy for him to say.

He embraced her and decided to say what Peggy used to tell him all those years ago—when he had a skinned knee or another wound from his father, or when he was about to have three teeth yanked out at one go:

'Everything's going to be all right. Everything . . . is going to be all right.'

Dooley met him in the driveway and told him the story of the baby delivered down the road, and the pestering news of the speeding ticket. They had a laugh about the volume of canned pumpkin circulating in this end of the county, then met in the office that smelled faintly of cats.

He showed Dooley the notice and didn't know what to expect.

Dooley sat for a moment, expressionless, then stood abruptly and turned away and looked out the window.

As a priest, perhaps the guilt he was feeling was pastoral, not personal. But guilt is guilt. He wished he had prayed more avidly over the years for the soul of Clyde Barlowe.

At the farmhouse, Jack was napping, Lace was painting, and Beth was assessing any yard sale potential of the junk room contents. Such domestic information came from Lily, who was rinsing her mop in a bucket on the porch.

Declining to disturb the household, he emptied his pocket of change and left it on the kitchen table as a nod toward Jack's savings for a bike helmet. A satisfying investment!

He hailed Blake, who was latching the run gate to the sound of barking, and a lot of it.

'I have a question if you have a minute.'

'Shoot, Father. Good to see you.'

'Would you know of anything the business needs that would help out in some . . . I don't know . . . some special way?'

'Don't even have to think about it. Sure is.'

They stepped away from the barking and sat for a few minutes on a bench by the clinic door.

'Don't mention that we talked about this,' he told Blake.

'Nossir. Not a word. Any idea when you'll get another dog?'

'Don't plan to. I had the best.'

Blake watched Dooley's dad walk to the car. That, he thought, is what everybody thinks when they lose a good dog. We'll see.

Before pulling onto the state road, he checked his phone, which he'd left on the passenger seat.

Three messages.

J.C., Otis, Omer.

All with the same hard news.

H e gleaned what he could from the charge nurse.

Mr. Packard's immune system was compromised and perhaps completely shot.

Bacterial pneumonia. The really bad one.

Drips of heavy-duty antibiotics off and running.

No visitors allowed except Father Tim and one employee from the patient's place of business, all required to wear a mask and wash their hands before and after each visit.

Visits limited to five minutes. Dr. Wilson had pronounced this a law, not a suggestion.

He must not touch the patient nor tire the patient.

Upcoming tests would include X-ray of the lungs for possible damage by excessive tobacco use.

Avis's breath whistled in, whistled out as he presented his plan to the priest and concluded with an offer. 'Ten dollars an hour.'

A convulsion of coughing that shook the bed.

'I don't know, Avis, I can't say right now.'

'Or fryers, roasters, chops, fresh produce. You name it, it's yours. You like a good ham . . .' Th' pain was a blowtorch in his chest, but he had to get this deal settled. 'Fresh pasta. All you need.' But who would make th' pasta? He was th' pasta man. Otis and Lisa could not make pasta. 'If I was to . . . maybe . . . you know.'

'Die?' said Father Tim. 'I don't think that's where you're headed.'

But if he did die, Avis thought, where was he headed? Up? Down? He didn't want to get into that. 'If I pass . . . maybe you could find where Chucky's at . . . an' check on him once in a while?'

'I'll do my best. Do you ever talk to God, Avis?'

'Nossir. I don't bother God.' Wait a minute. He'd asked God for somethin' th' other day, but couldn't remember what it was.

Lungs concrete; his head mostly air. He was glad the preacher was here; he saw him through some kind of cloud. His mother had eyes the color of clouds.

She was blue an' puffed up an' wet an' layin' on th' kitchen table where she rolled out her biscuit dough, where they sat and ate their dinner.

'Why?' he asked his daddy.

'Troubled,' he said. 'She was troubled.'

People talkin' in low voices, spittin' tobacco juice in her flower beds, hammerin' in the shed, tap, tap.

'Troubled about what?' He was afraid of the answer.

His daddy shrugged an' stared out to their three head of beef cattle standin' in th' field. 'I don't know nothin' about it, boy. God only knows.' He had wondered why God seemed to know so much an' people didn't know nothin'.

'Lisa and Otis, they don't have a way with th' public. But they'll give you backup. They're hard workers. Otis'll get his daddy to come up an' butcher for us.'

'We'll figure it out.' The rattle in Avis's chest was unsettling. 'You need to rest now.'

'They can't pay th' bills or write checks or place orders.'

'It's going to work out. We'll get Marcie Guthrie to run your books. She did some work for you a while back; she'll know the ropes.'

'Lisa an' Otis know how to price an' shelve an' run a card an' open th' refrigerator . . . I mean th' cash drawer. As for orderin' supplies, no, an' Thanksgivin' comin'.' This was a terrible thing. He could not afford to let his business go haywire with Thanksgivin' comin'. A wave of coughing churned in his chest, exploded, cracked open the concrete.

'If . . . anything . . . happens . . .' Avis forced out air to shape each word. '. . . you'll know . . . how to handle it.'

The five minutes were up. Father Tim crossed himself, prayed for words. The old petition came to mind like a bird to the outstretched palm.

'Heavenly Father, watch with us over your child Avis, and grant that he may be restored to that perfect health which is yours alone to give. Through Christ our Lord. Amen.'

He said *amen* in the way of the Baptists, with the long *a*, as it was pronounced when he was a boy in Holly Springs. It was a simple comfort to him, a priest who felt he had little comfort to give.

Seven-fifteen. Lights on in the town at the foot of the hill, stars on in the great bowl above.

Six days a week—Monday through Saturday—until other help could be found. Eight to four with a break for lunch. How could he possibly want to do this fool thing?

He huddled into his topcoat as he walked across the hospital parking lot to the car.

Maybe it wasn't about wanting or not wanting. Though he was beyond serving the mission field, wasn't his own town a mission field? No famine, no poverty, no war, thanks be to God, but a mission field, nonetheless. And didn't charity begin at home?

He had really enjoyed pitching in at Happy Endings a few years ago. For him, the bookstore had been part confessional, part community center, and more than part pleasure—all without the woes of the financial part.

In two years plus change, he would be eighty, and people could very well stop asking him to do anything. A terrifying thought if he let himself dwell on it. For decades, he'd been asked to do nearly everything, often including the impossible.

What did he know about the food business? Only what he'd learned from growing up with two great cooks and decades of doing his own grocery shopping—that should count for something. At the end of the day, as people liked to say, did he currently have anything better to do than pitch in at the Local?

He drove left on Old Church Lane and right on Main. Lights glowing in store windows. A wool cap at a jaunty angle on a mannequin head at the Woolen Shop.

She had turned the porch light on for him, though she knew he would come in from the garage. He liked seeing the porch light. The little things . . .

Their evening fire was embers as he shucked out of his coat.

He told her the whole story. Would he be nuts to do this?

'You're wonderful,' she said.

'It would be okay with you?'

'Absolutely! God equipped you perfectly for this job.'

'Come on!' he said, ironic.

'You know all about sautéing and frying and marinating and brining.

You're a regular font of culinary skills. Plus you're great with people. The very sort that come into a grocery store, dazed and frantic with no earthly idea what to make for dinner. And how about people who must cook on a shoestring? There's your famous Rector's Meatloaf, to name but one money-saver. All these qualifications are exceptional. But, honey . . .'

He loved it when she called him honey.

'. . . here's the plus that puts all else to shame. You've been in sales for half a century. Avis is getting a pro!'

She looked pleased with her observations. 'It's perfect, Timothy! I'm so proud of you.'

He turned off the lamp by the sofa, laid two sticks of kindling on the grate, and added a log. He watched the kindling catch and the flames leap up, then went to the sofa and sat next to her and looked at his deacon in the firelight.

They were grinning at each other like two kids. 'Thanks,' he said.

He had a job again. And it had come at the very time he thought he didn't need one.

THURSDAY, OCTOBER 22

He knew it was crazy, but he'd planned to ask Father Tim to make th' speech in place of hisself.

All those things th' Kavanaghs said about what th' Local does that other stores don't do—that's what he would've asked Father Tim to go to Charlotte an' say. Now he didn't have to ask such a fool thing. The torment he was goin' through had got him off th' hook.

He hoped th' dope he was on wouldn't fog his mind permanently; he wanted to remember always what th' Kavanaghs said.

'Chucky. I mean Father.'

'Right here.'

'You know th' way I like to answer th' phone every mornin'.'

'I can't do that, Avis. Sorry.'

'It's a . . . tradition,' said Avis. He tried to raise his head, but it was a brick.

'I'll do my best at everything else. But I can't do that.' No, indeed. He had his limits.

W e hope today's session, though decidedly unofficial,' said Father Brad, 'will be a step toward helping you begin to discern your future.'

Pooh, dressed in a knit shirt and khakis, sat with the group in a circle of chairs borrowed from the Sunday school.

'So we're just going to talk, Pooh, the five of us. Lilah Bowen, my assistant, Paul Huffman, our senior warden, and Father Tim will join me in asking a few questions. Nothing life or death here. Maybe it will give you, give us all, something more to think about in our faith.

'To begin, I often see you in the congregation with your parents. Have you had any other church experience?'

'After my mother and stepfather became Christians, we went to the Baptist Church in Wesley. We were there about a year before we joined Lord's Chapel.'

'What did you think of the Baptists?'

'The people were really nice, really glad to see us. And the food was great.'

Amused chuckles.

'There's only one thing I don't like about Baptists,' said Pooh. His face was flaming.

'What's that?'

'People say they won't speak to you in the liquor store.'

Startled, the group burst into laughter, Father Brad being the ringleader. They looked at each other, then at Pooh, whose coloring had gone from beet red to the pallor of a corpse.

'My English instructor advised me to make you laugh, up front.' His heart was pounding, his mouth dry. His English instructor was brilliant; he had always respected his advice. 'Trust me,' Joseph Kinley had said. 'It will work and it will be good for you and for them.'

'But this is . . . *religion*,' he had said, not knowing how else to put it.

'All the more reason,' said Kinley.

Pooh put his hands in his jacket pocket to disguise the trembling, though he'd been somewhat encouraged by the laughter.

'The pastor seemed to really care about us, was very knowledgeable, and usually gave an altar call. Most Sundays, a few people would go forward. I thought that was th' highlight of the service, but somethin' I would never do. And then one Sunday, I went forward.'

He had been terrified, but pulled as if by a cattle rope to the altar.

'How old were you?' asked Lilah Bowen.

'I was ten years old.'

'What do you think called you forward?'

'I believe God called me forward. I wanted to make a commitment to him, to the way he had loved my mom and stepdad, the way he had brought healing to them, and a kinder way of dealing with each other and with me. The love I saw in my mom and dad is how God first showed himself to me. I see th' way Father Tim has been an instrument of healing in my family. I see what Father Brad did for my brother Sammy. So he reveals himself to me through other people.'

There was a settling silence.

'Would you tell us about your prayer life?' said Father Tim.

Pooh drew a deeper breath. He had never talked like this to anyone before. Ever. He was a crater of nerves, but it was getting better.

'I pray every morning and every night. Sometimes during the day, just when it, like, crosses my mind, I might say, Hey. Or just thanks, or maybe just please. I hope that doesn't sound disrespectful.'

'Not at all,' said Father Tim. 'God is our truest friend. Does he speak back to you in any way?'

'Yessir. My heart gets warm, it feels full. And sometimes . . . it makes me cry.' He had not wanted to confess that, but it came out anyway. From reading the books Joseph Kinley loaned him, he figured that was the work of the Holy Spirit.

Father Tim thought he had never seen anything like this—a seventeen-year-old boy, feeling his way with candor and humility into subjects deep enough to challenge anyone in the room.

'What do you consider your weaknesses,' asked Lilah, 'for the calling you think you may pursue?'

Pooh thought a moment. 'I can be really shy. I don't always speak up when I should. And when I was a kid, I wanted to find my brothers, Sammy and Kenny, but I didn't have the guts to do anything about it. I would like to have more—I guess I'd call it courage.'

Father Tim saw that Pooh was doing the nervous jiggling of his right leg that was characteristic of Dooley. Blood will tell. How very extraordinary was the Barlowe family. He hoped to see the day when Pauline could be as happily astonished as himself at what marvelous people God had wrought through her. He wished Clyde Barlowe could have recognized this.

'Your strengths?' said Lilah.

'I'm a good listener.'

Father Brad nodded. 'It takes a great man to make a good listener.'

'And I can make a yo-yo sleep.'

They had a laugh.

'Fine,' said Paul Huffman, 'but can you make it walk?'

Pooh was grinning. His natural color had returned; he sat in the chair as if he might actually be comfortable.

'What is your hope,' said Paul, 'for any ministry you may undertake?'

'To help people love God so they can learn to love themselves and each other.'

'Is that it?'

'Yessir. Essentially.'

Father Brad looked pleased, even paternal.

They agreed to meet again in six months. In the meantime, they would pray for Pooh and Pooh for them.

They stood at the side door of the church as the lanky red-haired boy headed up Main Street.

'Who is that kid, anyway?' said Paul Huffman. 'Seems like the genuine article to me.'

'Deep,' said Lilah.

'Funny!' said Father Brad.

'Amazing,' said Father Tim.

Henry 'Pooh' Barlowe Leeper hardly felt his feet touch the pavement. He'd never done anything so frightening, and he was still alive to talk about it.

H e was walking from the hospital this evening, and taking a different route. Left on Old Church Lane, right on Church Hill Road, and left toward home. Stars blazing, the smell of woodsmoke.

The ringtone was muffled by his coat pocket.

'I'm on my way. A long road, they think . . . I won't be making any more night visits, I promise. Love you back.'

He was nearly home when he decided he could do it, after all. He hated to disappoint people.

His breath was a vapor on the air as he spoke aloud in the direction of the waxing moon. 'Red potatoes ninety-seven cents a pound today only. How may I help you?'

Something like that. But not a word more.

SATURDAY, OCTOBER 24

His first day at the Local had gone by in a blur of astonished faces, a confetti of coupons, trucks unloading at the rear platform, pumpkins being carved by a team of seventh graders under the store awning, and a good bit of feeling helpless.

He had, however, learned the root problem of the small-town grocery business:

Minimums.

To get free shipping and the best price, a store had to order a minimum of something or other. Say the canned-vegetables supplier wanted a minimum of $1,000—it could take a long time for a mom-and-pop operation to move that many cans and see a profit. Minimums were a rock and a hard place.

He was in and out of sleep. For some reason, learning the upgraded cash register system was a jawbreaker. Tossing, turning. Overall, the grocery business was looking like a can of worms. Think about it. Lettuce going limp. Fruit going soft. Meat going 'off.' Butter going rancid, milk going sour . . .

'Timothy.'

'What?'

'You're talking in your sleep.'

'What time is it?'

'Three o'clock.'

'What did I say?'

'Broccoli.'

Broccoli! He was supposed to print out his soup recipe to be given to anyone who bought broccoli today.

To its credit, Mitford was not altogether a Cheez Whiz town. There were a few accomplished cooks around, though they generally ignored the useful cannellini bean, disdained the avocado for anything but guacamole, and totally ruled out the fresh artichoke, which was considered 'too California.'

Walking to the Local on his second day, he designed his modus operandi. Starting tomorrow, he would drive up the hill for a five-minute consult with Avis, return the car to Cynthia, walk to work, and arrive at the store by eight. Avis was pretty doped up and miserable, so it was hard to get a straight answer, but he needed every crumb or tidbit he could cobble together.

'I told Avis about the broccoli that came in yesterday,' he said to Otis. 'A few stores in Wesley and Holding are asking one-ninety a pound. What do you think about *Fresh broccoli one-sixty-five a pound today only* for the phone ad?'

Otis adjusted his eyeglasses. 'I think we should get one-seventy-five,' said Otis, who had made up his mind to shoot straight. If the preacher ran this business off the rails, he and Lisa would be gluin' on labels at the canning factory.

'I think that's right,' said Lisa. 'One-seventy-five.'

'So be it.' He was George Washington in counsel with his generals. 'Make a sign for the window, please. And, Otis . . . '

'Yessir.'

'Where do we keep the broom?'

'Behind th' door in th' restroom.'

'I'll step out a few minutes,' he said. 'Is there a dustpan?'

'Attached to th' broom handle,' said Lisa. She was what his mother would have called 'a little bitty thing,' well seasoned with freckles. 'I do a good cleanup every evenin', you don't need to bother.'

'There's something I'd like to take care of on the street.'

He walked around to the side of the building where cigarette butts had made their forlorn accumulation and began sweeping them into the dustpan.

'Esther,' he said aloud to their former mayor, 'this one's for you.'

H e didn't need an hour for lunch. He hung a right and walked to Feel Good.

'Takeout,' he said to Wanda. 'The usual.'

She yelled the order through to the kitchen. 'And put legs on it!

'I hear you'll be runnin' th' Local.'

'No, no, it will be running me, wait and see. This is my second day.'

'Who's helpin' you?'

'We have a butcher coming up next week from the Valley. There's Lisa and Otis. And we may have some help from Otis's family. They smoke pork.'

She gave him a dark look. 'They smoke what?'

'*Pork.*'

'When you get through pitchin' in for Avis, come pitch in for me. I need to get out to Oklahoma to see my daddy.'

'I pitch in only when there's a medical emergency. You don't want to go there.'

'I hear it's gon' be a while for Avis. If you get desperate, I can send one of my girls. They're honest and hardworkin'. But only after th' lunch cleanup and only for two hours. And never on Friday or Saturday.'

'Thank you, Wanda. Very kind of you.'

'Mitford takes care of its own, right?'

It had been a while since he'd heard that. He gave her a thumbs-up.

MONDAY, OCTOBER 26

Good morning! Sweet Vidalia onions, five-pound bag, two-ninety-five today only. How may I help you?'

'Ahhh. Avis?'

'Tim Kanvanagh. Avis is out for a bit.' A few weeks? A couple of months? It was daunting not to know.

'I'm a longtime fan of th' Local. Hey, I need an eight-pound beef tenderloin for tonight. I'm drivin' down from Abingdon. Is that a problem?'

'I don't know. I don't think so. Can you hold?'

'I'm ten minutes out.'

He laid the phone down, located Otis. 'Need an eight-pound beef tenderloin.'

'I can give you pork, but no beef, not today.'

Back to the phone, reporting his findings.

Sayonara to the customer who wanted beef and was now motoring to Holding's Fresh Market, forty minutes south. He should have romanced what they had, shared his no-fail pork tenderloin recipe. Avis could not afford to lose a customer. He would have to do better, think faster.

As for today's phone ad, it was good to promote what had to go out of here, but onions? He needed something to stir the imagination, lift the spirit, inspire!

Possibly something foreign. Like—Italian sausage! Store-made! There you go.

'We don't have any Italian sausage,' said Otis. 'No Italian sausage.'

'Can you grind us some pork shoulder?'

'Yessir. We've got plenty in th' locker.'

'Grind us ten pounds, and in an hour or two, we'll have Italian sausage.' Otis gave him an alarmed look. 'Mild, I hope. We can't sell hot.'

'Mild, of course,' he said. 'This is Mitford. And I'll need two pounds of pork fat.'

'I can do that. But it's frozen.'

'Perfect. I'll need sugar and salt . . . '

'In th' break room.'

'And sherry. A little sherry.'

'Wine section.'

'I'll need big bowls.'

'In th' cabinet above th' sink. Avis ran his test kitchen back there.' Otis was noticeably wringing his hands over any possible bad decisions by the preacher. Sherry, pork shoulder, pork fat. These were big-money ingredients.

'How about four bucks a pound?' he asked Otis.

'Harris Teeter in Wesley gets four ninety-nine.'

'Good. Another reason to make it four bucks. But only for a limited time.' He knew something about loss leaders. Lose a little on a big item to get people in the store, right?

The only problem with this job is that he flat-out didn't know what he was doing. But he did know how to make sausage. They had made a lot of sausage at Whitefield; Peggy taught him how when he was ten years old, just before she disappeared.

He went to the spice rack. Crossed himself.

Took down the parsley, the garlic powder, the fennel seeds, the cracked pepper . . .

A nd there it was in the butcher's case. A great mound of it, garnished with sprigs of fresh sage. He looked at it each time he passed that way.

In two hours, they sold five pounds. This was not mere grocery sales, this was theater.

He was happy when the phone rang.

'Delicious store-made Italian sausage, four dollars a pound now through Thursday only. Bellissimo! How may I help you?' In his gleeful pulpit voice.

'Timothy?'

'Cynthia!'

Dead silence. But wait. The silence was not dead. His wife had put her hand over the phone, a tactic that failed to entirely conceal her hilarity.

R ay Cunningham was on his way out with a bag of collards, winter squash, broccoli, Brussels sprouts, and four bananas.

'Potassium!' said Ray. 'Lowers high blood pressure, helps with your heart problems, clears up confusion, irritability, and fatigue!'

Ray was once famous for dishes said to *cause* confusion, irritability,

and fatigue. 'I believe you're the fellow who was legendary for his barbecue, country-style ribs, fried chicken . . . '

'You *can* teach an ol' dog new tricks, Father. So you come up an'
see 'er, you hear? She's a honey, she's a real honey. Guaranteed to deliver
pure happiness. Where you gon' get a guarantee like that? But come
early, before th' queen starts linin' up her household staff!'

'Seven too early?'

'Slip in th' side door.'

In Ray's wake came Vanita Bentley, looking for a Helpful Hint for
the *Muse.* He was rearranging avocados that had been squeezed unnec-
essarily.

Do not squeeze the avocados was the sign he was hand-lettering in his
imagination. That would fix the overzealous shopper! But come to think
of it, he was himself a squeezer.

'I know you're a Hint fan,' she said. 'If you could just give me somethin' on par with usin' a banana peel to polish your shoes. That was big.'

'No time for Hints,' he said. 'You give me a hint.'

'About what?' she said.

'How to help run a small-town grocery without any knowledge of the
food business.'

'Keep smilin',' she said.

'That's good for starters. Thank you.'

He moved on to the broccoli, which was looking despondent.

'I know your wife is a fan of th' classifieds,' said Vanita. 'You should
see what we have in the can for next week! *Mars Bar Looking for Tootsie
Roll.*' Her eyes were enormous behind her tortoise-rim glasses. 'What do
you think of that?'

'Makes me nervous,' he said.

'Okay, so listen. Let me write up a piece on you doin' this wonderful
civic act for Avis. I know you're shy about publicity, but . . . '

'Vanita. Do not start with me.'

'Just one teeny tiny story.'

Out from her purse the size of a small car came the point-and-shoot.

'Or maybe just a smiley-face shot with a caption? Like, *Father Tim Kavanagh Bags New Job?*'

'Stop right there,' he said.

'So I can't do a story?'

'Vanita Bentley. Listen to me.' He leaned closer for emphasis. 'No story.'

'Okay,' she said, and away she went in her spike-heel shoes, *tik, tik, tik*.

'Vanita!'

She turned around and smiled, then waved, as if to say she was not giving up. Oh, she was an intrepid slip of a thing and he was fond of her for it. 'Thanks for asking!

'Now,' he said to Lisa. 'About the broccoli. Can we crisp it?' Avis was known to crisp certain produce in a sink of cold water, then transfer it to the refrigerator where it regained its soigné.

'Goes out this evenin' to th' Food Bank. Did you know broccoli is versatile? You can use it for a truly elegant centerpiece. My niece did that for her weddin' dinner. Just tie a bunch together with raffia an' set on th' table with candles. You'd be surprised how . . .'

Not up to the banana-peel polisher, but still . . .

'Vanita!' He did a fast trot to the front, but Vanita was out of there.

H e heard a good deal of merriment as a flock of ninth graders blew in from Mitford School.

Right behind them, Fancy Skinner—in pink capri pants and spike heels. He'd rather go out to the garden and eat worms. 'Pushing seventy-three and still no sensible shoes,' his wife once said.

'Oh, Lord, there you are,' she said. 'You're everywhere. Up at th' bookstore, down at th' church, workin' in th' food business. Busy, busy.'

He recognized her cool stare as a review of his haircut.

'Fancy! What timing! We've got Italian sausage, store-made fresh today, just four dollars a pound.'

'Too much grease in sausage. I have Mule offa grease, offa cheese, offa sugar. An' offa anything with white flour.'

Ha. His wife did not have him offa anything. He was a free agent!

'Is Avis comin' back?'

'Eventually, yes. We don't have a date.'

'I tried to tell 'im. Smokin', forgettin' to eat, runnin' himself ragged. Go across th' street, I said, an' jump in th' tannin' booth; get rid of that pasty look. Oh, that pasty look, Father, it's a *mark*, plain and simple, of bein' indoors and sickly. You have that look yourself, sorry to say. Preachers mostly seem to have that indoor look. Maybe it's because you have to be inside to read books an' study th' Bible, all by artificial light. You take Father Brad, he's naturally tan from bein' *outside*.' She gave him a smirk. 'That Father Brad—there's a total hunk for you.'

A collective whoop of insane laughter up front.

'It used to be peaceful in here,' said Fancy.

'Quoth the raven,' he said, dry as a crust.

We were just talking about you,' he told Father Brad.

The priest pushed a can of chewing tobacco across the counter. 'Positive, I hope.'

'You decide. You were spoken of as a total hunk.'

Father Brad burst into his famous unhindered laugher, the kind that can fill up a small store. 'Oh, boy. Okay, on to higher thinking. Jessie is in. Pray for snow.'

'This is great news. Count on me for prayer.'

'I always count on you for prayer. If I couldn't count on you, who could I count on?'

'Mary Ellen?' Grinning like a monkey; he couldn't help it.

Father Brad laughed. 'Father, Father. You're not giving up, are you?'

'Not if I can help it. What's with the chewing tobacco?'

'Our youth group is going to look at it through a microscope. Discuss the ingredients—nuclear waste, embalming fluid, cyanide, arsenic, lead, to name a few—and find out for ourselves how rotten this stuff is. Parents invited.'

He dropped the can into a small paper bag and handed it to his colleague. 'You're the best.'

Father Brad's face colored. 'No. No, I'm not, Father. Not at all. Please. Don't think that. No.'

Father Brad, who seldom seemed in a hurry, left in a hurry.

He had the sense that, for whatever reason, his friend was being harder on himself than God might choose to be.

A vis had said that Lisa and Otis couldn't place orders. Though quite a few pallets had been off-loaded on Friday, stock looked low in several places.

'I noticed we're low on bacon,' he said. He was a great noticer of bacon, a comestible long denied the diabetic.

'Yessir, we're low on my daddy's applewood smoked an' Timmy Proffit's uncured. Our livermush is way down, too. Avis don't like to let th' livermush get down. But that's all on our list.'

'What list is that?'

'We keep th' Valley list separate,' said Lisa. 'We don't need a minimum down there. Me an' Otis pick up what we need from everybody an' bring it to work in our van.'

'So when are we going to order what we need?'

'Avis liked to do th' orderin',' said Otis. 'We've never done th' orderin'.'

'Avis liked to do it all,' said Lisa. 'That's th' main reason he's sick. But that's just my two cents.'

'So, Father . . .' Otis had never called a preacher Father; this was his first time to say it. 'We were waitin' for you to do th' orderin'.'

'Otis, Otis, I am not Avis. What I am, I cannot say, but it is no grocery maven. I am Little League, not the Orioles. Do you know how to place orders?'

'Oh, yessir, I've watched Avis do it for fifteen years. I know all th'
distributors he does business with. I know what Avis likes.'

'Yessir,' said Lisa. 'He knows all that.'

He took a deep breath. 'So let's place some orders. And God be
with us!'

A vis had asked him to go to his house for the letter from the Association. Key under the top log of the woodpile on the back porch.
Please call the person who wrote the letter and say that he couldn't
make the talk.

He walked over before dark, leaving Otis and Lisa to close up at
seven.

He'd never been to Avis's house, which was set out back from the
street on a lot of considerable depth and heavy tree cover.

Gloomy. The perimeter of the yard was badly grown up and the
house didn't look so good, either. He was surprised. Avis was straight as
a shot about the details of his business dealings, which, as far as he
knew, were fastidious.

The hollow chill of an empty house had always made him uneasy.
He had felt it after his mother's death, when he spent days going through
her things, earmarking boxes, and for whom? Peggy had vanished years
ago, his father was long deceased, his aunts and uncles were installed in
Hill Crest Cemetery or otherwise dispersed, and all but one cousin was
flung to the four winds. He had hauled the boxes to Christ Church,
destined for their own version of the Bane and Blessing.

He found a bedroom that, although spare, possessed some spirit of
warmth and humanity. A squeaky toy on the night table. Chucky. The
whole sad scenario of the little guy on the leash . . .

Shame on him for walking through these rooms uninvited, making
his cool observations. But he did it anyway.

In the dark kitchen, he peered through the window over the sink.

Trees were overhanging the house. He was admittedly fond of the clean gutter, and God only knows what shape these gutters may be in. And the privet hedge—amok! For more than a decade he had tried to make something out of the privet at Children's Hospital . . .

He was leaving when he noticed the wall calendar by the door.

Avis would definitely not be coming home in October.

Though rushing time, which he could ill afford to do, he lifted October onto the nail and there was November.

If you're afraid of butter, use cream.

—JULIA CHILD

TUESDAY, OCTOBER 27

The call came around nine-fifteen. Avis not doing well. They were moving him to Charlotte by ambulance, immediately. Further information to follow.

Avis had been nearly incoherent this morning. The nurse had not allowed the full five minutes.

He rounded up Otis and Lisa.

'He's on his way to Charlotte.'

They looked at each other.

'It's just us.'

They were out to sea in a small boat.

He called Marcie Guthrie, mother of their police chief and one of Esther Cunningham's four daughters.

'How soon can you get over here?'

'I've got to do th' books at Woolen Shop, then get up to Mama's and fix her lunch because Daddy's at th' doctor—think I'll do pimiento cheese, but I probably shouldn't do cheese, maybe just a salad—then run by th' drugstore and do payroll, then pick up th' grans from school. I could be there at four.'

'Great! Four it is.'

He supposed Avis had chosen him because of his experience at Happy Endings. During that stint, Hope had run the inventory, planned the monthly sales, and ordered what was out of stock, all from the confinement of her bed and with help from Marcie Guthrie. He had been strictly sales, with a dash of window dressing thrown in. Nevertheless, selling a book was one thing, selling Brussels sprouts another.

He had avoided discussing the elephant in the room. Namely, the Laying In of Turkeys. He knew they kept a few turkeys on hand year-round, but that would soon change. Avis once said they'd be getting in a hundred free-range birds this year. A hundred! Scary.

'If I was a free-range turkey,' Cynthia said, 'I'd be going AWOL right now.'

'Th' whole hundred won't come in at one time,' said Lisa, trying to keep the grin off her face. 'They come in separate shipments. Mainly in our van.'

He figured the upcoming phone ad should promote the preordering of turkeys.

He took refuge in the break room. Scribbled a few lines. Looked up and saw his reflection in the drink box.

Good grief. Speaking of turkeys . . .

He walked toward home, carrying a pumpkin.

Maybe he would carve the thing, or maybe not. He wasn't a fan of Halloween. All Hallow's Eve, yes; Halloween, no. But c'est la vie, it was on sale, and they had to start making room for winter squash and a vast pile of warty gourds.

The Local was a kind of town treasure, really.

How good was it to live a block or two from a pint of Ben & Jerry's?

How good was it to have had fresh pasta and not really appreciate it till it wasn't available anymore and its maker was in a hospital bed in a distant city, with lights flashing and machines beeping and his chest filled with something damning and detestable and possibly life-threatening?

He thought about the maple top of the checkout counter. He liked how the hard wood was worn in the center, sloping into a shallow bowl where countless hands had rested, groceries were bagged, cash was laid out, cards were swiped, tales told, jokes enjoyed.

Avis was in Charlotte now, but not to preach his small-town grocer's sermon. His sermon had been preached 24/7 on the floor of the Local, for more than three and a half decades.

Who could know where this scenario was headed, or for how long? He said to Cynthia on the phone a while ago that he'd gotten himself into this scrape and he would stick with it. He would not be afraid; he would do his level best.

H e was tossing a bag of garbage in the trash can when Harley drove in next door.

He popped through the hedge. 'Yo, Harley!'

Harley rolled down the truck window. 'Rev'rend!'

'Good to see you, buddy.'

'I'm just droppin' somethin' off to Miss Pringle. She's got a piano lesson across town. How you doin'?'

'Good, thanks.' The lethal fragrance of Harley's cologne wafted from the truck cab.

'You want t' git in an' visit where it's warm?'

'Sure. I'll sit with you a minute, then get back to the house.' Cynthia didn't like him to 'vaporize,' as she called it.

He climbed in. 'You heard about Avis?'

'Yessir. I hated t' hear it.'

He nearly sat on something covered with foil.

'Let me move that. It's banana puddin'. Gon' leave it at her back door f'r a early trick or treat an' git on home—we're startin' work on th' barn shed in th' mornin'.'

Banana pudding, collard greens, brownies—always something for Miss Pringle! Years had gone by and not once had he asked a burning question of Harley Welch, much less Helene. Better still, he had never kept tabs on Harley's coming and going practically at his doorstep. He had restrained himself, respecting the privacy of others.

But he couldn't take it anymore. Unlike Father Brad, whose affinity for meddling was middling, he was accustomed to sticking his nose into other people's affairs. As his bishop once said, *Meddling comes with the territory.* It was time to make hay while the sun shines.

'I'm sure Miss Pringle appreciates your cooking.'

'She says she does, yessir.'

'You and Miss Pringle must have some interesting conversations.' It was a fishing line with a hook. He cast it out there.

'Yessir, we do.'

The hook dipped, noiseless, into the creek of the truck cab. Sank. Long silence.

No bait! That was the problem.

'I know Miss Pringle lapses into a good bit of French when she speaks. Learned anything yet?'

'Parley voo frahnsay?'

'Oui, s'il vous plaît.'

They had a laugh.

He could see by the dash light that Harley was not wearing his dentures. And on a visit to Miss Pringle!

'I guess you talk about what's going on in the world. We're in a mess, for sure.'

'Nossir, we don't talk about what's goin' on in th' world. Because we can't do nothin' about it.'

This was wringing blood from the proverbial turnip. What *do* you talk about? he wanted to say. That was the burning question! His wife would give him a gold star if he could find out. But the way things were progressing, he may as well pack it in and go home.

'Miss Pringle, she does most of the talkin'.'

'Is that right?' He would hardly call Miss Pringle a chatterbox.

'An' a good bit of it in French. I like it when she talks French.'

'You do?'

'Ain't able to make heads n'r tails of it, but I like t' hear it.'

'I'm sure she's interested in what you have to say.'

'She likes to hear about my liquor-runnin' days, how I growed up poor in Kentucky, about th' time I wore one shoe to school. Th' teacher said, Harley, you've lost a shoe! I said, no ma'am, I found one.'

Two guys in a truck, laughing.

'Such as that. She calls it *th' old ways of America.*'

'So she likes American history?'

'She showed me 'er citizenship papers. She's proud to be American.'

In the gleam of the porch light, he saw the professor's Audi parked in the backyard. 'I hear her new tenant is French. Or maybe Italian?'

'I don't know nothin' about her new tenant an' don't aim to ask.'

And here came car lights bouncing into the driveway—Miss Pringle in the ancient vehicle in which he once rode with her, sans brake pads, down the mountain.

'Lord help, now I'm blocked in!' said Harley. 'She'll want me t' come in an' set awhile.'

Harley dug into his shirt pocket, whipped out his dentures, popped them in; ran his fingers through his hair and, serious as stone, inquired of his seatmate: 'How'm I lookin'?'

Nine-fifteen. He banked the fire, drank a glass of water.

Historically, it was the most information ever quarried from the Harley Welch/Helene Pringle mines. He was a hero with his wife.

He checked his email.

From: snickersbar37@aol.com
To: whitefieldtim@gmail.com
Today at 1:08 p.m.

> Dear Father,
>
> I am thrilled you would ask!
> Unusual requests are my specialty!
> I promise to cross every i and dot every t.
>
> Tell me more!
> Emma

On October 27 at 7:15 a.m., Tim Kavanagh wrote:

From: whitefieldtim@gmail.com
To: Emma Newland <snickersbar37@aol.com

> Emma,
>
> Are your services still for hire?
> I have an unusual request.
>
> Fr Tim

14

L ace sat at the table with Lily and Jack; Dooley paged through one of the vet books he kept at the house.

'You an' Dooley an' Jack an' Sammy an' Pooh an' Jessie, that's six,' said Lily, making notes. 'An' Willie an' Harley an' Cynthia an' Father Tim an' Doc Harper an' Miss Olivia an' Puny an' her bunch—that's six at one whack—an' Tommy an' Beth and Father Brad an' Mary Ellen an' Doc Owen an' Miz Owen an' Rebecca Jane, that's twenty-five, an' Blake an' Amanda, that's twenty-seven. With these numbers, most people would go potluck in a heartbeat, but you don't want nothin' to do with that. Any time you're tempted, think back to your weddin' dinner.'

They had a laugh.

'But you've got a while to figure it out,' said Lily. 'It's not till December.'

'I like to get it fixed in my mind.'

'Who did we leave out?'

'We need to count Dooley's mom and stepdad,' said Lace. 'That's twenty-nine. And we need to count you, too, Lily, and Violet if she comes. You have to sit down with us, it's Name Day!'

'I don't set down.'

'You have to this time. So what can we cook that will feed that many?'

'You know I like to cook for crowds, so not to worry. Chicken potpie, you'd need three. Lasagna, oven kabobs, shrimp an' grits. Or I could do my apricot-glazed turkey with roasted onion an' shallot gravy.'

'You're showing off.'

'I have to keep up, honey, it's dog eat dog in th' caterin' world. Plus you'll definitely want my breakfast casserole for people sleepin' over.'

'I vote for cherry pie,' said Dooley, thumbing through the index.

'Beth will have the junk room finished in time. We'll put in two cots and start calling it the guest room.' Goose bumps along her legs; she was excited.

'An' you've got those two sleepin' bags,' said Lily. 'You could poke some poor soul down in them.'

'Mom, I need more money to buy my helmet.' Jack showed her his piggy bank. 'Look at th' counter; it's not a three an' a oh.'

'You're eight dollars away from your helmet. You still have six weeks before you get your bike, okay? So there's plenty of time to find the rest of the money.'

'But there's no more in th' driveway. I *searched*.'

'You're using your new big word. Very good! Remember the plumbers gave you two dollars—in your pajama drawer. That means you're only six dollars away from a helmet.'

'I could call Granpa Tim. He would give me six dollars—it could be a five an' a one an' you could put it in change.'

'He would love to hear from you. Can you dial?'

'No, I can't dial! I jus' learned Dad's surprise! I can't do everything, I'm a little kid!' He heaved a sigh and dropped his forehead onto the table.

She and Lily exchanged a look.

Dooley was half listening. When he had the nerve to talk to Lace again about adopting—maybe the first of the year—he would suggest a girl. A little sister. Yes. Definitely.

OCTOBER~ *don't know the date, maybe 30th?*

I never get to write here anymore. Stealing this time just for me. Beth taking an active role in Jack's teaching . . . He used his new big word, search, in the past tense! He is quick to learn and loves to learn. He occasionally wets the bed and is terribly regretful and apologetic. I hide the pad under the sheet because he is sensitive about it. I read that it is okay if they sometimes wet the bed at four years~ it isn't the end of the world!

It's hard to teach him good grammar with Willie and Harley as models, but I love Willie and Harley just as they are.

I am trying to keep a record here because he will grow up so fast. Dooley did an iPad video the other night and I have tons of photos on my phone.

J loves to be read to and loves to play like he can read. He goes into long narratives inspired by a book and does it at the top of his lungs~ he just devours books. At bathtime he washes his feet over and over. I don't know why. I kiss them good night when I tuck him in after his story. I love his feet and his toes~ everything about him.

Sometimes I think it would be wonderful to give him a brother or sister, but I don't think Dooley is ready. There are so many hoops to jump through I don't know how we could make it happen any time soon. And maybe I don't really want to share my love~ I'd rather give it all to Jack, who had no love for four whole years of his life.

When I talked with the social worker, I asked again how he could be so bright and loving and funny to have come from such a background. She said, 'It happens more often than you would think.'

Beth and I are doing a crazy thing~ because we need to get our junk out of the junk room and make it a guest room and because it is cold weather, we're going to have the yard sale in the living room! We will start with a preview sale for our neighbors and put a sign at the co-op for what's left and Beth will handle that on a Saturday. If we make any money we will buy a sofa. Yay! And maybe a chair!

Thank you Lord for Beth!!!

. . .

M om, when comes Christmas?'
          'Christmas comes two weeks after Name Day. It's when we
celebrate the birth of our Lord Jesus.'

'With th' cows an' sheep?'

'Yes, lying next to the manger, in a kind of barn.'

'What's a manger?'

'It's a trough that animals ate from back then. It was their dinner
plate. There's an old manger in our barn; we'll go look soon.'

There were times she loved his chatter as she worked, and times
when it made her crazy.

Today the sound of his voice helped ease her mind. She was mixing
acrylics to capture the sun-baked, unpainted timbers of their barn. She
preferred oils, but acrylics dried faster—too fast, really, for her work habits,
but when the final moment came to roll up the canvas and ship it across
the country, the acrylics would be dry and ready to travel. Not so with oils.

'Will there be presents?'

'You'll get presents on Name Day. At Christmas, there won't be so
many presents.'

'Could I tell my presents now?'

'What do you mean?'

'The presents to get from Santa, I could tell you?'

'Well, sure, but there's no way to know what you'll actually get.
Where Santa is involved, that's always a big secret.'

'I could get a pony because I would already have a bike.'

She smiled. No comment.

'I could get a police car with pedals, with a siren like made Dad stop
in th' rain after th' baby angel's house.'

No comment.

'Or! Or!' He tugged on her shirt. 'This would be my favorite thing in
th' whole wide world.'

Her son was a charmer. Totally.

'Come down an' listen, Mom, please!'

She stooped; he whispered. 'Forty books!'

'Forty books!' she said. She liked the idea of forty books, but it was way too expensive.

She looked down into his brown eyes. He tugged again, for emphasis. 'Don't please say it so people could hear or it might not come true.'

D oc and Marge Owen had taken Dooley in every summer for years, and Father Tim used to come out all the time when he was a bachelor. Meadowgate had a history of hospitality.

So she and Dooley had offered to have Thanksgiving at Meadowgate, but Cynthia wanted to do it at their place. 'You have enough to do,' Cynthia said.

She was relieved. The mural somehow filled up the farmhouse; there was no getting away from it or from the reality of the deadline. Though her work was upstairs and out of sight, it was almost never out of her head. She was happy to go to somebody else's house.

She was giving thanks, for sure, that her dad would be home for Thanksgiving and then forever. Cynthia had invited her mom and dad and Mary Ellen and Father Brad and Beth and the Owens. Father Tim was baking a ham, no surprise, and Cynthia would make yeast rolls and buy an OMC.

It wasn't a potluck in the true sense, but some insisted on pitching in. Mary Ellen, who would be staying with Father Tim and Cynthia, was doing smashed potatoes with garlic and cheese, and roasted Brussels sprouts, which Dooley totally would not eat. Father Brad was bringing cranberry relish made by one of his daughters, and four bottles of Argentinean wine. Her mom was bringing two cherry pies, and Beth, who was not 'versatile in the kitchen,' was contributing a Valley-made pumpkin pie from the Local. As for yours truly, she was making the proverbial

green bean casserole in a completely updated version. 'How updated?'
said Dooley, who was dubious about 'messing with a classic.'

She loved getting ready for the holidays. But Thanksgiving, Finish-
the-Mural-and-Ship-It Day, Name Day, and Christmas Day all in a row?

R ebecca Jane had come over to say hello and walk home with Doc
 Owen. She plopped herself down in the surgery where Dooley was
prepping the table for tomorrow.

When he was a kid coming out to Meadowgate every summer, Rebecca Jane had followed him around like a pup. Word was, she had a
crush on Uncle Dools. He kind of liked that, as nobody had ever had
a crush on him before.

As she got older, he had a chance to watch her help around the
clinic. She took it seriously, doing whatever she was asked, plus she
could watch her dad in surgery and not flinch. The kid was as at home
in a vet clinic as anybody he'd ever seen.

But she didn't come around much these days. A tough sophomore
year, plus her mom was working at the college and Rebecca Jane had
responsibilities at home.

'So, how did the Danny Hershell scheme play out?'

'It took four dimes, three quarters, five nickels, a half dollar, and
fifteen pennies. I robbed my savings drawer an' totally hated lettin' th'
half dollar go, but it was worth it because Danny loves findin' money.
So I swept th' concrete floor in that old building where he keeps his
arrowheads an' scattered th' money around and glued all down. Th' glue
was industrial. I mean, he cannot get up a single penny without a jackhammer! Because he would never ruin th' floor, it will torment him
forever.'

'Ah, Beck,' he said. 'I want to stay on your good side.'

'I'm gettin' even, I just am. It will be worth th' investment of two dollars and five cents.'

'What else is goin' on?'

'I finish my homework and check Facebook and Instagram and do stuff around th' house till Mom gets home from college, and then what else is there to *do*?'

'How are your grades?'

'You know I always make straight As. An' I have not been to the principal's office one time this whole entire year.'

'It's only October,' he said. 'You need a job.'

'What kind of job?'

'Fill in for us at the clinic next summer. You grew up helping your dad—turn some of that experience my way. You know how to answer the phone and take care of clients; Amanda can walk you through what else you'll need to do. I'll talk to your mom and dad, I'm sure it'll be fine. Deal?'

She was beaming. 'Uncle Dools! I thought you'd never ask!'

I didn't know about your grandmother,' said Beth, 'until Lace told me. I'm so sorry. I wish I'd known.'

Tommy was strapping his guitar around his neck. 'When we texted, you said you were going through a tough time at work. I didn't want to bother you.'

'It wouldn't have bothered me.'

'You didn't talk about what was going on with you. I didn't want to cross any lines and spill my stuff.'

'I hardly ever talk about what's going on with me. I guess I can be pretty closed about my feelings.'

'Your feelings aren't closed when you sing.'

'Yes.' She caught her breath. 'That's true. That's when I feel . . . that anything is possible.'

'Do you think it would be possible to . . . '

To give you a hug right now? She had never really wanted to comfort

Freddie, she felt he had all the comfort he needed from his mother and eight sisters. But Tommy . . .

'. . . possible to maybe listen to a couple of my songs?'

'Yes!' she said. 'I'd like that a lot.'

L ace could hear them singing in the living room, then cracking up and singing again.

So, okay, the living room was shabby, but it had the best acoustics in the house. She was starting to sort of like it, if only a little. Music—and laughter, too—were making it a space she enjoyed passing through to answer the door or run to the mailbox.

You're the CEO of my true affections
You're my heart's top-dollar VP
But listen to me, honey,
I'm tellin' you good
You're not the boss of me . . .

In the eight years she'd been best friends with Beth, she had never seen her so happy. Transitioning from Manhattan to a farm in North Carolina could be a serious adjustment for most people, but Beth seemed to belong here. She had seamlessly picked up the lessons with Jack and cleaned out the garden with Willie and started on the junk room. Best of all, with the junk-room project, she seemed to know what could go and what truly had to stay.

Now Tommy doing the vocals.

What can I say
That hasn't been said
About livin' alone
With hungry thoughts in my head
Dreamin' of you walkin'

In through my door
A stranger I'd never seen before
Yes, you were the one in my dreams, all right
Now here you are in my song tonight.

What did I do to deserve you?
I'd never been the man I could be
Till you walked into my life . . . [Word garbled, Tommy and Beth laughing]
An' started dreamin' with me . . .

She went to the living room and stood in the doorway, listening. Beth's back was to her, but she could see Tommy and the way he raised one eyebrow as he sang, as if he had questions that weren't yet answered and maybe never would be.

H e was beat as he came in from a long day and checking his cattle. Somebody else's cow had given him a kick in the groin this morning; he was hobbling like an old guy. And two dog poisonings in the neighborhood in four days. He hated this, he especially hated this.

Charley licked his hand; he gave her a head scratch.

'Jack has a wonderful surprise for you.' Lace handed him his favorite all-season libation—sweet tea with lemon.

'I need a surprise,' he said.

'You'll like it to th' *moon*, Dad! It will be a big huge jelly-belly *monster* surprise!'

'Come here, buddy.' He sat in his chair by the fire and opened his arms. He wanted to hold his boy and tease him and make him laugh, he wanted the chunk of him close; the little guy would be in college before they knew it.

'To do th' su'prise, I have to see your watch, okay?'

'Okay.' He took off the watch Lace gave him when he cycled from UGA to State.

Jack studied the watch face for a long moment, then threw back his head and shouted. '*Seventeen minutes till seven!*'

'What? No way do you know how to tell time. But it's seventeen minutes till seven on th' dot. How did you do that?'

Jack looked again at the watch, took his time, moving his lips.

'*Sixteen minutes till seven!*' he yelled.

'We've been working hard on this the last few days,' said Lace. 'He's amazingly fast, and great at keeping a secret.'

'See, Dad. Th' little hand's at th' seven an' th' big hand's at th' nine. *Fifteen minutes til seven!*'

'Good job!' He pulled Jack close. 'Proud of you. This is big. Why don't I take you fishin' Saturday? Deal?'

'I'll catch a whole bejoobie of fishes. Can Charley go?'

'Charley can go.'

'What if it's a snake out there?'

'There will always be a snake out there. Wear your boots and keep an eye on Charley.'

So here was something his dad and Cynthia or Doc and Olivia could give Jack for his Name Day; they'd all been asking. A watch! He was oddly moved.

'You know what?' said Dooley.

'What?' said Jack.

'I love you big.'

'I love you bigger, bigger, *booger, booger!*' More laughing. General hilarity.

'You're the best,' Dooley said to Lace. He needed her, the feel of her skin, a Tylenol, something. She came and stooped to him and kissed him. 'Supper in ten minutes.'

What did I do to deserve you?
I'd never been the man I could be . . .

'Tommy's having supper with us,' she said. She liked it that her husband had a best friend, too.

Jack's attention had turned to the kitchen clock. *Fourteen minutes till seven! I'm about starvin'!*

F loyd, Virgina,' said Tommy, forking a slice of meatloaf. 'Took th' whole band, a two-hour gig. They know how to have a good time in Floyd.' He looked at Beth. 'Do you like to dance?'

'Well, not the tango or anything.'

'Flatfoot,' said Tommy. 'And a little swing. That's as exotic as it gets in Floyd. We could all go up in th' van.'

'Or we could just go to the Crossroads,' said Dooley. 'It was great the other night. Thanks for sending your guys down.'

'How much money for th' shelter?'

'Two hundred and thirty bucks.'

'Dooley just delivered a baby,' Lace told Tommy. 'An emergency.'

'Dad made a angel come out!' said Jack.

'Man. Were you scared?'

'Shakin',' said Dooley, and passed the mashed potatoes.

Jack wrinkled his brow, puzzled. 'But I don't know where it come out from. Where did it come out from, Dad?'

Tommy looked at Dooley. Dooley looked at Lace.

'Did it jist . . .' Jack lifted his palms, struggled to find a word. '. . . *appear?*'

Lace stood up. 'There's no fancy dessert tonight, but we have ice cream!'

'Manilla!' said Jack, who liked whatever his dad liked.

'I could sure use some cherry pie,' said Dooley.

Tommy laughed. 'Dude, you've been fixated on cherry pie since I first met you.'

Charley barking at the front door. 'Somebody's knockin'!' Jack slid off the bench and was down the hall. Voices, farm dogs going berserk.

Teddy shot into the kitchen, followed by Jack, who was followed by Lucy.

'Sorry to come in on you so late,' said Lucy. 'I was at Mama's house all day, bakin'. Brought your cherry pie, Doc, I aim to keep 'im!'

All dogs barking; everyone stood to greet Lucy.

'Dooley casually mentions cherry pie,' said Tommy, 'and here comes cherry pie. Just like that! Awesome.'

'It's an old trick,' he said.

Dooley gave Lucy a kiss on the cheek.

B eth was heading downstairs.
      'So?' she asked Beth.

'So what?'

'You know what.'

'Just friends, Laceyface. *Friends.*'

'What is he doing for Thanksgiving?'

'On the road. Concerts in Asheville and Memphis.'

'He likes you a lot.'

'Do you really think so?'

'I know so. Tommy can't hide his feelings; they're out there all over the place. And you sound great together. Truly.'

'It's too good. It's too wonderful. I'm scared of wonderful.'

'Get over it,' said Lace. 'I was scared of it, too.'

Beth started to say something, but changed her mind. 'Sweet dreams,' she said, flying down the stairs.

D ooley was sitting on the side of the bed in an old T-shirt, thought-
      ful.

'That shirt is a hundred years old,' she said, toweling her hair.

'Don't even think about throwin' it out.'

'I won't. Lily can use it for rags.'

He gave her a look and she laughed.

'I'm seeing that Jack is a pretty acquisitive little guy,' he said. 'Not sure that's good for him.'

'I think it comes from watching TV for four years; that was his reality. A lot of it was what his grandmother watched, which wouldn't exactly set high standards. And besides, he's a little boy who's excited about everything. I think we need to just listen and don't say much. Just don't buy into it.'

'Did I tell you he wants forty books for Christmas? He has no idea what that number means and we can't afford it, but honestly, I could sign off on that.'

'Forty books.' Dooley shook his head, grinned.

'It's a secret, so don't tell him I told you. He thinks if something is kept secret, it comes true.'

'How's your work?'

'Run up and see it tomorrow before dinner. Tomorrow is Choo-Choo's day, I'll be painting him into the lower right-hand corner. Big!'

'You're happy with what's going on.'

'I love it. I'm not scared to death anymore. It is what it is; I'm giving it my best. That's all I can do.'

She wrapped her head with the damp towel, making a turban, and sat beside him.

'Let me ask you something.' He looked at his bare feet for a time, then looked at her. 'What did I do to deserve you?'

She rubbed salve on the wicked bruise. Black, blue, yellow. A very colorful mark for a simple country cow.

Though it had been a day of surprises, she had saved the best for last.

'There's one more surprise, Doc. It's so good, you will totally fall out. Guess what?'

'No guessing.' An inch or two to the left and that heifer would have turned him into a soprano.

She enjoyed a suspenseful pause. 'Julie and Kenny are being transferred. She called this afternoon.'

'Where? Ow. Easy.'

'To North Carolina.'

'You're kidding!'

'And soon. The end of November. Before Name Day. Can you believe it?'

This was beyond great. 'Let me guess,' he said. 'Winston-Salem. That
would be good. Just down the mountain.'

'Not even close. Where do people need bridges? Clue: like, near
water.'

'The Outer Banks?'

'You wish. Keep going.'

'Tell me.'

'Wilmington. They're so excited.'

'Wilmington!' Five, maybe six hours' drive time. Awesome. Kenny
was coming home; their family was coming together. Little drops
of water, little grains of sand, his dad used to say. And the cousins. Jack
would have onboard cousins.

'She said they'll all come for Name Day. Her due date is December
thirtieth, the doctor says it's okay to travel that weekend.'

'Jack will be over th' moon.'

'There.' She put the cap on the salve. 'Take an aspirin and call me in
the morning.'

'Guess how I'm goin' to repay you for your nursing skills.'

'Tell me.'

'I'm goin' to take you fishin' Saturday. Jack and I'll pack lunch and I'll
bait th' hooks. Be there or be square.'

Kenny and Julie and Etta and Ethan. Coming home. The last time
he'd been this happy was when Jack jumped down from the truck and
everybody came to their wedding. He was drowsy as she recounted heads
for their big day.

'. . . Julie and Kenny and Etta and Ethan and Sammy and Pooh and

Jessie . . . and Beth and Tommy and Father Brad and Mary Ellen and your parents and my parents and Pauline and Buck. Oh, and Lil who's coming with a sister. Violet, I think . . . '

A grill. He needed to buy a grill. Sammy was good on the grill, his dad could wrangle a grill . . .

'With us, that's nineteen!' she said, brushing her hair. 'Your dad is doing a ham and Lil thinks sixteen pounds for the turkey, which maybe is leftovers for sandwiches.'

She put the brush in the drawer. 'Wait a minute. I forgot. The band! That makes twenty-three. Oh, and Willie and Harley, twenty-five. And Doc and Marge and Rebecca Jane, twenty-eight. Can you believe it? I guess there won't be leftovers. Who have I left out?'

But Dooley was sleeping.

When she came to bed, she heard his snore. It was very low-key; she'd never heard it before. She loved everything about her husband, even this—it was new, and somehow . . . sort of fun.

She got in bed and pulled the blanket over his bare shoulders and did their two-spoons-in-a-drawer and gave thanks and was soon asleep.

15

He walked to the Local at first light.

Like him, Wilson was an early riser, and he managed to catch his doctor at seven A.M. While he knew bacterial pneumonia was dead serious, Wilson hammered that truth in somewhat colorful terms: 'It's like this, Tim. A strong immune system delivers heavy artillery to decimate pneumonia. No immune system and you've got an underfed guerrilla corps hiding in the woods with no ammo.'

Charlotte was employing antibiotics, oxygen, IV fluids, chest physiotherapy, and the alarming amenities of ICU. But there was no guarantee.

He flipped on the light switch in the back, checked yesterday's receipts without concentration. For Avis to battle rapid heart rate, searing chest pain, depression, racking chills, and lungs filling with fluid, something more was needed.

Something radical.

He unrolled and cut a large portion of brown butcher paper, inscribed a message in all caps, took the poster to the front of the store, and taped it on the window facing Main.

. . .

A s he dumped change into the cash drawer, he glanced up to see
several people waiting for the store to open.

He'd never noticed anyone waiting for a Mitford store to open. He
squinted at the small gathering, but nobody looked familiar.

It was truly amazing what a little Italian sausage could do!

He opened the door to a blast of frigid air.

'Good morning! Good morning! Come in and get warm!'

'Are you Rev'rend Kavanagh?'

'I am, come in!'

'I'd like you to meet Billy and Johnsie Pope, Pedro and María Sanchez, an' me, Hank Griffin. We're all from th' Valley.'

A big fellow—big!—with a beard. Here was a mountain man in the
classic sense, with a hand the size of a Valley ham. And here were a
wizened elderly woman and her husband, and a younger couple in their
forties, all seemingly thrilled to be standing on the sidewalk in freezing
weather.

'Step right in, let's get this door closed.'

He shut the door as they gathered at the checkout counter.

Hank cleared his throat. He was nervous as a cat and wanted to get
this speech done with. 'Avis Packard is a good friend to us and we feel
like we owe him somethin'. But not money. Nossir. More like somethin'
of ourselves.'

Nods all around.

'We'd like to help out durin' this hard time. No pay, no pay at all, just
for a little while, if you'll have us. Whatever y'all need done up here,
we'll be glad to do it. We're not too proud to sweep, haul trash, whatever
it takes.'

The Popes and Sanchezes nodded in agreement. Hank had done due
diligence as spokesman and was visibly relieved.

'Thank you, Hank. Thank all of you. My goodness, this is a wonderful surprise! I'll have to think about it, of course. But take off your coats and make yourselves at home.'

They looked around the store with a kind of wonder.

'Th' Popes have never been up to Mitford,' said Hank.

'Never been to Mitford?' He thought everybody had been to Mitford.

'Not a single time,' said Johnsie Pope. 'It's like another world, ain't it, Billy?'

Billy removed his hat. 'We always go out th' Morganton way.'

Johnsie's eyes appeared to have cataracts, but she was hungry to see. 'Is it right here where our gourds is sellin'?'

'This is the place!' he said. 'I'll be putting a sign in the window to-morrow.'

'We seen your sign in th' winder about Avis. We do that ever' night, don't we, Billy?'

'We do. Reg'lar as clockwork.'

María Sanchez raised her hand. 'We, too.'

'My wife, my mother, we come with green card twenty-four years ago,' said Pedro. 'Mr. Avis give us a pig, we breed our pig and sell six first year. I work on tree farm, María clean for my boss family. With sale of pigs we buy blueberry bushes, plant on land we rent. Mr. Avis buy all we raise, very big, sweet blueberries. Nineteen years we sell Mr. Avis blue-berries for to eat in Mitford. With blueberry money, we buy chickens an' sell eggs.'

'An' goats,' said María.

'An' goats,' said Pedro, 'for cheese. Last year, we buy th' land of our blueberries an' build bigger house.'

'For gran'children when they visit,' said María, 'Jésus, Miguel, Chris-tina, José, an' Juan.'

Pedro and María beaming.

'Well done! I'm sure I've enjoyed your cheese and blueberries many times.'

'We have a blessed life,' said Pedro. 'Whatever you an' Mr. Avis need, we come every Saturday for November.'

He was verging on speechless. 'He'll be grateful, Pedro. Very grateful. Let's get some coffee going. Right this way!'

In the corner of the break room, to the Popes' uncommon delight, was the small sea of warty gourds, piled into a couple of wheelbarrows that would be stationed tomorrow at the front door.

Everyone sat, shy and overcome, using the room's full supply of plastic chairs; the coffeemaker issued a steady aroma of Antiguan beans.

'Me an' Johnsie, we can come up with Hank most anytime,' said Billy Pope.

'I cook an' clean,' said Johnsie. 'Billy rakes an' mows.'

'Very useful pursuits!' he said, opening a bag of donuts.

'Avis started us out with chickens 'way back,' said Billy. 'He give us two Rhode Island Reds and two Dominickers to start our flock.'

'It's our free-range eggs y'all been eatin' up here in Mitford.' Johnsie blinked, suddenly awed by this momentous truth. 'I only raise gourds on th' side.'

'Every little bit counts,' he said, pouring coffee.

'I had a home improvement business,' said Hank, 'but like everything else, it's took a good many knocks over th' years. I said, Avis, all we've got is this little half-acre, what could we do with it to help us along? So Avis says plant dwarf trees that give a full-size apple. You'll get more trees on less land an' a sweet, big apple in th' bargain! That was th' start of it. He's bought our apples for sixteen years, it sure helps us through th' hard places. I'm retired now, I cleaned gutters, painted houses, met a lot of people. But it's good to have a little time on my hands. Time is a wonderful thing to have on your hands, right, Rev'rend?'

He'd always been conflicted about that, but what could he say?

'Have a donut!'

Otis and Lisa were running late because of roadwork through the Gap. They arrived as the Valley contingent pulled away from the curb in Hank's van.

'We just hired five people!' He was dazed, dazzled, dumbfounded.

Otis blanched. 'Nossir, we can't do that. Oh, Lord, no!'

'Free, Otis! They want to work free, as a favor to Avis. Anything we need done. As a *tribute*.'

'Wow,' said Lisa. 'Free! Omigosh, th' produce bins is needin' a good cleanout an' all that stuff out back, old crates an' pallets an' all, need to be hauled to th' dump . . .'

Otis brightened. 'An' home delivery. We could go back to offerin' home delivery.' Otis was fond of home delivery, it made people smile. Usually.

As he worked on tomorrow's poster, he whistled a bit of Mozart's *Magic Flute*. The Valley had just proved that Mitford wasn't the only place taking care of its own.

Abe from Village Shoes was coming in as Fancy Skinner was leaving.

'Fancy Skinner!' Abe rolled his eyes. 'I was going to give her a mean look, but she already had one.

'She was in my place yesterday lookin' for dress shoes. Toe in, toe out, high heel, no heel, Velcro, no Velcro. After fifteen try-ons, no deal. Said everything was too expensive. Look, I said, I know where you can get a great pair of shoes for two bucks.'

'Really!' said Lisa. 'Where at?'

'Th' Wesley bowlin' alley!'

Otis didn't care for Ms. Skinner, but he didn't join in such talk. He would never speak disrespectfully of someone who just spent $43.79, cash money, at the Local.

'So, Abe,' said Father Tim, 'you're looking spiff.' The owner of Main Street's shoe store was a golf-shirt-and-khakis kind of guy. This was dark pants with a jacket.

'Meeting of th' Merchants Association this afternoon. I was goin' to wear my camouflage shirt, but couldn't find it.'

He gave Abe a good laugh, which was what his old buddy usually came in for.

'Any tomatoes?' said Abe.

'Not that I can recommend,' said Father Tim. 'Tomatoes in October, no; in August, yes.'

'Which brings to mind a question. If tomatoes are technically a fruit, is ketchup a smoothie?'

Lisa giggled.

'Abe, Abe,' he said. Every town needed an Abe.

G race liked birthdays.
In January, when she was seven, she would spend her birthday with her dad at Hope House and with the old people who she liked very much. She would take the Jack Russells, too, even though they were retired.

She did not have grandparents of her own because on her dad's side a grandmother and two grandfathers died at the same time in a huge car wreck and the other grandmother died of being old. On her mom's side her grandmother died before her mom got the bookstore. There were lots of dead people in her family. But she got to have a grand-mother, anyway.

She had picked Miss Louella at Hope House, who was maybe ninety-four or six. She liked to use the remote on Miss Louella's chair when Miss Louella went on her walker to the bathroom. She liked to lean back in the big blue recliner and pretend to be very, very old. Sometimes the nurse would take her temperature and listen to her heart, *mush, mush, mush.*

She visited twice a month and took peanut butter cookies that were soft and easy to chew that she made herself. Sometimes she and Miss Louella watched cartoons, but her favorite was when Miss Louella told stories of being pulled around Mitford in a red wagon—by a little white girl who grew up and built Hope House.

'It would make a good book!' she said to Miss Louella.

Miss Louella gave her a pat on the head and looked straight in her eyes. 'Maybe you write it down when you grow up. Yes, you be th' one to write my story down.'

A s she drove by the Local, Vanita Bentley was reminded that her husband, Donny, didn't like foreign food but was crazy about Father Tim's Italian sausage. And tomorrow it would be four-ninety-nine a pound! While it was still four dollars, she needed to buy two more pounds and stick 'em in the freezer.

She glanced at the display window to see what else was goin' on.

PRAY FOR AVIS

She wondered if people should come out so openly about prayer. On a poster in the window, for Pete's sake. Wasn't prayer a personal thing? And wasn't there somethin' about the separation of church and state or whatever?

She would pick up the sausage on her way home and order her Thanksgivin' turkey while she was at it. Had she prayed for Avis? Well, no, she hadn't even thought about it, and their preacher hadn't mentioned it either, but maybe—if it was okay to pray in the car—she would do it.

M ule and J.C. were dropping by for a quick bite in the break room. He bought a loaf of seven-grain bread, sliced turkey, sliced provolone, sliced ham, a jar of mayo, a jar of mustard, a jar of pickles, and two Snickers bars. He was making sandwiches when Mule and J.C. blew in.

'Freezin' out there,' said J.C. 'Adele's in Wisconsin for a couple of days, so I'm batchin'—not to mention starvin'.'

Mule pointed to a large pile in the corner. 'What's that?'

'Warty gourds,' said Father Tim. 'On special tomorrow.'

'Good luck,' said Mule, peeling off a faux sheepskin hoodie from a yard sale.

'Mustard or mayo?'

'Both,' said J.C.

'Mustard!' said Mule. 'No, wait. I don't like mustard. Just mayo. Any lettuce?'

'No lettuce.'

'How 'bout tomato?'

'No tomato.'

'Chips?'

'Outside on the rack. Barbecue, sour cream, vinegar and salt. A buck twenty-nine.'

Mule sat down.

'There is such a thing as the free lunch, but this is not completely it.' He put a sandwich and pickle on paper plates and handed them off.

J.C. glanced at the unplugged coffeemaker. 'Any coffee?'

'No coffee. This is not a fully catered event.'

'Dr Pepper?' said Mule. 'Cheerwine?'

'In the box. Ninety-nine cents.'

'Okay, water,' said Mule.

A good bit of chewing sounds. None of the communal rabble and roar of the Feel Good.

'You're mighty quiet, J.C. What's going on?'

J.C. threw up his hands, wagged his head, sighed deeply.

'What did he say?' said Mule.

'Something maybe like *all hope is lost*.'

'That's it,' said J.C. 'All hope is lost, I give up.'

Mule leaned in. 'We're here to help.'

'I've got a problem. Like, at home. This is private, okay? Very personal stuff.'

'Okay,' said Mule. 'Count on us.'

J.C. wiped his forehead with the lunch napkin. 'It's like . . . party's over, you know what I mean?'

'Can't help you there,' said Mule. 'I have th' same problem.'

'No, I mean she comes home, fixes supper, watches the *Wheel*, maybe *Jeopardy*, then boom, out like a light. I'm chopped liver.'

As for himself, he had not done marriage counseling in a very long time. He'd forgotten everything but the basics. Or maybe the basics weren't basic anymore, he didn't know.

He cleared his throat. 'Some hide the occasional note.' This came straight out of the seminars. 'Women love a note, and heck, men, too, love a . . . ah, love note.' He was babbling; this was awkward.

Silence.

'You know, in a drawer she uses often, the pocket of a favorite jacket. That sort of thing.' He regretted that this sounded autobiographical. He looked at his tablemates. Was this not headed in the right direction?

He soldiered on. 'Actually, under her pillow can be a very good place. In the hidden note department, that's your ace right there.'

'Are we talkin' about th' same thing?' said Mule.

J.C. gave his forehead a swipe with the napkin. 'She says I don't pay her any attention, I'm not romantic, I don't know she's alive, yada yada.'

'Is that true?'

'I'm no Casanova, but I do my part. If she cooks, I clean up th' kitchen, I take out the trash, I keep her feet warm at night.'

'How do you do that?' said Mule.

J.C. gave Mule a look. 'I fill up a hot water bottle and put it in th' bed.'

'Where's this conversation goin'?' said Mule. 'Nowhere. What are you tryin' to tell us? Let's get down to it. Life in th' raw. We're here to help.'

'Maybe she's just exhausted,' said J.C. 'All that gear hangin' off her all day—th' badge, th' revolver, th' two-way radio, th' nightstick, th' holster, th' Taser, th' flashlight, th' medic kit, th' ammo—fifteen, sixteen pounds of stuff—in a town where nothin' happens.'

He couldn't remember the last criminal activity in Mitford. A few years ago, Tim Kavanagh and his wife had broken into Irene McGraw's house, but it wasn't really a break-in—her door had been left standin' open while Irene drove to Georgia and the Kavanaghs were just tryin' to be helpful.

And a while back, they had some goon walk out of Shoe Barn in a pair of work boots without paying. 'These Boots Were Made for Walkin'' was the genius headline in the *Muse*.

'She never even caught season six of *Downton Abbey*,' said J.C., 'because she was pullin' the Sunday-night shift.'

'Bless her heart,' said Mule.

'What about evening activity?' said Father Tim, presenting the Snickers bars, which were a hit. 'Is it all TV all the time?'

'As for evenin' activity,' said J.C., 'there's no TV in th' bedroom; it's in our livin' room, where we otherwise never live. We lie head to toe on a sofa which is really a loveseat.' He was embarrassed to talk about this. He was reminded again that a TV in the bedroom would be a luxury. Big screen. High def . . .

Mule yawned. 'If I was a shrink, I could write off this lunch.'

Father Tim looked at his watch. 'I've got root vegetables coming in before long. All I can tell you for sure, buddyroe, is that you need to do something positive.'

'Right,' said Mule. 'Like, immediately would be good.' What he was going to do to liven up his own marital circumstance was still a mystery. No way was he writing Fancy Skinner a love note. He peeled back the Snickers wrapper. Fancy had him off sugar, but say la vee.

'Bottom line,' said Father Tim, 'remind her that you love her. Tell her why. We all need that. I vote for the note.'

J.C. grunted. It would be a pain in the rear for him to write a note, much less a love note.

'But you got to remember this,' said Mule.

'What?'

'I don't know much but I do know this, and this is key.' Mule leaned in, gave J.C. a look. 'Make it mushy.'

Mushy.
      He had a couple of days to do this before Adele came home, but better to do it now and get it over with.

He sat at his kitchen table and considered the free advice.

He'd written only one mushy note in his life and where did it get him? To the principal's office, where he was chewed out to the max for passing a friendly note to Sylvia Wooten, who wasn't even that good-looking.

There was an idea right there. He picked up the pen and wrote.

Hey Good Looking,

*   What you got cooking? How's about cooking something up with me?*

*   Tonight, pork chops and season 6 on the big screen. What a combo! Be there or be square.*

Okay. He was great with salutations, but not so cool with valedictions. Yours truly, sincerely yours, ever thine, whatever, it was a minefield. He could possibly do *love always*, which felt binding, but as they were married and that was pretty much in the vows, he'd already said that. He closed his eyes and wrote, *Your Teddy Bear.*

He drove to Walmart in Wesley.

Bought a 43-inch flat-screen HD TV, a 12-pack of Orville Redenbacher's popcorn, DVDs of season six, fifty percent off, and a 24-pack of socks, one size fits all. His wife liked socks. Then he swung by the Local and bought two pork chops the size of his head.

Came home and prepped their bedroom wall facing the bed—took down a picture of his home place in West Virginia, their wedding picture at the altar in Lord's Chapel, and a photo of him with his Schwinn when he was ten years old and delivering newspapers. He would recycle these to the hall.

Removed the nails. Used a dab of toothpaste to disguise the holes. Not the best idea—he would tell Vanita that her recent Hint did not totally work. He stood back and considered what comes next.

He had installed a couple of TVs in this lifetime, he could do this. And just think. When she had the night shift and was resting in the afternoon, she could watch Dr. Phil nail some creep to the floor for stealing his current wife's car to go on a date with his ex.

Walmart had been a workout. He mopped his face with a kitchen towel. If this didn't do it for his marriage, it couldn't be done. He would install the TV tomorrow.

He put the popcorn in the pantry, shucked the wrapper off the socks, and opened her sock drawer.

He wouldn't be able to get the new socks in without taking out the old socks and reorganizing the whole drawer.

A pink slip. A warning.

From the MPD.

Name and occupation: *Captain Adele Leanne Hogan, Mitford Police Department*

Describe offense: *Running traffic light. Speeding within Mitford town limits.*

But why was it made out to her? And in her own handwriting?

He stood at the open drawer, scratching his head.

Well, well, well. He knew his wife was as honest as the day is long. She had written *herself* a warning! In a day when police were getting some really bad press, this would make a great little human interest story. But if he printed it, his wife would be in jail for first-degree manslaughter and it just wasn't worth it.

He tore the pink slip in half, went back to the kitchen table, and wrote another note.

Dear Hardened Criminal,

As punishment for your crime, I am making a citizen's arrest.
You will be confined to your room tonight with a new TV, DA's season 6, new socks, and a supper of pork chops cooked by your parole officer.

He tossed the old note and placed the destroyed pink slip beside the new note.

He had no idea how to cook pork chops; Adele was the one who cooked their favorite thing in this life every first Tuesday of the month. He would ask Father Tim, who was a cook. Tim would do a step-by-step phone walkthrough and J. C. Hogan would be a hero.

He was pretty excited. He liked planning ahead. He found his smartphone in the pantry next to the popcorn.

Tim was not in the store, Lisa said he was on the loading platform with a delivery of spaghetti squash and could not talk.

Otis didn't have a clue about cooking pork in any form. 'My family smokes it,' he said, 'But we don't cook it. We're beef people.'

Maybe they should be marinated for a couple of days, for starters. Adele had recently marinated chicken thighs in buttermilk. He opened the door of the fridge and shook the carton. About a half-pint left in the container.

He put the chops in a bowl and poured in the buttermilk. Took the tongs out of the drawer and made sure the chops were coated. Covered the bowl with Saran Wrap and stuck it in the fridge.

Adele would be home around five-fifteen Sunday evening. Supper at six. Season six at seven. A little romance at eight.

He could do this.

On October 29 at 3:17 PM, Emma Newland wrote:

From: snickersbar37@aol.com

To: Tim Kavanagh <whitefieldtim@gmail.com

>H and I not home tonite from bingo till late.

>See u in the morning at ten.

On October 29 at 7:04 AM, Tim Kavanagh wrote:

From: whitefieldtim@gmail.com

To: Emma Newland <snickersbar37@aol.com

>Can you meet me at ten in the morning? The Local.

>Or call me this evening. Hoping for good news.

On October 29 at 7:00 AM, Emma Newland wrote:

From: snickersbar37@aol.com

To: Tim Kavanagh <whitefieldtim@gmail.com

>Dear Father Tim.

>I snooped around and found out everything I could.

>Your place or mine? ha ha.

>Sherlock

He shut down the computer and turned off all lights save those on the stair. Light from the full moon flooded in.

Not that he had killed himself today, but a full-time job takes a particular toll.

'So, Truman,' he said. 'Are you coming up?'

He hoped the word would never get out that he was sleeping with a cat at the foot of his bed.

C ynthia was in the bathroom putting cream on her face.

She held up the jar. 'You should use this. Men use night cream, too, you know.'

He did not know that.

'I need a donor gift,' he said.

'Now what?'

'House paint. Maybe six gallons? I'm not good at estimating these things. Avis's house needs a facelift.'

Had he no shame to beg from his wife? Oh, he'd had shame the first time or two. But he was used to it now.

FRIDAY, OCTOBER 30

He liked the simple act of walking to work.

He'd spoken to Wilson this morning—Avis would be released to rehab tomorrow. Could be a week or more before they sent him home.

At seven, he had driven up to Ray Cunningham's, then returned the car to Cynthia and headed to the Local. The visit with Ray reminded him of something that a fellow named Ross once said.

Everybody needs something to do—he certainly had that. *Someone to love*—big check mark. *And something to look forward to.* Now he had all three.

He quickened his step in the stinging October wind.

'Oh, yes,' Ray had said, 'she's a honey. Just you wait an' see.'

. . .

YOU'LL LOVE OUR
GOURDS.
WARTS AND ALL.
4 FOR $10.00

Because of an early rush of customers, getting the poster up had been delayed. He was taping it to the window when Emma came in.

'No trail,' said Emma. 'Poof! Into thin air.'

'*Nothing?*'

'Moved to Bryson City. That's all they know.'

Blast. Bryson City. Roughly a two-and-a-half-hour drive.

'Bryson City should have a golf club, a country club, something. Call around.'

'I don't know her name.'

'You didn't get her *name?*'

'You didn't ask me to get a name. I just called the golf club in Wesley and told them I was looking for a blond gal in her forties who works in accounting and they said she moved to Bryson City.'

'Emma, Emma, we need a *name*. What did they say about Chucky?'

'They didn't know she had a dog.'

'Who would have a dog that nobody knows about?' he said, peeved. 'People have a dog, they love their dog, everybody *knows* they have a dog, end of discussion.'

'Right!' she said. He was ticked off; she liked it when he got mad, just not at her.

'Get her name from the Wesley people, please.'

'Will do.'

'I'll pay you for your time so far,' he said, taking out his wallet.

'No charge. If it's about dogs, I work free. In memory of Snickers.'

'Snickers is *dead*? Why didn't you tell me?'

'No, not dead! Just, you know, in memory of 'im while he's still livin'.'

A t lunch break, he walked over to Avis's place and checked the driveway. Hank's van was backed in next to the house, ladders off the rack. Good. Great. Terrific.

E sther Cunningham pressed what Ray called the Dump Button on her recliner remote, and was deposited on her feet at her walker.

She used the walker to navigate her way to the corner where her cane was propped. She would use her cane for this mission. The walker made her look vulnerable and bent over. She was not vulnerable, and she was not bent over.

She whipped the cane into use and went looking for Ray. This house was a whole lot bigger than it used to be. But no way were they puttin' it on the market and movin' to an old folks home. Not in this lifetime.

She had been thinking hard all morning. This would do it. At a time of year when people's hearts craved tradition, this would deliver it in spades, and remind one and all of th' *real* American values.

She wouldn't invite th' Father up for lunch, she would see him on his own turf, which, she had been shocked to learn, was the Local. A grocery clerk! She had no idea he needed the money. And there was his wife, rich as Croesus on all those little books . . .

'Ray!' she called.

He was probably in th' johnny, readin' *National Geo*. He could be in there for hours.

'*Ray!*'

'*What?*' He came out of the laundry room with a stack of folded towels.

'I have an idea.'

Just the other day, Marcie said, 'Daddy, I don't know if you can sur-vive another one of Mama's ideas. So if she gets one, have her call me, okay?' Lord knows, he hated to bother his girls, but . . .

'Call Marcie,' he said, stomping down the hall to the linen closet.

'Call her for *what?*'

'To tell her your idea!' he shouted.

I t was the Queen Mary, sailing into their humble port.

'I need to talk to you,' she said. 'Where's a private place?'

The break room wasn't up to a royal visit, but so be it. "Right this way,' he said. He knew better than to offer his arm; Esther did not enjoy the offer of an arm.

'Ray,' she said, 'remember to squeeze th' avocados, we want a ripe one for supper.'

He made a quick adjustment of his clerical collar and escorted her to the cubby behind the meat locker.

She eyed the room with suspicion, then lowered herself into a chair at the break table.

'Anybody,' she said, 'can ride in a parade in a Cadillac.'

He did not want to go wherever this was headed.

"What we need is somethin' completely unique. A cut above! T-model Fords with ooga horns an' Cadillacs with flags on th' hood—such folderol will not cut it for a mayoral bid.'

She moved the salt and pepper shakers and leaned across the table.

'What do people really want, Father? You should know, bein' clergy.'

'Umm,' he said, frozen as a herring.

'What we all want,' she said, 'is somethin' no politician can ever give us.'

'Amen to that!'

'What we all want is a sense of community,' she said. 'We want a sense of be*longin*'.'

Now came the Big Lean-in. Esther Cunningham was pretty much literally in his face. 'Long story short, what we want . . . is *family*!'

'That,' he conceded, 'is true.'

'So, you know that big favor you asked Ray to do for you?'

'No, no, Esther. I didn't ask Ray to do *anything.* He *volunteered.*'

'Same thing,' she said. 'So we do that for you, you do this for me, an' look who gets th' good end of th' stick!'

Ha. The only good end of any stick was Esther's end. 'What's on your mind?' he said, snappish.

She sat back, looked him in the eye. 'Here's how I see this thing rollin'.'

She had him by the scruff of the neck. Why couldn't he stand up to Esther Cunningham?

For years, he'd stopped by her office once or twice a week. They had a cup of coffee, she had a sausage biscuit, they prayed for the business of the mayor's office and petitioned God to show them who, among its own, Mitford should take care of—whose oil tank to fill, whose light bill to pay, whose prescription to fill anonymously.

She had been a great mayor, but there was nothing that suggested she could do it again. So this whole thing was a travesty. Nonetheless, in light of Ray's generosity, he was bound to play along. Let the woman have her fun, she was gaining on ninety. When he gained on ninety, he hoped somebody somewhere would let him have his own bit of harmless self-deception.

He called the Cadillac dealership and reeled out his tale, embarrassed.

Jake Tulley clearing his throat. 'This is, ah, a game-changer, Father. I can't let you have Tammy's vehicle for this particular purpose. Sorry. But here's the deal—we appreciate it when you supply down at our place and just for you, I'll let you have our best lightly used model. Nice, very nice. A very sharp ride. Tammy will sit this one out. But I'll drive it up and be at th' wheel for you. How about it?'

'Fine, fine. Of course, Jake. Absolutely.' All his life he'd allowed himself to be rooked into capers like this.

• • •

Mama,' said Grace Murphy, 'I don't want to finish writing my book.'
      She could tell her mother was truly shocked.

'But I thought it was going so well.'

'I didn't like it when Miz Ogleby knocked everything over in the china shop. I could not draw that scene, it was so messy with all the broken dishes. But here is the real reason—Miz Ogleby's story doesn't mean anything real.'

It was hard to say that her story didn't mean anything real. She had seven whole pages, both sides, and it had been hard to write that much and erase and draw and color pictures, too.

'I don't understand.'

'I mean that telling a story about a tiny town and a lady buying a cow doesn't end up *important*.' She could feel a lots of tears coming to her eyes.

Hope Murphy was always surprised by the earnestness of her amazing daughter. She sat down on the footstool in the poetry section. 'But a copy of your book was to be your Christmas present to everyone.'

'I have another story I want to write. And I will have to hurry really fast to do it for Christmas. Will you help me?' Tears were rolling down her cheeks. She was sad to give up her old book about Miz Ogleby and scared to write a new one, but it had to be done.

Hope took Grace on her lap. It broke her heart to see her almost-seven-year-old child so distressed. Seven-year-old children should not be distressed. 'I will help you always. No matter what. You can believe in that. Have you prayed about what you must do?'

Grace wiped her eyes on her mother's cardigan. 'A lots.'

'Then you must do it, of course. If it's in your heart to write another story, then that is the story you must write. Perhaps you don't need to illustrate your new story. Perhaps it can stand on its own and people can use their imaginations which is always a good thing.'

'It's a really important story.'

'Then you can do this, Grace Murphy! And I'll help you and Dad will help you and Aunt Louise and Coot. We will be your cheering section, a whole army of helpers.'

'Okay!' Grace slid off her mama's lap.

Something warm was working in her; she couldn't wait to begin. She would sharpen her pencils right away.

'What will your new book be about?'

'I'm going to tell Miss Louella's story!'

MONDAY, NOVEMBER 2

'Are we making any money?' he asked Marcie.

'Holding our own,' she said.

He considered this good news.

At ten-thirty, Mule ducked in to say he tried to call J.C. about lunch. Getting no answer, he stopped by J.C.'s house, which was currently his office while the old one was being painted. No answer to his knock at the front door and no answer at the back, though Adele's patrol car was in the drive and so was J.C.'s jalopy.

'I think Friday's her day off,' said Mule. 'But it didn't look like anybody was home.'

'Mule.'

'What?'

'*Note. Under. Pillow.* Trust me.'

Turkey orders flying in. Gourds flying out. Italian sausage backordered. He looked forward to whipping up another batch, say fifteen pounds, in the test kitchen cum break room.

At two-thirty, J.C. blew in, looking . . . what? Upbeat! Smiling! Joking with Lisa! This side of J. C. Hogan was as rarely seen as Halley's comet.

The *Muse* editor handed him an envelope. 'Th' recipe, my friend, for a long and lively marriage is not necessarily created by mushy notes. Here's th' real deal, in black and white. I say print it, circulate it to your customers.'

Saluting, J.C. was out the door.

He looked at the inscription on the envelope, penned in block letters:

J. C. HOGAN'S

MAGICAL MARITAL

MARINATED PORK CHOPS

16

He was latching the cattle gate and thinking it would be great to get away.

Maybe even go on a honeymoon.

He'd never thought much about honeymoons. Why not just get on with life instead of going off somewhere? That's what he and Lace had done and it seemed pretty sexy to him, all things considered.

Still, it would be good to kick back and catch their breath. But where would they go? He'd been camping more than a few times and this wasn't a time for camping. As for spring, he had five calves on the way and he couldn't miss that. Willie was a natural with cattle, but Harley was no help in that department. Harley was strictly repair and improvement, being one of the best carpenters on the planet. There you have it—he and Lace weren't going anywhere anytime soon. Maybe a long weekend with Jack. In June.

He was tired. People get tired. But this would pass.

Thank God for Beth, who was helping Lace keep her head above water, and for Lily and Willie and Harley and the tractor not breaking down and the barn shed as good as new for less than a thousand bucks.

'And thanks,' he said, 'for this land and th' practice and our little herd and th' mountains and two deep springs and our creek.'

She stood at the studio window, looking away to the winter woods where they would soon find their Christmas tree.

She would not have missed this ride, even if it was a roller coaster and not the merry-go-round. Even if she had gotten up at midnight last night and worked until two in the worst imaginable light.

Painting their trees and pastures, mountains and sky, had driven her deeper. There had been a few scary mistakes, like what happened with the girls grazing around the cottonwood trees—the repainting, the overpainting, and the long wait for them to come forth as muscle and bone. As for the clouds—clouds were a language that, until the mural, she thought she had learned. But she'd had to wring the truth from them, force them to reveal their mystery, as she had no time to beg for it.

It was not to be like a poster that gives fleeting pleasure, or a painting on the side of a barn that fades with time, it was not to be ephemeral. It was to be an actual place to the onlooker, impervious to time, with chickens scratching in a dust that never settles.

In less than four weeks, they would be taking it down, rolling it up, sending it off.

There were a few days when the image had been as real to her, more real, even, than Meadowgate itself, and she could keep moving forward, trusting her instincts. She had called Cynthia then to come out and speak the truth, and Cynthia had uplifted and encouraged her.

There was also the time she sat on the floor and cried, bawled, really. Jack had come in and, not saying a word, had climbed into her lap and they had cried together and she told him how things couldn't always be perfect, some things in life would be hard, and somehow he understood, maybe because he'd known hard things.

She washed her brushes and walked across the hall to the junk room with its neat piles ready to be recycled in Wesley, given to Lily's church, or moved to the living room sale. She noticed the window for the first time, really saw it, and stepped between the piles and took the beat-up window shade down and tossed it in the trash pile. Let there be light!

She went poking around in the yard-sale goods.

Their former lives. All in one room.

Textbooks. Novels. A torrent of jeans. Sweatshirts. Throw pillows. Curtains from the years she had roomed with four other girls. Flip-flops, sandals, work boots, running shoes, tennis shoes. His beanbag chair from UGA. The backpacks they took on the first leg of the Appalachian Trail. A point-and-shoot. A thermos. A nylon windbreaker with a broken zipper.

She opened the box tied with red string. Her white shirts! Bleached, starched, ironed, and folded. She had treated her white shirts as fondly as fair linen and had worn them nearly to tatters. As often as she could, she wore what she had.

It had taught her something to be thrifty. Not cheap, no, she was not cheap. She had learned how to look smart and self-confident in less instead of more—even when she didn't feel smart or self-confident at all.

And there was Dooley's jacket with the missing top button. The one he wore home the weekend she knew for the first time and without any doubt that she loved him more than life and they could make it.

And Jack's first boots, the ones in the box he opened the day he came home to Meadowgate. She would never forget that moment, just the two of them in Dooley's old room off the glider porch. And then he grew so fast he needed new ones in just four months.

How could people let go of their old things, when each told a part of their story? Old things were a literature, a narrative.

In a few days, there would be two cots in the room, made up with quilts, and a night table with a lamp, and a chair from the library. A rug, they would need a rug.

She put the lid on the box of shirts and retied the string. 'Let them go,' she said.

But no. Not yet.

She put the blouses and the jacket and the boots in a pile, then gathered them in her arms and took them to her closet and in they went.

I could've stayed home an' helped Harley,' said Jack.

He was riding to town with Beth and did not like looking out the window at people's cows.

'But you wanted to come with me.'

'I changed my mind.'

'You're going to have Granny C's famous pimiento cheese sandwich for lunch,' said Beth. 'You love her pimiento cheese. And Granny O is coming over with your favorite cookies.'

'I don't want to.'

'What do you want to do?'

'I could stay with you an' do grocery shoppin'.'

'You know you don't like to grocery shop.'

'I could ride in th' cart. I don't have to like it.'

'You are grumpy today. Do you know what grumpy means?'

'No.'

'Grumpy is a big old pouty face. Grumpy is not liking something wonderful, like a grilled cheese and cookies from your grannies. Grumpy is being no fun to go to town with, not even one bit!'

He crossed his arms and gave her a look. 'That is too much information.'

Cynthia waved from the front door as Jack climbed into Beth's car. Beth waved back.

He handed over a brown paper bag.

'From Granny O,' he said. 'I could have another one if you have one left over, which you might.'

'You get first dibs,' she said. 'I promise. Did you have a good time?'

'Yeah. I mean, yes! We played hide-and-seek.'

'You an' the *grannies?*'

'I hid under Granpa Tim's desk and they couldn't find me.'

'Oh, fun. Could you find them?'

'I found Granny C, she was layin' under th' table . . . '

'*Lying* under the table.'

'. . . an' I saw her feet stickin' out!' Gales of laughter.

'How about Granny O?'

'She was in th' kitchen an' said here I am, you don't have to find me, I am right here eatin' cookies!' More unbridled laughter.

'I will play hide-and-seek with you.'

'Would you do it tonight?'

'I can't do it tonight. I have a date.'

'What is a date?'

'Mostly, it's when two people spend special time together. They sit and talk or have dinner or maybe go out dancing or see a movie or go for a walk in the woods. In the fall is the best time for walking in the woods. Or they could go horseback riding together. Or take a hike and maybe hold hands or even tell jokes! And in the summer, they could go swimming in the lake and have a picnic after . . .'

'Aunt Beth.' He gave her a frowny look and said his new favorite thing: 'That is too much information.'

L ace was at the stove; her boys loved stir-fry.

'Jack has a loose tooth,' she told Dooley. 'Bottom front. I think it's going be a tooth-fairy tooth.'

'Isn't it early for that?'

'I Googled it. A little early but not abnormal.'

She didn't want to cry, but . . .

'Come on,' he said, laughing.

'You don't understand. He just got here. And he's growing up so fast.'

Jack was running his dump trucks around the room and parking them on the hearth.

'Hey, buddy. Do you think you could stop growin' up for a few minutes? I mean, just stay a kid for a while, okay?'

'No. I'm goin' to grow up really fast an' be a big huge dinosaur that eats shoes!'

'Really?'

'And poops in th' yard!'

Dooley gave Lace a look.

'Creative,' he said.

Dooley in a deep, hard sleep; her own sleep reluctant.

Lights flashed across their bedroom ceiling. A vehicle turning in the drive. She lay still, waiting, the vet's wife taking into herself the reality of a knock on their door at three in the morning.

She put on her old robe and went down before the knock came and turned on the porch light and opened the door. Old Man Teague was stepping onto the porch with his redbone hound in his arms, and he was weeping.

'She's dyin'. Redeemer's dyin'.'

The forcible shock of grief at her door.

'You take 'er. You take 'er.' He handed over his dog and she took the weight of the hound, speechless.

'She saved my life. She was my friend all these years.' Sobbing. 'Make it easy on 'er. Don't let me know.'

Teague turned and went down the porch steps, stumbled a little at the bottom. 'Don't let me know!' he cried as he literally vanished into the night yard.

She was conscious of the warm, stunning flesh pressing hers, of the old man's keening, a kind of desolate howl, as he went to his truck. Then the closing of the truck door and headlights moving in reverse down the drive and onto the road and gone.

She nudged the door closed with her shoulder and stood there, try-ing to find her breath.

The hound panted but didn't flinch as she carried her to the kitchen and squatted, careful with what she figured to be less than forty pounds of debilitated bone and muscle, and eased her down by the stove where the kittens had been. She went to the laundry then, and took the dog bed off the shelf and came back to the kitchen illumined by a waxing moon and put the bed down and rolled Redeemer onto it. The dog yelped.

She palpated her abdomen. A lump. Large. The dog opened her eyes and in the near darkness seemed to reveal whatever pain or resignation was stirring in her. In that look, Lace found a connection. She had con-nected in that way before with animals, and knew that it mattered.

She offered water, but it was refused. Peanut butter on her finger. Refused.

She took the afghan and a throw pillow from the window seat and made a pallet and stretched out beside Redeemer, a hand on the hound's flank.

'Lord, here is your servant, Redeemer, made with love and bound by your grace. Thank you for your mercy.'

FRIDAY, NOVEMBER 20

At first light she went again to the kitchen and covered the body with a towel and made coffee and spoke with Dooley when he came down.

'Our cemetery,' she said.

Not to the crematorium in Wesley. Not to some remote spot near the woods. Harley and Willie would dig a place for her in the Meadowgate pet cemetery, enclosed by a fence and entered by a gate. Barnabas was out there, and a lamb, a pet crow, and more than a few farm dogs and Owen family cats. It was important to acknowledge the beauty of Redeemer's devotion to a lonely old man.

And Mr. Teague, if he ever wanted to, could come and sit on the bench and visit.

MONDAY, NOVEMBER 23

Willie watched Harley get in his truck and head to town.

He fanned the front door for a minute, airing out the place. He'd never been a man to wear cologne, but Harley, he was different.

He closed the door, sniffed the air, and opened a window.

He knew it would take gumption to ask a man about his romantic life, but he wanted to know, maybe even had a right to know, bein' as how him an' Harley shared expenses. He remembered his mama sayin' it was curiosity that killed th' cat. As a young'un, he expected to die a sudden death every day or two.

What if Harley up an' moved out to git hitched? Now they'd got his room all settled an' had their meal times runnin' by th' clock—Harley generally cookin', him cleanin' up th' kitchen an' Swifferin'—it would be a letdown. That was th' word. They had finally settled on th' History Channel an' th' Weather Channel as their go-to entertainment, an' shook hands on no CNN, no Fox News, nossir, they wadn't neither one of them fallin' out over politics. So the thing is, he'd already got used to this arrangement, never mind that he was suspicious of it at th' start.

Harley spoke a good bit about Miss Pringle, how she was born in Paris, France, and brought up by her granny in the country an' about her daddy bein' a rich man who'd built that big white house in Mitford. He talked about how smart she was with her piano music an' all, and how she spoke French a good bit when he went to visit.

'Fret, fret, fret,' his wife used to say—he'd always been a worrier. But it made him nervous to think Harley could turn around an' move out an' tear up this whole scheme. All he wanted was a word, a sign, so he wouldn't be took by surprise.

Miss Pringle's place, that rock house where Father Tim used to live, that was a nice house for a man to put his feet up in. So he couldn't blame Harley if that was the way this was headed. There was one thing, though, that he might have to speak to Harley about if he took a notion to marry Miss Pringle.

It was th' way Harley left his teeth layin' around in front of God an' ever'body. Out of respect, Harley had pretty much wore his teeth when he moved in. Then first thing you know, they'd show up on th' kitchen window sill, in a rocker on th' porch, on th' stove hood, most anyplace. He, Willie, had not said a word, and wadn't goin' to, as a man had to have one spot in this world where he let hisself go and could feel at home.

Maybe Dooley an' Lace had some notion of Harley's plan. But he wouldn't trouble them with such a question; nossir, them two was run plumb ragged, goin' at a trot all th' time. He had no idea how they kep' it up. But of course they were young. An' they could handle it.

I t was a relief that Dooley's biological dad was gone. She had always sensed the shadow of Clyde Barlowe hovering over her husband.

Sometimes she wondered what had happened to her own biological father.

Ironically, their dads had hoboed together, stayed drunk together, broken the law together. She didn't see how Clyde Barlowe had lasted as long as he did. Surely her own father was buried somewhere; maybe it would be good to know the truth, maybe it would help. Or maybe not. She never mentioned his name to Dooley.

She wished she could at least have a sofa for Name Day.

But so what if Lace Kavanagh had no decent living room furniture—

her mother never had money to buy anything at all. No sofa, no chairs, just a table and four Pepsi crates and a wash pan and a stove and a bed and a leaking refrigerator and walls covered with newspaper. When her brother moved out, he took nothing with him because there was nothing to take but his few clothes and a shave kit and the bedroll he carried under his arm. All he said when leaving was, 'Mama, Lacey,' and they never saw him again.

She and her mother hung their clothes on nails, a look Lace thought softened the bare walls. With the lamp burning, the draping fabric had given the room a certain texture and dimension, like in a photo by Walker Evans, who she came to know in books from the bookmobile.

The bookmobile had saved her life. But nothing and nobody could save her mother's life, though she had tried every day. She could count on one hand the little pleasures of her mother's time on this earth.

The porch swing was the most wonderful furnishing they ever had during those years at the Creek. Her daddy had made it for her mother when she got sick with the blood disease. Maybe it was his way of saying I'm sorry for being a drunk fool, a violent man to you and your children. She thought her mother took it that way, as a gesture of making up to her something good that he had scared away.

She had a memory of her mother's apology to visitors for lack of seating, other than the swing. 'Ye'll have to sit on y'r fist an' lean back on y'r thumb!'

That's the way it would be for Name Day. A pile of people scooped together in the farmhouse, mostly in the kitchen, sitting on their fists and leaning back on their thumbs, laughing.

H ey, Lace, I can't let this go.'
        Dooley held up a sweatsuit that a wash had failed to improve.
'Why not?'
'It's still good.'

'A lot of stuff is still good. But it has to go, Dooley. Just let Beth and me do this, please. Look at the benefits—we gain a guest room and make extra money. You're giving your junk to a good cause.'

'I don't know. It seems crazy not to go through everything.'

'Beth and I have been through everything. If you want to go through it again, you need to do it now.'

He looked around the room, checked his watch. A surgery in twenty minutes. 'Do what you want to, then. It's all yours.'

'But remember what you just said. Okay?'

He was glad she was making him skip the torment; he would never get around to going through this mess.

'We're giving ten percent of the proceeds to the Food Bank,' she said. 'It's not about us all the time.'

He hesitated.

'It's not all about us,' she said.

I t looks beautiful!' she told Beth.

'It's a store!' said Jack. 'You should have toys.'

Their junk looked pretty good, displayed on sheets of plywood laid over sawhorses. Lace had called around the neighborhood, drumming up business.

'All that washing, ironing, and folding,' said Beth. 'All that dusting and sneezing! This simple country life is not to be missed.'

'You are such a good sport,' said Lace.

After supper, there was Dooley Kavanagh picking through stuff like he owned it, and bringing them an armload.

'I'm sorry,' said Lace. 'But those things are not free, you know.'

'I know, I know.' He laid the items by the cash box. 'How much?'

'You have a shirt, four pairs of tennis shoes in shreds, a camera, and two pairs of jeans.' She consulted Beth's list. 'That is . . . '

'Thirty-six dollars,' said Beth. Lace held out her hand.

'And this radio,' he said. 'But I shouldn't have to pay for it; we could use it in the break room. I should get it free, this is my radio.'

'It was your radio,' said Lace. 'You haven't used it since college. Remember you said we could have everything and do whatever we wanted with it.'

'They make you pay for stuff, Dad.'

'Maybe I'll pass on th' radio.'

'How much does it cost?' said Jack. 'I could pay!'

'Ten dollars,' said Beth.

Jack looked at his dad. 'I don't have ten dollars. I only have three left from my helmet.'

'Thanks anyway, buddy. You're a good guy. So does it work? Buyer beware.'

'Cleaned up, tested, and set on High Country Classics,' said Beth. 'A steal!'

He shuffled through a few bills, handed Beth the money, grinned. 'Hard-nosed women.'

'Thank you for your business,' said his wife, having a laugh.

They heard footsteps on the front porch, and voices, and the door opened and in rushed the frigid air with the Hershells and Danny from the next farm. Then the Owens and Rebecca Jane, who would be helping with the sale, and truck lights turning off the road into the driveway, which would be Harley and Willie with drinks and nachos from the co-op.

'A bonanza!' said Beth.

'Hey, Beck,' said Danny Hershell. 'I'd like to buy somethin'.'

Danny Hershell was twelve years old now, and proud of it. When his daddy told his granpaw that Danny had growed a foot last year, his granpaw said, 'Oh, Lord, now we've got a freak in th' family.'

'What are you lookin' for?' said Rebecca Jane. She had fixed him good with her trick, but would he let on? Not in a hundred years, the cretin.

He shrugged. 'I don't know. A belt, maybe? Or I could use a pocketknife.'

'Willie got our only pocketknife,' said Beth.

Danny stood by the table a certain way so they could see the birth-day T-shirt his uncle had sent from Chicago. Navy blue with a red bear head. Truly cool.

'How much money are you willin' to spend?' said Rebecca Jane. She knew he did not spend money if he could help it.

Danny dug into his jeans pocket and brought out a fistful of change. He opened his hand and grinned big. 'Two dollars and five cents. Found it on th' barn floor where somebody must've dropped it.'

S o?' said Dooley, leaning over the cash box.
'Guess,' said Lace.

'Eighty, ninety bucks?'

'Guess again.'

'I give up.'

'A hundred and sixty-two dollars and five cents. Can you believe it? And more to go next Saturday.'

His wife and Beth were jubilant.

'Look, Dad, what I bought!'

A vintage eggbeater with a red handle, the kind with a crank on the side. He remembered it from Lace's apartment in Chapel Hill.

'Man! What did you pay for that piece of machinery?'

'Two quarters. It was on sale jis' for me.' Jack whizzed the beaters. 'Look at it go!'

Dooley laughed his cackling laugh. It didn't take much for them, liv-ing out here in the sticks.

T wo-thirty and not much sleep so far.
Days ago, she had finally come awake to a hard fact: For Name Day weekend, her studio needed to be a bedroom again, the perfect spot for Kenny and Julie and Etta and Ethan.

TO BE WHERE YOU ARE

She would have to finish the mural early and ship it out of here. The tight deadline was now tighter, if only by a few days.

She had painted Choo-Choo but it wasn't right. It was some other bull from some other pasture. No matter how hard she tried, the eyes fought her; she couldn't get that special gleam, the nearly conversational gaze so peculiar to Choo-Choo. And the forehead—it should be broader. She had kidded herself that this rendering would work, she did not have time to repaint it. But it wasn't Choo-Choo.

Who would know? She would know. Eyes speak, and they needed to say the right thing. The bull was a huge feature of the mural, a muscular block of color in the lower right foreground, a kingly guard at the gate.

The fun for the viewer would be to get by Choo-Choo and walk into the life of the mural as if it were real. In her childhood, even in the hell of it, her imagination had been pure and eager. She could enter into the illustrations in a book and lose herself completely. This is what she wanted for the children who would visit Kim—that they would go away with the vision of a beautiful life in the country, taken into themselves without knowing.

Dooley sleeping hard.

In her mind, she squeezed titanium white, carbon black, cadmium red, cerulean blue onto the palette . . .

Now would be good.

She slipped out of bed and went along the creaking floorboards and ascended the twenty steps to Heaven.

TUESDAY, NOVEMBER 24

It was a jumbo-size postcard with a closeup photo of Jack. Big smile, big eyes, the slight dimple in his chin. She kissed one of the cards, which would go in the album she would make when there was nothing else to do, ha ha.

ON FRIDAY, DECEMBER 11,

THE WORLD WILL WELCOME

A NEW KAVANAGH.

ON SATURDAY, DECEMBER 12,

WE WILL WELCOME *YOU!*

❖ ❖ ❖

Celebrate Jack's Name Day
at Meadowgate Farm
Farmville Road
4 p.m. ~ Casual
The only thing you can bring is a present.
Thank you!

Everybody was so not asking for presents these days, but Name Day was huge, and presents would be okay just this once.

She drove to the post office and bought thirteen stamps.

'Thank you for your business,' said Sugar, who always made the post office window smell like hot dogs with mustard.

now movin' in on th' eleventh,' said Willie, grim as the Reaper. He was famous for dumping bad weather news on Meadowgate's special occasions.

He set his desiccated hat on the farm table.

'Two inches,' he said.

She took the eggs from his hat and placed them in the blue bowl. She had no intention of getting worked up over Willie's weather predictions. He had driven them crazy before the wedding, but he'd been right. It rained *and* blew a gale, knocking limbs down which they had to clean up. But it all passed over before the ceremony and everything was gorgeous.

'Two inches isn't such big deal. Besides, it's too early for an accurate forecast.'

Willie returned his hat to his head and headed for the door.

'Could be four, they're sayin'.' Once snow got started in these mountains, you never knew when it would stop.

J ack had worn his red helmet all morning.

'Look at you, look at *you*!' said Violet, who was in to do a major cook-and-freeze-off with Lily.

'We went to get my bike yesterday. They let me get on it to see does it fit.'

'So does it fit?'

'Yep. We brought it home an' it's hid so it'll be brand-new on Name Day. Do you know where it's hid, Lil?'

'I do not, an' don't want to know or you'd worm it out of me.'

'If you knew, I could just go look at it. I wouldn't ride it or anything.'

'Awww,' said Violet. 'Ain't that sweet? Gimme some sugar.'

'No,' said Jack.

'He don't do sugar,' said Lily.

L ace was brushing her hair; his wife took forever to brush her hair.

He lay on his back with the covers kicked off. Though the thermostat was cranked way down, it was hot as th' hinges up here. Their old furnace could make it happen; it was a bulldog.

In five and a half months—the wedding, their little guy, a puppy, the plumbing disaster, the business start-up plus the pounding they were taking with large animals since Joanna's sellout, the mural . . .

He rolled over.

. . . not to mention a ton of people and five sleepovers coming up.

Not to mention the jaw-dropping payout to the pharmaceutical companies on the fifteenth, not to mention the upcoming quarterly insurance payment, not to mention Christmas. They had hardly thought about Christmas.

'We've got a lot goin' on.' Call him the master of understatement.

She was numb with fatigue. She had asked Violet to come with Lily on the twelfth. That would help. And when would she start running again? When would she stop sleeping in this stupid ragged T-shirt and buy something grown-up? 'They say we're young, we can handle it.'

'Bull.'

She thought that one of the hardest parts of marriage was being loving when both partners were exhausted or wounded at the same time. When you had the least strength, that's when you had to dig beyond your limits and grab whatever could be found and give it away.

She put the brush in the drawer and lay down beside him and with her finger outlined a heart on his back and he turned to her and smiled. Her husband laughed, grinned, whatever, but didn't often smile. He had dug beyond to give her this.

'Love you deep,' he said.

The owl hooting in the tree by the kitchen porch . . .

17

On the day after Thanksgiving, promptly at dusk, the Christmas lights had switched on.

In a blink, the sullen winter street became a gleaming boulevard. Simultaneously, Christmas music coursed from the speakers at town hall—joyful stories everyone had somehow forgotten during the year, stories they craved to hear once again.

Until midnight each night through Christmas, trumpets would play, choirs rejoice, lights glitter beneath cold stars, and those who lived near Main Street would hear the voices of angels in their dreams.

Though lights and music were on time, the Christmas parade had been rescheduled.

The *Mitford Muse* had earlier announced in a front-page headline that the parade, traditionally held the Saturday after Thanksgiving at eleven o'clock, would be held Saturday, December 5, at two o'clock. There was a problem with the water main; details would follow from the town manager.

Such news was ill received. Phones rang at the *Muse*, the town office, the mayor's office, and two or three inquiries ended up in the lap of the priest at Lord's Chapel. People had plans for the *traditional* date; families were coming from *out of town*; food already bought for the Saturday after Thanksgiving would not *last* until the fifth of December. Some were still hacked over a Christmas parade in years past that had happened *before Thanksgiving*. What was the *matter* with people?

In a carefully prepared statement, the town manager released a flurry of broadsides to be installed on lampposts, taped on store windows, and available at checkout counters.

The street would be jackhammered at Wisteria and Main and repairs made to 'a water pipe which had busted.' The southbound lane would be closed. They would excavate the hole, requiring an excavator, an operator, two flaggers, two dump trucks, and the equipment truck from the fire department to keep the work site lit for men doing night work. 'And that,' wrote the manager, 'is just the tip of the iceburg.' Bottom line, they would be 'dern lucky to get the job done by midnight of the fourth. Please detour to the highway or practice courtesy in the single lane. Thank you for your patience.' End of discussion.

He sat at the kitchen island and ate a bowl of oatmeal with dried cranberries and honey. Drank a cup of strong tea, pined for caffeine.

Bong . . .

The chiming of the church bells. Seven A.M. Fifty degrees. A cold rain predicted for evening.

Bong . . .

It was one of those mornings when he craved the breakfast of his boyhood—country ham, two fried eggs, a buttered biscuit, grits salted by redeye gravy, chicory coffee perked on the stove and served straight up, thick as mud.

Though being a grocery guy was not up there with climbing Everest, it was rigorous in its own way. The run-up to Thanksgiving had half killed him, but he hadn't mentioned it to anyone. He was seventy-seven and being half killed was interpreted as a sign of declining years.

In any case, he was beat at the end of the day, and a dash mindless. He had forgotten, for example, to open yesterday's mail, something he rarely neglected to do. His wife was indifferent to mail, but he liked mail; he had high expectations of mail. Something wonderful would be revealed, a truth of some sort, or maybe a check for a large amount.

He grabbed the stack from his desk and took it to the sofa with a letter opener.

Is it earwax? Or is it hearing loss?

The usual from the Scooter Store.

Water bill, power bill.

Henry! His elegant, old-school handwriting and the Holly Springs postmark.

His wife floated in, hair every whichaway, gave him a kiss on the cheek. Having the uncommon ability to sleep like a teenager, she had lately been dead to the world when he came up to bed.

'I haven't seen much of you,' she said.

'You're painting, I'm selling cabbages.'

'Starting now, I'm taking a complete break. Irene and I have more than half our work done. Besides, Christmas is coming, you know.'

'Tell me about it,' he said. Yesterday they had rigged the store windows with lights, fake wreaths, and a plastic tree that shot open like an umbrella and spewed last year's tinsel into the produce bins. They had also changed the music from elevator to Mormon Tabernacle. Though Advent was upon them, there was no trace of it to be found in the marketplace. Advent was a waiting period and no one liked to wait. Period.

'I'll get the Advent wreath today,' she said. 'We have candles.'

'A letter from Henry!' He held it aloft, like a trophy.

'Read it to me while I get the coffee going. Did you have your banana?'

'I forgot.'

She brought him a banana from the fruit bowl. 'Your potassium,' she said, but he was already reading the letter. He regretted that it was briefer than usual; they had spoiled each other with lengthy letters.

'Dear Brother . . .

'Holy smoke, listen to this. Henry and Lucille are herewith announc-
ing their engagement!'

'Hooray!'

'He knows this is all happening quickly, but he says he loves her very
much . . . and realizes he has no time to waste.'

'Amen to that,' she said. 'When is the wedding?'

'Next June.'

'I thought he had no time to waste.'

'Ah, let's see. Lucille is having hip surgery in January and wishes to
walk down the aisle, so June it is. Only six months, Kav'na, not much
waste there. He asks us to save the date. June fourteenth.'

'Dooley's and Lace's anniversary,' she said. 'Lovely!'

He could smell the coffee. 'The timing, he says, works well for another reason. Lucille wants to carry a bouquet of Eva's roses, which
should be in full bloom for the wedding.'

'I'm going to love Lucille.'

He let the whole notion sink in, feeling the astonishing happiness of
it. Henry in love. Henry walking down the aisle. Henry, like himself, a
late bloomer in the marriage department. 'I'm thinking that he did his
half by coming to the kids' wedding; we can do our half and go to his.
What do you say?'

'Two halves make a whole! Yes! Absolutely.'

To think that he'd been a bachelor nodding over his books with but
one known blood kinsman to his name—Walter. Now here he was with
a wife, a son, a daughter-in-law, a grandson, a brother, and soon, a sister-
in-law. He was excited.

She sat on the sofa with her mug of Arabica.

'So, what are we doing for Christmas?' he said. 'Have you thought
about it?' In priestly days of yore, he was thinking about Christmas by
mid-August.

'The kids are asking us out for an early supper Christmas afternoon.
I think they don't want us to be lonely.'

'We're never lonely,' he said. 'Are we?'

They had a laugh.

'They've just been here for Thanksgiving and we'll have been there on the twelfth,' he said, 'and they're coming in for the parade and going with us to Lucera. It would be good if they could get a break from us on Christmas Day . . .' He was grinning big. '. . . but no way.'

'You're wonderful.' She gave him a smooch. 'I have goose bumps just thinking about it.'

When it came to the seventy-some Christmases of his life, this would be the Big One. All his ducks were in a row. He sat back, happy.

'Other than that,' she said, 'being quiet would suit me this year.'

'Quiet like how?'

'On Christmas Eve, our little fir with colored lights, a fire, oyster pie, and midnight mass. On Christmas Day, up to see Louella, out to see the kids, and pull off our caper—I'll tell Lace we won't stay for supper. Then straight home. Just us and Truman.'

He was starved for everything she mentioned.

'You'll get no argument from me. Tomorrow I've got to get cracking and set up the crèche.' A few years ago, he had fully restored the twenty-some pieces, hand-painting each figure, including camels, wise men, angels, sheep, and shepherd, several being two feet tall. All that to lug from the attic and down the hall stairs, then lug back again in January.

'I've been meaning to tell you,' she said. 'The kids would love to borrow the nativity figures this year. Lace promises not to ask again. She would like to use them for illustrating the Christmas story for Jack. She wondered if she and Harley could come for them today. They'll do all the hauling down from the attic and into the truck. Would that be okay?'

'Done!' He would miss the colorful troupe crowding into the study, but he could see Jack's face and the wonderment in his brown eyes.

'Moving right along,' she said, 'I have a great idea. How about no gifts this year, you and I? Let's just empty our pockets into the Children's Hospital. What do you think?'

'Not a completely great idea. How about just one gift? I mean, something to open, Kav'na. Something to *open*.'

'Okay, okay. And I'll show you my paintings then.'

His adrenaline was up again. They had a plan. The grocer could go to his cabbages a new man. Well, almost.

'A blessed Advent!' he said, and kissed her cheek.

He whistled a little on his way to the Local.

In the family photos taken last June at Meadowgate, Henry had stood out. One dark skin among the pale. In Holly Springs, it would be the reverse. Two pale skins among the dark. He wondered how that would feel. But there was only one way to know. And that was to be there.

A t the fire station, Hamp Floyd, formerly retired Mitford fire chief and interim since the departure of his successor, worried about the news from Clovis Baillie, their go-to Santa for the Christmas parade.

Clovis had missed his family's Thanksgiving blowout, an annual reunion of forty-six Baillies—to which at least one wore a kilt—because of a shingles outbreak. The burning rash had occurred with especial ferocity around his waist and he still could not bear the touch of clothing, especially a heavy fake velvet coat with fake fur and pants that were a size too tight last year. Plus he was getting a sore throat and a cough.

'If you get out there in th' cold, you'll be dead,' said his wife who appeared to enjoy the idea.

The antibiotics for th' shingles were working okay, but slow as molasses, and there was no way he could be cured in time for the parade. He would just have to sit this one out, with a Bud Light and a sandwich of leftover turkey and cranberry relish on white.

For Hamp Floyd, choosing a Santy was no laughing matter; it was serious business. You wanted a Santy who looked the part, fit in the suit, and seemed to everybody, especially kids, like the real thing—not just some guy playacting on a fire engine.

He would do it himself, but was only five-two in his sock feet and 128 pounds soaking wet. 'No Mickey Rooneys,' said a town council know-it-all from up north. He'd never understood how people from other places got elected to this town's governing body—proof right there that Mitford could not take care of its own; they had to have the help of New Jersey, Michigan, and Florida.

He didn't ask who Mickey Rooney was.

H ope Murphy put the finishing touches on the D for December window display.

At the foot of the fresh-cut Fraser fir, she placed books tied with ribbon. *Death Comes for the Archbishop*, a personal favorite, *Dictionary of Modern Quotations*, *Don Quixote*, *Dear Tooth Fairy*, *The Dot*, which was Grace's pick, and *Don't Forget I Love You*, which was Louise's pick.

On the floor by the leather wing chair, she placed a pair of slippers belonging to Scott. At the slipcovered chair, she placed a pair of her own. Was the scene too corny? Window display was not her forte. Actually, she would give anything to sit in a comfy chair and read a book.

Margaret Anne the Bookstore Cat wandered in, looked around, jumped into the leather chair, and curled up.

'Perfect!' she said. 'Thank you!'

At ten A.M. sharp, Louise turned the OPEN sign around. 'Okay!' Louise shouted. Hope plugged in the tree.

The star at the top of the fir flickered on; the train began its eager circle around the miniature Alpine village. Hope felt a tremor of some sort, perhaps of excitement, then realized the old bookstore was literally shuddering from the excavation of a vast hole at Main and Wisteria.

W hy was his cell phone doing that electric-buzzer-shock thing? What had happened to his ringtone?

'So, three hostile teenage girls,' said Father Brad, 'and snow coming the night of the eleventh! God be with us. Our youth counselor can't leave 'til one. That puts us in camp at two-thirty and gives us two and a half hours to set up—a challenge right there, as these kids have never seen a tent. Wish you'd come along.'

He laughed. All the years he had said yes, yes, and more yes to nearly everything—and now, the consolation of no. Even if he could manage the ascent to camp, he wasn't keen to freeze his digits off in a tent or a ramshackle cabin where the worst and best came out in people.

'And thanks again for taking Mary Ellen in at Thanksgiving. She loved being with you and Cynthia.'

'She's great company. Any time. We mean it.'

'She'll be bunking in Irene McGraw's guesthouse this trip, then going back to Boston after camp.'

Back to Boston after camp? When was Father Brad going to make his move?

'How's Jessie feeling about this?'

'Bullying the other two. Doing what many of us do when feeling inferior—acting the know-it-all. She'd never say it, but she's keen on the idea of a challenge. I love these crazy kids—this is a true Advent for me, the expectation that something wonderful will happen.'

'And it always does!' Father Brad hadn't been called the 'youth whisperer' for nothing.

'God may speak, hearts may open, heads may roll, including mine! Who knows? It's Divine Dice!'

He was mildly envious of the younger priest's enthusiasm. Where had his own fled? Something to look forward to, that's what he needed. But wait. Of course. Albeit a few months out, he had something—the spring fling with Cynthia. The problem was getting enthusiastic about the general format of it.

Otis's dad, the butcher, had come up yesterday to help out. As far as he knew, Lynwood had spoken all of four words. When taking off his cap, he said, 'Good mornin'.' When asked how he was doing, he said, 'Can't complain.'

Lynwood had brought with him a nephew who heaved boxes around, straightened up the loading dock, and moved the sidewalk bins to storage.

At noon, Hank came by to give a hand and make his informal reservation for a spot on the roof for the parade. He would climb up with a picnic lunch, his wife, three kids, and two grans, an annual arrangement he'd enjoyed with Avis for some years.

Ham orders were flooding in. Due for next week's delivery from Otis's dad were nineteen large boneless and five bone-in, with their big inventory rolling in midmonth. And sweet potatoes! He'd never seen so many sweet potatoes fly out of a place. What was going on with the sweet potato? And why were Brussels sprouts predicted to take a hit this year?

'You hadn't took your break,' said Otis, who was a firm believer in breaks, fifteen minutes on the dot.

'Consider it done.'

He went to the break room and called Emma.

'What did you learn?'

'Her name is Nancy Drew.'

'Come, now.'

'Can you believe it? And guess what? She's a mystery!'

'In what way?'

'Her old boss wouldn't tell me anything but her name. I immediately called all th' golf-related places an' country clubs in Bryson City. I ran th' full gambit.'

'And?'

'They never heard of her. And no phone listed. But get this. You said she was a dresser.'

'I said that?'

'You said she was dressed up. So you know that ladies' shop in Wesley?'

'I don't.'

'It's th' best. When you head into town, you turn right after th' drugstore, then left at th' movie theater—they're playin' *Th' Green Mile* for a dollar. Did you ever see it? Tom Hanks. I love Tom Hanks. Then you turn left at th' pizza place and go about two blocks or maybe three, an' it's out there somewhere around—you know where th' old Tastee Freez used to be?'

'Emma,' he said in his pulpit voice.

'Okay, so I went in an' took Snickers because dogs soften people up. And I said I was lookin' for somethin' smart like Nancy Drew wears. I dropped that name like I'd known Nancy Drew for a hundred years.'

She employed the theatrical effect of the pause.

'*And?*' he said. '*So?*'

'So they said they knew it was a book, but they hadn't read it. They never heard of Nancy Drew as a real person. So I guess she shops online. What do you want me to do now?'

'Let's drop it.' He breathed out. 'Let me know your hours, I'll take care of it.'

'No problem. But I hope you need somethin' else, it gets me out of th' house.'

A dead end. And Avis was looking like death warmed over. In addition to his medical circumstances, something was pestering Avis's spirit.

He, Timothy, hoped to supply an anodyne, but no way could he supply the cure.

T he Feel Good was slammed. Coats overloaded the coatrack; a third coffeemaker was fired up. It was cold out there.

According to J.C., all was bliss in the Hogan marital realm, with credit duly given to his newfound culinary passion.

'Troubles at home?' said J.C. 'Take my advice. Th' solution is not what you think. It's cornbread with a crispy crust served with fried green tomatoes, aioli, and grilled mahimahi.'

'Grilled what?' said Mule.

'*Fish.* Wake up, buddy. It's the twentieth century.'

'Twenty-first,' said Father Tim.

'I'm no good in th' kitchen,' said Mule.

'You can grill!' said J.C.

'I don't do th' grill.'

'Why not?'

'I'm scared of gas. It can blow up.'

'Listen to me. Th' grill is what a man *does*. A man *cooks on th' grill*. Wives don't like to cook anymore, but guys love it because they can ride a grill like a buckin' horse—steak, chicken, fish, shrimp, onions, potatoes, you name it. All done in th' open air under th' big blue sky. Boom, supper's ready, everybody's happy. And believe me, th' wife is thrilled to do th' cleanup, which is minimal. Th' grill is th' best thing since cornstarch.'

'Cornstarch?' said Mule. 'Are you drinkin'?'

'You got a knot you can't untangle, sprinkle on a little cornstarch. Want to polish your silver? Mix a little cornstarch with water, rub it on, there you go. Smelly shoes? Sprinkle in a little . . . '

'What are we talkin' about?' said Mule.

'Something tells me it's his Hint for the week,' said Father Tim.

'I don't know.' Mule shook his head. 'I can't cook, I can't grill, an' no way am I writin' a mushy note. So what should I do?'

J.C. mopped his face with a paper napkin. 'Say la vee, buddyroe. You'll have to take care of business the old-fashioned way.'

F ather Brad had called for an appointment 'in whatever confession booth you may have on hand.'

'Look for me in the rutabagas.'

He latched the break-room door and poured coffee straight up for his visitor.

'I've been wanting to do this; should have arranged it when we met. I hope it isn't interfering . . . '

'Not at all. Take your time.'

Father Brad sat back, drew a breath, exhaled. 'Easter was going to be full-on that year at St. Peter's. Trumpets. Thuribles. New choir robes. Three hundred lilies given by a parishioner.'

He had been there, done that, but never with three hundred lilies.

'Katie died March tenth. Easter Sunday fell on March thirtieth that year.

'The whole horror came out of the blue. Fine on Tuesday. Shaky and confused on Wednesday. Thursday morning, couldn't complete sentences; brain tumor diagnosed in the afternoon and pronounced inoperable. Deceased on Monday.

'A blur. It was all a blur.'

'We couldn't find anybody to supply the Easter service. My girls didn't go for it, but I insisted I would carry on with the celebration. There was no way I could walk away from a service everyone had worked on for months.

'I took a few days off to prepare, I was a fish washed up on the beach, gasping. Katie was the sunshine, the rain, absolutely everything.

'I don't remember much of what happened Easter Sunday, except for the choir. The music was genuinely celestial. The Holy Spirit was moving at St. Pete's. As we were celebrating Christ, I felt he was celebrating Katie, that this was for her, too. After it was over, I crashed.

'They gave me a month's sabbatical, more if I needed it.

'Told the girls where I was going. Rented a one-room cabin in the backcountry, above the tree line. Eleven thousand feet plus change—a lung-crusher. And a pretty challenging ski-in even for an old powder hound.

'It was what I needed. Three hundred and fifty miles of trail with killer hikes. A geyser basin, a lake, a summit with a three-sixty view of Mount Sherman. Wilderness is good, it gives me perspective. I get small again, the ego deflates.'

He sipped his coffee.

'I realized there would be no getting over losing her. What I had to do was learn a healthy way to live with it. Did God remove Paul's thorn? Not that we know. But even with the physical exertion and the altitude,

I didn't sleep well. Every day, every night was a struggle. I was in pretty constant prayer, trying to figure it out, trying to reconcile something that maybe couldn't be reconciled.

'Three weeks in, I met a man on the trail.

'He didn't look like any hiker I'd ever seen. Let's say haggard, underweight. Forty, maybe fifty. I noticed he was wearing the wrong shoes for hiking. He seemed to come out of nowhere.

'He asked if I had a match. He was holding a cigarette; I noticed his hand was shaking. It was like running into somebody on a dicey urban back street. I didn't have a match and didn't want to be bothered; I was in a cocoon of questioning and dialogue. I told him I didn't have a match and walked on.

'He came after me. Here's what he said: What can I do to know God?

'*Do you have a match, what can I do to know God?*—at eleven thousand feet in the Rockies?

'I wasn't wearing a collar, so why did he ask me that? Was he standing there asking this of anyone who came along? I didn't want this conversation. I felt like, this is my time, I just lost the love of my life, *please*.

'I walked on and he followed me.

'Hey,' he said. 'You need to tell me.'

'I picked up speed, almost a jog, and when I looked around, he was standing there, looking after me. Something didn't feel right about running out on him. But it didn't feel right to join his conversation, either. The whole incident bothered me for miles; I brought it back to the cabin with me. How would I have answered him? Maybe I'd see him again.

'The next morning at the same place, I ran into a mountain rescue team and a few hikers. They were carrying him up on a litter. The ledge he fell to was easily a hundred-foot drop from the trail. One of the hikers said it looked like a suicide.'

Father Brad put his elbows on his knees, stared at the floor for a long moment, then sat up.

'The bitterest irony. A man walks up to a priest and asks how to know God and the priest runs away. It haunts me. I long ago made my peace with losing Katie, but not with this, Father. Not with this.'

'How would you have answered him?'

'Maybe we could have sat down in the grass together. Snow was melting then, the green was coming on. We could have looked at Mount Sherman and maybe shared something of its vast serenity, and then talked.

'I would have told him that God was in love with him, that he made us for himself. As hard as that is to imagine, the power of it speaks to people, gives a certain comfort. I would have said that God isn't just up there, he's down here with us, knowing the beating of our hearts. I would have told him that governing truth, the bottom line—that what we must do is empty ourselves, surrender everything, asking his guidance in our lives.

'As far as I could tell, Mount Sherman had no ego, no desire to create its own destiny. It was surrendered, as all of nature is surrendered. The wilderness gives us that example continually.

'I believe there's somebody like him in every pew—asking a simple question, needing a simple answer. I've preached to him for years now. Though I can't remember his face, I imagine him sitting out there, waiting to hear. I've tried; I've really tried to make up for what I failed to do.'

He handed a box of tissues to the younger cleric.

'The guilt and shame you feel—do you allow it to serve as your punishment? Maybe you think you don't deserve to let it go. Judgment is God's job, though we try all the time to make that job our own.

'He may not remove the thorn, but we know he wants you to find a healthy way to live with this. And though we can't know what he wrought from it, I'm confident that he has wrought good. Much good. That's his nature.

'I'll say what you might have said to the man on the trail. God is in love with you, brother. He made you for himself. Trust that he has used and is using that episode in your life for good.'

He could hear voices outside the door. Mamie Houser talking to Otis about a pound of bacon gone wrong. Life. It was all about eleven thousand feet of altitude in the Rockies and bacon gone wrong. Who can know the winsome ways of God?

He glanced up from restocking sardines and saw Otis cleaning the glass of the butcher case. Otis rarely had to be asked to do something; he was on the lookout for a need before it actually became one. Small of stature, balding, rimless specs, always a shy but pleasant attitude. They still make them like Otis, he thought, but few and far between.

And Lisa. Over by the bread rack, chatting up Lance Poovey, who was hard-pressed to find anyone willing to chat him up. She took care of people, was genuinely interested in them.

He had praised her for this. 'Oh, gosh, I can't take no credit, it's how all ten of us was raised.'

If push came to shove, and he hated to even think about it, Otis, Lisa, and Marcie could run the place with part-time help. Otis had a head for economy, was good with the distributors and at tying up loose ends—he could be the manager. Managers didn't have to be drill sergeants; they could be nice guys with rimless specs.

At Avis Packard's house, Johnsie Pope lifted the December calendar page and hooked it on the nail.

The secret of success in life is to eat what you like
and let the food fight it out inside.
—MARK TWAIN

She had tried to get Avis to lie down after lunch an' take a nap, which was doctor's orders. But no, he dragged hisself out of th' chair an' dressed and out the door he went.

'I cain't lay up sick th' rest of my days,' he said, 'I have a store to run.'

She sighed. He was weak as pond water an' still wobbly on his legs, but what could she do? She was not the boss of Avis Packard, just what you call th' caregiver who rode up th' mountain of a mornin' with Hank who had a paint job in Wesley, then went home of an evenin' feelin' like she'd done somethin' that made a difference.

She went to the kitchen and warshed th' lunch dishes and checked his meds box and set Lois Burton's casserole out to thaw—mac an' cheese with bacon—which would go in th' oven right before she left.

As cheese was bindin', he would need somethin' green, so she tossed together a little romaine with a sliced carrot an' diced up some sweet pepper an' covered th' bowl an' set it in th' fridge. All he'd have to do is add dressin'.

Wouldn't she be happy to set home tonight an' think of Avis up here havin' hisself a good dinner and growin' strong? He had tried to pay her for settin' with him, but she wouldn't take it, nossir. An' he'd tried to run her off, too, but she wadn't goin'.

Hank had done a mighty job with this place. Took down two trees— 'Root rot,' he said. 'They was comin' down theirself before long'—cleaned th' gutters an' painted th' outside of th' house. And Pedro an' María, they'd cleaned an' scrubbed an' warshed curtains an' changed bedsheets an' she didn't know what all, an' her own husband, bless 'is heart, had mowed an' raked an' pruned th' bushes.

Everybody's job was done but hers, as th' doc said somebody needed to watch Avis like a hawk. She was good at doin' that an' knew for a fact he wadn't smokin'. Nossir, not one butt did she find an' not one whiff of smoke did she smell. Whether he was right in th' head she couldn't say, but he had called out somethin' durin' his naptime once or twice. Sounded like chunky, so she went over to th' store an' got him some peanut butter, which was good protein, an' put it on crackers.

Write down what you can, said the doc, and remind him to check his sputum for blood.

Terrified of cursive since childhood, she recorded daily all pertinent information in block letters. DEC. 1 HE ET SUPPER LAST NITE BUT PICKED AT HIS LUNCH TODAY. COFFIN NOT AS BAD. HANDS SHAKEY.

JOHNSIE

At three o'clock, she heard a commotion at the front door and went out to the hall.

Otis was on one side of Avis an' Father Tim on th' other, keepin' Avis on his feet. They got him to 'is bedroom and set him on the bed an' she squatted down an' unlaced his shoes an' took 'em off.

'His ankles is swelled,' she said. An' he groaned an' laid back on th' pillow, his face th' color of dishrags.

Three words is all Father Tim said. 'Rest, Avis. *Rest!*'

'Th' preacher's right,' said Otis. 'It's th' only way you gon' get better.'

P. S. HE COME HOME NEAR DEAD AFTER GOIN TO HIS STORE

Two big things was happenin' today.

The first big thing was, him an' Hope and Sister Louise had decorated th' Fraser fir in th' upstairs window of his apartment at Happy Endings; it was a nine-footer. They had started at ten-thirty an' went off an' on all day till four o'clock, they was that many things to hang on th' branches plus untangle th' lights. It has been him an' Hope on th' ladder, as Sister Louise had a bad ankle.

Hope an' Scott, they could have rented out his two rooms over th' bookstore with a toilet an' hot plate, but nossir, they give it to him for livin' there to look after th' place, help out in th' store, an' keep things clean as a whistle. It was also his job to work on th' furnace when it went to bangin' an' scarin' th' customers.

At five o'clock on th' dot, he stuck his head around th' tree an' looked out th' window an' seen Hope an' Scott an' Grace an' Sister Louise an' a bunch of other people all lookin' up an' wavin'. Then he throwed th' switch, so to speak, an' it was official.

The room exploded with light. Ribbons of color danced on th' walls an' ceilin'. There was th' sound of cheers across th' street.

He let out his breath, stunned by it all. That right there was th' most excitement he'd had since th' Christmas he played Saint Nick.

Th' other big thing was—right after supper, he was startin' his last picture book before he changed over to chapter books. It was by his favorite picture book author, who had passed. He hoped he wouldn't be causin' him to roll over in his grave because of not readin' picture books anymore.

L ew Boyd was nervous.

He was about to drop a huge wad on a Class A Sportscoach Cross Country 405FK. Used, of course, if that was any consolation. And he'd have to move fast, because this little number was mint condition and priced to sell.

When you figure that he'd never been much of anywhere, takin' this rig to Missouri would be a big deal. If somebody had said he'd sell his business in two weeks an' be goin' to Missouri in a RV, he would have laughed in their face. Until he married Earlene, he had no idea where Missouri was. And then he learned that even the people who live there couldn't pronounce it—some sayin' Missour*ah* an' some sayin' Missour*ee*.

But his wife had kin in Hannibal, and given the fact that kin could be pretty scarce in today's world, they were goin'. They would see th' fence Tom Sawyer made his buddies paint, visit th' Mark Twain cave, and go on a riverboat.

Though they couldn't make the trip till springtime, they had started a list of what to take. Earlene wanted to impress her relatives and carry a Valley beef roast the size of a South Carolina watermelon. As for hisself, he would make sure he loaded up with a crate of Cheerwine, which maybe they couldn't find in Missourah or Missouree, whichever.

You want to ride down and see th' bookstore tree?" said J.C.

He was in his skivvies because as usual, she had th' heat cranked up to sixty-eight.

'Not really,' said Adele. 'Th' lights'll still be on in th' mornin' when I check in.'

She was cleaning her Sig Sauer in the bedroom where the *Wheel* was giving th' clue of 'A Thing,' but he noticed she wasn't watching. Why people cleaned a gun they never used was totally beyond him. All th' MPD guys did it; it was regulation. Just in case, they said.

'They stung you with th' early shift?'

Head down, cleanin' her equipment, lookin' like she lost her best friend.

Th' honeymoon was over. Again. He had romanced her with a forty-two-inch screen, then his top-of-the-line grill, a strategy that had lasted about, what? Three, maybe four weeks? All had been rosy, hunky-dory, life was good, and now look. What did he have to do to stay on her A-list? Tonight, ravioli stuffed with rosemary an' Gouda, an' no, not from scratch, he was not th' Barefoot Countess or whatever, but still—with a nice salad an' a *bun*.

Coot took the lid off the candy jar by his chair, eyed the contents, and picked out his one piece for th' evenin'. He peeled back th' red wrapper. Chocolate! His lucky day!

He let it melt in his mouth while he looked at th' lights.

Then he commenced to read out loud, as th' sound of his own voice was comp'ny.

'How th' Grinch Stole Christmas!'

'By Dr. Seuss.'

Then he turned to th' first page, set back, cleared his throat, and kep' goin'.

It didn't take hardly a minute for him to get mad at th' Grinch for hatin' Christmas. An' nobody even knowed a good reason why!

'That's 'cause they *ain't* a good reason!' he shouted to his book.

Grace had said, 'You will not like it at first. You must keep reading and then you will like it.'

Him an' his mama had been crazy about Christmas, though they never had a tree but one time. They got their fill of Christmas trees on TV. Right after Halloween, you turned on th' TV and there was Christmas trees and Santy Clauses pilin' up. They seen colored lights and white lights, an' heard carols an' sleigh bells an' whatnot, 'til by th' time Christmas come around, they was both wore out.

'We don't need no Christmas tree,' his mama said. 'All a tree does is catch f'ar an' burn th' house down.' She had told him this since he was little, and never had he seen anybody's house burn down at Christmas. It was more like Easter when their neighbor's house caught f'ar, but they put it out an' kep' on livin' there.

As he read, the tree in the window shone its many-colored lights onto the street. It was as tall as the big window, which reached nearly to the ceiling, and dressed with forty-two strings of lights and more than two hundred ornaments and seven boxes of gold tinsel, and small candles that winked and glimmered like the real thing.

There had never been an official town tree. Instead, what was generally called 'the war monument' was decorated with lights. That was a very good thing and the council was keen to keep it that way. But as anyone would tell you, 'the bookstore tree' was a town favorite. All year long, the big upstairs window was as blank as paper, and then on the night of December first, the blank became a radiance of color and light that illuminated the street and reflected on the hoods of cars and when it rained, turned puddles into patches of crimson and sapphire, amber and emerald.

'Awesome!' was Shirlene Cunningham's take on the tree.

'Thrilling!' said Dr. Harper, recently returned from South Sudan.

Lois Burton admitted that it made her cry, but not sob or anything, when the lights came on.

From where he sat, he could look up an' see th' tree about three yards from his sock feet. An' people on the street passin' by, they could look up an' see th' tree! He felt the intimacy of this shared experience in a way he couldn't put into words.

He shook his head, read on. Cars passed. Rain whispered at th' windowpanes.

In a little bit, he come to th' part where th' Grinch got a *idea!* Th' book called it a wonderful, AWFUL idea!

He slammed the book shut and laid it on the table next to his chair and set th' candy jar on top. That was a close call; he had nearabout let hisself read what th' wonderful, awful idea was. He did not like to do what you call *gobble* a book, he would read that part tomorrow night. Yessir, he would make his last picture book *last.*

Father Tim told him th' other day that everybody needed three things:

Somebody to love—he had Grace and her mama an' daddy an' Sister Louise an' all manner of people who come in th' bookstore.

Somethin' to do—look at th' job he had, livin' up here like he was ol' Croesus hisself.

An' somethin' to look forward to—as for that part, he had solved it by always, always keepin' a good book underneath his candy jar.

SATURDAY, DECEMBER 5

She had her coffee, he had his tea; they had their Advent reading.

Although the Lord gives you the bread of adversity and the water of affliction, your teachers will be hidden no more; with your own eyes you will see them. Whether you turn to the right or to the left, your ears will hear a voice behind you saying, 'This is the way; walk you in it.'

G race stopped by the office of her dad, the chaplain, to give him a hug and a cookie from home.

'You are amazing,' said her dad for the hundredth time. She smiled big to show off where she had lost a tooth three days ago.

Then she took the elevator, which opened next to room 101.

She looked in and saw that Miss Louella's eyes were closed, but she wasn't snoring.

'If she's sleeping,' said a nurse, 'wake her easy.'

Grace went to the blue recliner and leaned close to Miss Louella's ear. She liked Miss Louella's safe, happy smell of hand lotion and face powder. She was going to say I'm here, Miss Louella, but what she really wanted to say was I'm here, Grandma. When she opened her mouth, out came the strangest thing:

'I'm here, Miss Grandma!'

She could have fainted from embarrassment. Miss Louella did not know she had been secretly adopted as her grandma. What if Miss Louella did not want to be her grandma?

Miss Louella opened her eyes and looked at her and smiled the biggest smile she ever saw.

'What you say?'

Her heart pounded. 'I said I'm here, Miss Grandma.'

Louella laughed. When she laughed, her body shook all over. 'Say it again, honey!'

'I'm here, Miss Grandma!' Oh, her face was burning hot, but she said it big this time because of the happy laugh it got.

'From this day on, that gon' be my favorite name fo' myself! Miss Grandma!' Louella laughed some more and held out her hand and drew Grace close. 'I be yo' grandma an' you be my baby!'

Grace did not want to be a baby; she was not a baby at all. But it would be okay to be Miss Grandma's baby, it would be okay. She shivered a little with a certain happiness.

'You loss a tooth!'

'Yes, ma'am.'

'I give you a dime fo' you leave. You here to write my story down?'

'I have one whole hour, then I have to go to the Christmas parade.'

'I hope you bring me some candy if you catch any.'

'Yes, ma'am, I will.'

'Sit on th' stool, then. What us gon' talk about?'

'Everything, Mama said.'

'Everything?' Louella gave Grace a look. 'You gon' take notes?'

'I don't know how to take notes. But I will listen really hard.'

'Miss Sadie, when she was talkin' on th' phone to her money man, she take notes. She know 'xactly what he's sayin', uh-huh.'

'I tried at home and can't write as fast as people talk, but I have a great memory, I promise. My dad says so.'

'Where we gon' start?'

'I think you just start anywhere? And things work out?' She posed this as a question because she honestly did not know.

Louella rearranged the knit shawl over her knees and leaned back in the recliner.

Grace caught her breath. A story was like opening a door; you never knew what you would find on the other side.

'My mama was China Mae an' my daddy, he was Soot. Soot Tobin. Black as soot, is how he got his name. He lived in Atlanta, Georgia, and worked in Mitford every summer.'

Louella closed her eyes, as if she was fixing to tell the story to herself.

'I never knew my daddy, but oh, how I wish I did. They say he wore a long black coat an' bow tie an' white gloves, to serve dinner at th' Boxwood House. You too young to know that Boxwood House used t' stan' down where th' Baptists is.

'They say my daddy was a han'some man. He could drive a Packard car, mos' any thing wit' wheels, even a bicycle. He had his own bicycle with a basket on it for food shoppin'. They say he come down Main jus' a-flyin', with his coattails standin' out behin'. He could cook, speak words in French, fix a car motor, an' preach at th' colored church. My daddy stuttered pretty bad, so his sermons ran long. But they say it was worth whatever it took, as he preached with a mighty conviction. Some say he was anointed.

'They had a little church back then jus' for colored, it wadn't big as this room. Ten colored come up th' mountain in th' summer with their white families, so it was enough people fo' a church. My daddy's white family built it down yonder where th' Methodists is now. They was good people, name of Thompson, had a daughter Lureen. When her mama an' daddy passed, she gave my daddy their Packard car, free an' clear. He drove it to Atlanta, Georgia, an' never came back. It was a sad thing how they passed.'

'How did they?' She did not like to say the words *pass* and *die*.

'Miss Lureen's mama and daddy fell off a rock an' was killed outright. Th' rock was tall as a chimbley, you had to climb a real high bank on one side to git out on it. It had a flat place on top over a gorge that went halfway to China. I seen that rock many times. They was havin' a picnic up there an' maybe not payin' attention. But some say they held hands an' jumped.'

'Jumped?'

Grace's eyes behind her round glasses was big as silver dollars. Louella realized there were things she could not tell this child—things too dark and heavy for a child to carry.

'That was just talk, honey, Lord Jesus, I shouldn't said it. Those good people didn't jump a'tall, it was a accident. Nossir. They was happy people.'

Grace breathed out.

'My little mama—she was a pretty woman an' a good woman, everybody say that. Miss Sadie's mama say she was slow in her mind, like a child. My mama was my bes' friend next to Sadie.'

A nurse peered in, waved to Grace. 'Miss Louella, time for your pain meds.'

'Go on away,' said Louella. 'I got comp'ny now. Young Grace be my meds.'

Grace sat up taller on the stool.

'I was jus' a baby when I got another kind of mama. She wadn't but fo' years older than me.'

Grace scooted to the edge of the stool. This was the part she liked.

'She was th' onliest child of th' white folks my mama worked fo'. Sadie Baxter took me on as her own, yes she did, said I was her baby sister.'

Louella was smiling with her eyes closed. 'She gave me a bath in a tub big enough for a Packard car, cornrowed my hair, let me play with her beautiful dolls. Oh, law, her dolls were th' prettiest things I ever seen. I said I want to be like this doll whose name was Annie. Sadie say you want to be like this doll, we got to straighten yo' hair. You never seen such a mess! Used vinegar an' *lard*. Lord help us, I was ruint.

'I cried, yes I did, jus' bawled. I said I ain't gon' be yo' baby sister no more ag'in!'

Louella and Grace laughing.

'Then Sadie, she cried, too. She say, oh, please, I won't do it no more, you cain't jus' up an' quit bein' my sister, that's ag'in th' law!

'So I say okay, an' we went off an' cooked us a supper of acorns and clover tops in our little playhouse in th' orchard. Her daddy had Mister Ned make us a playhouse with a chimbley on th' side an' what they call a Dutch door.'

'Tell about the red wagon!'

'Th' red wagon got a happy story an' a sad story, both. Which you want?'

'Both!' said Grace.

Louella's eyes closed again. She let out a long breath.

'Not many colored was in these hills back then. Colored don' generally like mountains. Too cold. Too hid back. Hard to earn a livin'. No, you got to go to a town where th' jobs is. So colored was rare in Mitford back in th' day, 'cept for them who come up in th' summer.

'October after th' leaves turned, th' white fam'lies an' their help went back where they come from an' I was th' only dark skin on this mountain. Some people here was bad to call me by a ugly name. Start with a n. You know it, honey?'

She knew the bad word people used to say. Somebody said it in her class just last week and got sent home. She thought being sent home was a treat; the person should have been sent to the principal or made to eat worms.

'You can use that word to let people know how it was back then. Ain't nothin' wrong with th' word itself, it come off of th' word *negro*, is all, which is Spanish fo' black. It's a ugly word 'cause of the mean spirit behind it. It was said all th' time to me fo' I moved to be with my grandma in Atlanta. You can let people see how it was back then.'

Grace didn't know how she could possibly write all this down. She did not know it would be so much. But Miss Grandma had lived a long time, which was why it was so much.

She would have to do what they talked about in her favorite magazine, *Stone Soup*. She would have to *edit*.

I ain't never played Santy,' Coot said to Hamp Floyd.
    'Nothin' to it. Ride on th' truck, throw out th' candy, wave to everybody. Piece of cake.'

The phone call from th' chief had come early this morning at th' bookstore. He'd been amazed that somebody was callin' him on th' phone, which nobody ever did. He had walked down to the station, not knowin' what was goin' on.

'We'll be ridin' you on th' cover of th' hose bed behind th' cab. We got a Santy chair we rig on th' cover every year. That sets you up pretty high, so people can see you comin'.'

'How about you play Santy?' he asked the chief.

'I'm too low to th' ground for that suit. It's perfect for you, an' you're perfect for th' part. Me an' th' wife saw you play Saint Nick down at th' bookstore one year. You nailed it.'

Coot nodded, sick with fear.

'Clovis did a lot of research on Santy Claus. Said Saint Nick was th' start of Santy, sack an' all. You're in.'

The fire chief said this as if it was law. End of discussion.

'Here's what you do,' said Hamp. 'Say *Ho ho ho* and throw candy. Simple. A baby could do it. Try sayin' it. Loud.'

'Ho ho ho,' said Coot.

'No, no. LOUD!'

'HO HO HO!'

'Good. Real good. There's no pay in this, it's volunteer, okay? As in *volunteer* fire department.'

Coot went to the back room where the firemen were suiting up. He carried the red garb, which had been sent over by Clovis's oldest boy.

A fireman slapped him on the back, whop! 'Get y'r red on, Buddy. We're rollin' out of here in twenty minutes.'

He went into a stall and took off most of his clothes but kept on his *I'd Rather Be in Mitford* T-shirt and his drawers and socks and lace-ups. It was freezin' in here.

'Here's your sack of candy.' The chief stuck his head into the stall and handed off a heavy burlap sack. 'Compliments of th' mayor's office. Bring it back empty, an' wear your britches under your Santy suit. You'll thank me.'

He pulled his britches back on. And his undershirt an' sweater, while he was at it, an' his jacket. Santy would look extra fat.

The chief stuck his head in again. 'Every once in a while, touch your finger to th' side of your nose. Like this.' The chief touched his finger to the side of his nose.

'Why?' said Coot.

'Beats me, it's somethin' Clovis liked to do.'

The costume smelled like popcorn or maybe chili dogs. And the boots were not real, they were thin as a paper bag. His hands was shakin' as he pulled 'em on over his lace-ups.

He was buttonin' the fur-trimmed jacket when somehow the fog started liftin' inside of his head. He could picture Santy settin' up on th' yellow fire truck—an' it was him! *Him*, Coot Hendrick, the great-great-great-great-great-grandson of th' man who rode up th' mountain with his English bride settin' behind him on his horse, and founded th' town of Mitford.

The notion of all this struck him so profoundly that he sat for a moment on the chair in the stall and whispered what Father Tim told him to say when he felt grateful but couldn't find words.

'Jesus.'

Town was packed, cars bumper to bumper, and the great maw at Main and Wisteria was commemorated only by a fresh patch of asphalt.

Alleluias rang from the town speaker system; store windows advertised a sale, a special promo, or the traditional free cider and cookies for parade day.

STEP IN AND WARM UP, read the hand-printed sign on the door of the Woolen Shop. No promises for anything more than seventy-two degrees Fahrenheit.

FREE CIDER AND COOKIES was Sweet Stuff's marketing ploy.

HOT CIDER AND COOKIES was the deal at Dora Pugh's hardware.

CIDER, COOKIES, AND A JOKE, read the sign at Village Shoes. 'It's a one-up,' said Abe.

At the Local, Hank and his family were seated to the right of the sign on the roof, waving to anybody who would look their way. Otis had warned Hank that it would be a really big insurance problem if anybody fell off. 'I hope you'll remember that,' he said, giving Hank a look. He did not want a tragedy occurring on his watch.

Otis was running things today. Th' preacher hadn't been much account since he came in at seven-thirty; he was excited as a kid. 'Ants in his pants,' said Lisa.

'We got you covered, Father.' Otis was proud to say it.

'You go on with your family,' said Lisa.

Go on with your family. Yes! He grabbed his jacket off the coatrack. He was out of there.

J ake Tulley smiled the smile reserved for the customer rollin' out of his showroom in a brand-new ride, but Jake Tulley did not like the idea of hitching his Escalade ESV to something with the square footage of a cattle car. This was a deal for a Dodge Ram, not a Cadillac.

'Only for you, Father,' he told the priest. 'Only for you.'

'You're the best, Jake!' He had to shout over the hubbub. 'The best!'

The Baptist parking lot was a spasm of kids, stressed-out parents, dogs in costume, crazed volunteers, tricycles, MPD, two llamas, and tourists who had stumbled on the circus at the assembly site.

'Stand back!' hollered Hamp Floyd. 'Get over behind th' line yonder. If you're not in this parade, stand back!'

Captain Hogan wheeled her patrol car into the lot and onto the grass. 'Cars parked every whichaway,' she told Hamp. 'Have you seen what a mess it is out there?' Out there was the zoo, the anarchy, the craven horde. 'Why do tourists think they can park on our grass when they'd never park on their own grass? Answer me that.'

He was just a fire chief, he could not answer that.

'Onboard!' yelled Hamp. 'All Cunnin'hams on board and make it snappy. Number thirty-two! Cunnin'ham! Number thirty-two, onboard!'

He had to dispatch number thirty-two before he could deal with the rest of the entries, as thirty-two would take forever to load. 'Line up, thirty-two! Line up, for crap's sake.'

Lord knows he had a fire engine to roll out of here, a pep talk for Santy in case it was needed, and this entire wacko zoo to wrangle. The good news was, last night's rain had cleared out, and there were no weather worries for today, zero—snow was comin' later, on the eleventh. Though he'd given up predicting snowfall dates and inches—he had bombed five years in a row—he could feel this one in his bones.

A llama sidled over, sniffed his hair. 'Whoa! Whose llama is this? Get away, dadgummit!' A llama had spit on him one time, which would be th' last time.

Though proud of his ability to project vocally, he used his bullhorn. 'WHOSE LLAMA IS THIS? Don't do that again, buster! SOMEBODY COME GET THIS LLAMA!'

He helped Esther up the makeshift steps.

'This is a creation of great proportion!' he said.

'This, Father, is a float. What we have here is a *float*! The first float ever to ride in a Mitford Christmas parade!'

And up went the jubilant queen, trailed by what she occasionally called her 'begats.' Moving along the jostling line behind were a slew of Cunningham family granddaughters and in-laws, all wiping noses, buttoning jackets, threatening the troops.

Puny's twins were starched, ironed, and receiving orders. 'Do not stand up, you hear me? These side rails are plastic. You could fall off this thing an' be squashed flat. If I see a single one of you standin' up . . . '

The lead band had bused in from Wesley and was tuning their instruments. There went the tuba.

'She'll never get elected,' said Hamp. 'Half the people here don't know who she is.'

'I think she just likes to be remembered, which is something we all hope to be, wouldn't you say? Let her have her day, and many more, if that's what it takes.' He was a little sentimental at the moment, though only yesterday he made an early New Year's resolution, which was to steer clear of Esther Cunningham for all eternity. As the sap who had hunted down and engineered this entire rig, including the rug, he could not deal with another bid for reelection.

'What's her platform this time?'

'Controlling growth, she says.'

'Ain't no way to do that,' said Hamp. 'Fat lady's done sung.'

And there went the trombone and the trumpet and the drum line with its raspy snares and throaty tenors.

I can see the world! I'm tall as the world!'

Riding on his dad's shoulders was his favorite thing. He bounced up and down and waved at the clown on stilts, who was tall like him. The clown waved back.

'Hey, dude, hold it down up there.'

'Th' clown waved back, Dad!'

'Wavin' back is good,' said Dooley.

He loved riding his boy on his shoulders, the feel of Jack's strong, sturdy legs tight around his neck. Since he was a kid, he loved the Christmas parade, too, and who ever thought he'd be watching it with his little guy and Lace? He looked at her and silently formed with his lips the two words she liked to be told, and she formed three words for him and smiled and took his hand.

'There's another band comin'!' said Jack.

He was the lookout tower, the one who could see what nobody else could see except maybe the clown on stilts. This would make three bands even if it was just a lots of kids smashing things together and blowing horns. It was the Mitford school band and the music was 'Rudolph the Red-Nosed Reindeer,' which he knew all the words to.

He bounced some more and sang the words as loud as he could. 'An' if you ever saw it, you would even say it GLOWS . . . '

. . .

U nrestrained cheers as an enormous entity hove into view along the parade route.

'Well, I'll be,' said Harold Mincer, who was using his army field glasses. 'There's th' old mayor. I thought she was dead.'

'Old mayors never die,' said his wife, Dannye Lee.

'How do that many young'uns ride a float an' not break it down?' said Harold.

'It's somethin' to do with th' suspension system,' said Dannye Lee.

All these years, Harold had believed everything Dannye Lee Mincer said. He had a scientific turn of mind, though he had not cultivated it.

'How does a Cadillac haul that much freight?'

'It's a big vehicle,' said his wife, done with the subject.

The SUV passed by, slow as molasses. The driver waved, everybody was waving. Somebody recognized Jake Tulley, though it appeared he'd had his teeth whitened and was now doing a comb-over.

On the flatbed trailer he was pulling, an artificial tree trimmed with strings of popcorn and a star stood by a cardboard chimney and mantel hung with stockings shuddering in a light breeze.

On a vast hooked rug, courtesy of Wesley Floor Coverings, sat twenty-seven Cunningham great-grandchildren of various ages, waving madly. And there was Herself enthroned in an armchair, one hand tossing something to the masses, the other waving in concert with the begats. Ray stood by the throne, proudly enjoying fifteen minutes of Warhol's allotted fame, and deserving more.

Grace Murphy dodged through the crowd. 'Me! Me!' she cried, walking fast beside the float. 'It's for my *grandma!*'

The old woman in the wing chair reached over the side rail. 'Hold out both hands!' Esther yelled above the tuba, and Grace did. It was a plastic bag with lots of chocolate Kisses! A whole bag!

'Tell your grandma to vote for Esther!' shouted Ray.

Though the ensuing tricycle fleet—with a dozen riders dressed as

reindeer—had many supporters in the crowd, some did not want to see
the float vanish. They ran after it, waving and scooping up candy and
reading the huge banner that floated from the bumper like a bridal train.

HAVE A GREAT GRAND CHRISTMAS!
ESTHER CUNNINGHAM AND FAMILY

Omer Cunningham noted that everybody seemed glad to be alive.

He threw up a hand and waved at all the kids sittin' around th' cardboard fireplace, and at his big brother, Ray, bless his heart, and his sister-
in-law, the former mayor, whom he once took for a spin in his tail-dragger.

He had no idea what to get his wife, Shirlene, for Christmas. She was
crazy about caftans, but he would not go near buyin' a caftan, online or
otherwise. She liked palm trees, which she had painted and hung
throughout the house he had lived in as a bachelor. It was a novel thing
to look at palm trees indoors and step out and see his four acres of Fraser
firs, which he could finally cut and sell next year. But he liked that
about Shirlene, who had brought something fresh and full of beans into
the life of a crazy old Nam vet.

Father Tim threw up his hand to Doc Wilson, who was out in shorts,
a sweatshirt, and a bandanna, running the parade line.

Wilson pulled up to him, panting, clapped him on the shoulder.

'What's up with you, Father? Haven't seen you filling that prescription I gave you. Come on. A measly five miles three times a week?'

'I'll be back,' he said. 'Have a minute to tell me about Avis?'

'Don't know what to say. He's slow on the uptake, but there is uptake. The problem is severe depression. The Local has been his passion
all these years. Now there's no passion for anything. I don't know where
this is going, but I'm workin' on it. Gotta catch up with Esther, I hear
she's throwin' th' good stuff. Okay, Father, see you out here, no excuses.'

He and countless others had prayed, were praying. Why did he feel
that somehow it was up to him? He had been riddled with this mistaken
notion all his life. Avis was up to God; Avis was up to Wilson.

• • •

Comin' out of th' Baptist lot, they made a left turn an' there went th' horn, it nearly blowed him off th' truck.

He throwed candy an' hollered. 'Ho ho ho, Merry Christmas!' It was his first time hollerin' and it come out in a squawk.

'Ramp it up, Santy!' said one of the guys on th' tailboard.

The yellow truck made a left on Main, and boy howdy, they was lined up like ants on both sides, hollerin' to beat th' band.

'HO HO HO HO!' he said. 'MERRY CHRISTMAS!'

He felt the cold on his face and the itch of the beard and the deep hum of the engine beneath. They was passin' the bookstore and there was Hope an' Sister Louise and a good many customers, lookin' happy as pigs in mud. An' up ahead was a little young'un settin' on his daddy's shoulders, near about as high as Santy hisself, an' they went to wavin' at each other.

He felt the tears on his cheeks, hot against the cold, and went to laughin' an' touchin' th' side of his nose all at th' same time an' sayin' HO HO HO HO, MERRY CHRISTMAS so they could hear it in Franklin, Tennessee, where his granpaw had been born at.

He heard th' band a-playin' an' th' horn a-blowin' an' he dug into his sack an' lifted his hand an' th' candy rose up an' scattered among th' crowd like a shower of rain.

'Santy, Santy, bring me a fire engine big as yours!'

'Could I have a doll with real hair, please, please?'

If Dr. Seuss was to see him now, he would write a book.

Avis lay on top of the covers.

It was cold and he was shivering, but he didn't want to get up and mess with the thermostat, or put on his sleep gear, which was his *I'd Rather Be in Mitford* T-shirt and a pair of long drawers.

He was tired of gettin' up. Get up, lay down, get up, lay down, it was a whole lifetime of th' same business. Maybe he would freeze and Johnsie would find him on Monday, a human Popsicle layin' curled up in a ball.

He would hate to do that to Johnsie. Or even Otis and Lisa. But Father Tim, he was a whole other deal. If Father Tim came to check on him this afternoon and found his remains, fine. He was th' type who could handle findin' a man dead as a doorknob.

Love came down at Christmas,
love all lovely, Love divine;
love was born at Christmas,
star and angels . . .

Th' music circled in his head all day and half the night. He didn't know how he could make it through th' trumpets an' people singin' high notes. He had covered up his head a while ago to keep out th' parade music, faint as it was.

His teeth chattered.

'We're prayin' for you,' people told him. They wrote it in cards, left messages on his phone.

'Save your breath,' he wanted to say. Oh, he was a mean sucker. He never knew he had a mean bone in his body, but he knew it now. He was a dead man forced to live and breathe and try to get well whether he wanted to or not.

H e had thanked Jake Tulley for a fare-the-well and was on his way home to help Cynthia with dinner when he met Ray Cunningham in Sweet Stuff. Where grans and great-grans were concerned, there was usually a stop by Sweet Stuff.

Ray was positively beaming.

'Oh, Father, there you are!' Ray shook his hand, then grabbed it and shook it again. 'When I think of all you've done for us . . . the happiness of it . . . you are a saint. A saint!'

'You've got the wrong man, Ray. You're the saint.'

Hamp Floyd, who was leaving with a bag of chocolate donuts and a relieved grin, overheard this remark.

'Takes one to know one, don't it, boys?'

18

Meadowgate Farm was shaped on the county plat like a snow shovel with a T handle.

Occupying the handle was a fenced plot known as the North Strip. Though the strip lay due south on Meadowgate property, it was thus named in 1802 as the north tip of eight hundred acres then owned by a Scotsman.

In the shaft were the century-old farmhouse, the clinic with attached dog run, a corncrib cobbled together around the turn of the last century, a woodshed, a holding pen, a chicken house with fenced run, and the caretaker's cottage, aka Willie's house.

The blade was comprised of a six-stall barn with hayloft, two run-in sheds, a three-acre pond, a bold creek flowing from a springhead in the west, and three pastures sown in fescue and clover mingled with rogue lespedeza. Of the precisely hundred acres, roughly twenty were comprised of a mature woodland. Oak, walnut, maple, dogwood, beech, cedar, the native eastern redbud—and no, they would never cut timber in there, not a single tree. And they'd leave most of the fallen trees for habitat and humus.

He liked ticking off the features of their land as he ran around the
pond with Charley.

He had gone soft. Too many second helpings at the table, too many
hours at the clinic. He had promised God he would do better and here
he was doing it. At dawn, in forty-four degrees.

Today was a celebratory run. Because the wait was over and the paperwork done. As of today, Jack was legally theirs and they were legally
his for all time. Hard to believe.

Kenny and Julie and the kids would pull in this afternoon, never
mind the forecast. Less than two inches, starting tonight, with a prediction of slush by Sunday morning. Kenny had Monday off and they would
drive back to Wilmington first thing. Around three, Sammy was flying
into Holding from Chicago and renting a car to drive up the mountain.
It was all coming together.

He looked up as he ran. Cirrostratus—snow clouds. They could use
the moisture. 'Thanks,' he said. The chill air received his breath, vapor-
ized it.

He slowed as he approached the cedar tree. It was eight feet tall and
self-decorated with blue fruit. They would ride over in the truck on Sunday and take the cedar home to the kitchen. The house rule was no
Christmas tree 'til after Name Day. These were two separate life events,
to be celebrated on their own merits.

He broke off a few needles, crushed them between his fingers and
inhaled the sharp, resinous scent. Over by the tree line—three does,
two fawns, ears up, alert.

Life was good.

'Thanks!' he said again, and ran on.

Harley and Willie had put everything in place—the bed, the ragtag
furniture she used when the studio was her bedroom, the pictures
drawn by kids she taught at the nonprofit.

Yesterday afternoon, they watched the long tube being loaded onto the truck; Dooley walked over from the clinic to see it happen.

She had worked extra hard and long and was nearly ten days ahead of schedule. It was the very best she could do, she could not have done more. She was exhilarated but exhausted; the whole thing imprinted in her bones.

Along the way, she had sent pictures from her phone. In her unstudied, even childlike way, Kim had liked everything, with only one request for change. 'Please paint in your old tractor,' she said. 'It's charming!'

'That wouldn't be my word for it,' said Dooley.

He was wearing his green scrubs; there were surgeries today.

'We're solvent,' she said. 'It sounds like something to open the drains, but we're solvent.' They were actually well beyond solvent, and that would go into Jack's education fund, too.

He put his arms around her, touched his forehead to hers. 'You're brilliant. I owe you.'

'Start paying now,' she said.

He kissed her. The truck drivers whistled.

'In installments.'

She laughed and he kissed her again.

She was in the kitchen, feeding the latest batch of kittens, when she saw the Mitford Blossoms truck pull up to the porch.

That Tommy, she thought. He was crazy wild about Beth . . .

She opened the door. A huge, fabulous arrangement! Tommy's pockets were obviously getting deeper with so many gigs.

'Miz Kavanagh?'

'That's me!'

The delivery woman held forth a profusion of roses, hydrangeas, green berries . . .

'For you.'

'For *me?*'

The woman grinned. 'That's what a lot of people say.'

She carried the flowers to the kitchen, found the envelope among the blush of roses. Her mom was wonderful to help them get ready for a houseful of company.

She slipped out the card.

Forever.
Dooley, Jack, and Choo-Choo.

She sank into Dooley's chair, feeling raw and somehow exposed, after the ardor—and the finality—of her work. And now flowers from her husband. She loved getting love in installments.

This wasn't a good day for a doctor's appointment, but they had recently done tests and wanted her to come in.

So she would run to Mitford and hurry home. Lily was here, everything was moving in the right direction. They would lose Jessie and Mary Ellen and Father Brad, thanks to the snow, and Puny had called to say Sissy and Sassy had colds and Timmy and Tommy were coughing, so that brought the number to maybe twenty-nine? She could not keep up with the numbers, but there might be leftovers, after all. She did not like the snow forecast, but so far everyone else was coming, and everyone had four-wheel drive.

She drove to Mitford, listening to Tommy's new CD.

She could not believe that Harley's teeth were missing again, which means he would be a toothless wonder for Name Day. It drove her crazy and she did not have the time or patience to deal with it. Leave it alone, she told herself. Think positive! Okay, she would go over her Christmas list for her parents.

They never expected her to give them a really nice gift, but this year would be different.

For her dad, a sander. He would be working on his projects again, making a bookcase for the Meadowgate living room, and shelves for the clinic. His old sander was 'going south,' he said.

For her mom, the Library of America editions of James Agee and Robert Frost and a three-volume set of Thornton Wilder.

For Dooley, warm running clothes and maybe she would join him on his run around the lake, so something for herself, too.

She had never given such wonderful gifts. She was intoxicated; sang along with Tommy, tried to control her miles per hour.

I n the hospital parking lot, she spotted a penny. Picked it up. Felt faint when she stood.

Not once had she let herself worry about the fact that something really strange was going on with her.

H er dad respected Dr. Wilson, yet where his family was concerned, he always wanted to know what Wilson said and did. *What about your lipids? Did he order tests? Why did he say that? I'll call Wilson in the morning.* If it was about her mom or Dooley or Jack or her, he always called Wilson in the morning.

She didn't text her parents that she was coming.

They were in the kitchen and she saw the happy look on their faces when she walked in. She tried to speak, but couldn't.

'Sit down,' her mom said.

'Tell us everything,' her dad said.

She told them everything. And they held her and wept.

S he ran over the brick edging when she turned out of their driveway. Her hands were trembling. She didn't remember the drive to Meadowgate, but came back to herself when she saw Dooley's truck parked at the co-op. She blew the horn, and four miles later saw smoke rising from their kitchen chimney and Charley and the farm dogs running out to meet her.

H ow many you need?' said Jake.
'Thirty-five,' said Dooley. 'Could get by with thirty if we have to.'

'Long as you get 'em back Sunday evenin' before dark. I'll meet you here at four on th' dot. Sunday-night football, plus I'm grillin' out for Sugar's kids an' grandkids.'

'I'll be here. And thanks. Thanks a lot.'

'Don't be throwin' any dances over at your place,' said Jake. 'I don't need th' competition.'

'No dances. Just a boy gettin' a new name. Besides, nobody could compete with you, buddy. You th' man out here in th' sticks.'

They had a laugh.

'Maybe you'll take a look at my cattle when you get a chance. Not much to look at, I'm down to a few steers.'

'Next week,' said Dooley. 'For sure.'

'Guess you heard the weather update.'

'What?'

'Could be a big one.'

'Better than two inches?'

'Maybe triple that.'

'We're wimps down here. Look what Buffalo, New York, just went through.'

Any time now, his sister would be leaving with Father Brad and the rest of the crew. Looks like the weather would give them what they wanted. And before it was too late, he hoped Jessie would get what she needed.

He was ready to pull onto the state road when he saw the green hatchback moving his way.

He choked up, hammered down on the horn. All those missing years, nobody knowing . . .

Kenny! Back on home ground. Complete with cousins.

The laughter until two A.M. didn't disturb the three farm dogs that slept in their corner in the kitchen. All three were going deaf, and one nearly blind. They had lived here all their lives and knew no other smells or comforts, table scraps or barn cats.

Every inch of the farm was their own, including the scent of cow patties baking in summer grass, the sheep smell still clinging to their old shade spot under the wild cherry trees, the urine and scat of bear, fox, bobcat, neighboring dogs. They were also imperial custodians of the woods, of trees smelling of velvet rubbed off by bucks, of lichen on fallen limbs, of doe beds in their brushy cover. Other creatures had marked this place ten thousand times over, but Meadowgate belonged to them.

There had been a concerted effort to move them to the new house at the end of the path in the woods. They were betrayed into climbing in Doc Owen's truck bed for a ride to the co-op, and were instead taken to the new place. They did not like it. The air in the house was sharp and acrid, the dirt had a strange odor, there was no barn with hay to lie in. They rolled in the decaying flesh of a crow and walked back along the path to Meadowgate.

Once more, the truck came and took them to the new place. And once more, they returned to Meadowgate, where they collapsed on the porch in the afternoon sun. The truck did not come again.

Indeed, the sense that their territory was theirs for all time was not greatly disturbed by the pup that came on board a while back. This, too, would pass. Live and let live.

Woven into the mélange of their dreams was the sound of laughter from the kitchen, and music. 'Gonna love you 'til the cows come home . . .'

Bone Meal, who in particular had enjoyed music and laughter, shivered a little in her sleep.

S ammy's plane had been delayed and he had arrived, ravenous, at ten P.M. Dooley had served him a mound of spaghetti and meatballs, the best he ever had, though he ate out frequently in Chicago, where he lived in a room with a shower down the hall. Chicago had a hot pool groove going on—you could make money, you could get somewhere, and he had his own home base for the first time.

He lay awake in one of the twin beds in the guest room, aware of the faint scent of lilac, maybe in the laundry soap used for the sheets. He had stolen a lilac bush when he lived with his dad; dug it up and moved it to their patch of red clay. He had planted it where no one would see it. It was a beautiful thing, not to be shamed by eyes that had no understanding of beauty. He was astonished that it survived and then actually bloomed. He had shown it only to Lon Birdie, who fought in Nam and raised orchids and lived in a gas station.

It was plain, this room, no frills, but it felt like home. It was like he'd been running a marathon and fallen across the finish line at Meadowgate, totally blanked, adrenaline shot.

He checked his watch, which he always wore to bed. Two-thirty. He would have to face his mother tomorrow, and he dreaded that to the point of being sick to his stomach. He would be ice; she would not get to him in any way, not by any route; he would see to that.

Even if he didn't make eye contact, he would feel the pressure of her longing. She would probably say again that she was sorry, but that could never make up for what she had done to him and to Kenny, to all of them. He didn't know if he would ever have a kid, but he knew he could not give it away like she did Kenny, to a total stranger for a gallon of bootleg whisky. Of all his sibs, Pooh seemed to have made it in a pretty positive way; he had hung in there, never detaching from their mother. How Pooh rode out the years before she got sober he couldn't imagine.

She loved Pooh more, he supposed; Pooh was her pet, he supposed, while the rest of the kids had been less than nothing to her.

He couldn't believe he'd been willing to die that time the Mustang slid off the highway and down the bank. He didn't try to purposely kill himself, he just stopped trying to control the skid. Why try any more to control anything? He let go of the wheel.

Everybody said it was a miracle that he lived, that he walked away with nothing but a cut on his forehead. He had felt shame at wrecking Father Tim's car, but it had taken a few years to apologize.

Then he went with Father Brad on the snow camp deal and took a fall down the side of a serious outcrop of rock and again nearly died, or felt sure he would, and God had spoken to him. *Turn your ass around.*

Dumb as he might be, he knew God did not talk like that, didn't use words like that, but that was exactly what had been said, clear as light, plain as day. It was as if the mountain, the sky, the trees, the rocks were speaking in a single voice, the scariest thing that had ever happened to him, worse than the skid down the bank. And then the truly weird, unbelievable peace that came into him like a warm flood. He lost all sense of muscle and bone; he was vapor on the freezing mountain air, momentarily free of some hell he had lived with since he was a kid.

He remembered saying 'Thank you, God,' and really meaning it.

He had waited several months before he told Father Brad, who started bawling and slapping him on the back and even picked him up and set him down again, laughing like a maniac. 'Wow,' the priest had said, wiping his eyes. 'Thanks be to God! Wow.'

He had expected that time on the mountain to solve everything. But it hadn't. He still could not forgive his mother; there was still plenty of stuff he did that he shouldn't do.

But he had come here to have a good time; he hadn't weighed himself down with his show stick, his break stick, or any of the other stuff. He was here to watch Jack growing up and to be with family.

He punched up the pillow and turned over. Having 'the ears of an animal,' as his backer liked to say, he heard the whisper of snow against the windowpane.

He would be ice, she would not get to him in any way, by any route; he would see to that.

19

The ham was in the oven.

He put his phone in his jacket pocket and walked over to Feel Good for an early breakfast. Snow had fallen in the night and was predicted to start again midmorning.

'I've got what you might call a marital problem,' said Omer.

'Must be somethin' in the water,' said J.C.

Omer leaned back in his chair. 'But other than that, I'm a happy man.'

'Good, good.' Don't tell us what the problem is, thought Father Tim.

'Problem is, my wife's makin' my dog fat.'

'Geez,' said Mule.

'When Shirlene and I got hitched, Patsy was fine. Then here comes th' biscuits, th' gravy, th' creamed rice, th' mashed potatoes.'

'That's a problem?' said Mule. He loved biscuits, gravy, and mashed potatoes, which were totally outlawed at his house.

'Don't give Patsy that hot dog, I say. Oh, she says, it's just a little bitty bite. An' there you go—Patsy's four pounds over fightin' weight.' Omer shook his head, looked at the priest. 'What can I do?'

'I don't know what to tell you, my training didn't touch on that marital issue. I admit I caved to Barnabas a time or two.' Liar, liar, pants on fire—way more than a time or two. Barnabas was nuts about fried oysters and popcorn and he, Tim Kavanagh, had given in regularly. He once went to the porch to eat popcorn while Barnabas stood at the glass door and eyed the consumption of every kernel.

Abe dropped by the table on his way out. 'Hey, guys, you know why Mayberry was so peaceful and quiet?'

'No,' said J.C., who didn't go for jokes before, say, noon.

'It was a small town,' said Omer. 'In th' South, in th' fifties. That'll give you peaceful and quiet.'

'The answer,' said Abe, 'is nobody was married.'

'I don't get it,' said Mule.

'Andy, Aunt Bee, Barney, Floyd, Howard,' said Abe. 'Goober, Gomer, Sam, Ernest T. Bass, Helen, Thelma Lou, Clara. All single.'

'Of course!' said Father Tim. 'The only married person was Otis!'

'Right,' said Abe. 'And he stayed drunk. Think about it.'

'That's not funny,' said J.C., who had just confessed that he slept on the sofa last night.

H is phone buzzed on the walk home.
    'Hey, Granpa!'
'Hey, buddy!'
'It's Name Day!'
'We know, we know. We'll be out soon.'
'Mom and Dad said be careful.'
'We will, I promise.'
'I got your back, Granpa, okay?'
'Okay!'

It was the first time Jack had ever called him. He was grinning all the way home. He remembered the countless photos of grandchildren he'd been forced to look at and admire over the years. He could never quite understand all the fuss. But things were different now. Really different.

According to local news, last evening's snowfall amounted to less than an inch in the Mitford area. But they could look for more, extending into the evening.

He stood by the study window, a mug of tea in his hand. No call yet from Father Brad.

He checked his watch. Everything was ready to go and piled at the door to the garage—everything except the ham, which in a half hour he could put in its carrier for the road. He might be the only man on the planet with a ham carrier.

'It's coming down.' He said this with some gravity.

She didn't respond.

'Pretty *heavy*,' he said. He wouldn't have to say more, as his wife was a mind reader.

'I can't imagine not going. We can't even think about it. All that food they made for everyone. And your beautiful ham. And our gift for Jack. And you're conducting the ceremony!'

'I wonder what Pauline and Buck and Pooh will do,' he said. As for Jessie, she was not due back to civilization until Sunday afternoon. He crossed himself, lifted another prayer for the snow campers.

He rang Hoppy, who was headed to the garage to warm up the car. Maybe he should call Dooley, to see what it was doing at Meadowgate. But Hoppy would have called Dooley, and he and Olivia were headed out, so . . .

'Remember,' said Cynthia. 'I have front-wheel drive.'

'True. And they're good about plowing the roads out there. And Willie will handle their driveway.'

Her husband was a worrier—with the southerner's alarm at a flake or two. She, however, was from Massachusetts. 'We should go,' she said.

He put his cup in the dishwasher. 'I'm a little concerned about the forecast. Four inches, maybe *six*? They can't seem to nail it. And what if it freezes?'

'We should go. The sooner, the better.'

Here was the clincher. 'What if we get stuck out there?'

She walked to the hall closet and took out her coat and hat and came back and put them on the sofa. 'We'll do what you're so fond of doing, sweetheart. We'll cross that bridge when we come to it.'

The phone was ringing as he latched the carrier.

'Whoever it is will leave a message,' she said.

'Probably Dooley.' He hurried to his desk. 'How much snow do you have?'

A pause. 'We have nine inches so far and more to come.'

'*Lace*? Who *is* this?'

'Brooke Logan in Stamford, Connecticut. Have I called at a wrong moment?'

Cynthia was jiggling the car keys.

'Well, yes, yes, you have, Ms. Logan. We're on our way to our son and his family and . . .'

'Sorry.'

'Is there something . . .'

'Sorry.'

'Call again if you . . .'

A click in Connecticut.

'Who is Ms. Logan?' said Cynthia.

'Actually,' he said, 'I don't have a clue.'

A siren. In the direction of Ivy Lane. He remembered hearing it fifteen or twenty minutes ago. There was nothing completely unusual about the sound except this one gave him a sick feeling.

The phone again; caller ID, the Local. Avis was headed to the hospital.

'We'll take care of it, Father,' said Otis. 'Abe has help today at his place, he'll fill in for you. You go on with your family.'

'What do you know?'

'Johnsie, she called th' ambulance, then called th' store. Seem like he couldn't get his words out.'

Stroke. His immediate instinct was to drop everything and get up there. He hesitated, torn. The priesthood had equipped him with a powerful pull to the siren call. But this wasn't just any day, it was Name Day. 'Thank you, Otis. I'll stay in touch.'

He picked up the carrier. 'This is not good,' he said to Cynthia. 'This is not good.'

He finished loading the hatch.

'I'll warm up the car,' she said.

He turned back to check on Truman's water bowl and lock the door to the kitchen. The phone again. Though his wife would be as steaming as the ham, he answered it.

'Helene!'

'Father, I know you and the young family are having a large affair this weekend.'

'We are, we are, yes!' He was breathless.

'I've just discovered the oddest thing on my back steps.'

'What . . .'

'I can only guess who they belong to, Father. A delicate subject, really.'

'What may I do for you, Helene? We're trying to get ahead of the snow.'

'It was a pair of . . . well, teeth. On my steps. It was . . . alarming, you might say, to come upon them, protruding from the snow.'

'We must go, Helene, truly.'

'I picked them up with my kitchen tongs and put them in a bag.'

'Helene . . .'

'I feel certain they belong to Mr. Welch, and wondered if you might possibly step over and fetch them? I'll just pass them out the front door.'

20

Snowfall had been fitful in their neck of the woods. Total accumulation, according to the Weather Channel: under three inches.

At six-thirty in the morning, Dooley had a fire going in the kitchen, the coffee was ready, Jack was still asleep.

'I'll use one of the sleeping bags,' said Beth, 'so you'll have a bed for two more people.'

'You do not want to crawl into one of those things,' said Lace. 'I promise!'

Willie and Harley came in, stomping snow on the mat at the kitchen door.

'Mornin',' said Willie, removing his hat.

'We're here for our marchin' orders,' said Harley. 'We're set to clear th' driveway whenever you say. They're workin' on th' roads.'

'We need the other two tables set up,' said Lace. 'But get a cup of coffee first and sit down.' Lace moved over on the bench. 'We have toast, fig jam, and bananas.'

'What's that in th' oven?' said Harley.

'Five dozen chocolate chip cookies,' said Beth, who could only hope they would be edible.

They heard thuds above. The Barlowe cousins were up.

'We're tryin' to work out sleeping arrangements if the snow gets heavy,' said Dooley. 'We're short on beds. Any chance you and Willie could bunk in together?'

Harley's pupils enlarged. 'Aint' no way I'm doin' that.'

'Ditto,' said Willie.

Dooley laughed his cackling laugh. 'Just seein' if y'all are awake yet.'

'I'll be makin' me a pallet on th' floor,' said Harley.

N ext to the fireplace, and surrounded by two angels, seven sheep, and a wizened shepherd, the Virgin Mother and Joseph knelt by a manger that would remain empty until Christmas morning.

Serene though the nativity figures were, the kitchen was upended by the business at hand.

Marge Owen was setting the tables. Lily had wrangled the turkey into the oven at eight A.M.—no stuffing, though a large pan of dressing was under way. Harley had been appointed to run a damp mop, which he claimed was not in his job description.

'I used to think this ol' house was a barn,' said Lily, weaving through the cluster of tables. 'But git this family together an' it's tight. No room to skin a cat!'

'I've never roasted a turkey,' said Julie, 'much less made a pan of dress-ing. You won't let me help, so may I watch?'

'Like my granmaw used to say, You're as welcome as th' flowers in May.'

'I remember there are lots of girls in your family, all named after flowers.'

'Rose, Pansy, Del for delphinium . . . a whole garden full. Eight girls, two boys, none dead. You take Violet, who's straightenin' th' upstairs. She's th' star of our family—th' Dolly Parton, th' Tammy Wynette rolled into one. Sings at parties all over, wearin' a cowgirl outfit like Patsy Cline.

'Violet an' me, we're a team. I cater, she sings, yodels, has a full what she calls repertory, but her signature number is 'Your Cheatin' Heart.' Did you ever know Hank Williams? He made it famous.'

'She ain't old enough to know Hank Williams!' said Harley. He had come in here an' held his hand out for a cookie, and what did he get? A Swiffer, an' him in his good clothes. He hoped Willie would not see him moppin' in here with th' women.

'Git in th' corners,' said Lily, 'specially over at th' dog bed. An' run it under th' tables.'

Lily stirred giblets into a bowl of crumbled cornbread. 'A pan of dressin' is tastier than stuffin',' she told Julie, 'plus stuffin' slows down th' roast time.'

'Lily,' said Marge, 'tell Julie about Johnny Cash.'

'So Violet met Johnny Cash when she was twelve years old. She went right up to 'im an' didn't say hey, how you doin' or nothin', just busted out singin' 'Cheatin' Heart,' an' he fell in an' sung it with her! Then gave her a quarter an' said call 'im when she grew up. Don't you love it?'

'Did she call him when she grew up?' said Julie, who liked knowing how other people live.

'No, bless 'is heart, by that time he was married. Anyway, she's hitched to Lloyd Goodnight, but barren like in th' Bible. That fireplace right there? When Father Tim an' Cynthia lived out here, th' chimney crashed down in a windstorm in th' middle of th' night! Just boom, down it goes in a cloud of dust like you never seen, pourin' bricks an' ashes all over th' floor! Lloyd rebuilt it, brick by brick.

'As for me, I am not currently married. It's weird, but all th' Flower girls who can't cook a lick, they're married. And us who can, we're single, divorced, walked out on, you name it.'

Into the bowl went sautéed celery, onion, and sausage.

'This dressin' should've set overnight to mix th' flavors, but it'll be good, anyhow. I baked th' cornbread yesterday evenin' so it'd dry out a little.

'Take our sister Arbutus, she lives in a brick house with two screen porches and is married to Junior Bentley. What does she do? Paints her nails, bleaches her hair, eats Raisinets, unloads th' dishwasher when the' notion strikes. Can't cook a lick, an' Junior *loves her to death.* It's a mystery.'

Lily looked around the kitchen. 'Where did Harley get to?'

'He slipped out,' said Marge. 'But the floor looks good.'

'Did he put th' mats back at th' door?'

'I'm doing it right now.'

'That's the way men are, they'll eat you out of house an' home but want nothin' to do with th' kitchen.'

Lily thought Julie was pretty an' very nice, but awful pale. Maybe because of carryin' around a baby predicted to weigh eight pounds. Or maybe she, Lily Flower, was talkin' too much. She had been accused of wearin' people out in that particular fashion.

Marge came over and put her arm around Julie. 'Are all the steps here okay for you?'

'Oh, yes, my doctor said steps would be fine.'

'I was running up and down these steps every day 'til the afternoon Rebecca Jane was born.'

'How was the delivery?'

'I was fifty-one! A huge surprise! But all went well.'

'You could go set over there in Dooley's chair,' said Lily.

'I'm okay, really. I guess it was the move across the country, and so many boxes. Thanks.'

'Now I'm cuttin' up a apple in here, I like to use a Gala when I can get it. You don't want th' apple to stand out, you just want a little sweetness. A little sweetness! That's what you're gon' have here in a couple of weeks. Got a name picked out?'

'We don't know if it's a boy or girl. We asked them not to tell us.'

'You're carryin' it high, looks like. That's when they say it's a boy.'

'Maybe James,' said Julie. 'Or Wesley, the middle name of Kenny's wonderful grandpa.'

Marge was filling water pitchers for the tables. 'James Wesley would be a handsome name.'

'James Wesley Barlowe!' said Lily, breaking two eggs into the bowl. 'There you go!'

Father Tim handed over the paper bag. 'From Miss Pringle.'

Harley looked into the bag with a mixture of relief and despair. Mostly despair; he had hoped the fact of his dentures was unknown to Miss Pringle.

'Where was they at?'

'On her back steps.'

'Lord help. She was off teachin' an' I taken 'em out when I was workin' on 'er porch rail! I guess that's th' end of that aggravation.'

'What aggravation?'

'All that French talk an' runnin' into town burnin' gas . . . '

Harley had as stern a look as he'd ever seen.

'To say nothin' of th' banana puddin's I've toted over there, an' th' pan of brownies last week. It'll be that perfessor now, fixin' up her porch. Well, let 'im have at it! Let that ol' geezer bust his thumb hammerin' down a loose board. We'll see how far education gits 'im on that deal.'

Harley popped in his dentures, made what could be called a grim grin. 'How's that?' he said, mad as a hornet.

'Joyful, joyful, we adore Thee,
God of glory, Lord of love;
Hearts unfold like flow'rs before Thee.
Opening to the Sun above.
Melt the clouds of sin and sadness;
Drive the dark of doubt away;*

Giver of immortal gladness,
Fill us with the light of day . . .'

Everyone processed from the kitchen to the living room. Beth and Tommy up front, leading the singing to Henry Van Dyke's hymn of joy.

Next were Dooley, Lace and Jack, then Hoppy, Olivia, Cynthia, Pauline and Buck. After Pauline and Buck, Sammy, Kenny, Julie, Etta, Ethan, Pooh, Rebecca Jane, Doc Owen, Marge Owen, Blake, Amanda, Harley, Willie, Lily, Violet, Beth, Tommy, and bringing up the rear, the priest, vested for the occasion in Advent color. He could have worn jeans and a collar, sure, but Jack liked vestments!

Beth and Tommy took their places with four band members, who were grouped beneath the stairwell. In the corner, wise men and camels en route across the desert to the Holy Family in the kitchen . . .

The congregation, each clutching a program, seated themselves in the Crossroads folding chairs. Jack in boots, new corduroys, checked shirt, navy blazer, and his first tie, sat between his mom and dad on the front row.

The service would be brief, informal, and simple. The family baptism ceremony in July had been properly ceremonious, but, reasoned the celebrant, far too long for a four-year-old.

Father Tim stood before them and signed the cross.

'Blessed be God: Father, Son, and Holy Spirit.'

'And blessed be his kingdom, now and forever. Amen!'

'It's said, Jack, that no Irish family can point to a more ancient background than the Kavanaghs. The name Kavanagh came down from the first king of Leinster in the twelfth century. That's eight hundred years ago.

'And because of your new name, you inherit the Kavanagh family motto, which we talked about the other day. It's a wonderful motto, and here's how it sounds in the old Irish: *Siochain agus Fairsinge.* Do you remember what that means?'

'Peace and plenty!' said Jack.

'That's it! As I look around, I see this motto fulfilled in every face in the room. Peace . . . and plenty . . . graciously provided by God who created us for himself, and who loves each of us devoutly, devotedly, steadfastly, forever.

'Let it be ordained that this child, Jack, be loved in like manner by each of us gathered here today. When he came to us just six months ago, we were all given the divine opportunity of joy, wonder, and delight in watching him grow, and of supporting him, however we can, in the changing seasons of his life.

'Will we promise to look out for Jack? Pray for him? Be family to him? And try to be there when he needs us? If so, let us say, We will.'

'*We will!*'

'He can play with my toyth!' said Etta.

Laughter.

'Thank you, Etta. That's the spirit! Will you come forward, Jack?'

Jack slid off this chair and stood by his granpa. He clasped his hands together, dropped them to his side, jiggled his legs, grinned at the congregation.

Father Tim leaned down and placed his hands on Jack's head. It was as warm as a melon in the sun.

'Into your hands, O God, we place your child, Jack Brady Kavanagh. Thank you for supporting him in his successes and in his failures, in his joys and in his sorrows. May he grow in grace and in the knowledge of our Savior Jesus Christ. Amen.'

'*Amen!*'

'Jack, may he bless you with his peace and keep you in plenty all the days of your life, that you might bring forth much fruit in his kingdom. Brothers and sisters, I present to you, Jack Brady *Kavanagh!*'

Applause. Tears. Laughter.

Tommy stood and strummed his guitar.

'Here are the chords,' said Tommy. 'Short an' easy, okay? Here they are again. The words are in your program. Clap twice where it says to, an' everybody sing big.

'Jack, Jack, we've got your back!'

Clap, clap. 'Jack Kavanagh!'

'Again!

'Jack, Jack, we've got your back!'

Clap, clap. 'Jack Kavanagh!'

Applause. Whistles. Jack laughing.

'That was fun,' said Father Tim. 'You know who else has your back?'

'Charley!'

Charley barked. More laughter.

'Jesus!' said Father Tim. 'Love him and trust him, for he will always be there for you.'

Jack tugged on his granpa's chasuble. 'I have a great idea, Granpa Tim! You an' Jesus could make my fake cousin an' fake aunts an' uncles be real.'

'Well, now, that is truly a great idea.' He took Jack's hand. 'We're going to have to pray again, everybody! As Saint Paul instructed us in Colossians, Be *instant* in prayer!

'Father, please help us all to be real with Jack and with one another. Help us to seek a true kinship of the heart, always. Through Christ our Lord. Amen!'

'Amen!'

Father Tim produced a small box from beneath his chasuble.

'We have something special for you today. It's from Granny Pauline, Granny Olivia, Granny Cynthia, Granpa Buck, Granpa Hoppy, and myself.'

'I have a *ton* of grannies and granpas!'

Laughter, applause.

He opened the lid of the box and showed the contents to Jack.

'A watch!'

'Take it out and look at the back. See your new name? With today's date? Let me help you latch it. Good fit, with room to grow! There, now. What time is it?'

Jack stared hard at the watch face. He wanted to get this perfect.

'Twenty . . . one . . . *minutes after twelve!*' he yelled. Charley barked. All applauded.

Father Tim laughed. 'But wait!' he said. 'There's more!'

To the clonking of a cowbell wielded by Rebecca Jane, up the hall rolled the red bike, Lace holding one handlebar, Dooley the other.

Just for the heck of it, Father Tim timed the jubilation. Four minutes plus change, which could have gone on till the cows came home, but he brought it to order with Jack at his side.

'Lunch is scheduled for twelve-thirty,' said Father Tim. 'And Jack has a message for us.'

'*Twenty-six minutes after twelve!*' yelled Jack.

'Time is always ticking away. May we choose, every moment, to love one another as God loves us. Go in peace, now, to love and serve the Lord.'

'*Thanks be to God!*'

The Biscuits played. Tommy and Beth sang an old Sunday school standard.

Jesus loves the little children,
All the children of the world,
Red and yellow, black and white,
They are precious in His sight . . . '

Everyone scrambled toward the kitchen; toward the turkey, the ham, the fire on the hearth, the tables with a place set for Miss Sadie . . .

And Jack yelled at the top of his lungs. '*Thirty minutes after twelve!*'

Whatever the man-cave notion may be, it wasn't for him. Put him outside in the weather, in the fresh air—with his cows, his dogs, with Lace and his boy, or alone. However you cut it, he did not like to be walled in. He had felt plenty walled in by what he owed the pharmaceutical companies, but he had put the checks in the mail yesterday. A truck had rolled off his back.

He and Sammy headed out after lunch to take a bucket of sweet feed to the cattle.

'Big day for th' little guy,' said Sammy. 'What if we'd had all that g-goin' on when we were four years old?'

'Maybe the point is bein' able to give it even though we didn't get it.'

'That's hard.'

'Uphill both ways sometimes.'

Snow and frozen grass crunching underfoot.

'How about with Lace?' said Sammy. 'How do you know how to l-love somebody in a really, you know, real way if you were never, like, loved as a k-kid?' He didn't know how to talk about this.

'It took us years to trust each other. There's no quick fix that I can see.'

'Nothin's easy. Right?' He wanted something to be easy—just one thing, just one thing. Maybe now, with Rio and one more sponsor . . .

'Dad quotes somebody who talks about *a long obedience in the same direction.* That's the magic. Look at you. How many trophies so far?'

'Thirty-two.'

'All because of stickin' to it.' He clapped his brother on the back.

Sammy grinned. 'It's all about th' hardware.'

'Not about the money?'

'Trophies are great, but yeah, it's really about th' m-money. I have to hustle. I want to play more in th' b-big tournaments, but no way could I afford it without Rio. They're th' cue maker I was tellin' you about; they called a few minutes ago. They're gonna sponsor me in some of th' b-big events.'

'Hey! Great news! Proud of you!' He hugged his brother, feeling a weight lift off—he worried about this guy.

'They'll cover entry fees and even some of the airfare. But I still need another sponsor.'

'How does that work?' Dooley unlatched the cattle gate.

'Somebody sees you play, they really like what they see, an' pretty soon you're w-wearin' their shirt an' shootin' with their cues.'

'You've got to tell everybody, this is big. Here, take th' bucket an' rattle it.'

Sammy made some noise with the feed bucket. The bull came running across the pasture; the heifers at a slow trot. 'I pray,' said Sammy.

'Me, too. Do I ever. Glad you're home. Everybody wants to shoot a game with you even though they're quakin' in their boots. Harley, Doc Harper, Blake, Rebecca Jane, Tommy . . . '

'Gonna sh-shoot just one game today. We'll draw names. I need to get offa pool for five minutes. Get my head in another place.'

'No pressure. You like it up there in the big city?'

Sammy looked across the field to the mountains. And back to where a really great vegetable garden could go in by the barn.

'I like bein' down here b-better, but no way to make a livin' doin' what I do. Chicago is t-total pool action.'

'Come home anytime,' said Dooley. 'Whenever you can. You'll always have a place with us.'

You'll always have a place with us. He liked hearing that; he needed to hear that.

T hereth a baby in there,' said Etta.

'A boy!' said Ethan.

'Mom, is that why Aunt Julie's tummy is so big?'

'I have a great idea,' said Lace. When would she and Dooley have what it takes to do what had to be done? 'Etta and Ethan brought you a jigsaw puzzle. You had a jigsaw last summer and loved it. We can put it on the table in the library where there are lots of people to help. And I'll help you set up.'

'How many pieces?' said Jack.

'Fifty. Do you think you could put together fifty pieces working as a team?'

'I can do fifhthy peethees,' said Etta.

'She can't,' said Ethan. 'Only this many.' He held up ten fingers.

H e stepped out to the kitchen porch and speed-dialed the nurses' station.

'Kennedy here.'

'Kennedy, you're always there. Do you never go home?'

'This is home, Father. I've been here a hundred years, remember?'

'I need to preach you a sermon about taking better care of yourself.'

'Do not preach me a sermon. So he's not doing much better than when he came in, he lost his speech, bless 'is heart, and no, you cannot talk to Dr. Wilson, he has been in to see Mr. Packard twice and things are stabilized. So please don't call the doctor, Father, this is the weekend, in case you haven't noticed. Let him take care of it.'

'What do you think, Kennedy?'

'I cannot answer that, medically speaking. All I'm prayin' for is a gleam in his eye.'

'For the nurses?'

'Ha ha, very funny. No. A spark of life is what I'd call it.'

A stroke with speech affected. He felt the long exhaustion of the whole thing.

A TV weather alert cited heavy snowfall at higher elevations. Buck, Pauline, Beth, everybody was concerned.

He tried Father Brad's cell, but got the voice message. He knew service was nearly impossible up there; that's why Father Brad had to find the sweet spot on the ridge before calling out. Beth had tried her mother's cell to no avail.

He didn't know the name of the youth counselor who was with them, but would try to make some calls and figure it out when they got home. In the meantime, he assured himself and the others with simple reasoning:

Wrangling teenagers was a handful. Being in love was a handful. Cooking a meal on a log must be a total handful. So in other words, they hadn't heard from the ridge because Father Brad's and Mary Ellen's hands were, like, full.

K enny needed a glass of water for Julie, who wasn't feeling well. But his mother was in the kitchen and he stood in the hall, trying to figure out what to do.

He felt the beating of his heart. Lily and Violet were in the living room, rearranging chairs for tonight's music. In a house full of people, this could be his only chance

Maybe he should quit thinking of her as his mother and regard her as a fellow human being who had made terrible mistakes as he had surely done and, God help him, could possibly do again. Maybe he needed to love her just for being another human being on the planet. He couldn't say he was thrilled with this idea, but it was the best he could do. He didn't know what to call her. Not Mother. Not Mama. So maybe he wouldn't call her anything; the point was to start somewhere.

Before he left, his grandma and grandpa in Oregon had said, *Forgive your mother, son.* No long-winded sermon. Just: *Forgive your mother, we love you, and you and the family come home safe.*

Had he deserved people like his adopted grandparents, who weren't even kin? People who literally saved his life? God had been merciful. He wanted to be merciful, too. He was the only one who could open the channel between his children and their grandmother. If he could do this with his head, maybe later it would move to his heart.

'Jesus,' he whispered.

His mother was washing dishes at the sink.

He couldn't speak, even though he had nothing to say. She turned and wiped her hands with a cloth, and moved toward him and offered her hand, warm from the dishwater. He took it, but could not look into her eyes.

Somewhere in her flesh, he felt a mild flutter, a trembling as of wings. His instinct was to draw back. But he held on. Held on to the fluttering thing in the faraway universe of this other person, and then he was weeping. He could not look up but knew that she was also. He held on as the flutter dissolved into a beat, the pumping engine of their hearts.

He glanced at her briefly, and went to the library and asked Lace if she would take Julie a glass of water.

Then he left the house and walked across the field, into the hollow of silence that comes with snow.

Sammy was sitting on the kitchen porch when he came back from the field.

He stamped snow off his boots. He needed to get in there to check on Julie. 'What's goin' on, brother?'

'Tryin' to g-get my head together.'

'Who isn't?'

They were silent for a time.

'Forgive her, Sam.'

'No way.'

'She made choices people suffered for. But she was sick. At least try to forgive her for what happened to the rest of us. I know that what she did to me was really hard on you, but don't hold out because of that. If she hadn't swapped me for the jug, God knows where I'd be now.'

Sammy stood and went inside. His mind was made up. And he didn't like people trying to change it.

Tell you what,' said Dooley. 'Sammy's here to enjoy some family time, so he's gonna shoot just one game. We're gonna draw the name of his opponent, so get ready to show him what you've got. Willie, can we use your hat?'

Willie handed off his beat-up headgear, pleased to be asked.

'Somebody pass around a sheet of paper and a pen.'

'I will!' said Rebecca Jane.

'Okay, write your name, tear it off, fold it up and drop it in th' hat. This is big-time, folks. Somebody in this room will get to challenge the Shark of Chicago. Ace this game and you'll win th' first annual Meadowgate eight-ball championship! See th' shirt Sam's wearing? Rio is his new sponsor. A cue maker. Thinks Sammy has th' magic.'

Whistles. Applause. Cowbell.

'So Jack will draw a name and if you can beat Sam Barlowe . . .' He paused, looked around the room. ' . . . you get to clean up th' supper dishes.'

Moans, groans.

'Ain't nobody in this room gon' beat Sammy,' said Willie, 'so ain't no supper dishes gettin' washed t'night.'

S he may never have a chance to actually exchange words with her son. If she could shoot a game with him, somehow that might be a kind of communication—all the guilt and sorrow and love becoming its own language in the flow of the game. She hadn't played pool in years, but a long time ago, before she started blacking out and getting fired from work, she'd been good at it; it was instinctive to her. She had actually won a few matches.

The trembling was uncontrollable. How could she possibly . . . ?

She looked at Buck. He nodded, put his hand on her shoulder.

She tried to control the trembling as she inscribed her name on the small slip of paper.

Pauline Barlowe Leeper

J ack drew a name and handed it to Dooley.

Cynthia was sitting on the sofa with Marge and Doc. Etta and Ethan perched like birds on the back, and Jack climbed up there, too.

She loved the excitement in the room, the good tension. This was the Barlowe family lottery.

Dooley looked at the slip of paper, unable for a moment to speak. He blinked, felt the breath go out of him.

'Pauline Barlowe Leeper.'

No whistles, no applause. Silence. No one moved. Cynthia thought it was like the game of Freeze, which she had played with friends at school.

Sammy took a stick from the rack, the one he had used at the wedding, and chalked the tip. His heartbeat was deafening. He would never have figured this.

She was just standing there. What was she waiting for?

'G-grab a stick,' he said, angry for having to say it.

He remembered almost nothing about being a kid before she made him go live with his goon-head daddy. Those years had wiped out the memory of nearly everything that went before. He remembered only the violence of his life with Clyde Barlowe, the humiliation, the disgrace he felt for having been shoved into it with no one to turn to, no one to come looking for him. Dooley would definitely have come, but who could know where he'd gone with a stone-crazy highwayman who was liable to end up anywhere?

He did remember his kid brother Henry, who carried around a pool ball that he called a *pooh baw*. The memory flashed back to him, now, sharp. His mother had brought it home—it was maroon; it was a seven ball.

So what she'd been an alcoholic and didn't know what she was doing. He knew plenty of booze heads and a few of them had gotten help. She could have done something; plenty of people did something—got off drugs, got off gambling.

She had loved booze more than she loved her kids, how could that be okay? Was that just the way things roll, life goes on? Thank God he was one sober dude when it came to drugs of any kind. No dopehead pool for him. He was going to make it into the Hall of Fame, no question, and he'd have to keep his head straight to do it.

And now here she was, wanting into his life. He had spent most of his years longing for what he figured other kids had—something he'd missed but couldn't have said what it was. If he truly forgave her, whatever that meant, he would have to stop feeling everything he had constructed. He was used to the old feelings; they played in a loop, over and over, indelible now.

But if Kenny could do it—

He didn't look at her as he spoke. 'Let's lag.'

The players stood side by side at the head rail. Each placed a ball behind the head string, then bent over the table and sighted their ball.

Almost in unison, the balls rolled forward, hitting the foot rail, then rolled back.

There was a murmur in the room.

'Man!' said Harley.

'What happened?' she whispered to Marge.

'Pauline won the lag.'

Sammy racked the balls. He didn't know if somebody in their twenties could have a heart attack. He should have brought his own cue, he knew better than to travel without his sticks. He'd like to walk away from the table, grab his duffel, get into his rental and ride. But no—in the game he chased, he had totally learned rule number one: Keep your cool.

Pauline bent over the table. She was immobile for a long moment.

The break.

'Yay!' said Jack, who liked to see the balls scatter.

Pauline stood and pushed her hair behind her ears.

Cynthia saw the old scarring around her left ear, surprised that Pauline had revealed it in what appeared to be a natural gesture. The burn had been serious, disfiguring her ear and requiring grafts that only rudely matched the color of her facial skin. She always disguised it with her hair.

Though this pool table had stood in their dining room for several years, Cynthia admitted that she had never even remotely understood the game. She had happily cheered for both players, and right now was no exception.

She looked up as Kenny came to the door. She saw that he signaled Dooley, who left the room.

Sammy sank a ball, then another.

Dooley came back to the door, caught Hoppy's eye, and Hoppy went out.

No one else appeared to notice the comings and goings; their attention was riveted on the table and the players. Even the children were absorbed.

Now Dooley came into the library again and left with Lace.

She glanced at Timothy, who stood near the table and hadn't seemed to notice. Since childhood, her modus operandi had been to put two and two together. Julie hadn't felt well or looked well. Kenny had come for Dooley, Dooley had come for Hoppy, then for Lace. And just now, she saw Timothy looking toward the door and slipping out to the hall. A doctor *and* a cleric . . .

She felt a momentary panic. What should she do? She would do nothing; she had not been called out. She moved to sit on the arm of the sofa for a better view, prayed for the unknown, and forced herself to study the faces in the library.

Clearly, the game in this room was about more than pool. It was about the future of a family.

He was sweating like a horse. He was used to sweat. But this was different. He didn't feel stressed as he might if he was baggin' five hundred bucks; he didn't feel anything. He was numb, playing by numbers. The sweat poured out of something he didn't understand.

He hunkered over the table, shot the seven ball into the side pocket. Shot the five ball into the left corner pocket.

'Gon' clear th' table,' muttered Harley.

Pauline was strangely relaxed in her shoulders, in her back, all the tight places that had stored so much dread and self-hatred. Whatever strategies she was using seemed given to her, fluid and full of a certain happiness. It was not a competition; it was nothing she would ever have expected. It was as if she and her son were teammates, conspiring toward the same goal, the same win.

D ooley literally ran down the stairs, drying his hands on a towel. 'What happened?'

'Mom won,' said Pooh.

'No way. Come on.'

'Sammy made a beautiful cut on his last ball,' said Doc Owen, 'but it didn't fall. He got lucky and left your mom behind the two ball so she didn't have a clear shot on the eight.'

'So Mom called the eight in the corner pocket,' said Pooh, 'and massé'd around the two, hittin' both cushions and barely missin' the eight.'

'It was a great shot, just came up a little short,' said Doc. 'It gave Sammy ball in hand on the two, which he put in the pocket and then it was straight in on the eight.'

'There's no way he would have followed the eight in,' said Dooley.

'Not that he missed the shot, because he didn't,' said Pooh. 'He made it, and followed the cue in behind it.'

'Did he let her win?' he asked his brother.

'All we know is, she played amazing pool.'

'Now we know where Sammy got his pool gene,' said Doc. 'The apple never falls far from the tree.'

'But did he let her win? There's no way he could have missed th' shot you just described.'

'Sammy don't let people win,' said Harley.

'Where were you, anyway?' Pooh asked Dooley.

'I'll let Kenny tell you. Great news goin' on up there.'

Willie held his hat close to his heart as if were a trophy. He didn't say much, but he felt he had to say this. 'Give it to 'er, boys. Your mama won th' game.'

H oppy washed up.
        It had been a comparatively easy delivery among the couple thousand he'd done. Mother fine, baby fine. There was no need that he could see for Julie and the baby to make a trek to the hospital. Let them rest, for Pete's sake.

Dooley had been a good scrub nurse, Lily and Violet had changed the bed linens and dealt with the basin, Julie had drunk water, the baby was nursing. Beautiful!

Julie held out her hand to Kenny, beaming. 'It's not James Wesley!'

He kissed her damp forehead, touched the cheek of the newest Barlowe. 'There's red in her hair,' he said with a kind of wonder. 'Colleen? Or Daisy? We liked both of those.'

'You can send Etta and Ethan in,' Hoppy told Kenny. 'This is a big event. They'll remember it for a lifetime.'

'Ask your mom to come up, too,' said Julie.

Kenny hesitated.

'Please,' said Julie.

E tta clattering down the stairs, shouting.
        'Ith a thithster! Ith a thithster!'

Etta tugged on Lace's shirt. 'Aunt Lathe, we could put it in th' manger till th' baby Jeseth comths!'

'It's another angel!' said Jack. 'Dad said Granpa Hoppy made this one come out! But where did it come out from? In your whole studio, there's no place for angels to come out from 'cept th' closet or th' bathroom. Was it stayin' in there an' we didn't know it?'

'In a minute, honey. Please help Ethan get the top off his juice. Let me talk with Dad.'

She drew Dooley into the hall room and closed the door.

'Where's Mom?' he said.

'She was here a minute ago, I don't know. They say it was an incredible game. Listen, Dooley, we have to tell Jack soon. Right away. He's terribly bright and curious and asking all these questions. He's a little farm boy, after all, he needs to know these things. Especially since . . . '

'Soon,' said Dooley. 'Soon.'

She looked skeptical.

'I promise,' he said.

'Jack thinks if something is kept secret, it comes true. Maybe we should keep it a secret for now to see how . . .' With all their heart and soul, they wanted it to come true. It had to come true. But there was a chance it wouldn't come true. 'What if . . . ?'

'We're not thinking what if,' he said. 'We're thinkin' when. And we can't keep it a secret. We need to do it today, before people leave. Who knows when we'll all be together again?'

'He's already exhausted by this whole incredible day. It would be too much excitement for him.' It was too much excitement for her; she was ready to be where nothing life-changing was going on.

'Rebecca Jane's getting ready to put the kids down for a nap,' he said. 'If she can make that happen, that'll be another miracle—they're wired to the max. So let's tell everybody while he's asleep and tell him in the morning, just the three of us.'

'Let's pray,' she said, relieved.

Jack opened the door and looked in.

'What are you doin', Dad?'

'We're praying.'

'*Thirty minutes to four!*' Jack shouted, and closed the door.

'He's my new timer,' said Dooley. 'Five hungry patients to feed at th' clinic.'

They held hands, prayed the few words together.

'Thank you, Jesus, for all you have done and are about to do in our lives.

'*Amen!*'

He kissed her, quick. 'Love you deep.'

'Love you good.'

He was out the door.

H e saw Sammy at the corncrib, facing the mountains.

'Go on over,' he said to Jack, 'and give everybody clean water. I'm right behind you.'

Sammy didn't turn around.

Dooley put his hand on his brother's shoulder. 'We're uncles again. It's a girl.'

Sammy liked kids. One day he would teach kids and old people how to shoot pool.

They stood together, wordless.

Did you let her win? he wanted to say. It was a question Sammy would be asked more than once.

'Don't ask me,' said Sammy.

And he didn't.

F ather Tim saw Pauline through the living room window, sitting in a rocker on the front porch.

He pulled on his jacket.

He had his church pension, his social security check, the monthly rent from Helene Pringle, his IRA, which due to age he was forced to dip into annually, and a few small stocks that had escaped the whiplash of a few years ago. He wasn't exactly on the dole. But there was no way he could do this alone, either.

Several things turned Cynthia's blue eyes a deeper, more ravishing blue. A tender word, roses in winter, children—and money talk.

A few days ago, he had given her the rundown and ended with a mini-sermon that was hardly needed.

'Pooh believes, and I believe with him,' he said, 'that his sole focus is to try and love others as unconditionally as God loves us. He may not become a great orator, but I believe he can become a great lover of those whose lives are broken. He has a true heart. I think he's the real deal. Maybe enough for the first two years of college? Till we see where this is headed?'

From cornflower blue to sapphire.

'I'm in,' she said.

He had kissed her hand. Both hands.

He went out to the front porch, which the others seldom used.

This was risky. He had been involved in one way or another in the lives of all Pauline's children, and felt there was some resentment or wounding from it. But he had prayed about what to say today and the answer was clear.

He thought she wasn't wearing enough to keep warm, so he removed his jacket and put it around her shoulders.

She looked up. 'You shouldn't . . . thank you.'

He sat in the rocker next to hers. 'Congratulations on your new granddaughter. Hoppy is convinced she looks like you.'

'Oh!' she said. Her cheeks colored. 'It's all so . . . everything so . . . I saw her, I can't even begin . . .'

'And congratulations on winning the game. They say you shoot a mean stick.'

'I don't know how to do what I did; it seemed to come out of nowhere. I didn't think about winning, I was just trying to shoot a game that wouldn't embarrass him. He shouldn't have let me win.'

'Who says he did?'

'He could have made that shot.'

'We don't really know that. And in the end, does it really matter?'

'The game was one of the most wonderful moments of my life. So many wonderful moments today. All so . . . wonderful.'

She was quiet, then laughed a little. 'It would be nice to feel good about winning, but I can't because I don't know.'

'Feel good anyway would be my suggestion. You shot a great game.' It was freezing out here. 'There's something important I'd like to discuss with you. Is this a good time?'

She looked away. Maybe the mention of an important discussion. He outlined the plan and kept it simple.

'I hope you'll let us do it, Pauline. Just say yes. He's a special kid. This is not for you and Buck. We're doing it for God and Pooh. Please allow us.'

Snow cascaded from the branch of a cedar tree.

This would mean, she thought, that all four of her sons had in some way at some time been rescued by this good man. It was a constant reminder that she was unable, unfit, but this was wrong thinking and she was desperately trying to move beyond that. What it was really about was Father Tim's caring example in the lives of her sons, which was changing their lives for good, forever.

She looked at him. 'What we all owe you, Father, we could never repay.'

'This is grace, Pauline. Grace to you and Buck and Pooh, and grace to Cynthia and me that we have it to give. Grace can never be earned and it can never be repaid. It's a win-win, Pauline. We should go for it.'

She was weeping, but he felt these weren't the old tears. This was a flood of relief.

And after a time, her smile.

'Thank you, Father.' She put her hand on his arm for a moment, and then stood. 'I must get back inside. There's a lot of life going on in there.'

She handed him his jacket and he reached into the pocket and gave her his handkerchief—then said what sounded like a platitude, but he believed it to be true.

'Everything's going to be all right, Pauline. Everything's going to be all right.'

Sammy was entering the kitchen as Pauline came out.

He thought he'd said *Great game* after it was over, but he wasn't sure. Maybe not. He didn't remember much of what happened.

From the world of words needing to be spoken, she couldn't sort even one from the millions.

'G-Great game,' he said in a voice he didn't recognize.

She had not addressed him by name at the wedding or at any time today, though she had longed to say it.

'Sammy. With all my heart, I thank you. Not for letting me win, if that's what you did, but for treating me like an equal at the table. For going through with it when you could have walked away. I will never forget our time today. It has given me great joy.'

She was trying not to cry, he could see that. He couldn't believe this woman with gray hair was his mother. At the wedding, she had said *I'm sorry*. That's all. She had not asked him to forgive her, which was fine with him.

But she had played an amazing game. The least he could do was shake her hand. He felt drawn to do this now, but he could not. Instead, he put his right hand on his left shoulder, shielding himself.

His hands were like hers, she thought . . . broad with long fingers. She remembered now his long fingers when he was born. 'He'll play th' piano,' said her mother.

She needed to say it, it had to be said. She had never before asked this of her children because she had no right to ask anything of them.

'Forgive me, Sammy. You are a wonderful man and I am so proud of you. Please forgive me.'

He looked at her a long moment, and turned and walked up the stairs to his room and closed the door.

She leaned against the wall.

It could take years.

But she could love, she could pray, and she could wait.

He was zipping the ham pan and platters into their carryalls when his phone rang.

Cynthia took the phone from his shirt pocket. 'The hospital,' she said.

'Could I speak with Father Kav'na?'

'This is his wife, Cynthia. He's busy now. May I help?'

'This is Linda Pope at Mitford Hospital. We have two patients who're askin' for Father Kav'na. They said please come if he can.'

'Who are the patients?'

Cynthia held the phone so he could hear.

'I didn't get their names, they're not completely registered. I don't think it's life or death, but nobody said for sure.'

'Describe them if you can.'

'I didn't really see them yet. I just know they arrived in a police car a few minutes ago. An officer, I think it was th' chief, gave me this note to call you an' say th' father should come if he can.'

'Thank you, Nurse Pope.'

'I'm not a nurse, I just work ER check-in part-time.'

'Tell them we're on our way,' he said to Cynthia. 'Thirty minutes or so, depending.'

Now what? he thought. Now what?

People getting into coats and jackets and vests and scarves and hats and gloves. Musical gear collecting at the door. Vehicles warming in the driveway; cousins sleeping; Charley barking; cookies packaged to go with the homeward bound . . .

In the living room, Dooley rang the cowbell, a companion to the one rung at their wedding. His dad and Cynthia came in from the kitchen. The Biscuits stopped packing up their gear.

He stood by Lace, gripped her hand.

'We have an announcement to make, everybody.

'First of all, Mom, congratulations.'

Applause.

'Because of th' weather, you don't have to wash th' supper dishes.'

Cowbell. Laughter. A whistle or two.

'But when you and Buck come out next time, no excuses, okay?'

'Okay!' said Pauline.

Buck looked at his wife, drew her close.

'Okay. Here we go.' Dooley swallowed hard.

'Jack is going to have . . .'

Golf ball in his throat.

'Jack is going . . .'

It wouldn't go down.

'Jack . . .'

He couldn't do this.

Lace smiled; saw the tears of her mom and dad, the expectant look on the faces of Father Tim and Cynthia. She felt like a kite that had bumped along the ground for a long time and was lifting now and sailing . . .

'Jack,' she said, 'is going to have a little brother or sister.

'We're pregnant.'

21

Wilson called as they drove into town.

He dropped Cynthia at home to feed Truman and drove fast up the hill. Pauline and Buck were with Jessie; he was on his way to Father Brad and Mary Ellen.

'We must keep a cot in the hall for you, Father.'

'Kennedy, it's you!'

'No, this is a clone. I'm home sleeping or possibly watching Netflix in my bathrobe.'

'What's the scoop?'

'Dr. Wilson thinks it's a high ankle sprain for Father Brad, much worse than what Cynthia went through, so you can imagine. We're waiting to see X-rays. We'll make him comfortable tonight and off he goes in an ambulance first thing in the morning—to Holding, of course, to their fancy bone doc. Ms. Middleton will go also. She twisted her knee and must see an orthopedic specialist. Can't bend her leg; looks like ligament damage. Very painful, but the meds should help. They'll do an MRI on both. You should have seen them in their wheelchairs. Like bookends! Just darling!'

He had to laugh. 'Darling, is it? I must say you're someone who enjoys her work.'

She gave him a rare smile. 'Takes one to know one, Father.'

He found his colleague in bed; one leg in a sling, pointed vaguely toward heaven. Mary Ellen sat next to Father Brad in a wheelchair, a leg thrust out on the elevated leg rest.

He kissed Beth's mother on the cheek. 'How are you making it with the pain?'

She smiled. 'Minute by minute, grace by grace.'

'Beth and Tommy are on their way. And how about you, my friend?'

'Hurts like the dickens. But the med is kicking in. This was my swan song, Father. If I can't stay upright and take care of the kids . . . '

He sat in the visitor's chair. 'Might be best to cross that bridge when you get to it.'

'I tried several times to locate the blasted sweet spot on the ridge. The last time I went up there, I stumbled into a shallow place, like a bowl—it was covered with brush and snow—and dear God, the pain. A violent pain in my left ankle and calf, I thought my leg was broken. I tried to get out but couldn't. Then Mary Ellen came and tried to help and fell in with me.'

'I twisted my knee,' she said. 'It was terrifying, I couldn't bend my leg, couldn't move it at all. I started screaming for Jessie.'

'The so-called youth whisperer,' said Father Brad, 'was hollering, too, I assure you. It's a long story, but Jessie offered to go for help. I asked how she'd manage in the snow, with dark coming on.

'Trust me, she said.

'What if she wanted out just to get to the drug she was using? How can you trust a kid who's wrecking her life? But I did. Okay, we had to, but there was something about her I'd never seen before. She was scared and yet completely determined.

'If we'd waited till they came looking for us, we would have waited a long time. Drew gave up trying to get a signal. We weren't due back till Sunday afternoon, and in those temperatures, broken or fractured bones start doing their own thing. Honest to God, I thought we might be done for.'

'Hiking up,' said Mary Ellen, 'we noticed Jessie hanging back, always at the rear. You must ask her to tell you what she was doing.'

'She was going to dump us, Father!' Father Brad laughed, ironic. 'What if she had? A compass would have gotten Drew back to Mitford eventually, but only eventually, and we needed him desperately up there, we were helpless. Tiffany and Sarah kept the fire going, an amazing feat given that they had no past experience with campfires.'

Father Brad stiffened. 'Whoa. The pain. It's semper fi! How about you, sweetheart?'

'Okay for now,' she said.

Sweetheart! thought Father Tim. This train is moving.

'When we made camp, I found a Heath bar wrapper in the trash left behind in the cabin. That's Jessie's favorite bar, so I said, "You've been here before, I take it!" I thought I was making a joke, but she said, "Yes, my school chums and I smoke weed up here."

'She was willing to be open with me, also something I hadn't seen before. So I asked her what else she was using, and she told me. Crazy, dangerous stuff. I knew she'd need professional help.

'But what a scrapper she is. What a terrific young woman behind the iron mask! What did I tell you, Father? Hearts may open, heads may roll! Divine Dice!'

'Brad and I agree it was worth it,' said Mary Ellen. 'Worth it for everyone.'

'How did they get you down?'

'Three firemen and Hamp Floyd, four police, including Adele and the chief, and two EMT guys,' said Father Brad. 'They would have sent more, but a lot of people were off duty because of the snow.'

'They carried us out in what they call Stokes baskets,' said Mary

Ellen. 'I felt like we were being carried off Everest—every step those wonderful people took was excruciating, and it snowed most of the way down. What a ride!'

Father Brad took Mary Ellen's hand, kissed it.

'Now!' he said. 'Saving the best for last . . .

'What do you think this wonderful, remarkable woman and I did while waiting for help to arrive?'

'You made loud lamentations?'

'We got engaged!' they said in chorus.

Their visitor gave a spontaneous shout. 'Thanks be to God! Congratulations! Good job!'

'Will you do the honors, Father?'

'Absolutely, and thanks for the privilege. When do we herald this glad event?'

'May,' said Mary Ellen. 'When my mom has recovered from shoulder surgery, and when Brad's gardenias are in bloom.'

'My daughters don't know yet, or the parish. So mum's the word for a few days.'

'Count on me. I can safely say your parish will be over the moon.' And then he said what he always said in cases such as this.

'I'll bake a ham.'

I knew Father Brad, like, wanted me to turn my life around. That's what his campin' stuff is always about. To make people shut up, I said I'd go. But I'd be, like, ready to get out when I wanted to.

'I made trail markers—big tacks painted with reflective paint, in case I wanted to split at night. I stuck 'em on trees facin' east 'cause I'd be, like, hikin' east down th' mountain an' carryin' a flashlight.

'I figured I wouldn't go home when I left camp—I'd hitchhike to Charlotte and disappear. Everybody would think I was lost on th' mountain and send up helicopters.'

'You'd like it if people were searching for you?'

'That would be cool.'

'People will be searching for you. Starting tomorrow.'

She was startled. 'Why?'

'When word gets around, everybody will want to thank you, Jessie. Think about it. If you hadn't gone for help when you did, the injuries would have been far more complicated by the time help arrived, and the pain pretty unbearable. Drew knew how to keep them warm and hydrated, but God chose you to bring help, which was key. Sounds very cool to me.'

She shrugged.

'I know you must be beat. So no more talking unless you want to, I can be on my way.'

She gave him a look. Clearly, she wanted to talk.

'I was like tendin' th' fire. Mary Ellen and Father Brad had disappeared an' everybody else was scroungin' for a log we were supposed to learn to cook on. I hated sleepin' in th' tent with Tiff an' Sarah th' night before; I was so, like, ready to bust out of there.

'I was puttin' on my backpack when I heard Mary Ellen callin' me. She didn't call the other guys, she was callin' me. So I went up to th' ridge and . . .' She caught her breath. 'It was scary. No way could I pull anybody out of that hole.

'When Drew saw what was goin' on, he, like, freaked. There was so much pain . . . an' it was so hard to . . . to help them up an' . . .

'But we had to do it, we had to get 'em to th' fire an' heat rocks an' wrap 'em in blankets an' oh, my God, it was . . .

'I said I'd go for help an' Father Brad said he would, like, trust me to find my way down. He said there was a compass in his backpack; I said I wouldn't need it.'

She looked at the IV needle in her wrist as if just seeing it. 'An' I don't need this drip thing goin' on. Why am I in here anyway?'

'Mild hypothermia, dehydration, exhaustion. You'll be fine. I hear your mom and dad will check you out in the morning. By the way—congratulations. I guess you know you're an aunt again.'

'Yeah.'

'Do you know your mom won an eight-ball match?'

'No way. Who was she playin'?'

'Sammy.'

'Totally no way. He let 'er win.'

'We don't know that. She shot a great game. Even Sammy said so.'

She drew in her breath, stared at the ceiling.

'In the end, did you still want to hitchhike to Charlotte and disappear?'

She shook her head no.

'Were you scared hiking down the mountain with night coming on?'

'Yeah. It was totally dark in an hour. Old people say there are panthers up there. Painters, they call 'em, they scream like a woman.'

'It was a tough slog.'

'Yeah.'

'So the rescue people probably knew the mountain pretty well and could have found their way up. Why did you decide to go back with them? An even tougher slog.'

She shrugged, turned her gaze toward the wall.

'I'm just an old guy, Jessie, what do I know? But I think you cared about Father Brad and the others.

'I also think you might want to have a good cry.'

And she did.

SUNDAY, DECEMBER 13

At three in the afternoon, he walked to Avis's house to go through the mail.

They hadn't wanted to let him in the room this morning. But he had prevailed, knelt by Avis's bed, prayed from the heart. Wilson was looking older. 'We're being as aggressive as we reasonably can, but he's managing to play dead. What can I do with that?'

He riffled through the mail at Avis's kitchen table—stacked the bills, tossed the junk, set aside cards to take to the hospital and read aloud whenever the time came. He hoped the time would come. He felt a sudden despair.

He was staring at the kitchen wall when he heard a scratching sound. He opened the door; looked out, then down.

'*Chucky!*' he said. '*Chucky-y-y-y!*'

He carried Chucky into the hospital without interference and took the elevator to the second floor. Nurse Kennedy was leaving Avis's room.

She closed the door, bearing its OXYGEN IN USE sign, and stood squarely in front of it.

'Don't even think about it, Father.'

'Kennedy . . .'

'Dander.'

'I know, I know. But Avis is on oxygen, he won't be breathing any dander. To see this little guy will be the best medicine we could possibly give him. I challenge you, Kennedy, to name a pharmaceutical that has greater healing power than a good dog. Just look at that face.'

Kennedy did not look.

'Interacting with a dog slows the heart rate! Boosts the immune system! Can even improve mood and reduce pain. All scientific *fact*, Kennedy. And look at that tail wagging. I think he likes you.'

He was hell-bent on getting this dog through that door.

'This is no therapy dog, Father, and even if it was . . . '

He had known Kennedy for years, come on! 'Any good dog is a therapy dog,' he said, sticking to his guns. 'Besides, I just gave the little guy a hot bath in Avis's tub, and dander will not be a problem.'

'Why are two of his feet bandaged?'

'Sore pads. I cleaned them up and used antiseptic. He's been *walk-*

ing, Kennedy. He's very likely come all the way from *Tennessee!*' The miracle of it!

'That dog does not look healthy. I can see its ribs.'

'Of course you can. He's just had what may be his first decent meal in who knows when. He is perfectly healthy, I can assure you.'

'A white collar does not permit you to break rules.'

'Blast, Kennedy. This dog needs to *go in there.*'

'I've never seen you so pushy. Take him in, then, but do *not* let the patient handle him. Do you understand? Stay away from the patient!'

'Scout's honor.'

'You are a reasonable man—at least most of the time. Maintain a reasonable distance from the patient.'

'Consider it done.'

'This is a busy hospital, Father, and I don't have time to check back in two minutes. However, that's exactly what I'm going to do.' She looked at her watch. 'Two minutes,' she said. 'On the dot. Mr. Packard is a sick man, and if you ever tell this to Dr. Wilson, I will say . . . you prevaricated!'

He noticed that she narrowed her eyes to show who was boss.

With Chucky in firm grasp, he entered the room. 'Do not bark,' he said under his breath. 'Whatever you do.'

Avis looked spectral. That was the word. Chucky's tail whipped the air, and there went the straining to leap from his arms. He tightened his grip.

'Avis.'

Avis opened his eyes.

It was like trying to hold on to a rocket in blastoff. 'Chucky has come back, Avis! I think he walked all the way from Tennessee!'

A long stare. Then tears. Flowing onto a pillow made in a faraway factory and as hard as stone.

Avis smiled a ghost of a smile, held out his hand.

Could that be a spark of life he just saw in Avis's eyes? Only a flicker, but still . . .

'We can't touch you, Avis, or they'll have our heads.'

In a single leap, Chucky was out of his arms and onto the bed.

W ith a foolish grin on his face, and clutching Chucky with a death grip, he met Kennedy as she came in the room.

'No more of this,' she said in her Darth Vader mode.

'Righto,' he said, and walked up the hall at a trot.

Truman would not go for this arrangement. No way. And his wife wouldn't go for it either. He would be in the doghouse.

But he would cross that bridge when he got to it.

He talked to Chucky on the way home. Chattered like a magpie, as he did with Barnabas when they were in the car.

'Chucky, Chucky, where have you been? Round th' world an back again? Now listen up, buddy. We have a cat. Truman is not fond of dogs. I must ask you to be a gentleman. Keep your distance! Are you listening?'

Chucky looked at him, tail wagging, one ear up.

He wouldn't mind having a . . . but no. Never again. Barnabas had been the best of the best. And that was more than enough.

T ruman threw a double left jab at the nose, then a right to the head. Chucky appeared to think a moment, then powered a retaliation to Truman's left ear. Truman shook his head, looked bewildered.

'Boys, boys!' said Cynthia.

'Do you mind?' he said, fearing the truth.

His wife burst into laughter. 'You are so hilarious, honey. Really you are. Of course I mind!'

'But can we keep him till . . . you know . . . '

'Till kingdom come? Till the cows come home? Of course. But only for you and Avis.' She delivered a theatrical pause. 'There is a caveat.'

He felt his own tail between his legs, in a manner of speaking.

'Do not let him go beyond this puppy gate at any time.'

'Fine, fine.'

'At any time, Timothy.'

'Right.'

She gave him a look. 'You know what I mean?'

He knew, he knew.

He rang Dooley and told him about Chucky's homecoming.

'Bring him out, I'll look him over.'

'Many thanks. Have Kenny and Julie decided on a name?'

'Colleen Marie.'

'Good, good! So how did it go with Jack?'

'He's busy planning what they'll do together. Swing. Go fishing. Ride bikes. Learn to swim. By the way, he made several visits to the clinic today to announce th' time.'

'When you told him the facts of life, what did he say?'

'We didn't tell him everything. He stopped us somewhere in the middle and said, That is too much information.'

Talk about laughing your skin off.

TUESDAY, DECEMBER 15

At seven-thirty in the morning, he called for a report on the bookends. Father Brad could return to the pulpit for Christmas Eve Mass, albeit in a half cast and with crutches. Mary Ellen's knee surgery would happen today. She would remain through the holy days and undergo PT before returning to Boston.

Even with two bandaged paws and the restraint of a leash, Chucky led him a merry chase around the yard. Not to mention that he barked most of the night—again—because Truman was skulking on the other side of the gate.

After an ear-splitting barkfest at the sight of Otis and Lisa, Chucky was settled in the back room with a beef bone.

'I've got a problem at home,' he confessed to Otis.

Otis blanched. He did not like hearing people's personal problems.

'Our cat's going to make mincemeat of him. And my wife is, shall we say, on edge.' He had to tell *somebody*.

'We'll take 'im!' said Lisa.

'I didn't mean to suggest that you . . .'

'It's fine, we love Chucky. Don't think about it again, not for minute.'

He did think about it again, with some guilt, but only for a minute.

He talked with Pauline on her break at Hope House.

Jessie had agreed to get help in a detox program available in Holding and Pauline had arranged counseling of her own. They were driving down together in the morning. Tiffany and Sarah may—or may not—be considering the detox program.

A very, very long valley. Then one day the view of the mountain, and God willing, the beaten path to the summit where others had journeyed before.

He was breathing easier.

Raking ashes over the coals, turning out the lights . . .

The phone.

He went to his desk. Let's get this over with, he thought.

'There you are, Ms. Logan. How may I help you?'

'I need to talk, Father. With someone I won't run into at the post office or the food store. I don't know much about priests except that they hear confession.'

'I'm Anglican, so if you're Catholic, Ms. Logan, I can't hear your confession or offer absolution. Otherwise, yes.'

'I'm a lapsed everything; I'm nothing. Please call me Brooke. My husband suggests I spare you the fine details and remain unemotional. I rehearsed this but now I hardly know where to begin.'

'Jump in anywhere. That works.'

An intake of breath.

'My father is an important man. A four-hundred-thousand-acre beef cattle ranch near Sioux Falls, inherited from my grandfather. Oil interests, new visions for the cattle industry, philanthropy.

'He and my mom lived in Hartford, my two brothers and I grew up there. But Dad was always in South Dakota on business when we were kids. We adored him; my mother was completely devoted to him. He was prince, king, and saint to us. When I went away to college, he started going to Sioux Falls for even longer periods. By then his absences were normal to me, and I stopped paying attention.

'I'm a criminal defense attorney, Father, thus far unable to successfully argue my own case. Which is this:

'Three years ago, I flew to Sioux Falls on business. None of us had gone to the ranch since I was nine years old. It was strictly off-limits—it was where Dad 'worked very hard to give us all a beautiful life'—that was my mom's mantra.

'I took a car out to Star Creek. And there I met his other wife and his other three children.'

A long pause. 'Living happily at the family ranch,' she said. 'Can you imagine?'

'I can.' And he could.

'It was devastating. Completely.

'My mom was the most wonderful woman I ever knew. I didn't tell her; it would have destroyed her. But the cancer did it, anyway; she died two years ago. I haven't told my brothers—they're just finishing college and have their own issues. Only my husband knows. As for what this has done for me—it has wrecked my marriage and gone to work on my health.

'That's where you came in, Father.'

He sat down. This was not a phone call for standing.

'The journalist I was trying to call is writing a book about important ranchers in the West. The upside on these families is easy to find; he also wants the dark side. I said I would talk if I could remain anonymous. I was thrilled to have an opportunity to destroy my father's image. To grind him to dust. It gave me pleasure to know I would have power over one who abused his power over us.

'And then my husband asked for a divorce.

'Where I'm going with this is that maybe I didn't get the wrong number when I called you. Talking with you even briefly reminded me that I should pass this by someone else, a third party. My husband and I can't speak of it again.'

'You wish to . . . ?'

'To learn how to live with what I'm going to do. I'm meeting with the journalist next week. Telling the truth will be healing, but it frightens me, too. Somehow there should be another way.'

'There is another way, Brooke. But only one. Forgiveness.'

'You're going to talk about that?'

'I am.'

'That's out for me. Totally out. There has to be something else . . . '

'Something else to do what?'

'To help me live with what he's done. I'm bound and gagged by the rage I feel. I want to be able to love again—to give it and receive it and not sabotage it. How could I ever forgive him? Were his children nothing, that he had to have more? His devoted legal wife nothing, that he must have another? Please try to understand!'

'I do understand. My father had a relationship with another woman, and sixty years later, I learned that I have a brother. I, too, shall spare the details, but I was able to reap the fruit of this new relationship by forgiving my father. Forgiving him was the path to loving my brother.

'We'll never see each other at the post office, as you say, so I'm going to be very open here.

'You're clearly depressed. I imagine that all your relationships have

suffered, including those in your profession. You mention that your
health is affected and your marriage may be ending.'

'Yes.'

'Given that, Brooke, this is not about your father. This is about you.

'Confiding the dark side to the journalist won't alleviate the hurt. It
will only extend it, for you and countless others. It's important to remember, too, that it would dishonor the memory of your mother.

'So let's drop the notion of humiliating your father, and concentrate
on Brooke Logan.

'In nearly five decades of working with human souls, I've seen how
we can define ourselves by how we've been wounded. In every way, un-
forgiveness makes us the victim—nothing that an attorney would wish
to be, I'm sure.

'Surrender is the key that unlocks the hard heart and gives love the
liberty to enter. Where love enters, the possibilities for forgiveness go
viral.'

'I don't surrender, Father. I really don't. I think we need to end this
conversation, it's not going anywhere for me.'

'May I give you a few words more? By someone far wiser than either
of us?'

'If you must.' Snappish.

'Blaise Pascal was a brilliant mathematician, inventor, philosopher.
There is a God-shaped vacuum in the heart of every person, he said, *and it
cannot be filled by any created thing. It can only be filled by God, made
known through Jesus Christ.*

'At the age of forty, I was a priest who believed with the intellect, but
knew nothing of the intimacy with God that comes with surrender. I
was certifiably lost—holding on to my pain, trying to fill the God-shaped
vacuum. Then one day, standing in the backyard of the rectory, I was
moved to pray a simple prayer from the heart. I surrendered everything.
And everything changed.'

She laughed. 'So there's a trick prayer that solves all our problems?
You would be a poor candidate for the witness stand.'

'It has power to do what's intended.'

'What exactly is its intent?'

'To lead us out of ourselves. Liberate us from the gridlock of ego.'

'The gridlock of ego. You sound like my husband. Okay, you've been kind to listen to me. What is the prayer?'

'Thank you, God, for loving me and for sending your son to die for my sins. I repent of my sins and receive Christ as my savior. And now, as your child, I surrender my entire life to you.'

Long silence, and then laughter. 'Oh, no. I'm not ready for that, not at all, no. It's not my sins I'm calling about, Father. Or perhaps you have misunderstood.'

They were both exhausted

'Call me anytime. If I don't answer, you may get my deacon, Cynthia, who just happens to be my wife. She's wonderful. You'll love her, everybody does. She was betrayed, too, you see, and really gets it.'

He sat for a time after they said their goodbyes.

A few nights ago, Cynthia mentioned she was ready for him to retire once and for all.

But no. Old priests never retire; they just get the occasional wrong number.

22

MEADOWGATE

THURSDAY, DECEMBER 24

Tommy remembered saying it to only three people in his life. To his grandma, Ivy Amelia Sanderson, his granddaddy Milton, and when he was eighteen, to Adrienne Millhouse.

He had burned alive with love for Adrienne Millhouse, stayed in love with her long after she moved out west with her parents to a place he never heard of. He had tried a couple of times in college to love somebody else, and had tried again in Nashville. But trying isn't the magic. Maybe it sounded like a blurb on a refrigerator magnet, but love happens when you're not trying.

Now he needed to say it again, was dying to say it again. So why couldn't he say it again? Because all he had to offer besides a great sound system was a beat-up van, a run-down house, and forty acres needing lime and fertilizer.

Beth had made serious money in New York and she had no plans to stay here, which is where he wanted to live forever. Right now he was renting an apartment the size of a guitar case, chasing the dream, the dollar, the big break, so he could settle into the home place and make it what it used to be.

She would love what it used to be. Cherry trees, pear trees, apple trees bowed to the ground with fruit, walnuts lying thick in the grass, wild turkeys roaming where he had hunted and fished every summer as a kid.

But in the end, maybe the home place was getting in the way of his life. Maybe he was clinging to a dream that couldn't come true for years.

Maybe what he really needed to do is wake up and grow up. Or just man up—and take the risk—and say what he was crazy to say.

What he said was 'I have a gig in Nashville on Tuesday, and three hours in the best recording studio on the planet.' They were in a booth at Jake's and it was loud in here. 'Come with me. Cut a song with me.'

She had never thought of herself as spontaneous. She had her dad's let's-think-this-thing-through DNA that other people's money required. Money wasn't a dice roll. She had seen how Wall Street cowboys had done it and that wasn't her way. She should say she would think about it, because she really didn't know.

'We could drive up on Sunday,' said Tommy. 'I have friends with a horse farm. It's a beautiful place, they're great people. You could stay with Luke and Betsy.'

She didn't know how to stay in the home of strangers. She should say no.

But what she said was 'Thanks. Great! I'd love that.'

She caught her breath, laughed. Felt the heat in her face. She was rolling the dice.

They drove out to his grandmother's farm and wandered through the house. It was sunny today, but cold. There was no heat in the rooms and the water had been turned off. It was a winter house.

He smiled at her and touched the kitchen table covered with oilcloth, the kettle on the stove, the peeling wallpaper he had helped his grandma hang. They went upstairs to his bedroom and looked out the windows to the barn, and away to the deep blue hem of mountains on the robe of sky.

The bed he had slept in till college and afterward on visits was something like a cot. Above it, thumbtacked posters and album covers of Hank Williams, Bill Monroe, Patsy Cline in a cowgirl outfit, Tammy Wynette, Ronnie Lee Milsap, Bonnie Raitt, and a baseball glove hanging by its wrist strap.

She studied the faces of people she had never heard of, except Patsy Cline.

'Classics,' he said, nodding toward the posters. 'I grew up on those people.'

The smell of the house—walls and curtains infused with the scent of coffee and maybe fried bacon and ashes cold in the fireplace—all speaking kindly of the life of Ivy Amelia and the grandson she helped raise . . .

In the kitchen on a shelf were framed pictures. One of Tommy on his bike when he was ten, before the accident with Dooley. One when he graduated from high school and one when he was in college—the same determined look, she thought, the same beautiful smile. His mom and dad standing by a yellow convertible—his mother trim and smart, his dad wearing a fedora. His petite grandma and handsome grandpa in the vegetable garden out back, both in overalls and laughing. An uncle in California with a beard and a headband, signed Clyde 1976 San Francisco.

'So now you've met the family,' he said.

She was carrying a bottle of water and wet the tail of her shirt and cleaned the glass in the picture frames.

'You look like your grandpa.'

'A great man. Gone a long time. Couldn't have done it without them.'

Tommy walked out to the porch at one point and stood facing the mountains. When he came in, she could tell he had rubbed his eyes and she wanted to put her arms around him and say she was sorry about his grandmother, that she understood, which she truly did. It was hard to hold back her sudden feeling of tenderness, but what would happen if she didn't hold back? She couldn't live someone else's dream.

They walked around the garden, still patched by snow. 'I'm tillin' it up in the spring. Corn. Beans. Tomatoes. Lettuce . . .'

'What about rabbits?' she said. She knew that much about farming.

They had a picnic on the porch where the sun was, where vines were growing through cracks between the floorboards and she took pictures and they took selfies and sat on a blanket he had slept under as a boy.

It was a beautiful place. White oaks revealing enormous branches against a cloudless sky. The long, hard-packed driveway grown up with orchard grass in the middle. A bucket hanging on a nail by the door. His grandmother had filled the bucket with zinnias in summer, lilacs in May, Queen Anne's lace in September. A bucket on a nail. She was moved by its simple beauty against the faded green of the shingle boards.

She could imagine Ivy Amelia at the screen door, waiting to see her grandson walking up the drive from where his mother dropped him off at the road. Later, he would arrive in his pickup truck; later, still, in his van with the sound equipment and four hungry Biscuits. Ivy Amelia would walk out to the porch, waving . . .

He had brought his favorite guitar today, a 1956 Gibson, and they were singing together when their eyes met and she was suddenly lost— plunged to a depth she'd never reached before. She felt the beating of her heart in her throat, heard them singing the words as if this were not happening at all . . . then the sensation of coming up fast, as if breaking the surface of a lake, hungry for air.

After he took Beth to Meadowgate, he parked the van in his drive-way and dialed the radio to the country classics station.

He hammered out the dent in the rear left door. Soaped the whole thing and hosed it off. As for wax, that was a two-hour undertaking. So no wax.

'*You were always on my mind, you were always on my mind . . .* '

He would go out to Meadowgate this evening for supper, then pick her up on Sunday at eleven and head out to the town he was still counting on.

Funny, but he'd never kissed her. Before they met at the wedding, Dooley told him her income range. He'd never known a woman who made that kind of money; he thought it might be like kissin' the Bank of America. But that idea was definitely revised. How he felt when they sang together had nothing to do with financial; it was easier than breathing.

He had a gig tomorrow, Christmas Day, and one on Saturday, so he had to get the van cleaned up for her now and hose it off again Sunday morning for the trip to Nashville. The guys would ride to the venues with Lonnie.

He checked the air in the tires. Sprayed Armor All on the dashboard and wiped it down, hosed the floor mats, reorganized the sound equipment. Collected loose change from the console and put it in his jeans pocket for Jack. Installed two bottles of water in the cup rack, and her present in the glove compartment.

'*I fall to pieces, each time I see you again . . .* '

The gold bracelet was the only gold his grandma ever owned. He had wrapped it himself.

Maybe he should talk to Dooley about all this. Or maybe not.

His hands were shaking as he wiped down the seats and realized he was saying it—under his breath, over and over.

Beth didn't want to think about her life right now, about where she was going. Meadowgate was supposed to be a halfway house, a safe place where she could make sense of the connections she had severed and what the future may look like.

How could she leave behind forever what she was trained to do, good at doing? She hadn't expected to fall in love with Jack and the wonderful life Dooley and Lace were living—with family close by, and the old house so sweetly giving to all who come through the door. Surely she must be again what she had been in the city—but without the craziness, if that was possible. How easily she had surrendered to craziness by marrying Freddie.

Their marriage had lasted 'about the time it takes to pluck a chicken,' her mom's housekeeper said.

'All those expensive suits he left behind!' said her mom. 'And *pounds* of ties!'

She had been relieved but bewildered. It was like he walked into the night and was smuggled out of the country. Later she heard that he showed up at his office the following day, unfazed, in an Armani blazer.

The truth was, she had wanted to love somebody, thought it was time to be in love. And so she had worked to make love happen.

He was a clever attorney and popular with legions and called her *darling* like in the old movies they watched for hours. Shallow is what she had been. Lace was never shallow, she was real and true. Tommy was real and true, and Dooley and Harley and Willie.

She didn't know if Elizabeth Anne Middleton could be real and true.

L ace sat on the side of the bed with the journal open in her lap.
She had recorded their amazing news a few days ago. There was really no good explanation why women with adhesive disease can get pregnant. Her dad said that over time, adhesions can become thinned and give way without medical intervention, but there's no guarantee. Medical intervention can even make things worse. All she knew is that her dad and Dr. Wilson were really positive, and that somehow, much less of her biological father's cruelty haunted her body. Her body had revolted and laid claim again to itself.

She uncapped her pen.

DECEMBER 24~ *Once he was a little boy whose story was~*

I can watch tv anytime I want if Granny is sleeping and eat anything I want if there is anything to eat. Granny keeps me because she gets money and because my other mom went to California and my other dad is dead because of a train.

Tonight he wants to do the sweetest most wonderful thing. He wants to tell his story after supper to his mom and dad and Uncle Tommy and Aunt Beth. His story has grown to have a life apart from bedtime~ it is his "certification"~ and he is eager to share it. Thank you, Lord!

L ook,' said Lace.

Dooley stepped to the window.

Sunset burning the western sky; Beth, Tommy, and the farm dogs walking out the hay road, like he and Lace had done through hard times and easy. He remembered they were walking the hay road just before the wedding when his cell buzzed. The birth mother had given up rights and Jack would be coming to Meadowgate the following day.

'God help us,' he'd said. And his prayer had been answered in spades.

L ace, it's Kim! It's up and it's marvelous! The entire wall of the playroom—imagine how huge it will look to the children and how real it all will be. I feel I could walk into it and pet Choo-Choo.'

'You wouldn't want to do that!' This was bliss, this was surely bliss. That her work could bring such happiness . . .

'Everyone will be arriving next week. We're going to have a party in the playroom and churn ice cream and have a Christmas tree decorated with moss and berries and birds' nests and everything real and wonderful.

'I know you can imagine what joy I feel to have discovered my sister and her adorable family. I had no one, really, for so many years.

'So thank you, Lace, for bringing your world into my life and theirs, I feel like a kid myself. Oh, and a big tub of little ducks will be coming to the party. And a farmer in overalls with a wheelbarrow filled with presents! And a golden retriever like in the mural—I do hope he's properly trained.'

'So elaborate, Kim. So fabulous!'

Kim laughed. 'Ah, well! This is Hollywood, you know.'

I can read four whole books an' spell forty-eight whole words . . . ' . . . an' make peanut butter an' banana san'wiches an' say prayers to Jesus all by myself!

'With two dollars an' eighteen cents from Uncle Tommy, I have eleven dollars an' . . . how many cents, Mom?'

'Nine.'

'Eleven dollars an' nine cents in my pig bank!'

Jack looked at the floor. He was stuck.

'What happens in July?' said Dooley.

'In July, I get a baby brother!'

'Remember we don't know it will be a brother,' said Lace. 'We won't know till your little sister or brother is born, okay?'

'Okay, but it *could* be a brother.'

'Absolutely,' said Dooley. 'Keep movin' on your story.'

'My uncles are Uncle Pooh, Uncle Sammy, Uncle Kenny, Uncle Henry in Miss'ippi. Uncle Walter in New Jersey, Uncle Doc, an' Uncle Tommy.' Seven fingers.

'Proud to be included!' said Tommy.

'Uncles are hard 'cause there's a *lots*. For cousins, Etta, Ethan, Rebecca Jane, an' Colleen Marie makes this many cousins.' Four fingers.

'Mom or Aunt Beth or Dad teaches me somethin' every day. Like th' a'phabet an' makin' pizza. An' Dad showed me how to turbo my bike with a Pokémon card!'

Lace looked at Dooley looking at Jack. Her wonderful, handsome husband was smiling.

How far all their stories had come.

She placed her hands over her belly. And always, always, more stories waiting to happen.

H e and Beth were doing the supper dishes. He liked to wash, she liked to dry and put away.

'Where are you playing tomorrow?'

'Big family reunion in Holding,' said Tommy. 'Wish I didn't have to do it. I'll miss all the action at Meadowgate.' The bracelet was burning a hole in his pocket. Before he got the gig, he planned to give it to her on Christmas morning, but maybe he should do it tonight because he was rehearsing tomorrow morning.

'Could I go with you? I could help set up or something. I wouldn't get in the way.'

'Are you serious?'

'Dooley's mom and dad are coming out for the big surprise. It would be great for them if it could just be family. They won't miss me!'

She didn't know exactly how he was taking this.

'I could meet you in town to save time,' she said.

He was what Dooley said he'd been at the wedding: plastic in a microwave.

T hey walked out to the van. She was learning to love the big silence of a country winter night.

'I want to be like Jack,' he said.

Beth laughed. 'Me, too! But how do you mean?'

He took her hands in his. He was determined to say what he needed to say, what he had said only three times in his life.

But what he said was 'I'd like us to have a new story. One we could be in together.'

She had kissed before, but this was the first time.

23

G race Murphy had set her alarm for seven A.M. She wanted to be among the first to bring in the *Muse* from the porch.

She put on her glasses and sat in her pajamas by the front door until she heard the light thud, then ran with the newspaper to the dining room table.

The front page showed pictures from the parade, with Coot in his Santa suit the biggest picture of all! She would make sure he put it in the scrapbook she gave him last year for Christmas.

She drew in her breath when she saw the next page. They had used her story in her own handwriting! She thought it would be in *printing*!

She was embarrassed that she had not been more careful with the block letters, which had taken a very, very, very long time with lots of erasing.

On Tuesday, she had raced next door to deliver her story because Mr. Hogan called the bookstore and said hurry, it was a deadline. There was no time for her mom to spell-check and she had dashed through the shoe store and up the stairs as fast as she could. But Mr. Hogan was not there and Miss Vanita Bentley was not there, so she left it on the desk that was neat and not the messy one with things falling on the floor.

Her heart beat fast as she looked at her story, which spread across two pages! There was the picture of her with Miss Louella. It was good of Miss Louella but not good of her because she was smiling and you could see the gap where her tooth was missing.

She read the printed caption.

> Miss Louella Baxter Marshall, a longtime resident at Hope House with the author of this story, Miss Grace Murphy. When asked for her advice about life, Miss Louella says, 'Love whoever God sets down in front of you. Even the mean ones, 'cause they can sho use it.'

She could hardly breathe. She had never seen her name in a newspaper before and hoped people would like the story. She would never, ever write another story this long till she learned to type with both hands.

J. C. Hogan was quick to acknowledge that he wasn't a complete dunce. The 43-inch screen and the grill had both been disappointing in the long run. So maybe Tim Kavanagh was right.

He was in the office early this morning as he wanted to do this at his computer, in private.

He selected 14-point Century Schoolbook and typed:

> Have I told you lately that I love you?

So, okay, it was a song title, but it would work as an opener.

Your problem, said the article he read in a magazine at the Wesley barbershop, is that you have shut down your true feelings. You have no clue how you feel about anybody or anything. Long story short, you did not hang the moon, it is not all about you. Go to your gut—how do you really feel about her? Dig deep or call it a day.

So how did he feel about Adele—deep down? He sat back in his desk chair, closed his eyes. One thing he knew for sure—marrying her was the best thing he ever did. Didn't she keep him in decent clothes? Iron the occasional shirt? Stay after him about a sensible diet? Rub his feet after he had pounded the pavement all day?

And how about reading his editorials and cheering him on? And nursing him when he was sick as a dog with his blasted annual sinus infections?

Pre-Adele, he was a disaster. Maybe he was still a disaster, he didn't know. He sat up, typed, and added an underline for emphasis.

Marrying you was the best thing I ever did.

He took a deep breath and stared at the framed quote over his desk. _If a cluttered desk is a sign of a cluttered mind, of what, then, is an empty desk a sign?_ So much for the jerks who called his desk the Dumpster. That little nugget was from Albert Einstein, no less.

Eighteen words so far, and how long had he been sitting here? Twenty minutes? Thirty? Lord knows.

Speaking of—he could pray. Did prayer always have to be about ending war and feeding the hungry? Tim Kavanagh had said many times it was good to talk to God about th' little stuff as well as th' big stuff. So maybe compared to th' suffering in th' world, this was little stuff, but it was big to yours truly.

He felt awkward praying, but he did believe in God and Jesus and even th' Holy Spirit, though th' Trinity was tough to wrap your head around.

He made the sign of the cross as Father Brad did every Sunday before preaching. His mind went completely blank.

When he snapped back, he thought about her job. It was tough. Not that she ever had to take out any hardened criminals, but tough. And they'd never been anywhere to speak of, except Wisconsin twice to visit her family. People in this town were not world travelers except for Percy and Velma Mosely, who'd been on, like, four cruises where Percy learned to order drinks with umbrellas. Out of bed at four in the morning for thirty-five years, to open up th' Grill and fry livermush? Percy deserved it.

Maybe they should go somewhere romantic. Vanita could put out an edition if he left her with enough photo stock and ad backup.

But wait. He wouldn't mention a trip till later. That would be his ace.

He looked at the ceiling, sighed; studied his shoes. Brown.

Face it, he hadn't been the best husband. Feelings scared him. A few times in his life, he had gone to his gut as the magazine said, and did not want to go there again.

And yes, now that he really thought about it, he loved Adele Hogan. But what if she didn't love him anymore? 'Let that go from your mind,' Tim had said. 'If you love her, tell her about it. And see where the chips fall.'

He looked at her photo on his desk. She was in that dotted blouse she wore on their first date; he'd been nuts about her. The very thought made him feel . . . what? Mushy.

So if he could think up one more line, he'd be done. The operative word here was *note*, not letter. But the line had to be a closer, it had to have punch. *Had* he told her lately that he loved her? Not in maybe a year or two or three. Like, he thought the grill/TV combo would do th' talkin', but obviously not.

I love you . . .

Maybe he should add something like dearly or passionately? No. He was not going off the cliff here.

But wait. He felt his hair stand on end—yes!—and completed the declaration.

. . . forever

He looked at the words he had just written; added an exclamation mark. Call him butter, he was on a roll! So maybe a bonus line.

And I am very proud of you.

It was something he'd meant to tell her since she was promoted to captain a few years ago.

He sat back in the chair, out of breath. What had just happened here? He had stopped to really think about Adele. Maybe he'd actually gone to his gut, because something had just happened here.

He folded the note, put it in the envelope, and licked the flap. He would give it to her tomorrow morning with her gift which he hadn't decided on yet.

But no, he couldn't wait.

Heart hammering, he legged it to the station and sat across from her desk while she read it. What if it was too mushy? What if she didn't care anymore? When she looked up, he thought he'd never seen her so happy. Fact is, he couldn't remember being so happy himself.

'This is th' sweetest thing I ever read in my life.' There were tears in her eyes. 'Do you really mean it?'

'I really mean it,' he said with a knot in his throat. He got up and whipped around the desk and leaned down and kissed her. 'Yes, I do. I really mean it.'

The chief walked in and had a laugh. 'You're disturbin' th' peace there, Hogan.'

'Ten-four, Chief. Just kissin' your captain.' He could not wipe the grin off his face.

On the way to the *Muse* office, he stopped by the Local for a Snickers. An eighteen-wheeler was blocking the southbound lane, with Otis directing traffic. He found Tim Kavanagh signing off for thirty-five-pound bags of sweet potatoes and a stack of crates from the Sunshine State.

'I hate to admit this, buddyroe.'

'Admit it anyway,' said Father Tim.

'Just so you know. It's not pork chops.'

And out the door of the Local went J. C. Hogan—whistling, of all things.

. . .

There had been no time to check the *Muse* at home this morning, so he bought one out of the rack at the Local.

There was Jack on Dooley's shoulders. And the clown on stilts. And Esther and Ray and the begats on the float. And Coot waving and happy. It had been a very good day for Mitford.

At break time, he had a cup of tea and a quick read at the cash register.

MISS LOUELLA:
A True Story
By Grace Elizabeth Murphy

PART ONE
___

Miss Louella Baxter Marshall lives at Hope House. She says she is old as a mountain but she is only 97. She has seen a lots of things in her life. She was raised by Miss Sadie who used to live at Fernbank at the top of the hill with the orchard. Miss Sadie was four or five years older and called Miss Louella her baby.

Miss Louella said they were very close. She did not sometimes know where she stopped and Miss Sadie started!

When Miss Louella was little, Miss Sadie pulled Miss Louella around in a red wagin. They went all around the huge yard and through the orchard and to the playhouse Mister Ned built.

There is a happy story and a sad story about the wagin. Because it is Christmas, I will tell you the sad story first so you can read the happy story last and feel good when you finish.

One day Miss Sadie's mama gave them a quarter each and said they could go to town with the wagin for the very first time by theirself. Miss Louella was allowed to carry Miss Sadie's best baby doll that day because it was Miss Louella's birthday. She was three or maybe four. She could walk as good as anybody but Miss Sadie like to pull the wagin and Miss Louella like to ride.

Miss Louella said be careful on the bumps I don't want this baby doll name of Annie to fall out much less my own person.

They got to town and went to the drugstore that used to be where the Happy Endings bookstore is now which is my mom's bookstore. I can help you if you come in on Saturday.

Miss Sadie bought a vanilla ice cream soda with two straws.

Miss Sadie sat on the bench out front and Miss Louella sat in the wagin and they handed their soda backwards and forwards to each other. It was the best thing Miss Louella ever tasted.

Two mean boys walked up and one said you could give me a drink of that soda and Miss Sadie said no this is our soda and the boys stolen it away from them and said its ours now and called Miss Louella a very, very bad name and drank it all up. Then they grabbed Annie and ran off. Remember Miss Louella was only three or maybe four and she bust out in tears but Miss Sadie got screaming mad and ran after them hard as she could but she could not catch them.

I'll ride yall and your wagin home said the drugstore man. And off they went in a Buick car. Even in a car it seemed a long ride home and uphill all the way.

Miss Sadie ask the drugstore man what is the boys name and where do they live cause her daddy was what they called a FORCE in Mitford even if he was gone a lots on traveling. Their names was Lewis Young and Boid Bentley. Miss Louella said she never forgot those names.

Miss Sadie knew if she told her mama what happen her mama would not let them go to town again by theirself ever. So she told her mama because she and Miss Louella did not <u>want</u> to go to town again by theirself ever.

They were both heart brokened about Annie and cried half the night. But the next day as a treat they were going to play queen riding in a golden carriage. So they went out to the apple barn to get their wagin that would be a golden carriage and it was gone.

If you have a bike or a car and ride it all the time and it is your favorite thing that is how you would feel if it was stolened.

Miss Sadie's daddy was in Paris France and they could not sik her daddy on the thiefs. So Miss Sadie and Miss Louella made up a plot. An eye for an eye said Miss Sadie quoting the Bible her mama read to her—and a toothe for a toothe.

PART TWO

Miss Sadie's mama went to visit the sick so Miss Sadie ask Ned who wirked at Fernbank to take them to town. Miss Louella said Ned was a sweet white man who was kind to everybody.

Ned said who say I can take yall to town?

Mama said we could not take the wagin to town ever again so you will have to take us.

That was the truth, but Miss Sadie said it like he was supposed to take them to town because her mama said to.

Where you gon go in town said Ned?

Over back of Ivy Lane.

Ned's truck would do 35 miles an hour! They loved to ride in his truck.

So they drove by Boids house and saw his family had a barn. If you was to steal somebodys wagin where would you put it said Miss Sadie?

Let's see said Ned I would put it in my ole barn.

So Miss Sadie and Miss Louella jump down and run into Boids barn and there was the wagin but not their baby doll annie.

They went in and was going to take out their wagin and wait for Ned but they heard somebody comin and hid behind a lots of hay bales. They were scared to deathe. Do not cough or sneeze said Miss Sadie and Miss Louella did not cough or sneeze a single time but she said she wet her pants which were pink overalls.

It was Boid an Lewis. Boid said let's charge kids two cents apiece to ride over and back to the drugstore which now is my mama's bookstore name of Happy Endings.

Lewis said plus we can charge 2 cents extra for whoever wants to ride holdin th baby doll. But I will have to steal it from my sister who give me a dime for it.

They went off with the wagin, but Miss Sadie and miss Louella did not come out till they heard Ned's truck.

Please take us to the house next to Miss Angelina Haygood's house said Miss Sadie.

When they got there Miss Sadie said to Louella you sit in the truck and she went to the door and knocked. A woman came to the door. Miss Sadie said my baby doll Annie is here I would like to have her back.

The woman said we do not have your baby doll and slam the door.

Take us to the drugstore please said Miss Sadie.

She told Ned she would preciate it if he would ride in the red wagin for 4 cents. I will give you 4 cents.

Does I have to hold the baby doll said Ned.

The wagin come along after awhile pulled by Boid with Lewis walking behind and riding 2 kids with runny noses and one holdin Annie.

Miss Sadie gave Ned his 4 cents so he could ride and hold the baby doll at the same time. Ask to go down to the hardware and back again she said and when you get back we will put the wagin and the baby doll in the truck and go home.

Ned got in the wagin and said take me to the hardware and back and the mean boys stuck our their hand and got 4 cents.

'Have a nice ride!' said Miss Sadie.

Miss Louella said Ned was a powerful big man with long legs like a grandaddy spider and could not fold his legs all the way in the wagin. Plus he was too heavy to pull very far so Boid and Lewis took off runnin and kep the 4 cents.

Ned walked back laughin and pulling the wagin and holding the baby doll with people on the street clapping.

Miss Sadie said it is a shame they ran away because I did not get to give them my note. She took it out of her pinnafort pocket and read it to Miss Louella.

> *My daddy is on his way back from Paris France. If you ever tuch*
> *anything of mine and Louellas again what will happen to you*
> *will be so terrible I cannot even put it in words. You should learn*
> *how to be nice. It is easy if you have any brains.*
>
> *Yours sincerely,*
> *Sadie Eleanor Baxter*

Almost fifty years later Boid knocked on Miss Sadie's and Miss Louella's door in Mitford. It was Chirstmas Day and he said he was truly truly sorry. They invited him in and Miss Sadie set out peanut butter and crackers and Louella made fried chicken with green beans and mashed potatoes and gravy.

THE END

Otis hung up the phone.

'Daddy's on his way. So you can have th' rest of th' day off.'

'You needn't do that. Really.'

'Daddy likes to come up to th' store. He don't say much, but he gits th' job done. You go on with your family.'

He felt the muscles in his neck relax. 'Otis, do you know what you are?'

Otis did not care for personal questions.

'You are a champion. The real deal. Bless your heart. We love you and Lisa. You're the best.'

Otis turned red as a beet, but the grocery cleric had said what needed to be said.

Puny and the twins arrived at the house at one o'clock. He noted again how the Guthrie clan had an agreeable way of *pouring* into a room.

Puny presented them with a dozen eggs from the flock, a quart of apple butter, and her famous cheese wafers. Riches galore!

'Granpa, here's my gift!' Sassy handed him an egg decorated with a portrait of himself!

'My nose,' he said, 'looks like a rutabaga.'

This simple truth evoked hilarity.

Sassy handed an egg to Cynthia. Another portrait.

'Are these *wrinkles*?' said his wife in mock astonishment.

'Yes, ma'am, but just around your eyes an' mouth an' some on your forehead.'

Puny gasped. 'I cannot *believe* you said that! Miss Cynthy does *not* have wrinkles, she has laugh lines. I would give anything to have *laugh* lines.'

At that, the adults had a laugh.

'My gift is better!' Sissy held up a sheet of paper. 'I wrote you an' Granpa Tim a poem.'

'My present next!' said Tommy.

'No, mine next!' said Timmy.

'I was born first,' said Tommy.

'Would you like me to read my poem to you? Or just give it to you on paper?'

'Don't *read* it!' said Tommy. 'I've heard it a thousand times.'

'I'd *love* you to read it!' said Cynthia.

'Me, *too!*' said the ornery granpa.

Moans, groans, shrieks of laughter.

After the flurry of gift exchanges and cups of hot chocolate, the clan headed out to Mamaw and Papaw Cunningham's.

'Thank you for all their books,' said Puny, who was looking a little frayed around the edges. 'An' the hand vac, which I was dyin' for, an' the bonus an' everything. I love y'all to pieces! Merry Christmas!'

'We love you back,' said Cynthia. 'Merry Christmas!'

'You're the best!' said Father Tim.

'I'm tryin'!' said Puny.

. . .

H ow 'bout that Grace Murphy?'
   'How 'bout that Louella?' said Cynthia.
They were proud.

T onight they would each open their one small present, and in the
   morning, the big one. The whopper!

He had just finished wrapping the big one when she knocked on the bedroom door.

'Timothy! The tape?'

'Hold on.' She would be surprised. Really surprised. Hadn't she said 'practical'? He preferred practical. A few years ago, she had given him a custom-tailored tuxedo and had he worn it? Maybe twice.

'Okay.' He opened the door a crack, handed her the tape.

'Give me a clue!' she said.

He closed the door. 'No clues!'

Her present would go under the tree tonight; in the meantime, he hid it at the back of the closet. She wouldn't come looking for it, of course, but still . . .

S he tied the bow at the top of the box. Even though he wasn't a 'man
   who has everything,' her husband was hard to buy for. But this was perfect; it would make him happy. Which of course was the agenda all year long, the old sweetie.

I t's smelling good in here,' he said.
   At six-thirty, the oyster pie was in the oven and their laps were full of Christmas cards.

'From Marian and Sam Fieldwalker,' he read aloud. He and Cynthia had spent nearly a year supplying on an Outer Banks island, blessed by the friendship of these good people.

'*We hold you in our prayers, dear Father and Cynthia. Enclosed is Morris Love's new CD. It is selling like crab cakes at our new pier restaurant! We still miss you in Whitecap. Wishing you a blessed Christmas.*'

Morris Love. He was moved by the memory of the man behind the wall and the crucifying music that had poured forth to a curious cleric. He placed the cards on the table by his chair and put the CD in the player. Bach's Organ Chorale no. 3, 'Lord Jesus Christ, the Only Son of God . . .'

He was mindful of something like utter satisfaction as she chose a card from the pile.

From the Eire, that faraway, never-to-be-forgotten land where one's ancestors fought and died and somehow managed to live on in the very stones, she read:

> '*The light of the Christmas star to you*
> *The warmth of home and hearth to you*
> *The cheer and good will of friends to you*
> *The love of the Son and God's peace to you*
>
> '*Dear Father and Cynthia, Bella is being married at Broughadoon*
> *in March and moving to Dublin with a lovely husband. Wish you could*
> *be with us. We shall send an invite in any case. Evelyn and William*
> *sit in the sun on days when we have any sun at all and hold hands*
> *like children. One could not ask for better. Siochain agus Fairsinge!*
> *Your friends forevermore at Broughadoon. Anna and Liam.*'

The music soaring into the room, taking them willing captive . . .

From Agnes at Holy Trinity—across a creek and up a hill to a clearing that overlooks the billowing sea of mountains, he read:

*'Wishing you a blessed Christmastide from Holy Trinity, where to
our perfect amazement we have cobbled together an official choir of
thirteen voices! As you know, one must often wait a very long time
for one's prayers to be answered—and it was worth the waiting!
Climb above the clouds and break bread with us any time, we sorely
miss you.*

'In the love of Him Who loved us first, Agnes and Clarence'

Ha! Out of Henry's card fell a photograph. Henry and Lucille! Look
there! Both shining with happiness. Lucille in a very fine hat, the two of
them on a bench in a photographer's studio having such joy documented
for all time. 'Look!' he said, holding up the photo. 'Look at this miracle!'

'A very handsome pair. And I just realized I'll have a sister-in-law!
A first!'

Henry was going to meet Lucille's children and grans over Christmas, so he wouldn't call at Christmas, but catch up later with all details.

From Memphis, a postcard of a jolly Santa, the message in a script he
vaguely recognized:

Hey Buddy let's go climb a water tower! Your old pal, Tommy.

A card from George Gaynor, who lived undiscovered for many
months in the Lord's Chapel attic where he came to know the creator of
all that is seen and unseen.

*Father and Cynthia, I am a happily married man and soon to be
a father. Pray for me in this as I have no prior experience in either!
Continuing in prison ministry in Topeka. You are often in my
petitions. But for you, Father, but for you . . .*

Merry Christmas!

Yours in Christ, George

From Holly Springs, where he was born into this world so many years ago, and from whence he began his travels to this chair, this fire, this woman, this quiet pleasure:

> *'Father, I am spending my golden years doing the thing I love*
> *best—sorting through the countless photographs I have taken, first*
> *with my Kodak Brownie, then my Holiday Bakelite (I believe this*
> *was shot with the Bakelite) and later with the fancy Leicas and*
> *Nikons and now with my point-and-shoot! And just look what*
> *I found! Merry Christmas to you and yours, Jessica.'*

There he was in black and white, in all the skinniness and perplexity of youth, his knees as opalescent as bone china, his hair profuse, his hands too large for his frame, in track shorts and T-shirt, the sun bright on his face.

'You were adorable!' said Cynthia.

This was Christmas enough, he thought, right here, right now. With oyster pie soon coming, and at last her paintings.

He happened to glance out the side door and voilà. Harley's truck was pulling into Helene's driveway.

He had completely given up trying to figure this one out.

'Harley,' he told Cynthia.

'*La vie est belle!*' she said, clapping her hands.

She smiled a little, oddly anxious

'I'll leave you alone with them. I'd love to know what you think.'

With that, she had sent him padding down the hall to the living room.

He was startled. So many images swarming the room, standing against the sofa, leaning against chairs, lined up against the wall by the fireplace. A forest of paintings.

Her canvases were almost always large, but these appeared larger than life, full of viscera in this silent, unused room.

A great, stalking flamingo. Albino deer in a herd of five, all looking with solemnity into the eyes of the viewer. A rhino peering from behind a tree, the horned snout immense. A nest, greatly magnified, with speckled eggs and an infinitesimal red mushroom sprouting from the moss.

Portraits of people he had never seen but felt at once he knew. An old woman so black you could see the suggestion of blue, wearing a printed head rag and looking solemn with her Bible clasped over her heart. The hand, often a stumbling block for artists, beautifully rendered; he could see veining and blemishes, knuckles grown prominent with age and hard work. Black skin, black garment, black Bible—black on black, yet each component with exquisitely defined nuance.

He looked on the back of the canvas where she had handwritten the title: *Chosen.*

And there was William! William of Broughadoon, translated from the watercolor she did in Ireland. He was glad to see his friend William, with merriment in his eyes, and wrinkles as numerous as the fairies in Mayo.

At the close of the Christmas Eve Mass at Lord's Chapel, Father Brad cited that tonight was indeed the birth of Good News to all the world. And he had some good news to all of Mitford.

Then he asked Jessie, Sarah, Tiffany, and Drew, three policemen and their captain, three firemen and their chief, and two rescue volunteers to please join him up front. This was a big moment. By way of a seeming accident, God had fulfilled the entire purpose of snow camp for three hurting teens.

He guided Jessie to his side and held her hand.

'Brothers and sisters in Christ, you see before you, myself being the exception, a choir of angels. In the flesh!

'Most of you know the story of our emergency situation on the mountain. No cell service to call out for help. Two injuries needing immediate treatment. Drew kept us hydrated and prayed for. Tiffany and Sarah gathered firewood, made hot soup, and heated stones to keep us warm. And these good firemen, police, and rescue volunteers left home and family to haul us down the mountain in baskets. If you ever wondered if your priest is a basket case, now you know.'

Some had wondered, but all laughed.

'And though everyone in the choir did an amazing job in the nick of time, it is this young woman who made everything come together in perfect harmony. Jessie Leeper hiked two miles to Mitford, alone, at night, along a mountain trail covered by snow, to get help. Then she hiked back up the trail with the volunteers, to make sure we were okay.'

Spontaneous applause.

He spoke to those being recognized. 'Thanks be to God for his good favor, and to all of you for your hard work and sacrifice. May God mightily bless you and your families for your blessing to us.' He turned to the congregation. 'I'm asking our youth team and carryout team to stand at the door with me, so you can thank them. A hug or two would not be unwelcome.'

Hamp Floyd was fighting to keep his eyes open. He had not been up this late since he was a kid waitin' for Santy Claus. He was a believer in ecumenism, which he could not spell, even though he knew what it meant, so here he was—a flatfoot Baptist in th' middle of th' night, trapped in a church that didn't know when to say amen and go home.

'I am happy to tell you there's still more good news,' said Father Brad. 'I'll get you out of here in a moment, I know it's late.'

He limped on his crutches to Mary Ellen, who was sitting on the front row.

'But it is never too late . . .' Father Brad turned a slow red. 'For love! Right?'

Big applause.

He could hardly believe his flamboyance. But wasn't that the truth, after all? Wasn't that what the Good News is *about*?

Beth and Tommy helped Mary Ellen stand, splint and all, aided by crutches of her own.

A murmur rippled through the congregation. So! Just what they'd been expecting. And Boston, no less. A Yankee! Just like Father Tim did all those years ago. But nice, very nice, Mary Ellen, and certainly good-looking. Well, leave him alone, let him go his way, he was a good man, Father Brad, though he could be a trifle *different*. Maybe this would cool his ardor for the purchase of a motorcycle, which was occasionally rumored to be his heart's desire.

'Mary Ellen Middleton,' he said, 'has agreed to be my wife! Sunday, May fifteenth, at two in the afternoon! Weather permitting, dinner on the grounds!'

Unhindered applause. Made the rafters tremble.

'Go in peace, now, to love and serve the Lord! Alleluia!'

'Thanks be to God! Alleluia!'

The ringing of the bells, then, with what seemed a particularly joyful abandon, and the great flurry of greetings at the door and in the church-yard.

'Merry Christmas, Pauline, Buck!'

'Jessie, Pooh! Merry Christmas!'

'Merry Christmas, Captain!'

'Merry Christmas, Chief!'

'Father Tim! Cynthia! Merry Christmas!'

Advent was past. Christmas was official.

H e and Cynthia collapsed on the sofa, too spent to climb stairs. She put her head on his shoulder. 'How much happiness can one *take*, anyway? No, don't trouble yourself to answer, honey, that is a moot question.'

As a wind-down, they were having a little Mozart, a few of the irre-sistible cheese wafers, an unhurried look at their tree . . .

Together they had strung the lights and placed the ornaments, but he alone had flung the tinsel around. 'Maybe I was too heavy on the tinsel this year.'

'I love tinsel!'

'Tell me something, Kav'na.'

She smiled—waiting for the old familiar question from her husband. 'What don't you love?'

'The way I beat myself up about my work, always seeing the flaws. Flaws are good, we learn from flaws, so I should be grateful. But I can't seem to get a handle on that point of view.'

'Listen to me,' he said. 'That you could contain that imagery in your heart, in your soul—it's beyond understanding.'

'I know very little about art, but maybe it's what you call flaws that make your work so profoundly accessible—open, somehow, and eager. I can't believe I'm married to you. This is a dream. Do not wake me.'

A t 107 Wisteria Lane, Tim Kavanagh looked at the bedside clock— three A.M., his usual middle-of-the-night wake-up call by way of the golden years.

He remembered he was sleeping in his nightcap, but positively for tonight only. He was bewildered when they unwrapped their small presents after supper. He'd given her a pair of great sunglasses, but was mystified by her gift to him. Was it a potholder?

'It was going to be socks,' she said, 'but it turned into a sort of . . .' She couldn't find words.

'Aha.'

'They say body heat flies out the top of our heads. It might help.'

It was a mildly humiliating gift—who was he, anyway, Old Father Time? Scrooge in his night stocking? But for her, he would do it. At bedtime, he had turned out the lights and popped the thing on his head.

He eased out of bed. Actually, it felt pretty cozy up there on his bald pate. It was keeping him a tad warmer in a house currently at less than sixty degrees. But still . . .

Before she woke in the morning, he would take it to the front hall and pop it on the head of their bust of St. Francis—where henceforth it would remain.

A vis woke up, realizing he was hungry. Steak! That's what he was cravin'.

He rang for a nurse. By the wall clock, it was three-thirty in the morning. He thought the nurse would never come.

'I'm star-r-r-vin',' he said, pushing the words out. '*Steak*.'

The nurse gave him a look.

'Me . . . me . . . '

'Me what?' she said, mean as a rattler.

'Me-e-dium rare . . . an' thank you.'

'You're bein' released this mornin'. Have whatever you want when you get home, we don't do steak.'

What had he asked for, th' dern *moon*?

'Merry Christmas to . . . to you-u-u, too!' Ol' biddy.

24

They were driving up the hill to see Louella.

'So how did you feel when you opened your box with the smoothie blender?' he said.

'Probably the same way you felt when you opened *your* box with the smoothie blender.'

They were still amused when they pulled into the Hope House lot.

'So who gets the odious task of returning their blender?'

'I'm not returning mine,' she said, sly as a fox. 'It has sentimental value.'

Well, there you have it. He would be the one to scramble around for the box his came in and find the shipping label and fill out the return form and seal up the box and haul it to the PO, c'est la vie.

Taped to Louella's door was the double spread from the *Muse* and two pink balloons. The nurses, somewhat diminished in number because of the holiday, were thrilled with the excitement of it all.

'A wonderful, wonderful story!' said Cynthia. 'You're famous now!'

'That Grace, she be th' one famous. She didn' jot a single note, jus' carried it all aroun' in her curly head.'

'Grace got a puppy for Christmas,' said Father Tim. 'A Jack Russell. We called to congratulate her on the story. A truly remarkable achievement. One of my favorite stories ever!'

'I wouldn'a tol' th' part about wettin' my pants,' said Louella.

'That was one of the best parts!' said Cynthia.

They had a laugh.

Louella opened her new brush and comb and used them at once. And Cynthia slipped the blue bedroom shoes on Louella's feet. 'Merry Christmas, dear Louella!'

'An' Merry Christmas to y'all! I got some big feets. Come straight from my daddy, Soot Tobin.'

'What became of your father?' said Cynthia. 'I always wanted to ask.'

'Miss Sadie's daddy run him off. He loved my mama an' wanted to marry her, but Mr. Baxter run him off, said he better not show his black self in this town ag'in. Nobody wanted t' cross Mr. Baxter, nossir. That hurt my mama, she never got over it. An' I never laid eyes on my daddy.'

He was washing his hands at the sink, according to visitor regulations. That was the thing about Christmas, he thought. With all the joy and hope and laughter, there's always, somewhere, the sorrow—just as there was in the manger that pointed to the cross.

Louella held up her feet to see her shoes. 'They's a perfect fit! An' I thank you. I'll be wearin' th' hair offa these good shoes. Now I got somethin' for y'all. Right there on my dresser in th' envelope. Open it up; it's yours to keep. An' Merry Christmas!'

In the envelope, a photograph. Eight by ten. Sepia.

Miss Sadie and Louella as children, standing in front of their playhouse, happy and proud. A bandaged knee. Socks eaten up by their shoes. Ribbons in their hair.

'What you cryin' 'bout, honey?'

'Life,' he said. 'Sometimes it's too good. Thank you.'

He leaned down and kissed her cheek; Cynthia gave her a kiss on the other.

'Merry Christmas!' said Cynthia.

'And many more,' he said.

A good portion of his soul was forever bound to the two souls in the photograph.

O tis drove Avis home.
    Somebody had draped a string of colored lights above the kitchen sink. On the counter, a loaf of banana bread from Lois Burton. A bag of yesterday's donuts from Sweet Stuff. A sticky note on the fridge: MAC AN CHEESE INSIDE 350 20 MINNITS

'Johnsie sent the mac and cheese,' said Otis. 'She'll be up tomorrow.'

'No John . . . Johns. . . .' Avis couldn't get the word out and shook his head no.

As Avis didn't have any next of kin, the doctor had given him, Otis, an earful—here were prescriptions to pick up, here was a file folder full of stuff to read, here was a list of what th' patient could and couldn't eat, plus appointments for checkups an' an order for somebody to monitor the patient for the next few days.

Otis had never once told Avis what to do, but that was then and this was now.

'If you go up th' hill one more time, you prob'ly ain't gon' make it down here ag'in. You need to do what th' doctor says an' let somebody *look after you a day or two!*' Otis's heart thundered. He had raised his voice, but was glad he said it.

Avis fumbled with the oven knob as if he'd never seen it before. Otis took the mac and cheese out of the fridge.

'I'd 'preciate it if . . . you-u-u would run home an' bring Chuck . . . Chucky. I'll pay-y-y your gas.'

'No need to run to th' Valley, he's at th' store in his place by th' deer jerky. We didn't need to fool with a dog till I got you home.' He looked at the oven setting to make sure Avis had dialed it to 350. 'I'll be back in ten minutes.' Lord knows he was sick of foolin' with a man who wouldn't listen to nobody but hisself.

Avis opened the refrigerator door and stared in.

He took a package wrapped with butcher paper out of the freezer.

He filled Chucky's water bowl, put kibble in his food bowl.

He shuffled through his house.

In the bedroom, he found Chucky's blankets and made a nice spot at the foot of the bed. Seem like he wanted to whistle a tune but there wadn't enough air in his lungs yet.

'Whoa!'

He saw hisself in the mirror on the back of th' door. Looked like one eye was settin' lower than th' other an' his clothes were hangin' on him. He would have to kill a pint of rocky road every night or two to put meat on his bones. What he would do about his head, which was a dope bucket, he didn't know. Plus what would he do for Father Tim, who had done so much to get him over the worst hump of his life? He couldn't answer that right now, but it would have to be somethin' good.

In the kitchen, he started a list. *Kibble*. The best money can buy! Plus a couple dozen cans of soft, as life for Chucky had been hard.

Bacon. Free-range eggs. Two pork chops. He'd have to get hisself well an' go back to makin' pasta. No handmade pasta at th' Local was money goin' over to Wesley. *Basmati rice. Roasting hen*. Chucky would like a little white meat an' rice with his kibble. Some of Father Tim's Italian sausage, which he heard was tasty. *Four pints rocky road*. An' some kind of vegetable to make th' doc happy. *1 sweet potatoe*.

There you go! He was in th' grocery b'iness; life was good.

Over by th' door, his wall calendar was still parked on November.

He lifted what was left of December an' hooked it on the nail.

The only time to eat diet food is while you're waiting
for the steak to cook.

—JULIA CHILD

'Amen!' he hollered.

Speakin' of amen, what little time he was layin' in th' hospital with a clear head, he had thought about God. Well, not about God exactly, but how people talked about him all th' time. He realized he did th' same thing.

He said God A'mighty when somethin' rattled or surprised him.

He said God only knows when Avis Packard didn't.

He said Lord help when he didn't expect any help.

It was just words. You open your mouth and out comes stuff you hear other people say, then you say it, too, and it don't mean nothin'.

The thing was, he'd like it to mean somethin'.

I t was your wonderful idea,' said Cynthia. 'I think it should be just the two of you. This is so important, and you don't get much time together. I'll go in and give Lace a hand.'

He had checked his CDs and was surprised that, indeed, he had enough wherewithal to do this. He arranged the purchase with the help of Hal and delivery time through Blake. Not easy this time of year. But on Thursday, Hal had gotten Dooley up to the Crossroads for a cheeseburger, and by grace alone, literally, the truck had arrived at Meadowgate on time, and it all came together.

He and Dooley walked to the clinic. At the storage room door, he took the key from his pocket.

'So that's where the key went,' said Dooley. 'I was ready to get a locksmith out here.'

He inserted the key but didn't open the door.

'We know you asked us not to help you. And we're obeying that request. So we're not helping you, we're helping the cats and dogs and all those whose lives you may save because of what's in this room.

'The manufacturer will send someone at week's end to install it and do the tutorials. Blake and Amanda have all the details.

'It's an investment, son—in the lives of creatures who generously give so much joy and satisfaction to us. We present it to you in memory of Barnabas. He would have liked you to have it.'

He turned the key, opened the door.

Dooley laughed, Dooley cried. He threw his arms around his dad and slapped him on the back again and again and again.

'You're rattlin' my brain!' said his dad, doing some backslapping of his own. 'Merry Christmas!'

He had never held his son like this; his son had never held him like this. Years ago, he had legally adopted Dooley. In this moment, Dooley had completely, unilaterally, adopted him back.

The X-ray machine would run through a few parts as time went by, and would last between ten to fifteen years.

But this particular Christmas memory, he hoped, would last for the rest of their lives.

I can only read some words. That word is *forty*. That word is *Christmas*, that word is *books*, an' that is my name on th' top. You can read my card out loud if you want to.'

'Dear Jack,

'Here are ten books. In the spring, you will get ten more. In the fall, you will get ten more. Next Christmas, you will get ten more. That makes FORTY BOOKS!

'Love you to the clouds and back.

'Mom and Dad.'

Jack ran to the new bookcase. 'Granny C! You could read this one!'

He held up a large-format *Tale of Peter Rabbit*.

'Perfect!' Granny C helped her grandson climb into her lap. 'I can't think of anything I'd like better,' she said, meaning it.

The Owens had come over for the unveiling and returned home; all had marveled at the new technology. Tommy and Beth were doing a gig in Holding. Rebecca Jane was conducting a bike-maintenance tutorial in the living room.

Things were pretty quiet at Meadowgate.

'So, Dad, let's step out back a few minutes. I have somethin' for you, too. It's really special.'

'Give me a clue.'

'He isn't Barnabas, no other dog can ever be. This dog is just Gus. That's all he was made to be, all he wants to be.'

'A *dog*? No, no.'

'You'll like this little guy, I guarantee it. He's at the clinic, come take a look.'

'Truman,' he said. '*Truman.*'

'Gus loves cats, he grew up with cats. Give it a whirl. If it's not a good fit in ten days, back he comes. Two years old. Trained to grass. Great health. Great disposition. I'd take Gus myself, but I can't take 'em all.'

Gus. He'd had a great-uncle named Gus. He had to be clear here. 'The timing is *not* good. Not at all.'

'Try it for ten days. He'll get you out of the house.'

'Get me out of the house? Wait a minute, buddyroe, I *am* out of the house. Six days a week! I have no wheels of my own, I walk to work, I . . .'

'Sure, Dad. Right. Sorry. But trust me, the minute I saw him, I thought he's perfect for you. Plus he does a really amazing trick.'

'What's his breed?'

'Good bit of terrier. Franklin Roosevelt, Coolidge, Hoover, Harding— they all had terriers. Presidents love terriers.'

He did not remind Dooley that Barnabas's trick was unparalleled in

canine history. Any disobedience by his dog, he had rebuked with whatever Bible verse or passage came to mind. Instantly, his errant dog lay in
submission at his feet. He could have taken that show on the road.

To put a fine point on it, he had loved and been loved by the best.
There was no topping that, so why bother?

'What kind of trick?'

'Hard to describe. I'll bring him out to the yard. You can meet and
we'll see how it goes.'

He gave his son a look.

'I talked with Cynthia,' said Dooley. 'She met Gus, she's okay with
th' ten-day trial. She says you need a dog.'

He felt betrayed. Everyone knew he was not getting another dog . . .

Gus charged from the clinic ahead of Dooley.

Twenty-five pounds, he guessed. Muscular. Happy little guy. Bristling
white coat, nice coloring around face and ears . . .

'If it doesn't work,' said Dooley, 'I'll come get him. No problem. Got
kibble and a loaner crate ready to roll. You'll never get another deal like
this.'

Gus trotted up and looked at the man with the white collar who was
looking down at him. Very thoughtfully, it appeared, Gus raised his leg
and relieved himself, spattering a few drops on the Collar's right loafer.

Dooley was aghast.

'If that's his trick . . .' said Father Tim.

'Man. Sorry, Dad, sorry, totally uncharacteristic behavior . . .' Dooley
dug something from his jacket pocket. 'See this tennis ball? Watch this.'

Dooley pitched the ball toward the corncrib; Gus tore up some snow-
bound grass to retrieve it.

Back raced Gus, with the ball in his mouth—barking. He dropped it
at Dooley's feet.

'Have you ever seen anything like it?' said Dooley. 'Barking with a
ball in his mouth?'

'How does he do that?'

'That's his trick! Isn't it amazing? I mean, *look* at this little guy—teeth clenched on th' ball, barkin' like crazy. People go nuts over watchin' this.'

Father Tim looked down at his shoe.

'And loves cats, totally. We can take him out to the barn where there are at least a dozen, we'll prove it. And remember: a twenty-five-pound bag of kibble. Organic! Made in America! *Free!*' How long could he keep pitching this dog?

His son was absolutely determined to ship Gus out of here. What did he have to lose? Ten days would be over, after all, in ten days. He stooped down, offered Gus the back of his hand. Gus sniffed. Sat. Looked up, tail thrashing the snow.

'Okay,' he said. 'Consider it done.'

'Good job, Dad! You and Gus will be a great team!' He pitched the ball again.

'Ten days,' he said in his pulpit voice.

And there was Dooley's smile, every bit as good as his X-ray machine smile.

A light snow was beginning to fall. Lace and Cynthia watched through the kitchen window, heard their laughter.

'My husband the matchmaker,' said Lace.

'How are you?'

'Tired. Really tired. But I can rest a little now. Dad says it's already moving around, though I can't feel it. And he says fingers and toes are forming.'

Her beautiful daughter-in-law had already taken on the proverbial glow. Cynthia gave her a hug. 'You know I'll come anytime, any hour, for any reason.'

She had never been able to have a child, and occasionally the old disappointment still haunted. But somehow she knew this baby was for her, too. She would live all the days of all the stages of this new beating heart with a joy she hadn't known before.

• • •

He checked his email as they loaded the car. Maybe in the New Year he would learn to text, or at least type *u* for you.

> Avis settled at home with Chucky. Eating mac and cheese. Says
> they starved him at the hospital.

He hit Reply.

> Great news! I'll be at the store in the morning. You and Lisa take
> the day off. Don't worry. Omer will give a hand. Will check on A
> first thing. Merry Christmas!

It was time to have a heart-to-heart with Avis Packard. About more than the Local. He'd been praying about this for months.

They were installing the dog crate in the hatch when Old Man Teague drove in.

Dooley watched him climb down from his truck with a paper bag, and thought their neighbor looked more feeble than he'd noticed before.

'Somethin' for y'r boy.'

Dooley opened the bag and took out a duck call.

'Hit's signed,' said Teague.

'You made this? Wow. Good-looking work, Mr. Teague. Thank you very much. Jack's at the Owens' right now. He'll sure love it. Austin Teague, meet my dad, Reverend Tim Kavanagh.'

He liked that his dad was wearing the scarf he and Lace gave him.

'Pleased to meet you, Mr. Teague. I hear you're a very fine dancer.'

The old man shook his dad's hand, gave a curt nod.

'Will you come in?' said Dooley.

Teague wagged his head, he would not come in.

'I hope you'll walk out to visit Redeemer. She's in our pet cemetery behind th' corncrib. We gave her a nice sunny spot and a marker. It's easy to find.'

The old man turned away, removed a handkerchief from his overalls pocket. 'I thank you.'

'I'll bring Jack by one of these days. Would you come for supper sometime?'

Teague shook his head. He would not come for supper.

'Thanks for the great duck call. It's a wonder how anybody can make these things.' Dooley tested it. An actual smile on Austin Teague's face. He blew the call again. 'Beautiful!'

'That'll get you a raft of ducks on y'r pond.'

'Merry Christmas!' said his dad. 'Good to see you, Mr. Teague.'

Dooley watched the old man walk along the driveway toward the corncrib.

'Mr. Teague!'

He turned around.

'We'll call you about supper here in a week or two.'

He knew exactly what Austin Teague needed. It was a little soon yet, but when the time came . . .

Truman was pouting. Big-time.

Not one swipe had he taken at Gus, who seemed crazy about his new surroundings and totally dedicated to getting on the good side of the house cat.

Truman had removed himself from the lowlife by leaping from the floor to the desk chair and from the chair to the desk, where he ensconced himself in the out-box.

They were on the study sofa with a bowl of popcorn, couch potatoes par excellence. It was snowing again—what the Wesley TV station's weatherman had called 'a quixotic and somewhat indifferent snowfall.' Perhaps the meteorologist had been an English major.

'What do you feel ready for in the coming year?' he asked his couchmate.

Cynthia devoured a handful of popcorn and considered the question. 'Ready for you to retire again and stay retired.'

'Not just any woman would say that to her spouse.'

'Well, there you have it. Living proof that I'm not just any woman.'

'So what would we do?'

'I think we should learn to have more fun.'

'I'm not terribly good at that,' he said.

'Yes, but we can learn. It's not too late to learn.'

'Spring,' he said. 'I drive, you knit. That will be fun.' Liar, liar, pants
on fire. He had not yet adjusted to the idea that it might be *fun* to wheel
that thing around, but he was getting there.

'Look who's here,' he said.

Gus sat at their feet, amber eyes unblinking.

'I thought I latched his crate.'

'I unlatched it,' she said.

'But dogs *like* their crates. They're *den* animals.' Whose dog was this
supposed to be, anyway?

'It's Christmas, honey. Besides, the gate is still up from Chucky's
visit; he can't go anywhere. I think he wants popcorn.'

'No popcorn unless it's unbuttered, unsalted, and inspected for un-
popped kernels, which can lodge in the teeth or in the throat.'

'Textbook!' said his wife.

'That's what Dooley would tell you.'

'Gus really is darling, don't you think? Maybe he wants on the sofa
with us. If I were a dog, I would want on the sofa with us!'

'No, no, this is a *trial run*, we don't need to start any . . . '

In one tidy leap, Gus joined them on the sofa.

It was a awful idea, all right. Turned out th' Grinch stole everybody's
Christmas—roast beef dinners, stockin's hung on th' mantelpiece, all
th' presents for th' young'uns—everything!—an' piled it on his sled to
dump off a mountain.

But before th' ol' Grinch got to it, somethin' wonderful come to pass. It took up two whole pages of th' book!

He settled into the ending with renewed satisfaction.

He read the part where th' Grinch, after stealin' ever'thing he could git his hands on, brought back to Who-ville *everything he stole*—all the food, all th' toys, even th' Christmas tree!

He unwrapped a chocolate from the jar.

He did not like to go to doctors, but he would go to Dr. Seuss if he wadn't dead.

'Dead as an inkwell,' Grace had said, lookin' what you call final.

It's said that big cities never sleep, but little towns do.
Or maybe not.

Sometime after eleven on Christmas night, an eight-point buck, two does, and a fawn plowed south along Main in two inches of fresh snow. For economy, many shops were dark, but Dora Pugh's Hardware was not. In the lighted display window, two large stuffed brown bears sat at a table, ostensibly admiring a fake fire burning in a fake stove, and a fake, but nonetheless endearing, spruce tree strung with colored lights.

Disturbing the delicate lacework of red fox tracks, the deer veered left onto the sidewalk. where they gazed at the scene in the window.

God rest ye merry, gentlemen.

Let nothing you dismay . . .

On Ivy Lane, an actual bear, black in this case, clawed down the bird feeder at the Newland residence. Emma recognized the snuffling sound outside their bedroom, and the clank of the chain. She got up at once and rapped sharply on the windowpane.

'Get! Get out! Go away!' Snickers raised his head, barked once, and went back to sleep. Harold got up and made a beeline to the kitchen, where he polished off the last of a sweet potato soufflé.

O Holy Night! The stars are brightly shining . . .

Roused for his nightly trek to the bathroom, Abe looked out the window and in the light of the streetlamp saw snow falling. 'Oy,' he said, his breath steaming the glass. He had to sell sixteen pairs of work boots by next Tuesday, period. It was his first ever fifty percent off sale—he had done thirty-five percent off, but never fifty, and who would come out to shop in another snow?

Love came down at Christmas,
love all lovely, love divine;
Love was born at Christmas:
star and angels gave the sign . . .

At the Wesley College radio station, now annually contracted to transmit holiday music to the Mitford town hall, the psych major manning the turntable fell asleep. He was unaware of an unfortunate scratch, accidentally made by last night's biology major, in the hymn by Christina Rossetti.

'Love shall be our token, love shall be our token, love shall be our token' sounded through the nighttime village as if to say, If nothing more, remember this.

25

Stone fireplace, trout stream, hiking trails, the works.

Dooley and Lace were stealing time from their busy life to spend four days in a mountain cabin, with Jack in tow.

'Late honeymoon, early anniversary,' said Dooley.

The kids had stopped by Wisteria Lane this morning, to pick up a food basket Cynthia put together. After all the goodbyes were said, they saw Dooley hurrying back to the house from the Volvo.

'My keys. Thought I left 'em in the car. Gotta get gas at Lew's, run by her mom's, and we're out of here.'

He was glad for the extra moment with his son. He gave him another pounding on the back. 'Go and be as the butterfly!'

Dooley grinned. 'You've said that as long as I can remember. I'm not pullin' up what it means.'

It was what God had said to him, a small-town clergyman, another lifetime ago, and what he had tried and was still trying to do.

'I think it means to go unfettered by cares, by the infernal bondage of the mortal. Go with a light heart, trusting God and giving thanks. Go and gather unto yourselves so you can pour out to others.'

He took a deep breath. 'Go without looking back.'

Dooley laughed. 'That's a lot, Dad. Back atcha!'

He loved Dooley's laughter, though his smile was the magic.

He took out his wallet and found a twenty, just as he'd done for Dooley's first birthday at the rectory all those years ago when Dooley turned—was it twelve? He remembered the little guy looking solemn, it was his first such currency. 'I'll keep it forever!' Dooley had said, but it was gone in a day.

'We'll be close behind you to the exit,' said Father Tim. 'But praying for you all the way.'

Dooley gave him a hug. 'Praying for y'all. Have a great time. Thanks for everything. Stay in touch. We love you.'

'We love you back!'

And there went a tall kid with long legs, sprinting down the sidewalk.

Dooley turned, threw up his hand, the early morning light a coronation on his red hair.

Even from here, he could see it. His son was smiling.

Cynthia had historically called out the wild man in him, in a manner of speaking, and he had been pretty up for being called out. This, however, was wilder than he was used to. He encouraged himself by imagining the look on her face when she got a load of this rig.

He had written her a note two weeks ago, and stuck it in her favorite coffee mug.

> Pack one bag that will serve for one month.
> Warm climates. Casual.
> Depart our driveway Thursday after next, eight a.m.
> Be there or be square.

He swallowed hard when he wrote 'month.' Wouldn't two weeks be a better, more sensible deal for everybody? Then again, once they were out there, why not make full use of the investment and stay out for a month? He had never 'stayed out' much of anywhere, he was no Shackleton. But right around the corner, he'd be seventy-eight. Or was it seventy-nine? He could never do a quick recall of his age; there must be a medical term for this idiosyncrasy. Anyway, if the RV trip was going to happen, it needed to happen now.

Not that he planned to croak any time soon, but he needed to travel while he still remembered left from right. Plus Esther Cunningham and Ray, longtime veterans of the roadie lifestyle, were making him a loan he couldn't refuse.

Their 'baby' had been to New Mexico, Washington State, Wisconsin, and many points in between. Strike while the iron is hot! they said. Seize the moment, life is short, you only live once.

'Bring it back better than we left it,' said Esther. 'We might have another trip left in us.'

He looked at Ray, who did not have another trip left in him—zero— but what could the good fellow say? 'It's a honey,' said Ray.

He had read *Travels with Charley* and had had several tutorials with Ray, including three on the parkway to familiarize himself with sharp curves, steep grades, and few passing zones. The third time out, he actually enjoyed it. Why had he waited so long? What had he been afraid of?

Then came the parking business and the compost business and the awning business and the Wi-Fi terminals and the built-in charging stations, and where was Dooley to help him through all this? Dooley was busy; Dooley would be busy for the rest of his life and he must get used to that.

They would take it easy, they would not hurry. And of course there would be surprises—they could count on it—but that was precisely what She Who Loves Surprises craved. With the exception of his makeover of the nativity scene, she hadn't gotten a good deal of surprise out of him, but he'd gotten a great supply of it from her. He hoped this would make up for what had been lacking on his end in a way that would fulfill—possibly even exceed?—any future expectations.

Being able to leave with a clear conscience was, of course, a benefit not to be overlooked.

Dooley's business was thriving and so were Lace and the baby, due to arrive in July. The auction had raised a bundle for the Children's Hospital—nine of her paintings sold—and the generous check to the hospital from Avis had been a great boon; he was proud to deliver it to the development officer.

Harley would of course come in to mow and blow, and Truman had been readopted by Meadowgate and promised a cat door to the laundry room. Who could possibly ask for more?

He had driven the RV down to Holding and up again, and over to Wesley and beyond. He had backed it under Ray's jerry-rigged shed and had not sheared off the side mirrors. He was primed.

Last night he parked the RV in their driveway. 'Don't look,' he said to Cynthia. 'No fair looking.'

He had stocked the galley kitchen with their favorite skillet, their favorite saucepans and utensils, provender from the Local, and their smoothie blender.

Onto shelves over the sofa went *Travels with Charley, The Book of Common Prayer*, the King James, the Lewis and Clark diaries, *The Oxford Book of English Verse*, Allen and Greenough's *New Latin Grammar*, several novels by dead authors, plenty of Billy Collins, Mary Oliver, and Wendell Berry, maps galore of terra incognita, and a volume of Wordsworth for old times' sake.

This morning around seven, he had finished the move-in. Gus's crate was in place, the suitcases were stowed, and their wedding gear was hanging in the closet. He was buzzing like a kid at Christmas.

He invited his wife for a grand tour. Over the moon would be a good way to describe her approval.

At eight A.M. on the dime, he locked up the house, gave Gus a last hurrah at an unwilling nandina bush, and let him into his crate. Gus had ridden shotgun on the trip to Asheville and seemed to like the idea of wheels.

He prayed again for safe travels. Then climbed into the driver's seat, buckled up, turned the key in the ignition, and looked at his wife.

All she knew was, they would arrive for the wedding in Holly Springs in two weeks, and stay for two days.

Wearing jeans, tennis shoes, a ball cap, and her favorite plaid shirt, she was looking brand-new. On the floor at her feet was a workbag with miles of yarn and the ambitious beginnings of a sweater for Jack and one for the Kavanagh to come.

'Just for fun, sweetheart, can you tell me where we're going?'

He was ready for this inquiry.

'Into the wild blue yonder,' he said.

He had seldom seen her look so happy.

A vis and Chucky walked from the house to the Local and stood for a moment under the green awning. There came the Volvo and the two RVs motoring down Main, headed south. The dew was still on.

He knew th' Volvo would drive four miles, hook a left to th' interstate, an' exit south to Brevard.

Th' Freelander Coach would exit west to Tennessee an' eventually south to Holly Springs, Mississippi, where Father Tim was born at. Father Tim had said it was a family weddin' but wadn't specific about other destinations.

The Sportscoach diesel would exit west to Tennessee an' north to Missouri, which was a haul an' a half.

He knew these things because the drivers had provisioned at the Local.

Th' Sportscoach had taken on twenty-four large bags of Fritos, two cases of Cheerwine, a case of Bud Light, a 12-pack of Orville Redenbacher's buttered popcorn, tortilla chips and salsa, a 16-pack of deer jerky, which was ten percent off with a coupon, an' a seven-an'-a-half-pound beef roast. He had cut Lew th' extra half-pound to thank him for his business.

Th' Volvo had hardly any room to take on serious food items—it would be crammed to th' gills, according to Dooley, with a golden retriever, fishin' gear, an iron skillet, a coffeepot, a child's seat, two huge pieces of luggage, and a bunch of art supplies. Dooley had mostly provisioned with energy bars, coffee, tea, OJ, whole grain cereal, trail mix, banana chips, cheese, yogurt, almond milk, peanut butter, whole wheat bread, and three plastic forks for a pie Miz Harper baked for take-along.

Dooley tapped the horn three times. Avis waved, Chucky barked.

Th' Freelander was a mini-Local on wheels. Triple-virgin olive oil, grass-fed beef, dried fruit, three unripe avocados, romaine, merlot, two pounds of French roast in the bean, Earl Grey tea, whole grain bread and crackers, three cheeses, four lemons, two onions, eggs from uncaged birds, frozen North Pacific salmon, two dozen Gala apples, a hand of unripe bananas, and a quartet of organic raisins. He had refused payment. If he died broke, say la vee.

Th' Freelander blew th' horn; he squinted into th' light. Father Tim and Cynthia, with Gus hangin' his head out th' window . . .

He threw up his hand, Chucky barked.

'There they go. It's happenin'. Miz Kavanagh's big dream.'

He stepped to the curb and peered at the next vehicle. The diesel Sportscoach was so big it blocked the sun from his eyes, an' way up there was Lew an' Earlene gettin' a bird's-eye view of him an' Chucky.

He threw up his hand, Lew honked, Chucky barked.

Big suckers, those RVs, glidin' by like floats in a parade. Gas hogs! Plus, how did you back one up to th' gas tank without takin' out th' tank? Or what if you got someplace and th' RV park was full? Did you just keep goin' till you fell asleep at th' wheel?

'Everybody's headed someplace but us, Chucky.' He stooped down and gave his dog a scratch behind the ears. 'It's just me an' you, okay?'

He wondered why such a thought made him feel so happy.

This afternoon he would grind a pound of sirloin, pick up extra-sharp cheddar from the cooler, corn tortillas, the whole nine yards. 'Tacos tonight, how about it?'

Chucky's entire rear end was waggin'. Don't tell him dogs don't know what's goin' on. 'Miz Sanchez sent us her homemade hot sauce, but I'll hold th' sauce on yours.'

He thought he might put his feet up this evenin'. He'd never once put his feet up. He had an orange crate Johnsie told him he could use, but only if he topped it with a bed pillow, which would aid circulation.

'An' how about we build us a fire?'

It had been a cool spring and Lord knows, he hadn't built a fire in his fireplace in five, maybe ten years. 'If we burn th' house down, we'll get us another house, maybe one of those houses on wheels we just saw rollin' by. Me an' you, we'll head out to Wyoming, what do you think about Wyoming? We'll see us some cowboys ropin' steers. Maybe get us a job on a dude ranch.'

He didn't exactly know what he was feelin', seein' th' two RVs, solemn and immense, goin' off to other places. It was like some part of him was set free. But free for what he didn't know. Maybe free to do whatever he wanted, with th' best dog he ever had. Come to think of it, th' only dog he ever had.

He stepped to the front door of the Local and inserted the key in the lock and went inside and thought again how he loved the smell of this place. 'Thank you,' he said, looking up.

It was good to think you might go somewhere sometime if you wanted to, but right now it felt pretty good just to stay at home in Mitford.

He turned the sign around to read what everybody wanted to see:

OPEN.

ACKNOWLEDGMENTS

With eternal thanks to:

Ivan Held, my lovely, understanding, old-school publisher, aka grill maven.

The brilliant team who makes it all come together for the reader: Christine Pepe, editor supreme; Sally Kim; Alexis Welby; Katie McKee; Ashley McClay.

Candace Freeland: daughter, cheerleader, first reader, and hatcher of sublime ideas.

Dr. Mimi Cogliano: Hail to thee, blithe spirit.

Dr. Tim Short: As my grandmother would say, you're worth your weight in gold.

Tripp Stewart, DMV (this designation awarded only by the University of Pennsylvania): charming, ultra-generous Mitford vet in residence.

Dawn Buchanan and Marguerite Rueger, league operators, American Pool-players Association of Central Virginia. Let's lag!

Lincoln Perry: controversial, renowned, and generous muralist.

Everett Barrineau: one of Mitford's earliest and most ardent champions. Thank you, dear heart.

Amanda Brown Megargel: gifted writer of "Civil War," a brilliant country song that deserves a savvy publisher.

Woody Baker: friend, RVer, and cattleman of distinction.

Patrick Comyn, DVM: thanks for the cow that nearly got away.

Dannye Romine: poet par excellence (just call her Darling).

Nancy Bass: friend and cheerleader; David Bass for his introduction to *Beef Cattle Science*.

Dr. Gary Haines: my entertaining, skydiving dentist who doesn't know much about snow camping, but thanks for the laughs.

Gerry Newman: creator of pastry heaven.

Keturah Bracey; Reverend Jane Sigloh; Danny and Laurie Crigler of L&D Associates, Inc.; Margaret Leckrone, Foundations Child Development Center; Professor Christopher Bryan; Polly Hawkes; Sheridan Hill; Mike Barfoot, BRPD; Mike Wilcox, BRPD; Sharon Van Dyke, BRPD; Sarita Bennett, DO, CPM; Kim Kepchar; Reverend Sarah Kinney Gaventa; Sarita Bennet; Nadia Badr Cempre; Dan Nakas; Dr. Tom Daniel; Jim Childress; Dr. Sue Mueller; Audi Barlow; Bruce Sullivan; Tony Hancock; Mary Motley Kalergis; Mary Eckenrode Gibson; Patrick Brady; Jacki Bryant; Geoffrey S. Garbaccio; Gail Esterman; Nate and Scott of Blick Art Materials; Reverend Paul Walker; Graham Shannonhouse; Ahmet.

And to all the devoted readers who love Mitford, please know that Mitford loves you back. Always.

Applause for the legendary Edna Lewis (1916–2006) and Chef Scott Peacock, who developed the recipe for the Orange Marmalade Cake, aka OMC. Early on, it was clear that Mitford needed a baker of seriously high standards—somebody famous for a cake that everyone was nuts about. But it had to be off the grid, completely unique.

So how about a lusciously moist cake filled and topped with rough-cut orange marmalade? Done! Readers loved the much ado made over this cake by Father Tim and other Mitford characters and wanted the recipe. But there wasn't one.

So. When I was writer in residence with Hearst's *Victoria Magazine*, the editor hired Ms. Lewis and Chef Peacock to concoct the OMC recipe in their Atlanta home kitchen. Over the years, brave Mitford readers have baked this challenging cake and been awarded rave reviews. (You'll find the recipe in *Jan Karon's Mitford Cookbook and Kitchen Reader*, always available online, or ask your go-to bookstore.) It is my favorite cake of all time, and a funeral service with much ado about the OMC is precisely how one of my best-loved characters would wish to be remembered.

Speaking of remembering:

Chick McKinney (1933–2007), penultimate adman. *Gratia!*